PORT OF ORIGIN

LISA HARRIS
LYNNE GENTRY

HG

Cover design: Lisa Harris

To the brave souls who dare to care for those who cannot care for themselves.

PROLOGUE

OFF THE COAST OF CAMEROON, CENTRAL AFRICA

SINCE ANCIENT TIMES, THE SEA HAD BEEN GENEROUS. TUNA. SARDINES. Ocean prawns big as a man's hand. But those days of plenty had vanished in the wake of the foreign trawlers whose illegal fishing practices were destroying the coastline's natural resources. Dabir watched the moon slip behind a veil of clouds, leaving him and his brothers to navigate the vast Atlantic in an eerie shroud of darkness. From his position at the end of the boat, he could see little beyond the shadowy silhouettes of his father and his two younger brothers.

He stopped rowing for a moment as he waited for the sharp tug of the nylon fishing net that would signal the night's first catch. A wave smashed against the side of the narrow craft, reminding him of the dangers of straying too far into the open waters. He searched for the light of the trawlers that swept the sea's floor with their ghostlike underwater lights while their wide metal jaws devoured everything in sight, but tonight there was no sign of the floodlights used to lure the fish into their nets. Which meant the deadly boats could be anywhere, trying to avoid the overworked coastal patrols searching in vain for those illegal vessels that strayed into the zone reserved for the smaller vessels. All Dabir could do was pray his father's boat steered clear of the stealthy trawlers that prowled the darkness. And pray that they would catch enough fish to feed their family another day.

Except for the rhythmic slap of waves against the boat and the distant roar of the incoming tide against the shoreline, a silence settled between them. His brothers, Leiyo and Chomba, were too young to recall the sea's bounty or the fat prawns found where the river emptied into the ocean. Even he barely remembered the feel of a full belly and a nice profit. But so far their efforts, like the night before, and the one before that, had brought nothing but a meager catch of tiny fingerlings. No fish meant famine, which was why he'd left university in the capital in order to help provide for his family. And to ensure his son didn't have to do the same thing.

Anger rose, breaking the surface like the great blue marlin, but resentment would do nothing to fill the stomachs of his brothers or his wife and young son. Ignoring the gnawing emptiness in his gut, he waited for the dawn that would soon arrive, bringing with it the fiery ball that splashed pink across the distant horizon.

His wife would be among the women who lined the shoreline with their empty metal pans on their heads anticipating the dozens of small wooden canoes, with their colorful painted sides, to return with a better catch than the night before. Once again, he would disappoint her.

"We need to change our course," Dabir's father shouted and dug his paddle hard into the choppy water.

A spray of saltwater brushed his face, burning Dabir's chapped lips. He searched for the horizon as he rowed, but the black night made it impossible to see.

And his empty stomach made it impossible to go home too soon.

Dabir heard the low rumble of the trawler before he saw it.

A sliver of moonlight broke through the clouds and settled on the side of the rusty hull of the giant trawler that dwarfed their wooden pirogue. The small boat tipped in the wake of the larger vessel.

"Hold on," Dabir screamed.

Their wooden boat groaned then split in two. The smashed skiff plunged into the murky waters, sucking Dabir into its depths.

He gasped for air as the sea engulfed him. Panic flooded his chest. Disoriented, he searched for the surface, but only darkness surrounded him. Lungs threatened to burst. A trail of moonlight glistened above him, revealing a stream of tiny bubbles. He propelled himself upward, emerged, then filled his lungs with air.

Something thrashed in the water a boat length away.

Dabir grabbed a splintered piece of wood and bridged the distance between them. Leiyo and Chomba struggled to stay afloat on a jagged piece of wreckage.

"Where's Father?" Leiyo shouted.

"Don't let go," Dabir shouted back. "I'll find him."

Senses heightened, Dabir searched the dark, bobbing surface of the endless Gulf of Guinea for a sign of their father. His muscles cramped. Every second that passed pushed him and his brothers closer to succumbing to the deadly currents. But he would not return to his family's compound without his father.

He screamed his father's name over and over again. Silence greeted him. Something brushed across his arm and Dabir felt his heart plummet. The still body of his father floated to the surface. He reached out to grasp his cold hand as the trawler veered away from them, its foreign captain unaware of the fractured wreck beneath his ship's massive hull.

Dabir pulled the limp body against him and swore his revenge. They'd taken his livelihood, and now his father. The men in those giant ships would take nothing more.

CHAPTER ONE

SOUTHERN CALIFORNIA

Consider the problem. Execute the moves. Summit.

Josiah Allen mentally repeated his life's mantra as he hung from the hairline crack snaking up a crag of El Capitan. A chilly Pacific wind sanded his knuckles and his fingertips were blistered, but he'd never let pain slow him down. Getting to the top despite the obstacles was something he'd learned how to do a long time ago. Willpower had made him one of the best plastic surgeons in the country. Today, he intended to reach another one of his goals: climbing one of the toughest monoliths in the world.

He strained against the taut belay rope connecting him to his wife perched on a narrow ledge fifteen feet below.

"Slack, Camilla." Arms and legs burning from the lactic acid building up in his tense muscles, his feet scrambled to find a toehold. "Camilla?" His desperation bounced off the three-thousand-foot rock tower and came back to him silent.

Josiah risked a swift glance over his shoulder. Camilla, beautiful in her form-fitting spandex and helmet, studied him with an impish grin.

"Today, Monkey Shine," he shouted over the wind.

She shook her head and her black braid wrapped around the slender neck he loved to kiss. "I'm not letting you go any higher, *Dr. Allen*, until I'm sure you're as proficient with all of those shiny new cams racked on your harness as you are with a scalpel." Her brows lifted in a doubtful arch.

"Very funny, *Dr. Allen*."

Neither ever let the other off the hook when it came to their competitive nature. In fact, it was Camilla's drive and brilliance in the cadaver lab that had drawn him to the Venezuelan beauty their first year of medical school. Together, they'd climbed to the top of their chosen fields of practice. He, for one, was looking forward to their sharing the view from the top for many years to come. Summiting El Cap was only one mountain on his list of accomplishments he'd yet to achieve.

Josiah shifted his weight to his left hand and removed a medium-sized cam from his gear strap with his right. "When have I ever steered you wrong, my love?"

"Castle Rock." Her reply bounced off the granite.

He slotted the head of the cam into an overhead fissure. "That was a freak rainstorm."

"In Seattle?"

"Okay, so it ruined your hair." He pulled the trigger on the cam. The reassuring ping reverberating in the canyon told them both he'd chosen the perfect tool. In the ten years they'd been climbing together, he'd made plenty of mistakes. Camilla didn't need any more ammo to twist his impetuous nature into a noose around his neck, but he could tell from the way her dark brown eyes twinkled he'd just tossed her a rope. "That all you've got, woman?"

"Flatiron." Her grin was smug, her confidence as sexy as her long, shapely legs.

"Freak snow."

She jammed her rope-wrapped fist into one of the curves right above those perfect hips. "Colorado? In November?" Her laughter, like hot chocolate in front of a crackling fire on a snowy night warmed him to the core. Perfection with whipped cream. His Camilla.

Josiah jiggled the cam to make sure all four friction lobes had caught. "Early November. Really more late-ish October." He stretched his rope to clip into the carabiner hanging from the cam. Three inches short. He was stuck until she cut him some slack. "Your point?"

"What if I'm tired of getting wet?"

"Come on, admit it, Dr. Allen"—he cast his best provocative wink to egg her on—"you love it when I warm you up."

Her cheeks flushed the pink-grapefruit of a California sunset. "*Dr.* Allen." She placed a long slender finger to her lips, the same one that could slip inside a child's heart and fix a broken valve with lightning speed. "The neighbors." She jutted her perfect chin at the climbing party seventy-five feet above them. "Newbies," she mouthed.

He glanced at the two-man team huffing and hoisting a hundred-pound haul bag full of supplies. Loud, cocky, and loaded with more gear than ten people would need for a five-day climb, these newbies had been an irritant all day. He hated the snarled traffic jams inexperienced climbers and good weather invariably caused on the wall.

"Maybe it's time we bought our own slab. One so remote, I wouldn't have to share you with anyone but God."

"What's your hurry, big boy?" She tugged on the rope and it pulled his waist toward hers. "We've got the next five days."

"You know that by day three you'll be begging me to go home."

"I trust your sister with our little girl. Rachel will spoil Emma rotten."

"Plus, she'll have obliterated every germ from our house."

"I like having an infectious disease specialist in the family. I'll miss her when she goes to Africa."

"Hey, I said we'd go. . .someday," he said.

"Consider the problem. Execute the moves. Summit." His wife threw his own mantra back at him with a tone of challenge he found hard to resist.

"For you, I'd even get on a boat."

"That's a pretty serious promise for someone who's afraid of water," she teased.

"I'm not afraid. I just prefer clear heights to murky depths."

Camilla lifted her chin and dragged her hand seductively down her torso. "Then let's just sit back and enjoy the view, shall we Dr. Allen?"

"Woman, you're a view I could look at all day—"

Snap.

"Rock!" Freaked-out shouts from above jerked Josiah's head up.

An overloaded haul bag plummeted toward him.

"Camilla!" Josiah flung himself out of the way just before the duffel whizzed past him. The force spun him around and slammed his shoulder against the cliff face. He grabbed the rope that connected him to his wife and pulled back a limp, severed thread.

"Camilla!"

Josiah's frantic gaze careened off the ledge at the exact same moment a woman's body, the body he knew better than his own, catapulted through the void.

"Camilla!" His raw scream followed her twisty-turns and slow-motion somersaults. His hands clawed at the empty air.

One second, she was there. The next. . . "No! God! No!"

"Daddy?" A small hand shook his shoulder. "Daddy!"

Josiah sat straight up. His eyes flew open. Sweat dripped from his forehead. Expensive bedside tables and lamp-like shapes swirled in a gray fog that smelled of burnt toast. Head pounding and heart ricocheting against his chest, he tried to make out how he'd descended a mountain and ended up in their master bedroom.

Breath ragged, he squeezed his eyes shut. In a desperate attempt to remove the weight obstructing his air supply, he dragged his hands across his face. Stubble pricked the smooth palms that reeked of sweat and surgical latex.

Something poked at his leg. "Daddy?"

He dug at his sunken eye sockets, but no amount of rubbing could get at the jackhammer throb. He forced his eyes to open, cringing at the light shards piercing his corneas. He let his hand wander to *her* side of the bed. Empty and cold.

"Daddy, phone."

Slowly, his sleep-deprived vision cleared. "Emma?" The croaky and foreign voice surely didn't belong to him.

His daughter, dressed in a Barbie nightgown and a shiny plastic tiara, clutched his expensive new cell phone in one hand, a banana in the other. Her flawless face was a mini version of Camilla's—except for her eyes. Ocean-blue and narrowed with concern, they had him pegged for the loser he'd become.

He ran his tongue around the inside of his dry mouth, trying to work up enough saliva to speak. "Who is it, Cricket?"

"Aunt Rachel." Emma held out the phone. "She wants to talk to you."

He swallowed the chalky and bitter spit he'd mustered. "Can I call her back?"

"No. She says it's important." She prodded his leg with the banana. "Are you awake, Daddy?"

"I am now." Josiah tried to swing his feet to the floor, but the sweat-drenched top sheet had bound his scrub-clad legs in a twisted vine. He remembered eating a bowl of cereal when he dragged through the door around three am. He did not remember falling into bed in the same clothes he'd worn for ten hours in the OR.

"Give me a minute." He fought the bedding like the reoccurring nightmare that would not let him go.

His daughter put the phone to her ear. "Aunt Ray, Daddy has to potty, then he can talk."

"Em!"

Her face sobered and he immediately regretted raising his voice. "Sorry, Cricket." He patted the bed. "You know how I am before I have coffee."

She nodded. "Worse than a bear in spring."

Camilla's old sayings coming out of Emma's young mouth punched him in the gut every time. "You gonna share that banana?"

Emma eagerly broke the fruit in half. "I made toast, too." She used her half of the banana to point out the tray at the foot of his bed.

"Emma Grace." He crammed banana into his mouth. "We've talked about needing a grown-up present before you use electrical appliances."

"You also told me civilized people never talk with their mouths full." She scrambled up beside him, dragging the bruised fruit with her. She held out the phone. "You ready to talk?"

He shook his head.

Emma regarded him for a brief instant then raised the phone to her ear again. "Aunt Ray, I have a loose tooth."

Josiah couldn't believe he'd allowed himself to sink to such a pitiful state that he'd rather let a child cover for him than explain his decision to his sister.

He snagged a piece of toast from a princess plate. He could hear Rachel gushing on about what a big girl Emma was and promising her she would send the tooth fairy a notification email the moment it fell out.

Then he heard, "Let me talk to your father." Rachel's tone, no longer gushy had become all lab-geek serious.

He was in for the tongue-lashing his late-night text deserved. A real man would have called his only sister to explain his decision. Rachel's sacrifice of leaving her beloved medical ship for over a year in order to devote her attention to him and Emma had earned her that much consideration and much more after. . .He still couldn't say the words. *Camilla died.*

"Put him on now, Em!" Rachel's voice had risen to the same level he'd once heard her use on some CDC Director after he failed to take her advice on an outbreak that had hit and killed kids in several states.

Emma lowered the phone. Her gaze locked with his. She shrugged and held out the phone. "I tried, Daddy."

If he could take back the last twenty months and restore his little girl's innocence, he'd cut off his operating hand.

Steeling himself, he dropped his half-eaten piece of toast on the princess plate and took the call. He motioned for Emma to go on about her business. She acted like she didn't see the gesture and wiggled deeper into the pillows piled on Camilla's side of the bed. Since his wife's death, Emma had become more like his clone than his child. He watched her slender fingers set to work peeling back the banana's yellow skin, the precise movements of a skilled surgeon.

Thanks to Camilla, fixing what was wrong was in Emma's genes. Not a single detail would ever get past this inquisitive little stalker.

Josiah kissed the crooked part on the top of Emma's head, careful to avoid the bejeweled crown that Camilla had given her before...she died. The sweet smell of tear-free shampoo brought a lump to his throat. Camilla had insisted her baby would have very few reasons to cry.

He put his feet on the floor and raised the phone to his ear. "Hey, Ray."

"A text, Joey? Really?" Rachel growled. "When did you become such a coward?"

Josiah dragged his palm over the two-day stubble on his face. "Top of the morning to you, too, sis."

"I'm not going to take no for an answer," she shrilled. "This is your chance to do what Camilla always wanted the two of you to do together."

At the scorching reminder, he yanked the phone from his ear, counted to five, and went in to settle this thing. "I'm not following you out to sea."

"The *Liberty* ports in one place for months at a time."

"What about Emma?" he asked. "Think my six-year-old will be okay if I just leave her home with the keys to the Porsche and a no-limit credit card?"

"Lots of our docs bring their families."

"I'm not taking my daughter to Africa, Ray."

"You don't get to bail on life on my watch, brother."

"This isn't your watch. It's mine now." From the silence, his words had cut like a scalpel.

"I love you, Joey. But you've left me no choice. I have to consider the welfare of my niece above your need to hole up in an operating room."

He recoiled at the viper-strike accuracy of her diagnosis. The little sister who used to believe he walked on water knew he was sinking. Her disappointment was another stone crushing his chest.

A lonely burn radiated through him. "My work is no less important than yours."

"Emma still has one parent and she deserves to have him present in her life."

"Daddy?"

Josiah froze. He'd forgotten Emma was sitting right there, listening to every word. Again. Rachel was right, he wasn't fit to be a single parent.

He turned. "Cricket, I..."

She held out a jagged chunk of banana. "I saved you the biggest piece."

Guilty bricks were stacked so high on his shoulders he could barely lift his arm to take the banana. "Thanks, Cricket." He cleared his throat and returned to his phone conversation. "I'm sorry, Ray. That was out of line."

He heard Rachel release a pained sigh. "I know you think you won't be able to guarantee Emma's safety on some rusty bucket of bolts in a third-world country, but the *Liberty* is a first-rate, state-of-the-art American medical facility. We have a school, full-time childcare, and a movie theater. It's a floating suburb, complete with kids Emma's own age. Having someone besides her old man to talk to couldn't possibly put her at risk."

"What about exposing her to who-knows-what?" Fear tinged his voice. "You may be God's gift to infectious diseases, but there's stuff over there no one's seen, let alone developed a cure for."

"You know Camilla always wanted to do this."

"Camilla also wanted to climb Everest."

"Camilla loved adventure as much as we do," Rachel reminded him. "If she had this opportunity, what do you think she would do?"

Josiah pinched the bridge of his nose, but the guilt pulsed through his veins afresh. How many times had he second-guessed his decision to take Camilla climbing?

"We couldn't have stopped her," he mumbled.

"When Camilla set her mind to something..." Rachel paused. "She wasn't afraid of dying and she lived right up until she took her last breath. Your wife wouldn't stand for the way you've backed away from life and you know it, Joey."

"What about my practice?"

"Sell it. Plenty of greedy chumps out there are anxious to plump the wrinkles of the rich and famous."

"What about when I come back?"

"Start over. Maybe even open that free clinic Camilla always wanted."

"I can't."

"Take a leave of absence if you don't want to sell to your partners," Rachel said. "Heaven knows you haven't allowed yourself a day off since the funeral."

"No."

"I know how you feel, Joey."

"No offense little sister, but being stood up at the altar isn't quite the same as losing the mother of your child." He knew he couldn't have hurt her more if he'd taken his scalpel and cut her open. She'd struggled since Aiden Ballinger's betrayal, but she hadn't squirreled herself away in her lab. He hated how the inability to move on tasted in his mouth. "Ray, I'm—"

"At least say you'll think about it."

He couldn't stand the ache of loss that resonated in her voice. "Ray, I appreciate everything you've done for us. Really, I do. But Emma and I have to figure this out on our own now."

"Can you at least do one thing for me?"

"Sure."

"Ask Emma what *she* wants to do."

"She's six."

"Going on thirty," Rachel said. "You know she's been listening this whole time. Ask her."

Josiah sighed and looked at Emma. This little girl was all he had left of

Camilla. And when she stared at him with Camilla's same expectant expression, his guilt became unbearable.

"You don't want to go Africa, do you, Cricket?"

Emma threw her arms around his neck and wrapped her lanky little legs around his waist. "I do, Daddy!" In her hopeful gaze, it was as if every promise he'd ever made to Camilla waited to be fulfilled.

Against his better judgment, he swallowed his hesitation. "Africa it is." On the other end of the phone, Josiah could hear his sister cheering. "Two weeks, Ray. That's all I can give you."

"Only two weeks?"

He peeled his daughter off him and sat her on the bed. "Take it or leave it."

Rachel didn't hesitate. "I'll take it."

"You better pray I don't regret this, sister."

"Come to Africa, and I'll help you burn that ugly pile of regret you carry around, brother."

"On the water?" he scoffed. "Won't be much of a fire."

CHAPTER TWO

NIGERIAN COAST, ONE MONTH LATER

MACKENZIE SCOTT SHIFTED IN HER SEAT IN THE TRANSPORT HELICOPTER. She longed for an hour in the pool to work out the kinks from traversing six time zones on two commercial flights from Atlanta to Lagos, followed by a smaller chartered flight across the African country to the city of Warri. But relief was a luxury she could not afford. Not if she was going to be the first woman to earn the rank of team leader on the highly specialized extraction squad.

The helo banked to the left, and the Nigerian shoreline came into view. Endless miles of stunning blue ocean spread out in front of her, a beauty she hadn't expected in this dangerous part of the world.

Moses "Mo" Adams's elbow poked her side. "Next time we do this, I get the window seat."

She tightened her helmet and shot him a smile. "Not if I outrank you."

"Until then." He leaned past her and plastered his face against the window. She was glad someone had screwed up Mo's vacation paperwork. The delay had left him available for this assignment.

"Whoa. If this is the armpit of Africa, this stint isn't gonna be bad at all."

Mo fished his cell phone from his pocket. "Looks like paradise compared to Iraq."

"Don't let the trees fool you. Foliage can hide a multitude of sins," she shouted through the headset.

"Africa." The word rolled off Mo's tongue like he was some rich Wall Street Banker going on safari. He aimed his phone at the view below. "It's gonna be hard to convince the wife and kids that the old man is suffering while they're on vacation without me." He snapped a picture.

"What are you doing?"

"Little souvenir."

Mackenzie pushed his phone away. "You know this mission's classified."

"Don't worry." Mo nudged her with his elbow. "Susan thinks I'm training in the Bahamas."

"Why'd you tell her that?"

"How else am I going to explain the tan?" A lopsided grin split his brown face. "A little wishing-you-were-here pic would make her feel better." He stuffed his phone in his pocket and laughed. "Chill, Mac. I'm not going to actually send it."

Mo's wife and two young boys were the luckiest people Mackenzie knew, despite his tendency to preach. She'd given up on Mo's Sunday school God a long time ago and would plead her case for God's lack of concern for her life if she didn't secretly feed on Mo's eternal optimism. Some days the guy's belief that if *anyone can set the record straight God can* was all she had.

The helicopter continued its route, skimming the shoreline and white-capped waves of the coastline. Mackenzie pushed her doubts to the back of her mind and studied the terrain. The lush vegetation slowly gave way to a scattering of isolated, cinderblock facilities, no doubt built by the oil industry.

She'd done her homework on the flight over, and this was more what she'd expected to see. Far from the booming capital and the well-managed press coverage, a different picture emerged. There were signs of dying mangroves, and pools of water polluted with dark patches of oil. Here, as they headed toward the infamous Niger Delta, lay the center of an international controversy where tensions between foreign oil corporations and local militant groups had reached a boiling point. And from the air, she could see why. The blackened devastation seemed almost apocalyptic.

All because of the treasure that lay buried beneath the dozen or so oil platforms dotting the harbor like straws stuck in a milk carton.

Oil. Black gold. Lots of it.

Since the discovery of such vast quantities of fossil fuel back in the fifties, every nation in the world had made a run to stake their claim on the fortune. American dependence upon the energy source only helped drive the stampede.

The video clips she'd watched earlier showed how oil money had divided the country because of the lucrative profits that had all but vanished from the hands of the local people. Pictures of Africans struggling to survive and make the best of their situation replayed in Mackenzie's head. The combination of a lack of jobs, decaying infrastructure, and miles of pipelines and oil spills had resulted in gangs and armed groups demanding a share of the oil profits. When their demands were denied, they'd retaliated by attacking the tankers and taking hostages for ransom, resulting in a loss of hundreds of thousands of barrels per day.

The last hijacked tanker in the gulf had been held for six weeks and had purportedly cost insurance four million US dollars and three lives. This current situation they were headed for had been going on for twelve days. Drilling operations had been suspended by the Texas-based company who operated four off-shore rigs in the region.

Maybe she should have stayed off the computer during their short layover in Amsterdam, but whether or not the locals received their due was not her problem to solve today. She was here to extricate a shipload of hostages in an attempt to make international waters safe again.

Period.

The helo buzzed over another shantytown where dozens of houses were laid out in a row with their rusted corrugated metal roofs. The vegetation was no longer green and lush but blackened with oil. Endless creeks and canals snaked along the terrain, all unnatural shades of black, gray, and green.

"How do these people survive here—"

"Ladies and gentlemen, we're currently heading out over the gulf, and we'll be landing in the next couple minutes." The pilot's announcement swallowed Mackenzie's question and stopped any further conversation. "We've got a bit of a strong tailwind chasing us, so please make sure your seatbelts are fastened."

By the time she'd double checked her seat belt, they were circling the massive metal structure that loomed out of the water. Four bright orange legs supported the oil platform, its metal scaffolding, and mining cranes towering above the blue-gray waters. The pilot set the helo on the platform and a moment later, Mac stepped onto the landing pad, rattled but in one piece. The stifling heat of the Equator hit her full force. The increased humidity immediately transformed her crisp uniform into a sticky blanket she wanted to shed. She wiped her brow and gave her surroundings the once-over.

The salty breezes off the Gulf of Guinea were stronger and the sunrays more powerful than anything she'd encountered during her military training. But she'd spent her life proving to anyone who knew her Navy admiral father that she was as good as him. This was no different.

Tendrils of steam rose from the surface of the platform and moisture from the humidity seeped through her khaki pants and black T-shirt. Perspiration trickled from her neck and dripped down her back. The dark curls she'd pulled back tightly were already a tangled mess in this sauna. This was not her world. She was an alien, more than likely as unwanted as the oilmen she'd been sent to extract. She hoisted the strap of her duffel over her shoulder. Going against the odds was territory she knew better than Mo knew his God.

Mo elbowed her. "I don't think we're in Kansas anymore, Toto."

In the seventeen hours since she'd been given her orders, she'd slept maybe five. Jet lag and exhaustion would catch her fast in this oppressive heat. She followed Mo and the pilot toward an open door to the side of the helo pad where the rest of their team was waiting for them inside.

The oldest of the four soldiers stepped forward, his weathered skin and military stance indicated that this was not his first extraction. "I'm Commander Brandon Knight your team leader. Welcome aboard. For the next few days this oil platform will be your home. Hope you got some sleep on the way over here, because I've been given orders to brief you and then get to work."

"Not a problem," Mo said.

"I'll let you introduce yourselves."

The tallest of the remaining men stepped forward and shook their hands.

"Wayne Sloan. US Special Forces for seven years. Three years with SWAT in Dallas."

Gregory Benson was shorter, but had the physique of a wrestler. "Retired marine and sniper."

"Javier Díaz." The last man had a military haircut and tattoos covering his forearms. "Four overseas tours with the army and five years in diplomatic security detail."

Their resumes were impressive, but none of their work experience surprised her. In order to get a job like this, candidates couldn't even apply unless they had extensive military and/or law enforcement background that included being a member of a SWAT or another equivalent tactical response team. On top of the necessary credentials, everyone had been required to pass rigorous physical fitness tests and weapons qualifications.

Commander Knight strode toward Mackenzie after Mo introduced himself with an equally impressive resume. His displeasure was evident on his weathered face. "And you're Scott. I wasn't expecting a—"

"Woman?" she countered, holding the man's gaze.

He leaned in closer so she could hear him over the noise of the platform. "You're not afraid of the water, are you?"

"You tell me." Mackenzie tilted her head a couple degrees. "Two years training as an Aviation Rescue Swimmer, including water, land, and flight safety, Rescue Swimmer school, and then based on a helicopter command at sea with the US Navy for almost four years. Two tours in the Middle East, and oh. . .a perfect M4 qualification score. I think I'll be able to keep up with your boys."

The man's jaw slackened at her response, and she thought she saw the hint of a smile, but Mackenzie didn't blink. She was used to the surprised look on team members' faces when they realized a woman was going to be a part of their security team. But she was good at what she did and made no apologies.

"I was briefed that we've got a hostage situation with ransom demands that need to be settled," she said.

Knight took a step back. "Scott's right, men." Emphasis on men. "As soon as night falls, the six of us will be flying out toward the hijacked vessel."

"The report we read on our flight over was pretty sketchy. How many are on board the tanker?" Her commander might not like being pushed by a woman, but she didn't care. Going in blind was how people got killed.

"Twenty-four hours ago, one of the hostages was able to get out information confirming seven armed men holding thirty-three hostages in the mess hall."

"What about negotiations?" Mackenzie pressed.

"If negotiations had progressed, we wouldn't be here."

"What do they want?" Mo asked.

"Fifteen million dollars. And they're threatening to blow up the ship if their demands aren't met."

Her jaw tensed, but she refused to be intimidated by some higher-ranking guy with an ego. "It's a risky move to try to take them down physically."

"That's why the six of us were hired. To go in and put an end to this, quickly."

Mac plunged ahead with her theory. "This group—whoever has taken the hostages—has a different MO than the others."

"Different how?"

Knight's frown deepened, but she wasn't done yet.

"Typically, we've seen well-orchestrated attacks involving speed boats and plenty of firepower in this area. Sometimes they even utilize bombs in the pipelines to make sure they're being taken seriously. Often they take hostages to a separate location, so they have complete control of the situation."

"I'm not sure what your point is, Scott, but it's been twelve days. They're holding thirty-three hostages, including the captain and one of the oil executives. Are you saying we should just walk away because things have stalled with the negotiator?"

"Not at all." She glanced at Mo and caught a flash of warning in his eyes for her not to push the man, but if she was going to put her life on the line, she was going to see she had all the information needed to ensure things didn't go south. "I'm just saying that the negotiation might go better if we knew who was behind this. In the brief I read, none of the normal militant groups have claimed responsibility, and as far as we know from the proof-of-life videos given, there have been no injuries, which means—"

"We weren't hired to negotiate." Knight stepped up to her. "That's already been tried and failed. Our job is to go in and take down whoever's behind this. Period." He glanced at the rest of them. "Any questions?"

"No, sir," the team, including Mackenzie, shouted in unison.

"Good. Then let's get to work. We've only got a few hours to put an end to this situation."

CHAPTER THREE

DOUALA, CAMEROON, CENTRAL AFRICA

Tropical humidity hung on Josiah like a shroud as he tightened his grip on Emma's hand and surveyed the yellow taxis lined up outside baggage claim where his sister had told them to meet her. Someone jostled them from behind, and he pulled Emma closer to him. If they got separated, he'd never find her in this throng of people. After an hour of maneuvering through crowded health inspection lines, customs, and finally baggage claim, he was kicking himself. Coming to Africa was the biggest mistake he'd made in his life.

He glanced at his daughter. How could she be so wide awake after thirty-five hours of flying? He, on the other hand, needed either a shot of caffeine or a bed if he was going to make it. But the last thing he wanted was for Emma to notice his crabbiness. He'd made himself a promise once he'd agreed to come. For the next two weeks, he was going to try to put his guilt aside and be the father Emma deserved. It's what Camilla would have wanted. It's what he wanted.

"You see Aunt Rachel anywhere, Cricket?"

Emma tented her palm beneath her slipping tiara. "Maybe she got tired of waiting on us."

Josiah squeezed Emma's hand tighter still, as a man came up to them with an offer of a taxi ride, which he quickly declined. "My sister has the patience to watch a cell mutate. She didn't get tired of waiting on us."

It was true that he might have dragged his feet a bit since acquiescing to his sister's harebrained scheme. Rachel complained every time he pushed back his departure date. Every time, he reminded her that she'd agreed to giving him time to complete their immunizations, procure Emma's passport, and clear his surgery schedule. He wasn't surprised when his little sister called his overloaded operating-schedule excuse *flimsy*. After all, she lived in a lab with her eyes glued to a microscope and her nose in a petri dish. But cells didn't make angry calls when things didn't go their way. She had no idea the negative impact her little soul-revival experiment would have on a practice he'd worked hard to build. Hollywood A-listers expected their "touch-up" work to be done between films. He'd had to nip and tuck around the clock to accommodate his star-studded clientele.

"Emma! Joey!" The petite blonde hurrying toward them and calling their names wore blue scrubs and a huge, victorious smile.

"Aunt Ray!" Emma dropped his hand and dashed toward his sister. "We're here!"

Seeing Rachel's beaming face didn't cool the silent battle Josiah had been fighting as much with himself as with his sister. He knew Rachel persisted in these futile ploys because she loved him. But grief wasn't a virus to be cured. It was the cement overcoat he'd worn for almost two years. Some days the pain was so heavy he didn't think he could take another step. Yet he'd grown comfortable in its torment. He'd be naked without the burden. . .and still unhappy. If it weren't for the joy on his sister's face, he'd declare that he'd already seen enough of Africa and save himself the added weight of the mistake of staying.

Minutes later, they'd managed to weave their way to their transport vehicle. The white Land Cruiser was emblazoned on the sides with the *Liberty*'s logo. Rachel insisted Josiah sit up front with Samson, the broad-shouldered driver. "I don't have to be back in the lab for a couple of hours, so Samson and I thought you'd enjoy taking the scenic route."

"We're pretty beat, Ray."

"I'll give you the shortened tourist version then." She hopped in and helped Emma buckle up. "Douala has the chief port of the country, which is why the *Liberty* is here. It's actually located on the banks of the Wouri River, with the two sides of the city being linked by a bridge."

Emma pointed at a cluster of street vendors. "What are they selling, Mr. Samson?"

Samson's laugh was deep in response to Emma's question. "If you want it, someone will be selling it. Ground nuts, sugar cane, shoes, fried plantain, and the best fish rolls you've ever tasted."

"Can we try one?" Emma asked.

"I'll make sure you get one while you're here," Samson said.

Josiah tried to match his daughter's enthusiasm, but came up short. "Traffic's a bit crazy, and that's saying something coming from a guy from L.A."

The busy streets were filled with cars, motorcycles, and bikes, while pedestrians crowded the sidewalks.

"What's that big building?" Emma asked as they slowed to a stop at a light.

"A cathedral," Rachel said. "A big church."

"Oh," Emma sighed. "We drive by one of those back home."

"Maybe your daddy can take you to see it. Would you like that?"

"Daddy gets sad when he goes to church, because of Mama."

Rachel met Josiah's furtive gaze with an air of caution then quickly turned her attention to curbing Emma's disappointment with a promise. "You and I will slip away one day while your daddy's busy in the OR. We can visit the city and eat fish rolls."

"Can I wear my crown?" Emma asked.

"Absolutely." Rachel kissed Emma's forehead. "You're a daughter of the King, aren't you?"

He started to tell his sister to lay off the God-talk, but in keeping with his promise to make the most of this trip, he decided to keep his mouth shut. For now.

The oil money disappeared into the potholes that pocked the crumbling pavement and Josiah's guilt bounced around inside him like the Land Cruiser on the rough road. Camilla would not be pleased if he allowed his anger at God to rub off on their daughter.

Rachel lowered her window and Emma followed suit. A briny ocean breeze whipped their hair as Rachel tried to distract him from the neglected buildings, ramshackle high-rise apartments, and muddy slums by pointing out the bay on the other side of the narrow coastal road as they headed toward the port.

"Looks pretty rough here, Ray."

"Relax, big brother." Rachel reached up and patted his shoulder. "It's not the Amazon."

He shook free of her touch, but the terrifying memory of clinging to his father in the middle of the Amazon jungle didn't budge. "You can't hide a war-torn, third-world country beneath one shiny church steeple, Ray."

"Then you can understand why I'm here. These people are suffering. Most don't even have access to basic medical care." Rachel leaned between the seats and nodded toward a harbor filled with boats of varying sizes. "There she is. The *Liberty*. Your home for the next two weeks."

The gleaming white medical ship, a big blue cross splashed across its towering smokestack, dwarfed every other vessel in the busy port. Semis lined the pier, loaded with pallets of rice, rolls of wire, and frozen fish. Samson expertly maneuvered the car around a portside market abuzz with fisherman and sellers, then he slowed to a crawl as he waited for the hundreds of men, women, and children to step aside so that the car could pass. The line went on for several blocks. Finally, Samson got to the end of it and wheeled the Land Cruiser into a parking space beside three similar vehicles marked with the *Liberty*'s logo.

Emma unsnapped her seatbelt and stuck her head through the open window to study the crowd they'd passed. "Are all these people here to see my daddy?"

"They line up like this every evaluation day," Rachel said sadly.

The knot tightened in Josiah's stomach. This was not going to be the vacation he needed. "How can one small ship possibly have enough doctors to treat that many patients?"

"We don't." Rachel unsnapped her seat belt. "We see as many as we can. Unfortunately, some of the worst facial deformity cases have to be turned away." She looked at him. "But now that you're here, we won't have to disappoint them."

"I can't save the world, Ray."

"One good doctor can do more than a hundred politicians." Rachel didn't give him time to argue. Instead, she and Samson jumped into planning his life. Samson agreed to deliver the luggage to their quarters so that Rachel could show her family around. "Come on, kiddo." Rachel took Emma's hand. "Let's get you started on acquiring a set of sea legs."

The prospect of living on deep water was far more disconcerting than treating the long line of patients stretching out before him. "You said the ship would remain ported."

"Relax, Joey." Rachel's eyes sparkled with the same childhood mischief that had loved to purposely tip his canoe into the Amazon River. "See those huge tether chains? This ship's not going anywhere for several months."

Josiah slung the strap of his medical bag over his shoulder and hurried to catch up with his sister and daughter.

As he neared the crowd, a whiff of the tell-tale odor of neglected gynecological issues assaulted his nose. He told himself to ignore the stench of women rotting from the inside out. To mind his own business and to focus on protecting his daughter. But something inside him, a feeling he hadn't felt since Camilla died, wouldn't let him walk away. He stopped and quickly scanned the sea of brightly colored dresses. To his right, a woman rested a toddler with a cleft palate on her hip. To his left, another woman was trying to nurse an infant with a similar condition. The children he could help. The mothers suffered exhaustion, malnutrition, and possible anemia. He remembered enough from the surgeries he performed on a residency ob/gyn rotation that he could at least stop any uncontrolled hemorrhaging. His gaze leapt to a teenager whose neck and face had been distorted by a large tumor. He could do something about it, if the growth wasn't cancerous.

Everywhere he looked, the diseases of abject poverty stared back at him. Tumors and deformities easily corrected in the States were clearly commonplace. Coming here may not have been a mistake.

"Patients with tumors wait dockside under these portable tents," Rachel said as they continued down the dock toward the gangplank. "Doctors see them one at a time and determine whether or not we can treat them. We use the tents for admissions and outpatient services. Patients are screened, then given an appointment card if our team thinks we might be able to help."

"I have to say, I'm impressed."

She shot him a smile. "And you haven't even seen inside the *Liberty* yet."

"Daddy!" Emma's cry shifted his gaze.

"Emma!" Josiah raked the array of colorful clothing and scarf-wrapped heads. No silky-headed miniature brunette. Heart racing, he pushed through the crowd. "Emma!"

"Here, Daddy."

He found his daughter standing nose to nose with a bone-thin barefoot boy dressed in tattered shorts and a dirty shirt. The boy supported his windswept legs with a short stick.

Schwartz-Jampel syndrome. An abnormal outward turned deformity in one knee in association with an inward turning in the other. But these problems were also coupled with a snake-like deformity to his hips, knees, and ankles. In countries with decent medical care, these dysmorphic features led to a diagnosis by no later than the age of three. From the peach fuzz sprouting from his fixed facial expression of pursed lips and narrowed palpebral fissures, this boy was probably closer to thirteen. Because he'd lived so many years without treatment, his body had compressed into the shape of a lower-case Z.

Reading about a rare deformity in med school was one thing. Seeing an actual victim trying to stand despite his twisted body shook Josiah to the core.

"This is Faoudu, Daddy." Emma introduced the boy to him as if he was a Disney star and not a child who needed to be on someone's emergency surgery roster. "I told him you could fix his hurt legs." The compassion in Emma's face reflected her mother's. Whenever a sick child was presented to Camilla, she refused to see anything but possibilities. "Say hello, Daddy."

He hated when Emma looked at him like he could save the world. He didn't even know how to save himself.

Josiah squatted until he too was eye-to-eye with the hopeful gaze of the bent boy. "Faoudu." Josiah started to say that he hadn't done ortho since residency, but instead he said, "I'll see what I can do." The twinge in the corner of the boy's half-fixed smile chipped at the stone in Josiah's chest. "No promises, kid. Understand?"

The boy nodded.

Josiah rose and faced Rachel. "Do you have an orthopedic surgeon?"

"For another week," she said. "He's in the village doing some follow-up visits."

"We need to make sure that Faoudu is first on his schedule when he returns."

A pleased grin tugged at the corner of his sister's lip. She gave him a two-fingered salute. "Aye, aye, Doctor." Rachel led them toward the metal gangway.

At the security station at the base of the ramp leading to the ship, Josiah stopped and craned his neck backward. He counted four stories towering above the waterline. He owed his sister an apology. The *Liberty* was no rusty bucket of bolts.

Rachel flashed her badge and called each armed guard by name. "These are our Gurkhas," she told Emma. "They keep us safe."

The burly men required Josiah and Emma to empty their backpacks. Even Rachel had to take a turn walking through the free-standing metal detector.

"It's easier to get on an international flight than to get past those guys," Josiah said as he stuffed his laptop into his bag.

"I told you it would be safe." Rachel took Emma's hand. "The floors of a ship are called decks," she explained as she led them up the gangway. "The walls are called bulkheads, and the stairs are called ladders. There are no halls or corridors in a ship, only passageways. Openings to the outside of the ship are ports, not windows. Openings from one deck to another are called hatches. The handles on the watertight hatch or door are called dogs."

"Dogs. Got it," Emma said enthusiastically.

They stepped into the ship's bright and inviting reception area, then continued the tour through the internet café, coffee bar, and general store. The ship looked like an American mall inside. Bright, clean passages. The fresh scent of industrial cleaner. People hurrying from one end to the other. But the subtle roll of the Atlantic Ocean beneath his feet would not let Josiah forget he was on a boat. He rotated slowly as his thoughts about whether or not it was too late to rescind his idiotic decision to stay clashed with a growing desire to use his skills on the patients lined up along the dock.

Sensing his discomfort, Rachel said, "Let's check out the hospital deck, shall we?"

For the next hour, Rachel dragged them through narrow passageways and up and down even narrower stairs.

The hospital level, while tight on space, had five operating theaters with an adjoining scrub room and was stocked with everything he'd asked for.

There was also an up-to-date CT scanner, X-ray room, a full-scale lab, and the latest surgical instruments. The single-room accommodations he and Emma had been assigned were about the size of the pantry in his house in Beverly Hills, but he hadn't come here expecting to be comfortable. He only needed a place to sleep and shower. His time would be spent in the OR and trying to reconnect with his daughter. The latter scared him more than the likelihood that he would be expected to perform surgeries beyond his realm of expertise.

"Who wants ice cream?" Rachel asked when they returned to the café.

Before Emma could jump in with her order, Josiah cut her off. "We need sleep instead of sugar."

"You can crash once you get Emma enrolled in school."

"School?" Josiah scowled. "We're not going to be here long enough to worry about Emma missing a couple of weeks of school."

"Six-year-olds have to go to school every day, Daddy." Emma crossed her arms over her rumpled pink princess T-shirt. "Even in Africa."

"She can't just roam about unattended while you and I are working."

"I'm not suggesting we give her the keys to the Land Cruisers," Josiah said. "But I thought you promised a babysitter."

"I'm not a baby, Daddy."

He didn't like disappointing his daughter, but from the roll of her eyes, that's what he'd done. . .again. Since her mother's death, he felt like Emma had been searching his soul for something more. But there was nothing more. Maybe there never had been. Camilla had always been the one who bridged the gaps between their family life and his work commitments. Without her, he feared the divide would become an ocean neither he nor his daughter could cross.

Josiah pushed aside the guilt Emma had leveled on him and squatted so that he could explain his decision to her eye-to-eye. "Nobody's calling you a baby, Cricket." He balanced on the balls of his feet. "I just think you'd have more fun if you had some sort of one-on-one guide to show you around." He leaned in and whispered, "Who knows, you might even figure out how to run this place."

"Then what would the captain do if I took over his job?"

Encouraged by her grin, he reached for her hand. "If I buy you a strawberry cone, will you cut me some slack, let me figure out how I can help people, and keep you from causing a mutiny?"

Emma considered his offer only for a second. "If I went to school, they would teach me what mutiny means."

"Ray, can you help me out here?"

"After you meet someone." Rachel turned and motioned to an attractive black woman with a brightly flowered dress and silver streaks in her hair.

"Dr. Allen?" The woman held out her hand. "I'm Loraine Tanner, the ship's school principal. Rachel told me you were arriving today."

"Principal?" Josiah cast a glare Rachel's way.

"I need to check on some labs one of the surgeons ordered," Rachel chirped. "Loraine will fill you in on the school, then take you back to reception where they process new crew members, give you your badges and keys to your room, and do a final orientation. I'll meet you for dinner in the cafeteria at say. . .six?"

Josiah just nodded.

"My son's a doctor," Loraine said as Rachel disappeared around a corner, "so I have a great respect for your profession and your willingness to take time out of your busy schedule to bless the people here."

Josiah realized the principal was waiting for a response. "What's his field?"

"Internal medicine," she said proudly, then turned her full attention to Emma. "You must be the brilliant young lady I've heard so much about."

Emma beamed at the praise.

"Confident *and* bold is exactly how your aunt described you." Mrs. Tanner leaned in close. "I have a feeling you'll fit right in, Emma Grace." She nodded toward the café. "Let's sit down and fill out the paperwork over ice cream, shall we?"

Five minutes later, Mrs. Tanner handed Emma a double-scoop cone and offered Josiah one of the two cappuccinos she'd ordered. "To keep you going, Doctor, though you're not the only one needing a caffeine pick me up right now."

Josiah chuckled. "Not a bad idea."

"I've learned that the healing of these people is a slow and tedious process."

He inhaled the delicious fumes coming from his Styrofoam cup. "Are they expecting me in the OR today?"

"Not until tomorrow. Today is orientation. A bunch of paperwork, plus a muster call, along with your orientation on lifeboat procedures, quarantine regulations, invasion protocols—"

"Invasion protocols?" Josiah blurted. "You've got to be kidding."

Loraine smiled. "It's all standard procedure. Nothing to worry about, Dr. Allen. You've seen the security in place. No one's getting on this ship without going through the assigned security officers, our rotating Gurkha security guards, and metal detectors. There are even closed-circuit television cameras located around the vessel. The bridge and engine rooms are locked. We might not expect trouble, but if anything does happen, our captain wants his crew well prepared."

Talking about armed guards didn't make him feel any better, but he nodded.

"So, what do you think of our little port-side operation, Dr. Allen?" the older woman asked in what he assumed was an attempt to distract him from thoughts of pirates.

A wall-mounted TV tuned to the news played on the wall above the coffee bar. He didn't want to admit that he was a coward running from ghosts or that most of his operating experience had come from working on wealthy women choosing to reshape their noses or plump their lips. Seeing the need all around him made him feel as if he'd been wasting his talents considering his training as a pediatric cranial-facial surgeon.

But this seasoned educator had already seen straight through him, and from the penetrating set of her eyes, she expected the truth.

"Honestly, I'm extremely impressed. It's clean. Up to date. And, from the nurses I've talked to, adequately staffed."

"He's very good at fixing faces." Emma hoisted a hip up on a bar stool. "Mama used to say if Daddy can't make you look ten years younger, no one can."

He didn't know what surprised him more, that he'd completely failed to teach his child acceptable social skills with adults or that his daughter once again remembered word for word what her mother used to say.

"Em—"

"It's true," Emma continued. "He could even shave that bump off your nose, Mrs. Tanner."

"Em!"

"Really?" Loraine's hand flew to her nose. "Well, no wonder our organization was willing to bend the single-parent rule to snag such a talented surgeon."

Emma aimed her ice cream cone like a laser pointer at Loraine's face. "And if you're tired of those wrinkles—"

Josiah gave Emma a quick zip-the-lip sign.

Emma's nose scrunched. "I'm sorry, Mrs. Tanner—"

"Inquisitive minds are always welcome here, and I have a feeling your daughter has one of those."

"Why are *you* here, Mrs. Tanner?" Emma slurped a drip from her cone.

The principal cocked her head. "I believe you're the first student to ever ask that question." She went on to explain that she'd spent twenty years in the classroom, and another thirteen years in school administration. Five of those administrative years as a high school principal. "When I turned fifty-five, my sons were grown. So I decided it was time to retire and see the world." She wiped ice cream from Emma's chin. "But I love children, and working on a medical ship seemed the best way to combine my talents and goals." Her eyes twinkled over the rim of her glasses. "Be careful, Dr. Allen. Saving the world can get into your blood. Next thing you know, you'll be extending your commitment."

Josiah frowned. What did it matter if the world was saved when the one you loved the most was lost? Extending his commitment by even a minute was out of the question. He would concede to Rachel that he could do some good here. But in two weeks, no matter what kind of deformity waited in that long line on the dock, he was taking his daughter home.

He ripped his eyes from the principal's hopeful gaze and once again searched for the exit. His attention came to an abrupt halt at the television hanging on the wall. An aerial view of a large oil tanker flashed on the screen. Even with the sound muted he knew there was trouble. He scanned the close-captioned words scrolling at the bottom of the screen.

The twelve-day standoff in the Gulf of Guinea that has caught the attention of the world has taken yet another dramatic twist. While the details we've received are still sketchy, it has just been confirmed that ten of the thirty-three hostages being held aboard the Echo Atlantic were let go in a show of good faith about fifty-five minutes ago. This comes after two of the crew were killed on Monday in crossfire during a skirmish between the pirates holding them hostage.

Captain Bill Tillman and Sid Ramsey, an oil executive, still remain on the ship and according to our sources, no changes have been made to the fifteen-million dollar ransom the pirates are demanding in exchange for sparing the lives of these men...

Pirates? Seriously?

And he'd been worried about exposing his daughter to typhoid.

Josiah tore his gaze from the newscaster for a moment, hoping Emma, already an accomplished reader, was too absorbed in her ice cream and her conversation with Mrs. Tanner to notice the live footage streaming from the oil tanker's deck.

"Do they issue guns at that orientation?" he asked, only half joking.

Loraine chuckled. "If the *Liberty* was an oil tanker, I would have retired near my two boys and my grandkids a long time ago. But I've been here five years, Dr. Allen, and the worst trouble we've had aboard this ship is an outbreak of food poisoning from some bad chicken." She patted his arm. "These pirates aren't after a bunch of surgical equipment and medical volunteers who have to raise funds to support their time here. There is no money to be made by hijacking a medical ship."

Loraine's cell phone dinged, and she picked it up. "I'm sorry, but it's a message from my son asking me to call him." A frown furrowed her forehead. "My grandbaby isn't scheduled to arrive for another week. I hope this little one isn't coming early. That would really throw a wrench in my flight plans." She noticed the worried look on Emma's face. "Don't worry, Emma Grace. We'll get you settled."

"Okay."

"For now, we'll head on to reception so you can finish your orientation." She lifted Emma's downcast chin. "Starting tomorrow, you'll start school and your father will start changing lives."

CHAPTER FOUR

GULF OF GUINEA, CENTRAL AFRICA

It was a textbook plan. A helicopter would drop their team ten miles from the hijacked tanker by parachute. Their target at that point would be a Rigid-hull Inflatable Boat, or an RHIB, dispatched from the aircraft and waiting for them in the gulf below. They'd swim to the boat, haul in the chutes, then make their way to the oil tanker under the cover of darkness. Once the mission was successfully completed and the hostages secured, they'd radio for an extraction. If everything went as planned, the hostages would be home in forty-eight hours.

If everything went as planned.

Mackenzie grabbed her gear and walked out the door of the cramped quarters that separated her from the whoosh of testosterone crowding the narrow hall and shoved aside any lingering reservations. No plan was foolproof. She'd learned a long time ago that a plan was only as good as its execution. This was her first time working with most of her new teammates. She'd have to let go of her need to control if she was going to trust them with her life.

"Mac!" Mo's deep bass cut through the squadron's frenzied exit. "Wait up." He struggled with the straps of his backpack as he ran to catch her.

"Keep up, old man." She shot him a grin as they headed toward the civilian version of the Boeing Chinook. Used primarily by the US Army and the Royal Air Force, the helicopter was a perfect workhorse for a mission like this, already used for hundreds of tactical and airdrop missions. Just like the one they were about to implement.

Mo hurried alongside her. "You ready for this?"

"Always."

"I hear the water temp is nice."

"Then we're in luck."

"But once we're on the ship. . ."

She stopped and caught his gaze as they waited for the go ahead to board the helo. "You sound worried."

Which meant something was wrong. Mo was never worried.

"Not worried, just. . .cautious. I don't know. Some things aren't adding up, like the message one of the hostages was able to send. The intel was specific enough to justify this operation, but we can't verify who actually sent it."

"You think we're looking at some kind of ambush?"

He hesitated, then let out a low chuckle. "I think I'm beginning to sound like you." But the smile on his face quickly faded. "Susan thinks I made the wrong decision in taking this job."

"I know she misses you, but you're halfway through your contract. You'll be home soon."

He'd signed the six-month contract with the private security company, whose role included everything from crisis action planning to personnel rescue operations like they were doing now. The hefty paycheck offered would go a long way toward his sister's unexpected medical bills, but the personal cost to his family had been high.

"Forget I said anything," he said. "We'll talk about it once we're celebrating our victory on the plane ride back home."

She nodded, but she couldn't help wondering if he regretted letting her talk him into this. "Sure. It's a deal."

The pilot signaled the all clear, and soon they were ducking beneath the whirring blades of the chopper and jumping in through the open side panel. She strapped into one of the seats on the side, still trying to forget Mo's reservations. Now was not the time to lose her focus. She tugged the bulbous flight helmet onto her head and secured the strap under her chin. The rest of the team piled in around her. She let her adrenaline soar. She was ready to do this.

Compared to the mountain rescue training that had forced her to hang over jagged granite, dangling several hundred yards above water thrilled her. Water gave. Water welcomed her with its sweet embrace. Water offered a fighting chance. Stone was unforgiving. The one guy she'd ever dared to get serious about had used the same description to describe her heart when they broke up. Every time she bailed out over a solid surface, she had to fight off the feeling that like most of the relationships in her life, this encounter could be her last. Today, she'd have a chance to prove her stuff on turf she trusted.

The chopper lifted and sped farther out to sea. Mo's words continued to repeat in her mind, no matter how hard she tried to dismiss them. He was always the optimist. The one who saw the glass half full. The one who believed that saving lives was always worth the risks. Why was he suddenly hesitating?

"Stay alert, people."

The team leader's order terminated Mac's internalization and snapped her attention back to the watery terrain. She made a quick check of the sky. Jagged fingers of lightning poked holes in the distance, but the inky darkness shrouded moon and stars, which would give them yet another advantage. They couldn't go into this with any hesitations. Fear would get them killed.

The crewmen on that tanker were depending upon her ability to perform life-saving missions in remote areas under bad conditions. She directed her focus to the indiscernible horizon, searching for the lights of a ship, but they were still too far out. And more than likely, the hijacked tanker had gone dark, dousing any unnecessary lights that would give their location away.

The helicopter veered sharply to the right, slamming Mackenzie against Mo. A percussive *whap* of the blades pulsed in Mackenzie's helmet. She snapped her night vision goggles into place. A phosphorescent green glow outlined Mo's face. She craned her neck, adjusting her position to compensate for her limited field of vision.

The RHIB dropped into the water from the helo behind them. It was time to jump. She gathered her gear, then waited for the command.

"You're up , Scott."

"Yes, sir."

"Keep your eyes on the target."

Mackenzie moved to the open doorway. She perched with the tips of her boots supported by nothing but air, searching the cold black waters for the boat. Lightning flashed. Everything went red for a split second then the green glow returned directly below her.

"Go!"

The weight of her gear on her back added to gravity's deadly pull as she made the jump. Seconds later, her parachute ripped open, slowing her descent. Her lungs sucked in the salt-saturated wind as she aimed for the target. Her feet hit the water and her body sliced through the gulf's warm current. Relieved she'd stuck this landing, she shot back to the surface, then quickly swam toward the boat where three of the men, including Mo, were already on board. Another two minutes, and the six of them were headed toward the tanker in the RHIB, putting on their gear that had been waiting for them in the boat, and checking their radios.

The communication headsets they all wore were submersible and would allow them to communicate with each other as they carried out the rescue, but for the moment no one spoke. Instead, they made the ten-mile voyage in silence, each preparing mentally for what they were about to do. When the tanker finally came into view, silhouetted only by the pale light of the moon, Mac felt her pulse quicken.

"Let's go." Commander Knight whispered through their coms. "Clock's ticking."

The team's snipers assumed their positions at the front of the boat. They readied their weapons, pressing the monocular infra-red scopes tight against one eye. The tiniest flash of human heat would not go undetected. They were trained to take all the moving parts into consideration—the wind, the unsteady chopper, the rolling ship. Their job was to take out the hostage takers in the dark without harming the hostages.

They made their way up a metal ladder they'd thrown up to the sprawling deck, then spread out as planned. Mac yanked her pack from her back and extracted her weapon. Reining in her galloping heart, she did her best to allow the rhythms of her body to mesh with the harmonic motion of the ship. The sooner they synced, the better her aim would be. She did a visual sweep for shooters. She and Mo were to go directly to the mess hall and secure the hostages, while the other four men took out the hostiles and reestablished command of the vessel.

Her own sharp intake of breath sounded in her helmet. With hands tight on her weapon, she scrambled across the deck toward the bow. She'd memorized the schematics map of the vessel, because tracking down the hostiles before they were spotted was key. They were prepared for armed guards securing the upper deck. Unless Mo had somehow been right, and this was some kind of ambush.

Her heart pounded, but her senses stayed focused.

Bullets splintered the air.

"Two hostiles down," Knight said. "I repeat. Two hostiles down."

"Copy that," Mo said. "I just clipped a third, but he's still moving."

Mac heard more shots and dropped low again, needing to determine where they were coming from. Three more rounds came at her from above. One grazed her helmet. She saw another armed man and ducked behind a metal drum. She counted to three then raised and fired. Her .308 slug dropped a man. His AK-47 bounced across the deck. Red sparks. Green. Red.

"Deck clear," Sloan reported.

"Sloan and Benson," Knight said. "Clear the way for Adams and Scott. Díaz, we need to locate those other hostiles. I'm right behind you."

"Roger that."

She turned toward Mo who was to her right, and followed behind the two men. Seconds later, they hit the stairs and made their way toward the mess hall on the lower deck. They turned left. Stopped in front of two metal doors. Then kicked them open.

Mackenzie aimed her flashlight inside. Two dozen people stared back at her from along the far wall. All the tables in the room had been pushed to one side.

"The ship has been secured." Knight's terse voice sounded in Mac's headset. "But the remaining hostiles have escaped in a skiff, with possible hostages on board."

"Roger that," Sloan said. "We are in pursuit."

Mo stepped forward to address the terrified hostages while Mac counted them. "Our team was sent here by the oil company. I need each of you to kneel down with hands above you while we do an initial search, then I promise we'll get you back to your families."

She scanned the hostages, counting again.

Twenty-two.

"Who's missing?" she asked.

One of the men, wearing a button-down shirt and slacks but no shoes, raised his head. "They grabbed two of us when they heard the gunshots. The captain and Shannon Parker, one of the engineers. They headed out the far door."

"That should leave twenty-one," Mo said.

Mackenzie spoke into her headset. "How many hostiles were on that skiff?"

Silence.

"Repeat," Mac said. "How many hostiles on the skiff?"

"I can confirm three dead, and three on the escaping skiff."

That left one hostile unaccounted for.

A man on the far left pulled out a weapon and dragged the man next to him to his feet, the gun pointed at his temple.

"Nobody move!" he shouted.

Mackenzie automatically shifted her own weapon at the boy who didn't look a day over eighteen. How had he gotten involved in this? "It's over. Put your weapon down and let him go."

"No." He took a step toward the door. "I will leave this ship alive. You try to stop me, I will shoot him."

"Your men are gone, son." Mo's calm voice had a fatherly sound. "There's no one to help you. No way off this ship. Do as she said."

The boy pulled his hostage back another step.

"Do it now," Mackenzie shouted.

The boy fired her direction, and she returned the shot. A wave of nausea washed over her as he dropped to the ground and his hostage stumbled to safety.

"Last hostile is down," she said despite the taste of bile in her mouth.

"Roger that."

"You can all get up now." Mac took a step forward. Many of the hostages seemed confused, but none seemed seriously injured. "You'll all be able to get medical help. Start moving toward the upper deck."

She turned around as they started filing past her. Mo stood beside her with a strange look on his face.

"Mo?"

He held up his hand. It was covered with blood.

"Mo! What happened?"

He dropped to his knees. "I didn't even feel it, Mac."

"Man down. Mo's been shot," Mac shouted into her headset. "I repeat. Man down."

"What's his status?" crackled in her ear.

She helped Mo lie down, then grabbed her bandanna and pressed it against the wound where the bullet had hit his abdomen. No. No. No. This couldn't be happening.

"He's going to need an immediate medical evac," she shouted into the com. "He's losing too much blood."

"Copy that. Helo's two minutes out."

Her mind raced through their limited options. "Where's the nearest hospital?"

"I have confirmation that there's a ship docked just up the coast at Douala. A floating medical center based out of the US with state-of-the-art medical care."

"Advise them we're on the way." She turned back to Mo, her heart racing. "Looks like we found someone to patch you up, Mo, though I'm not sure why someone would be crazy enough to risk the lives of civilians in waters swarming with armed gangs and pirates."

"Have a little faith, Mac." Mo struggled to take a breath. "No matter what happens."

She frowned. "Oh, I have plenty of faith. Faith that our helo is going to get us to our destination. Faith that those docs are going to patch you up—"

Mo's eyes rolled back.

"Mo! You've got to stay with me. Susan will kill me if I don't bring you back in one piece. Talk to me."

"Tell Susan...Tell her and the boys I love her."

The room began to spin. He had to make it. He couldn't leave her to explain this to his wife and kids. She stumbled backward as two of the other men came to take him to the upper deck.

"Moses Adams, you're going to tell her that yourself, which means you can't quit on me. Not now. Not ever."

CHAPTER FIVE

DOUALA, CAMEROON

"DR. ALLEN." POUNDING STARTLED JOSIAH FROM A FITFUL SLEEP.

He sat up in bed and tried to pull himself away from the dream of a capsizing lifeboat dumping him into the dark waters of the ocean. He wouldn't have agreed to watching the orientation video if he'd known the message dwelt upon what to do if this ship went down.

"Dr. Allen, it's Samuel Methu." The African-accented English belonged to the chief medical officer from Cameroon he'd met yesterday. "I need your help. There's an emergency."

Emma's face dropped down over the top bunk, her eyes big in the glow of the clock flashing four o'clock. "Want me to get the door, Daddy?"

"Go back to sleep, Cricket." Josiah threw his legs over his bunk then stumbled to the door. "Samuel?"

The man, still dressed in scrubs, had a grave look to his dark-skinned face. "You're needed in surgery, doctor."

"Now?"

"Come." Samuel took his elbow. "I'll show you the fastest route."

"No offense, Samuel." Josiah stretched, still trying to clear his sleep-deprived brain. "But cleft palates aren't exactly an emergency."

"It's a gunshot wound."

Nerves that had lain dormant in Josiah since his surgical residency days snapped to full alert. "I'm not a trauma surgeon. Call someone else."

"There is no one else. Our ortho surgeon is onshore and currently without cell service. We cannot reach him. Our other surgeon is tied up with a complicated emergency C-section, and I'm a pediatrician with no surgical training."

"I can't leave my daughter."

"Bring her."

Josiah snatched up the bag containing his surgical instruments, slung the strap over his shoulder, then turned to summon Emma.

She was dressed and slipping into her shoes. "I'm ready, Daddy."

As the three of them raced to the stairs, Samuel phoned the head nurse. She cut off his inquiry with one word. "Hurry."

"I'm going to kill my sister," Josiah mumbled under his breath, squeezing Emma's hand tighter as they raced to the hospital deck.

The three of them burst out of the stairwell and into a wide, well-lit passageway. Samuel led the charge toward the surgical bays where two men wearing black tactical gear blocked the operating theater Josiah had seen during Rachel's proud tour of the facilities.

"Move," Josiah shouted at the group.

A tall woman, her curly dark hair wet, and green eyes flashing fire, shoved her way between the soldiers. Legs braced and fists jammed into her hips, she made her Kevlar-clad body into an unbreachable wall. "My partner's been shot." Blood splatter did not mar the perfect symmetry of her face. "I promised him I'd find a doctor who would make sure he lived."

"Then this is your lucky day." Josiah ripped his gaze from hers lest she see the doubt swirling beneath his boast. Bloodstains on her vest caught his attention. His triage followed the blood trail snaking down her legs. "Are you hurt?"

"No." Her gaze swept from him to Emma. "This isn't a place for a child."

"You're right." Josiah lifted Emma's hand that was fisted in his. "You look after my daughter, and I'll look after your partner."

"What?"

"Every second we stand here debating each other's obligations"—he inclined his head toward the operating room door— "decreases the probability that I can save your partner's life." He didn't wait for her agreement, but knelt and took Emma by the shoulders. "I need you to go with this nice lady."

Emma's gaze bounced from the glowering woman then back to him. "I told you, I don't need a babysitter, Daddy."

"No, but she does, Cricket."

He rose, pushed through the swinging door, and stepped into chaos.

Nurses fluttered around a large, bare-chested black man supine and unmoving on the operating table. An anesthesiologist stood at the patient's head, feeding the intubation tube into place and shouting orders for the blood protocol to be initiated.

Josiah stood immobile. He'd not operated on a ballistic trauma since his days as a surgical resident in a Dallas County hospital. Camilla used to tease him by telling him that for a man with his squeamish stomach, plastics was a much better career path. But he knew long before his days in the ER that he never wanted to be that guy again who did everything he could to save someone and then be forced to stand back and watch them die anyway. Controlled operating situations suited him better. Eyelift patients were far less likely to circle the drain. This man who was obviously suffering a massive hemorrhage from the AK-47 hole in his torso already had one foot in the grave.

The head nurse noticed him searching for the scrub sink and grabbed a clean gown. "Dr. Allen? Let me help."

She turned him around so she could secure the gown over his T-shirt and shorts then dropped his goggles and mask into place. Before he could find the words to say he wasn't the man for the job, he was already gowned and gloved.

"We did a CT." She spoke with the calm of someone experienced in trauma. "It appears a single round from an AK-47 struck him between the protective panels of his vest. The bullet entered his right side. Shredded the liver, then bounced around and ripped open the small intestine. There's a twenty-centimeter exit hole on his left side."

There was no time to sterilize the favorite tools of his trade. Besides, from the blood spilling on the floor, most of his specialized facial instruments would be of little use in this situation. The clock began ticking for this man the moment that bullet cut through him. Time was running out.

In the movies, people died quickly from these types of gunshot wounds, but in real life, dying from a hit to the abdomen was usually a slow, painful process.

Josiah stepped to the table. Blood soaked the packing someone had crammed into the large exit wound. "I've got to see what we can salvage inside." He held out his right palm. "Scalpel."

With one, steady slash, he cut through layers of well-defined muscle. This guy could probably bench press three hundred pounds and do sit ups all day long. He was too young and healthy to die. Josiah shoved the possibility aside. There was no way to make this pretty, but, for right now, all that mattered was keeping this man alive.

Josiah filleted his patient wide and stifled a gasp. The bullet's trajectory through the torso had created a pressure wave that had frayed tissue, severed blood vessels, and shattered organs.

"I'm going to need a hand to get all of these bleeders clamped." Josiah swiped at the blood splatter on his protective eyewear. "Get me another surgeon."

His nurse cleared his smeared goggles with a wipe. "There is no one else."

"Call my sister."

The nurse's brow furrowed over her glasses. "Rachel's not a surgeon."

He didn't have time to explain that Rachel had done a year of surgical residency before she switched her specialty to infectious diseases. "Get her!" He didn't look up from his prioritization of clamping gushing blood vessels over the removal of the compromised spleen or gaping hole in the small intestine.

Though tempted to rush from one gusher to the next, Josiah allowed his training to kick in. He sutured and clamped off with methodical precision. The nurse was sponging at the blood continuing to pool in the wreckage of this man's torso cavity when Rachel burst into the room.

"Tell me what you need," she said to Josiah as someone gloved her and tied a paper gown over her scrubs.

"Everything you've got."

Together they worked with the syncopation they'd developed as children, each anticipating the other's move a second before the move was made. Rachel tackled the removal of the spleen while he searched for the reason behind the continued loss of blood.

"We're losing him," the anesthesiologist announced.

"BP?" Josiah and Rachel asked at the same time.

"Fifty over thirty."

"He's in PEA arrest." Rachel lifted her hands from the bloody cavity.

"We need to do CPR." Josiah slapped his hands on the patient's chest and began to pump. "Come on, buddy. Stay with me."

Each pump brought back the memory of not knowing what to do as his father lay dying in a pool of blood on the jungle floor. Each pump was another day, another reminder, of watching his wife die in his arms.

"Josiah." Rachel tugged on his stiffened arms. "Josiah."

He didn't know how long he'd been pumping, demanding life to stay with this man he didn't know, but he was drenched in sweat. "What?"

"He's gone," Rachel whispered.

He stepped back from the table. His own heart pounding and his breath coming in the desperate gasps of a man who'd just ran a marathon, he tried to remember the last time someone had died on his operating table.

In the quiet that comes with death, he surveyed the bloody room. The staff, blinking tears from their eyes, looked to him for a word of comfort or explanation. All he could think to say was, "This isn't what I signed up for." He ripped off his gloves and stormed from the room.

"Daddy." Emma sprung from the waiting room chair. She skidded to a stop when she noticed the blood on his gown. "Is Mo okay?"

It took a second for her question to penetrate his angry fog. "Mo?"

"Mackenzie's friend."

"Mackenzie," he said, trying to sort the names.

"That's the lady's name, but she said I could call her Mac." By now, the woman who'd nailed him on his way into surgery had joined Emma. From her wary expression, she was prepared to nail him hard again if the results did not meet her expectations.

"Dr. Allen?" Mac's address was a question he did not want to answer.

Delivering bad news was the least favorite part of any doctor's job. Mackenzie—Mac—had expected a miracle, and he'd failed her. But he wasn't God. He knew that better than anyone.

He took a bold step forward and conveyed his condolences without offering details. Non-medicals rarely understood the ramifications of traumatic injuries or the exhausting efforts required to try to piece a person back together.

Except for a hard swallow, the woman allowed no reaction to show on her face. "Your daughter told me that you're new here. That this is your first day. That you normally spend your days ironing out wrinkles for aging Hollywood stars."

Josiah bit back the urge to tell her to leave his daughter out of this awful mess. He knew, from his own grief experiences that people suffering from loss often lashed out at the nearest target, which was almost always the unsuccessful doctor. He stepped forward to redirect her anger toward whoever had pulled the trigger when he felt a familiar hand slip through the exhausted arm that hung at his side and pull him back.

"My brother's a highly rated surgeon."

Mac's eyes flicked briefly toward the teammates standing beside her, then cut with a razor's edge back to him. "Mo didn't need a facelift. He needed a doctor who could save him."

Josiah bristled. "There's not a trauma surgeon on the planet who could have saved your friend. It looked like a bomb had gone off in his abdomen. Who shot him?"

"They weren't good guys." She blinked and, for a second, Josiah thought she was struggling to hold back tears. "Moses Adams was the last of those."

CHAPTER SIX

DOUALA, CAMEROON

MACKENZIE HUNG UP THE SKYPE CALL WITH MO'S WIFE AND STARED AT the screen. She'd not been able to shake the sickening feeling that had spread through her when she saw the surgeon's pale face. Mo was the one with the noble reason for being here. Her motivation on the other hand seemed shallow. And she'd been the one who had convinced him to sign on the dotted line and jump on that plane to Africa.

Now he was dead.

But guilt didn't play favorites. It found you no matter where you were, no matter who you were, no matter where you ran. Even on a medical ship that had traveled to the ends of the earth.

Mac fought back tears as she hurried down the ship's narrow passageway. Her boss would be calling soon with new orders, but she wasn't ready to walk away from this. Mo was dead, and someone needed to pay. Panic pressed against her chest until she couldn't breathe. She needed some fresh air. Needed to think.

She stopped in the middle of the passageway and realized she had no idea where she was. She leaned against the wall and took in a slow deep breath. There wasn't time to grieve. Not yet. She needed to find a way to pull herself together and find the rest of the men who'd hijacked the oil tanker. There would be time to fall apart later.

"Can I help you, ma'am?"

Mac looked up at a girl who didn't look old enough to be wearing medical scrubs. "I don't know. Which way to the cafeteria?"

"Straight ahead. One deck down. I could take you there—"

"I can find it. Thanks."

Mac hurried away from the girl. Not wanting to fall apart in front of a total stranger.

She found the cafeteria, but had no idea why she'd said she wanted to come here. The smell of coffee and breakfast sausage filled the air. There was no way she could eat.

But coffee. Maybe that would help.

Dozens of tables and chairs filled one side of the large room. The other side had a cafeteria where one could choose what one wanted to eat, as well as a coffee bar. About a fourth of the tables were filled with people talking and laughing.

Didn't they know Mo was dead?

"Miss Mackenzie?"

Mac paused at the sound of her name, then turned and saw Emma and her father sitting at one of the tables next to where she was standing.

"Do you want to sit with us?" the little girl asked.

Mac's gaze shifted from Emma to her father then back to Emma again. Being friendly with the man who'd failed to save Mo was the last thing she wanted to do. "Thank you, but I'm just going to grab some coffee."

Emma jumped up from her chair and clamped onto Mac's hand. "Sit down and I'll get you some. I'm good at ordering coffee. I get Daddy's all the time at home."

"Really, it's okay—"

"You might as well let her." The doctor with dark circles under his eyes looked as if he could use sleep instead of caffeine. "She's not good at taking no for an answer, especially when she's wanting to help."

"Okay, then. Thank you, Emma."

The smile on the dark-haired little girl faded. "I'm sorry that your friend died. My daddy's the best doctor, but sometimes people die and there's nothing a doctor can do."

Mac paused at the statement. How had someone so young acquired such a deep insight into death? "I'm sure your daddy is a wonderful doctor. Mo was hurt bad when he got here."

"What do you like in your coffee? Daddy takes his black, because he says it makes him smarter."

Mac's brow rose. "Smarter?"

Josiah cleared his throat. "There is some scientific evidence."

"You may be the doctor, but I'll take mine with two sugars and a splash of cream."

If Emma had caught the anger that still lingered in Mac's voice, she didn't let it sink her cheery spirits. "I'll be back."

Mac watched as Emma scurried off to the counter. "You've got quite a girl there."

"That's what I'm beginning to appreciate. She never ceases to amaze me, though sometimes that's the problem. She's not supposed to be the adult. I am."

Mac took measure of his honesty. She didn't know many men willing to risk their manhood by admitting they could be undone by a child. From his athletic physique and the confidence he'd displayed before and after Mo's surgery, his manhood was securely intact. She wanted to ask where Emma's mother was, but felt that wasn't any of her business. Clearly whatever had happened, the little girl seemed well adjusted and taken care of, though being a single parent—which she was assuming he was—on a ship like this couldn't be easy. She should know. Her mother had raised her on her own.

Josiah motioned to the empty chair at their table. Mac hesitated before finally sitting down. Guilt shot through her for chewing him out, but before she could admit she hadn't been at her best, he started talking.

"Listen, I want to apologize to you." He reached for his coffee that was still half full and cupped his hands around it. "I'm not sure I handled this morning the way I should have. But the bottom line is this: I'm so sorry for the loss of your friend. I wish I could have done more."

Mac looked across the room and blinked back the unwanted tears. She was used to being the strong one. Used to putting up a fight until she won. It was how she'd survived this long doing what she did. But having a man apologize was another chink in her initial impression of him.

"I'm sorry as well," she said. "Sorry I took it out on you. I just...I still can't believe he's gone. I had to call his wife and try to explain what had happened. How do you do that?"

She caught his gaze for a moment and saw the fatigue in his expression, but that wasn't all she saw. There was pain in his eyes, making her wonder if it was from losing a patient or from something more personal.

"Were you close?" he asked.

"We were. Mo wasn't just a coworker. He was a friend, and honestly, I don't make friends easy."

The words came out before she had a chance to stop them. The wall she'd erected around her heart had been put in place for a reason. The work she did was dangerous. Getting involved emotionally wasn't an option, and the last thing she needed to be doing was blubbering on about her relationship failures.

"I was the one who talked him into doing this," she continued like someone had pulled a cork out of her mouth. "He told me he needed money. I told him the pay was good. It was just supposed to be for six months. Long enough for him to get the money he needed to pay off his sister's medical debt."

Josiah set his coffee cup back down and leaned forward, his jaw tense. "This wasn't your fault."

"It wasn't yours either, as much as I wanted to blame you. I saw how much blood he'd lost before we were able to evacuate him off that boat. He knew it as well."

Tell my wife I love her.

If they'd have only come up with a better plan before boarding that ship. Been more cautious and ensured they'd accounted for all the hostiles.

"Two sugars and a splash of cream." Emma's voice yanked Mac back into the present. "And I asked Mary to add some whipped cream on top because whipped cream makes people happy."

Mac couldn't help but smile as Emma scooted in front of her eggs and sausage. "You did, did you?"

"Is that okay?"

"More than okay. In fact, I think I need to take you home with me. I could use someone like you to get my coffee every morning."

Emma giggled. "I can't drive."

"You can't?"

"I'm only six."

"Maybe ten years from now then." She took a sip of her coffee. "Because this is perfect."

"I'm glad." Emma beamed, then cocked her head. "I like your hair."

"Thanks, though this. . ." Mac said, pointing out its unruliness by tugging on a loose curl, "is thanks to my Scottish father and Jamaican mother."

"I wish I had curly hair."

"So you like curly hair. Let me guess something else about you," Mac said. "You like pink."

"It's my favorite color." Emma pointed at her pink princess shirt and matching pink shorts. "You must like pink too."

Mac glanced down at the pink scrubs covered with llamas someone had let her borrow while they washed her clothes that were stained with Mo's blood. She'd almost forgotten.

Josiah's phone buzzed and he grabbed it off the table. "I'm sorry. I've got to take this. I'll be right back, Cricket."

Mac watched him walk away, wondering what had brought someone like him to a place like this. And with his young daughter. She knew places like this did a tremendous work. It was one thing to sacrifice your own life for others, but to put your child at risk in a place infected with pirates and disease. She wasn't sure she could make that kind of sacrifice.

"You look sad."

Mac took another sip of her coffee while Emma finished her breakfast. "I suppose I am."

"It's sad when people die."

Mac hesitated, not knowing exactly how to respond. Talking to Emma about death and dying wasn't her place. "My heart is really sad to have lost my friend."

Emma cocked her head and caught Mac's gaze. "Why do people say someone is lost when they're really dead?"

Mac sat back, taken off guard by the question. "Maybe because when you say it that way, it doesn't sound quite as final."

"Except he's not lost. And he's not coming back."

Mac shook her head. "No, he's not."

"My mother died. She's not coming back either."

"Oh. I'm sorry."

She glanced toward the place where Emma's father was still talking on the phone, understanding better now Emma's knowledge of death and where her father's anger came from.

"Daddy's sorry too. Aunt Rachel thought coming on this ship would help him not be so sad anymore. She said it would give him a porpoise."

Mac couldn't contain a smile. "I think your aunt meant coming here would give your daddy a purpose."

"What's a purpose?"

It's what Mac thought she had, but now that Mo was gone, she didn't know. "It's a reason to do something really brave."

"Daddy's brave. He and Mama used to climb cliffs."

"Wow."

"After Mama fell, he burned his climbing stuff in the fire pit by the pool."

"I'm sorry about your mother."

"Me too. My daddy still cries sometimes. He tries not to let me hear him, but I know he does."

"Crying is okay. It helps us when we don't know what to say."

"I know. Aunt Rachel told me it's okay to feel sad and to cry. You can cry if you want. It won't upset me."

"I'm not sure I can right now, but I will. I promise."

But she knew it wasn't a promise she could keep. She'd given up crying a long time ago. She'd grieve in a way that would actually do some good. She'd get to work to right the wrong that had been done to Mo and make those pirates pay.

Emma picked up the last piece of sausage off her plate. "Did Mo have any children?"

The question sliced through her like a knife. "Two little boys."

How much did you tell a little girl who seemed more discerning than most adults?

"You can give this to them." Emma pulled off two string bracelets she'd been wearing on her wrist. A bright blue one and a bright yellow one. "And you can wear them until you see them, if you want."

"Emma, I couldn't—"

"It's okay. I want them to have them. What are their names?"

"Terrence and Jalen."

"Maybe they will help them not be so sad," Emma said as Mac slipped on the bracelets.

Maybe.

"Your father's going to help make a lot of people feel better working on this boat."

"I just don't like the sad parts. Like when people die. Like your friend. The good thing is that I'll get to see my daddy more. And I made a friend yesterday. His name is Faoudu and he has to walk with a stick. Daddy said he has jump. . ." Emma hesitated.

"Schwartz-Jampel syndrome." Josiah rubbed Emma's head, then sat back down.

"That's a mouthful," Mac said.

"Daddy's going to fix him."

"I'm going to try."

An awkward silence settled between them for a moment. Mac needed to go find her team and push them to go after the pirates. But, sitting in the cafeteria of an oversized medical ship with two people who understood loss better than she, somehow seemed the closest thing to normal she could imagine at the moment.

"Emma just told me she'll get to see you more while you're here working on the ship," she said, wanting to prolong the encounter a bit longer.

The smile slid from Josiah's face. "Someone begged to go to school, so I'm not sure how much time we'll have to hang out."

"That's okay. I love school," Emma said.

Mac caught the gleam in Emma's eyes. If only she could be six and so innocent again. "You sound excited."

"I am. Daddy's going to take me, and then Aunt Rachel promised to come during break and take me to the bridge to meet the captain."

Mac couldn't help but smile at the girl's enthusiasm. "Your aunt is on the ship?"

"She works in the lab here. Studied infectious diseases," Josiah hesitated. "She helped me in the OR last night."

The reminder hit like a punch in the gut. The walls of the cafeteria pressed in around her. She wasn't here to sip coffee and chat. She needed to find the rest of the pirates. They were just as guilty for Mo's death as the one who'd pulled the trigger.

Mac shoved her half empty cup of coffee back. "I need to go, but I have a feeling you're going to do great here, Emma. Thanks for the coffee."

"We need to get going to school as well, young lady, but once again. . ." He looked at Mac. "I really am sorry for your loss."

"Thank you."

"Will we get to see you again?" Emma asked.

"I don't think I'll be on board much longer, but I'm glad I got to meet you." Mac held up her wrist. "And thank you for the bracelets."

Mac stumbled out of her chair, anger quickly replacing the grief as she headed toward the exit.

Sloan was just walking into the cafeteria. "I was sent to find you. I heard the news about Mo. I'm sorry."

Mac nodded. "Did you find the rest of the pirates?"

"We located their speed boat, and the two hostages they took have been rescued." Sloan avoided her gaze. "But the three remaining pirates escaped."

Mac shoved back the irritation. The hostages might be safe, but as far as she was concerned, this was far from over.

CHAPTER SEVEN

DOUALA, CAMEROON

It had been an hour since Josiah took Emma to school. He rose from his bunk and checked his phone. He'd tried to go back to sleep, but he couldn't relax. Images of pumping Mo's chest kept replaying through his mind, but it was the conversation that he'd had with Mo's beautiful partner that weighted each step he took to the bathroom. She was a unique mix of attractive physicality and surprising sensibility. A razor's edge that could cut deep with an accusatory remark then just as easily pivot and offer an understanding ear to a child. She was unsettling and he hadn't felt unsettled by a woman in a very long time.

He decided to break the ship's rules and treat himself to a long shower. The tiny bathroom was a cloud of steam by the time he toweled off. He leaned against the sink to still his shaking hands. He'd scrubbed and scrubbed but they still felt covered in blood. He swiped the steam from the mirror. Instead of the guy who used to laugh in the face of tough situations, the sober face staring back at him had dark circles under the eyes and absolutely no desire to walk back into a surgical bay any time soon. But he also knew getting back on the bicycle so to speak was the best medicine for keeping his hands occupied and his mind from revisiting the anguish on the face of Mo's partner.

Josiah shaved, slipped into clean scrubs, and made his way to the surgical deck.

"Ah, Dr. Allen." The surgical coordinator met him in the corridor. She had a stack of files in her arms. "Just the man I was looking for. Hope you got some sleep."

"Some," he lied.

"Dr. Allen," she said kindly. "We can only do our best."

"My best wasn't good enough."

"I've learned there's only one God, and He's the one who decides who lives or dies."

Josiah frowned. Platitudes were as empty as prayers.

"Right." He pointed at the stack of files. "Don't tell me those are today's surgeries."

"No. I've scheduled your first surgery for this afternoon." She smiled. "These are patients in need of a morning round of post-operative."

"I'm confused," Josiah said, knowing his failure to save his patient meant that the surgical records of Moses Adams were not in that stack. "I don't have any patients in post-op."

"We all wear many hats here, Dr. Allen. One of the hats our surgeons must wear is doing post-op visits on each other's patients. It's not best for continuity of patient care, but it's the best method we have for filling the gaps when one surgeon leaves and a new one comes on."

Josiah's eyes narrowed. "You have that many post-ops?"

"Yes."

"All housed on the ship?"

"No," she said. "We have an off-site clinic set up about a fifteen-minute walk from the dock."

"Doesn't sound very efficient."

"We've learned to make do." She handed Josiah the files. "If you will stop by reception, you'll be given directions and a phone."

"Wait. Wh-what?" Josiah stuttered. "You want me to leave the ship and do rounds on patients I know nothing about?"

"There's a full staff there, and Dr. DeMarcus should be back from his visit to an upriver village by now. He'll be happy to show you the ropes." She turned and left him standing in the middle of the passageway.

"But my kid gets out of school at three."

"You'll be back on the ship by then, but I'll keep Loraine updated on your schedule. She'll see to it that your child's care is covered while you're busy," she said over her shoulder.

Josiah let out a long, slow breath. He might not be ready to go back in the OR yet, but maybe a little fresh air and the mindless tasks of checking incision sites, bandages, and vitals were exactly what the doctor ordered.

He swung by his room, picked up his medical backpack, and slid the files inside. Twenty minutes later, he was checking out at reception and had the clinic site directions pulled up on the new phone he'd been given.

"Anything else I should worry about?" Josiah asked the receptionist.

"Violent crime is rare. Just watch out for pickpockets, but that could happen anywhere in the world, right?" The woman noticed Josiah's widened eyes and added, "Stick to the main route and you should be fine. If not, call one of the two numbers in your phone's contact list."

"Who am I calling?"

"The first one is ship's security."

"And the second?"

"The local police." She leaned over the counter and whispered. "But their response time is. . .slow."

"Good thing I updated my will." Josiah headed down the gangplank, through security, then past the dozens of potential patients waiting in line outside, hoping he didn't look as unsettled as he felt.

Gulls circled close, dropped a few feet from him, and begged for scraps. Their squawking added to the clamor of the horns of the freighter ships coming and going from the port in the stifling heat of Douala.

A fishy smell hit Josiah's nose hard. He turned to see a rusty boat with Chinese lettering on the side pull into the small space beside the *Liberty*. Next to the massive medical ship, the fishing vessel appeared small, but it was good-sized compared to what he'd seen of the locally owned vessels. This trawler was so heavily loaded with silvery fish that its hull sat low in the water. Tired men threw their mooring ropes ashore. They jumped to the dock, shouting orders to each other in Chinese as they began tying off the boat without giving him any notice.

After Josiah left the dock, the female voice on his phone's mapping system informed him to take the next right. Women hawked fruit and vegetables on the sides of the street. Men, young and old, sat on stoops or leaned against buildings and watched him pass with as much wariness of him as he was feeling about them.

Josiah checked his phone and pressed on. When the voice announced that he had arrived, he looked around for a building resembling an outpatient clinic. Instead, what he found was a big, canvas tent. The door was a flap tied open with a thick rope. He followed a dirt path and stepped inside.

He stood at the doorway and took in the situation. While the space appeared clean, heavy tarps covered the dirt floor. Cots filled almost every available inch of space and patients filled every cot. He could see four people dressed in scrubs and busy caring for patients. Two were busy trying to bathe a small boy wearing a full body cast that was probably compliments of the ortho doc he was supposed to meet. They were joking and the boy was laughing despite his obvious discomfort. The heat inside the tent was even worse than outside. That child had to be miserable inside that cast, and yet he was smiling.

Josiah cleared his throat.

One of the nurses, a thin woman with a gray ponytail and skin wrinkled by years in the sun, looked up. "Can I help you?" Her drawl was southern, maybe Texas. He couldn't be sure, but it was patient and kind and lacking the put-out vibe he sometimes got whenever he interrupted a nurse.

"I'm Dr. Allen." Josiah hadn't moved from his position at the door. "Dr. DeMarcus is supposed to show me the post-op ropes."

"I'm sorry, but Dr. DeMarcus isn't here."

"Where is he?"

"I don't know. He's late." She frowned. "Which isn't like him."

"Guess it's up to you to train the rookie then." Josiah rallied a smile.

With no fanfare, the nurse launched into the procedure the patient she was tending had undergone. At each bed, Josiah was hit not with the poverty or suffering of the patient or their attending family member, but with an overwhelming sense of resilience and gratitude. Each patient, even when in obvious pain, did their best to smile.

Josiah did his work, checking casts, wound sites, and updating med schedules. At the bed of a small girl who'd had cleft palate work, he took extra care. A maxillofacial surgeon from North Carolina whom Josiah had never heard of had done an excellent job. According to the chart, this child had not been able to eat. But now, after only one surgery, it wouldn't be long before she was chowing down on ribs and smiling from ear to ear.

"Excellent work," Josiah said. "Excellent."

"Dr. Allen?" The nurse tugged at his sleeve. "We need you for a moment to help us with a patient who is febrile."

"Have you given acetaminophen?" The moment he said it, he hated how condescending it sounded. "Of course you have," he corrected at the slight rise in her brows. "Let's take a look."

"Her temp's gone up two degrees. She also has a headache, sweating, and vomiting."

Josiah went to the young woman lying on a cot in the corner. She was drenched in sweat and complaining of a headache. From the incision on the side of her neck, he suspected she'd had a benign tumor removed. "Let's see your chart." A neurofibroma, just as he'd thought. Removed two days ago. A dangerous procedure, but it wasn't cancer, and she was young. According to the record, she'd handled the surgery beautifully.

"Malaria, you think?" Josiah asked the nurse.

"I tested her. It came back negative."

"Let's get some more blood cultures drawn, and I'll run your concerns past my sister. Nothing jazzes her like tracking down a good pathogen." He jotted the order then handed the nurse the chart.

While he was waiting on the blood draw, he stepped outside and phoned Rachel.

"What's up?" Rachel was obviously at her computer and distracted.

"I've got a suspicious fever down here at the post-op clinic."

"Fever?" Her attention was all his now. "Any other symptoms?"

"Headache, sweating, and vomiting. She had a large neurofibroma removed from her neck two days ago, so a headache isn't that disconcerting," he said. "A malaria test came back negative."

"You sound worried."

"Perplexed."

"Get a few vials of blood."

"Already ordered the draw." Josiah peeked inside the tent to see if the blood was ready for transport. “Oh, and Ray, Dr. DeMarcus never showed up at the post-op clinic.”

“That’s odd.” She hesitated. “He probably got hung up somewhere. The roads in and out of the villages aren’t always the best. I’m sure he’ll check in soon. Bring me that blood,” she said. “I’ll see if security’s heard from the doc.”

CHAPTER EIGHT

GULF OF GUINEA, COASTAL REGION

Dabir felt a stab of anger course through him as he steered the speedboat through the delta. He could still see Leiyo's body bleeding out on the deck of the boat. Balik had promised no one would get hurt. Dabir knew that what he was doing was illegal. His father would have forbidden him from becoming involved in something so morally detestable, but both hunger and revenge had a way of blurring the lines between right and wrong.

Still, watching his brother, along with three of their men die, had made him question again what he was doing. The disappointment on his wife's face when he'd boarded Balik's skiff and picked up a gun had left an imprint on his soul. She never told him what to do. Never asked him where he was going. But the last time he'd left, she'd begged him to stay. He'd brushed her off and told her he didn't have a choice. He'd be back in a few days.

"This is the only way I know to take care of my family," he'd said.

Wasn't it? What would have happened if he'd listened to her? Would Leiyo still be alive?

He'd read the news about the attacks on the ships bobbing in the gulf. About the millions of dollars waiting to be taken. And yet, what about the part of the story no one told? The part about the need to stop the illegal fishing and dumping of toxins and fuels into their waters? How else was he supposed to combat his village's inability to survive with no work, no resources, no doctors, and now more of their men dead? The authorities didn't care. Instead, they continued to make deals with the oil tankers and the Chinese fishermen. Corrupt leaders let the foreigners do what they pleased on their waters. And the money they received as payment never made it past their own pockets.

He'd lost a part of himself today, and on top of that, there would be no windfall of money.

Everything he'd attempted had failed.

Water splashed against his face as he steered the boat toward the shoreline. He couldn't tell his wife what he'd done. He feared that the soldiers in black with their weapons and night vision goggles would come after him. That he'd put his family in danger. If they found him, Abeje and his son would have nothing. He jumped off the boat.

Cédric followed him up the embankment with Wilson. "We might have lost this time, but we need to go after another ship. This can't end here."

"And then what?" Dabir stopped at the edge of the shore, his feet caked with mud. "We just lost four of our men, including my brother, and I can't even bury his body. How am I going to explain that to my family?"

Cédric grabbed his arm. "I don't know, but we need to regroup and strike again."

"He's right," Wilson said. "Your brother isn't the only one gone. So is Balik. You need to take his place. There are plenty of men who want to join us."

Dabir pulled away without answering.

Chomba was waiting for him at the top. "I know where you've been, brother, and I want to go with you next time."

Dabir frowned. The boy did as well in school as Dabir had. If Dabir could secure enough money, Chomba would get the education Dabir had to give up when the fishing went bad and his father called him home to help.

He brushed Chomba off, just like he'd brushed off Cédric. "You don't know what you're asking."

"I know that the last time you came back with Balik," Chomba said, "you had enough money to buy a fishing boat and send Leiyo and me out into the waters again with brand new nets."

"And that is where I expect you to be every night."

"Dabir, wait." Chomba looked into his eyes. "Where is Leiyo? And Balik?"

Dabir glanced down at the narrow trough where a bullet had ripped across his shoulder then told the news he could hardly bear to speak. "They're dead."

His little brother's eye's widened. "Dead?"

Dabir caught the disbelief in his brother's gaze. He would never say it out loud, but he knew what his brother was thinking. Everything they'd done lately felt as if it had been cursed. Men were dead. Their ransom demands shattered. But it wasn't a curse that put a bullet in Leiyo's chest.

"And the ransom?" Chomba asked.

Dabir avoided his brother's gaze. "There is nothing."

The veins in Chomba's neck pulsed. "Then I will go back out there with you so we can get what is ours. Make them pay for what we have lost."

"And then what?" Dabir countered. "I lose you as well?"

"Are your people not worth fighting for?" Chomba challenged. "Because if they are not, your wife may die. Abeje's worse, and she's not the only one. The sickness that has come to our village is spreading."

Dabir felt his heart sink. He'd lost his brother. His friends. He couldn't lose his wife too. She'd looked tired before he left, but she'd said nothing.

"How many?" Dabir asked.

"I have lost count. Two days ago, a man died upriver. Yesterday, three died. Three more had to be buried this morning."

Dabir glanced up the hill to his house he was building. He'd thought that by the time he returned she would be fine, but he'd been wrong.

"I did what you said and bought her medicine from the healer, but she's not getting better," Chomba said. "I think it's like you said. The sickness is coming from what the big ships are dumping."

Dabir frowned. That might be true, but what was he supposed to do? The traditional healer and his potions had failed them, but he also had reason not to trust the doctors in the capital. No one would listen to him. He marched up the hill, then ducked inside the two-room cinderblock house he and his wife shared with their son and his brothers.

"Abeje?"

She lay on a mat on the dirt floor, her forehead glistening with perspiration. She was always up before the sun. Never stopped until the sun went down. Something was terribly wrong.

His wife opened her eyes. "I'm sorry. I was going to have something for you to eat when you arrived, but I'm so tired."

"Chomba said you are still sick."

"I'm getting better."

He held the back of his hand against her forehead. "You're burning up."

"I'm fine."

But she wasn't fine.

"There is a medical ship at the port in Douala," he told Chomba and Cédric who'd followed him into the house. "I'm going to take her there."

Chomba shook his head. "She's too sick—"

"And if I don't? If she dies like the others? I can't let that happen."

"I'll go with you," Cédric said.

"So will I," Chomba said.

"No." Dabir turned to his brother. "I need you to stay here with Taiwo. Pull him out of school until I get back and keep him at home."

"Dabir—"

"Don't argue. Just do as I say."

Two hours later, Dabir's boat motored into the capital's port and headed toward the medical ship. The line outside the ship was long, snaking along the dock, and filled with dozens of desperate people. But he was desperate too, and he wasn't going to take no for an answer. The three men he'd brought with him helped press a path through the crowd for Abeje. His wife leaned heavy upon his arm. She was growing weaker, and he feared that soon she would not be able to stand.

A young white woman dressed in a blue uniform stepped in front of them. "Do you have an appointment?"

"An appointment. . ." Dabir glanced frantically at his wife. "No."

"I'm sorry, sir, but without an appointment there's nothing we can do. There's a local clinic—"

He read her name badge. "Harper, my wife is sick. She needs to see a doctor."

He knew how it worked in the city. You went to the clinic, and half the time they had no medicine. Or they sent you to the private hospitals, but he couldn't afford that. And he wasn't going to lose his wife.

"Everyone is sick here, sir," she said. "These people have appointments."

"I just need someone to look at her." Dabir tried to keep his anger in check. "We live two hours up the river. There are no doctors there and here in Douala. . ."

How could he trust the doctors who'd let his first wife die? How did he make the woman understand he was out of options?

"Ask the doctor to look at her, please," he begged, something he swore he would never do again.

"You could go to the back of the line and if we have time today—"

"No!" Dabir argued. "She can't wait."

"Sir, please," the woman said. "I'm going to have to call security if you don't step away from the line. I'm sorry."

Dabir looked around. The crowds were pressing around them. He'd heard the doctors on this ship had good medicine. People who couldn't walk had their legs straightened. Children with mouths split could eat. Old men who couldn't see had their eyes made like new. He had to get Abeje on this ship.

Someone jostled against him, causing Abeje to almost lose her balance. Dabir tightened his arm around her waist. Couldn't they see she needed help? Anger rippled through him. He wasn't going to move until they let him on board.

Harper started talking into her radio to someone.

Cédric stepped closer to Dabir. "We're going to have to board the ship in order to get help."

Dabir caught the man's gaze. "Forget it. We're not forcing our way onto a medical ship."

"Why not? It's the perfect solution. You get the medical help you need, and we have a ship load of hostages. They will pay."

Dabir shook off the crazy idea. "I said forget it."

"It's the perfect scenario, Dabir. We came prepared. We have a jammer, and we're armed."

Dabir glanced at his wife as a uniformed security guard ran up to them and addressed Harper.

"What's going on?" the guard asked.

"I've told him our procedure, but he won't leave."

Dabir tried to push away Cédric's plan, but Abeje would die without some kind of treatment. He was tired of no one listening. Tired of everyone saying no. And if they did things right this time...

Cédric pulled out the gun he was carrying under his shirt, grabbed Harper, and pressed the gun to her temple. "My friend needs to see a doctor."

Wilson and Alec followed suit and pulled out their weapons.

A woman in line screamed.

Someone started shouting.

"All of you, please. Put the guns down." The uniformed guard held up his hands. "Everyone here needs to see a doctor, and this isn't going to change anything."

Abeje tugged on his arm. "Dabir, we'll go to the clinic. It's fine."

Something deep within Dabir snapped. "No!" He whipped out his weapon. "It's not fine!" He knew it was a bad choice, but sometimes there were only bad choices left. "Here's what's going to happen," he told the guard. "You're going to take me on board with my wife and my friends. Once she's seen someone, we'll let Harper go. No one has to get hurt, but you will let us onboard."

"Sir, I understand your frustration," the guard said, "but I can't do that."

"Then take us to the captain." Cédric jerked Harper's arm. "Now!"

"Sir—"

Cédric turned and shot the guard point blank in the head. Chaos erupted around them, as the man fell to the ground. Dabir froze. This wasn't what he'd wanted. Two more guards made their way toward them. Cédric shot them without hesitation.

"All I wanted was to see a doctor!" Dabir shouted as the people scattered.

Sweat poured down his face as he fought to keep Abeje upright. He wasn't sure how he'd gotten to this point, but there was no going back now.

CHAPTER NINE

DOUALA, CAMEROON

"EDDIE!" THE BOOMING VOICE RATTLED THE LOCKED DOOR TO THE SHIP'S bridge. "I can see you in there, Scott." He pounded on the glass.

Captain Edmonton Scott took a deep breath and swiveled his chair away from his maintenance logs. He gave a nod to Ricardo Nunes, his second officer from Brazil, to let the man in.

"Eddie," the American oil executive said as he pushed past the officer.

"At ease, Ricardo. Sid Ramsey's welcome on my bridge anytime." Captain Scott rose from his command post and extended a hand to Sid while Ricardo stepped off the bridge to give them their privacy as requested. "I'm glad you made it off the tanker in one piece, Sid. Sorry about the man you lost."

The normally well-groomed man looked like he hadn't slept in a week. He grabbed the Captain's hand and pulled him into a tight embrace. They hugged for a second then clapped each other on the back. "Moses Adams was a good man. These pirates are getting bolder and bolder."

"They're hungry, Sid. Frustrated with foreign trawlers who come in and destroy their fishing lanes. Oil tankers polluting their water ways—"

"That's no excuse for what's happening. The bottom line is they found a way to line their pockets with ransom money." Sid stormed to the control console and gazed out the bank of windows. "Besides, we pump a good bit of our profits right back into whatever country we're drilling in. You wouldn't believe how much busier this port is now compared to when we first arrived."

"But how much of that money actually trickles down to the people?"

Sid spun back around. "You know as well as I that most of the governments here are corrupt. What happens to the money after we put it into their greedy little hands is their problem not ours."

"That's a rather convenient, self-serving view of life."

"You always were the bleeding heart."

Edmonton studied the man pacing before him. Fifty-five-years old and the president of the African division of one of the world's largest oil companies. Suit tailored to show off the muscle mass of a man who knew his way around the gym. Thinning dark hair, colored and styled to hide the balding patch at his crown. A dazzling porcelain-veneer smile that gave him a reputation of having a way with the ladies. And one of the *Liberty's* biggest donors.

Sid had also spent the last twelve days on a hijacked oil tanker terrified for his life.

Even though they'd been friends since college, they'd rarely seen eye to eye on things, but being the captain of the *Liberty* had given Edmonton a second chance, and he was determined not to blow it. There was nothing to gain by arguing with the man he owed. He'd learned that the hard way.

"Something tells me you didn't come here to talk African politics, Sid."

"Your medical staff did a fine job patching up my team this morning." Sid clapped a hand on Edmonton's shoulder. "I don't know what we would have done had the *Liberty* not been docked within flying distance. I just wanted to thank you. I'll make sure the *Liberty* receives another generous check."

Edmonton frowned. "Still trying to keep me in your debt?"

"It never hurts to have someone beholden to you."

He had a feeling Sid Ramsey would never let him forget his indebtedness.

"Captain!" Ricardo burst into the bridge, terror in his eyes. "Armed locals have breached security, and at least three of the Gurkhas are down. They're holding Dr. DeMarcus's daughter hostage and making demands to see a doctor. . . Or they will start shooting hostages."

CHAPTER TEN

DOUALA, CAMEROON

MAC STOOD IN THE MIDDLE OF THE TINY ROOM LOCATED NEXT TO THE surgery bay where Mo had taken his last breath and stared at his gear. Everything he'd had on him had fit into his backpack. A backpack he'd never use again.

How had it ended this way?

Another casualty in a war that would never be won. And it wasn't even their war.

"Ma'am?"

Mac turned around. A woman in her early thirties stood in the doorway, wearing blue scrubs, her long hair pulled up into a ponytail.

"My name's Lacy. Is there anything I can do for you?"

"I was just. . .collecting his personal things."

"I'm so sorry. I was told he was a friend of yours."

"He was." The walls of the room seemed to close in around her and the air couldn't seem to reach her lungs. She struggled for a breath, wanting to somehow go back in time and erase everything that had happened. "How long have you been working on this ship?"

"Six months. I work here in the surgical bays."

"I can't imagine what you've seen."

"It can be hard, like today, but most of the time we're able to fix and repair rather than deal with life and death situations like your friend." She shook her head. "I'm really sorry."

Mac nodded, acknowledging the woman's response. "I had to talk to his wife. Tell her he wasn't coming home. It's hard enough for me, but what about her? How is she going to tell their little boys?" She hesitated. "I'm sorry. . .this isn't your problem."

"It's fine. I lost my mother last year. I know how hard it can be to lose someone you care about."

"It is. There is one thing you can do." Mac looked up and caught the woman's gaze. "Can I see him again?"

"If you'd like. We don't use it very often, but we have a holding place for. . .for bodies. We'll keep him there until arrangements are made for him to return to the US. I know that the captain is already coordinating the transfer."

Mac nodded. "I appreciate that."

She followed Lacy into another small, cold room with green tiled walls and three metal refrigerated drawers for bodies. Lacy pulled one open, then slowly unzipped the black body bag. Mac took a step back, the pressure on her chest so tight she was sure her heart might explode.

For a moment, she could almost convince herself Mo was sleeping. He lay there, eyes closed, the familiar hint of gray in his goatee and kinky hair. She ran her finger across his cheek and blinked back the tears. She should have been the one who took the bullet. She had no one to go home to. No family waiting for her except her mother, who suffered from such bad dementia she wouldn't know if Mac was there or not. And yet, for some reason, God had let this happen.

"Where's his dog tag?" Mac looked toward the door of the other room where his backpack still sat. The tag hadn't been in Mo's things the nurses had given her. She was sure of that. Mac pulled down the zipper another six inches and searched next to his broad shoulders, wondering if it was possible the tag had fallen. Because if it wasn't with his things, it had to be here. With him.

Panic bubbled in Mac's gut. "I need his tag."

Lacy laid her hand on Mac's shoulder. "If he came here with it on, we'll find it."

Mac shook her head. "You don't understand. I can't send him home without it. He buried one of his dog tags with an army buddy who died in the Middle East, and the other one... Mo never takes it off. Never."

"They would have had to cut it off before surgery," Lacy said, "I can check the OR bay."

Maybe it was crazy, but the loss felt like another blow that threatened to pull her under. "Please do."

"The captain has asked if you would meet him on the bridge when it's convenient for you. He wanted to offer his condolence. In the meantime, I'll find the tag and make sure you get it."

Mac slowly zipped the body bag. "Thank you."

"Of course. Do you need an escort to the bridge? It's easy to get lost."

"I'll be fine if you just tell me how to get there."

Lacy gave her directions, then slid Mo's body back into the hollow chamber. The door clicked shut, a sound of finality. Mo was gone, and nothing could change what had happened.

The narrow passageway was quiet as Mackenzie went up a flight of stairs then hurried down the deck reserved for the general crew accommodations. Emma walked toward her, holding the hand of her aunt Rachel.

"Miss Mackenzie!"

Mac tried to swallow the lump stuck in her throat, and forced a smile at Emma. "We just keep running into each other, don't we?"

"Aunt Rachel showed me where she worked, and now she's taking me to the bridge."

"You've had quite a day."

"So have you." Rachel's gaze was filled with more of the irritating sympathy that was rampant on this ship. "I'm really sorry about your friend."

"Thank you," Mac swallowed. "I'm actually headed to the bridge as well. The captain wanted to see me."

"You can come with us," Emma said.

"I'd like that." She smiled at the little girl who had already stolen a piece of her heart. "Especially, since there's a good chance I'd get lost on my own."

Emma's laugh got lost as movement at the end of the passage behind

Rachel caught Mac's eye. An armed man dressed in black headed down the stairs.

"Rachel, wait." Mac snagged the pretty blonde's arm. "You have Gurkhas on this ship, right?"

"Yes. They run our security. Why?"

"What do they wear?"

"White uniforms. Black berets."

She'd seen these officers when they'd landed on the ship. The man she'd just seen wasn't in a Gurkha uniform. And he was carrying an AK-47.

Mac lowered her voice. "We need to get out of this hallway and somewhere safe."

Rachel pulled Emma close. "What's going on?"

Mac glanced at Emma. She didn't want to scare the little girl, but she didn't see another option. "I just saw an armed man in black heading down the stairs from the deck above."

"That's not a Gurkha."

Mac shook her head slowly. "We need to get to security."

Rachel didn't move. "We all go through training, but we've never had an issue with intruders."

"What's wrong?" Emma asked.

"I'm not sure, sweetie," Mac said.

"There's a number we can call in an emergency, or if we have to report something." Rachel pulled her phone out of her pocket, looked at the screen, then held it up. "I don't understand. I don't have a signal."

Mac grabbed her radio earpiece out of her pocket and slipped it on. "Knight...Sloan... Benson...Díaz...Can any of you hear me?"

Silence greeted her. Her mind immediately searched for a solution. They didn't know how many intruders were on this ship or where they were, and without the ability to contact security, they were on their own.

"Where would they be going?" Mac asked.

"The only thing below us is the engine room."

Mac touched the radio and tried calling her team again. "Knight...Sloan...Requesting emergency assistance immediately."

Still nothing. If they'd left the *Liberty* to work on the arrangements of shipping Mo's body, they'd be out of range.

"I can't get through to my team. Come on." She hurried down the passageway to the first door and knocked. No answer.

"Like I said," Rachel said as she and Emma caught up to her, "most people are working right now."

"What happens in an armed attack?"

"There are anti-piracy protocols and equipment in place."

"Meaning?"

"There's a ship alert system. It's in case pirates attack, or if there's an act of terrorism."

"What happens?"

"I don't know. I—"

"Rachel." Mac turned to her and caught her frozen gaze. "I need you to tell me what happens."

Rachel nodded. "Um...There's...there's a beacon that can be activated if there's a piracy attempt or any other threat to the ship. Then law enforcement or military forces are alerted and dispatched."

"What kind of beacon?"

"It's a silent security system. There's a central location that's notified, and then a rescue is coordinated."

It made sense. "That's what happened on that tanker we just boarded."

"But all we have on the *Liberty* are doctors and sick patients. What do they think they're going to get?"

"I don't know. Where can we activate the beacon?"

"Two places. One switch is on the bridge. The other is under the reception desk. The whole crew has been trained on where to find them and when to turn them on."

"So chances are someone has already activated the alarm." Mac glanced down at Emma and wondered again why a father would bring his child on a ship with ship-hijacking pirates in the area. "We need to get Emma somewhere safe."

A rumbling sound shook the boat.

"What is that?" Mac asked.

Rachel gripped the handrail next to her. "They've started the engines."

Mac's mind clicked through the short list of options. This was no drill. Someone had boarded this ship who shouldn't be here. Armed men with AK-47s. The entire crew and patients on board were at risk.

Mac knocked on three more doors, but there was still no answer. She kept walking, then stopped at a square grill on the wall. Pulling out the tactical knife she carried, she pried off the metal cover. She examined the small crawl space. This would work.

Mac turned to Emma. “Sweetie, Rachel and I need to make sure that the boat is safe. And while we do, we need you to wait for us inside this crawl space.”

Emma’s eyes widened as she pressed against her aunt. “In there?”

“Wait a minute...” Rachel’s face had paled. “We can’t leave her.”

“Just until we’ve figured out what’s going on.” She turned back to Emma. “I know this might be a little scary, but you’ll be safe here. I promise.”

Emma’s eyes widened. “Are there bad guys on the ship?”

“That’s what I’m going to find out.”

“Are they the bad guys that killed your friend Mo?”

“It’s possible.”

“Why do they want to hurt people?”

How was she supposed to answer that question?

“I’m not sure,” Rachel said. “Do you know how to play hide n’ seek?”

Emma nodded.

“Then crawl in here and hide. Promise you’ll stay here and stay quiet until I tell you it’s safe to come out. Understand?”

Emma nodded again, but Mac didn’t miss the fear in her eyes.

“We won’t be long and the bad guys. . .they would never think to look here. Trust me?”

“I trust you.”

Mac stood, Emma’s words gouging through her heart. She couldn’t promise the little girl that she’d be safe. Mo had trusted her to have his back, and he was dead. If anything happened to Emma. . .

She pushed away the battering waves of doubt. “We’ll be back soon.”

Mac fitted the grill back in place, then motioned Rachel to follow her down the hallway. “Where’s reception?”

“Deck five, but you need to understand something.” Rachel hurried to keep up. “I know she acts grown up, but Emma is only six. This is going to traumatize her.”

“And if those armed men find us? Find her? What then?”

“Fine.” Rachel stopped for a moment. “What do we do once we get to reception and the gunmen are there? All we have is your knife."

"You need to keep knocking on doors until you find someone who answers."

"We stay together," Rachel said. "I know the layout of the ship and you don't."

"Point taken," Mac conceded. "Stick close to me. We need to make sure the beacon has been activated. If the ship has been breached, whoever is behind it won't get far. Not with all the security and protocols put into place. Plus, if they don't know the ship, we have the advantage." She started for the door marked *stairs*.

Rachel hurried after her. "But what if they've been patients and they do know their way around?"

Mac paused. "Brief me on the ship's layout."

"There are eight decks. The lower four decks house the actual hospital—the operating rooms, labs, an ophthalmology unit, x-rays and recovery rooms. Above them is reception."

"Where's the bridge?" Mac asked, working on a plan.

"Deck seven."

"How many crew members?"

"Around four hundred."

"Patients?"

"On any given day, at least a hundred."

She'd known it was a massive ship, but hadn't realized just how big. And they were looking at about five hundred people on board. She knew there were intruders on the ship, but she had no idea how many hostiles, or how many people knew what was going on.

And there was something else that was bothering her. Emma had asked if the men on the boat were the same men who had killed Mo. The conclusion made sense. Her team had killed four of their men. What if they'd somehow found out that the injured had been brought to the ship for medical care and now they wanted revenge for their fallen comrades? It was also possible that one or more of them had been injured and needed medical help. Either option was disconcerting, because it would mean that this was personal.

But she wasn't going to jump to any conclusions. Not yet. Hopefully, with the security measures already in place, it should only be a matter of time before the authorities arrived and took them down.

Mac pulled off her visitor badge. "Take off your ID."

"Why?"

"If we run into them, I don't want them to know who we are."

They hurried up another flight of stairs then headed outside toward the bow of the ship and the bridge. She could feel the ship moving beneath them now, slowly away from port. She blew out a short breath. Whoever was behind this had to know that a ship this big couldn't simply disappear.

"Mac—" Rachel's scream was cut off by two men rushing at them.

Acting on instinct, Mac slashed at the first man with her knife, cutting him across his arm, but her speed wasn't enough. One of them grabbed her wrist and threw her against the wall. She fought the pain, struggling to catch her breath.

"Mac!" Rachel screamed again.

"I'm fine."

Except she wasn't. She was the one who was supposed to stop this, and all she could do was stand there, helpless. But she knew a false move could get her—or Rachel—shot. She held up her hands, and a moment later, the men forced them up the staircase.

Mac masked her expression, frustration searing through her as she stumbled up the steps and onto the bridge.

A shorter man, also armed with an AK-47, crossed the bridge. "What are you doing?"

"Found these two down below. I thought we could use more hostages—"

"We have a ship full of hostages. But right now, our focus has to be on getting this ship out to sea."

"Dabir—"

"What happened to your arm?" Dabir asked.

The man she'd slashed was holding his arm. "She had a knife."

"I thought doctors were supposed to help people." Dabir caught her gaze.

There were nine people on the bridge besides her and Rachel. Four armed pirates, an African woman sitting on the floor who looked as if she were about to fall over, a young woman in a uniform whose name tag said *Harper*, and three other men.

But Mac's attention zoomed in on the man standing in the corner of the room, wearing a captain's uniform and steering the boat out of the port.

Edmonton Scott. Her father.

CHAPTER ELEVEN

DOUALA, CAMEROON

JOSIAH GATHERED THE PATIENT FILES AND THE VIALS OF BLOOD DRAWN from the febrile patient. He'd watched the uncomfortable woman for a couple of hours while finishing rounds on shore. She seemed stable, but the continued spike in her temperature meant something wasn't right. He needed to get these blood samples to Rachel ASAP. Post-surgery infections were nothing to mess around with. The sooner she was put on the proper antibiotic, the better.

"Need anything else?" he asked the nurse who'd forgiven him his crankiness. It had taken a bit of effort, effort he really didn't have the heart or energy to expend, but he was pleased that he'd scraped up enough of his old charm to finally bring her around. Maybe Rachel was right. A change of scenery and focus was what he needed.

"Just let us know what her test results come up with." She nodded toward the woman drenched in sweat.

Josiah pulled out his borrowed phone. "Text me your questions and concerns as they arise, and I'll do what I can from the ship." They traded numbers, then he flashed a smile for good measure.

Sunlight, bright enough to make him squint and hot enough to make him long for a nice cold shower, hit him the moment he stepped from the tent. Around him the street vendors were selling fruit, roasted meat, and something that looked like fried dough.

Just as promised, Rachel's number was in his new phone. He texted to ask if he could risk eating something bought on the street, or if he should stick to the ship's cafeteria.

Children raced around him, offering handmade bracelets and boiled eggs for sale. Their distended bellies made it hard for him to keep walking, but the orientation video had clearly warned against pulling money out of his wallet. It would be like feeding sea gulls. Feed one, and he'd get swamped. There were just too many for one person to help.

At the next food cart, Josiah checked his phone. Rachel hadn't answered him. Probably up to her elbows in amoebas and other nasty organisms. He texted her again. "Still on for lunch?"

He kept walking and waited a few minutes, but still no response. He reached in his pocket, checked to see if anyone was watching, then secretly pulled out a folded bill and bought a grilled plantain. The man handed him a handful of coins, but Josiah shook his head and motioned for him to keep it.

Munching on the plantain, Josiah retraced his steps to the port. With each twist and turn in the path, he felt his responsibility for last night's tragedy of losing a man on the operating table lessen. He wasn't the one who'd sent a security operative in to rescue some oil company's bottom line. He hadn't made the pirates so financially desperate that they'd hijack a ship. And he certainly hadn't pulled the trigger on that AK-47 that put an irreparable hole in a man.

He'd just been at the wrong place at the wrong time. And whose fault was that? His sister's. As much as he'd enjoyed his post-op clinic work this morning, after lunch he was going to tell Rachel that he and Emma were going home. This had been an experience. He'd gotten to see where Rachel lived and worked. He appreciated his sister's passion and even admired how she was living up to her calling, but Africa was not for him. And this was certainly not the place for his daughter. Cameroon might have great fried plantains, but they also had unexplained fevers and pirates, for Pete's sake.

He knew Rachel had high hopes for this little experiment. And, if he were honest with himself, he'd admit he was tired of living in a dark tunnel. Today was the first pinprick of light he'd seen since Camilla died. A better man would stick this out. See if there was something to this caring for those who were unable to care for themselves. But sadly, he'd given up on ever being a better man again.

Josiah plotted his arguments in his head as he neared the shipping yard. He knew better than to face Rachel without a bevy of well thought out reasons for his decision to cut bait and run.

Smells of saltwater and rotting fish overwhelmed his senses. Multi-colored shipping containers stacked five and ten high obscured his ability to spot the *Liberty*. Big blue cranes thrummed with the effort to load the containers onto the large transport barges parked parallel with the dock. An air horn sounded behind him. He wheeled to see a large semi loaded with timber barreling toward him. He dropped the greasy newsprint his plantain had been wrapped in and jumped out of the way.

The truck whizzed past in a cloud of black diesel. Peeling himself off the shipping container he'd thrown himself against, Josiah checked to see if the traffic lane was clear. He would never get used to a place with so little regard for human safety, and he'd been a fool to expose his daughter to unnecessary dangers. He started again for the direction of the medical ship.

The ship?

Where was the ship?

Josiah stopped and scanned the harbor. He could have sworn the *Liberty* had been parked right alongside the smelly Chinese fishing boat loaded with full fishing nets when he'd left this morning. The trawler was still docked. Its deck had been hosed off and the lights in the cabin were dark, but this had to be the right place. A crowd of people milled around the dock, patients still sat inside portable tents. The boy with the windswept legs cast a long-deformed s-shape silhouette shadow across Josiah's path, but the looming medical ship was nowhere in sight. Where the massive medical ship had been parked, sea gulls dove for fish floating in the dirty waves that beat against the dock.

His heart seized in his chest. Blood pounded in his ears. His thoughts spun like a tire stuck in the mud as he searched the shoreline. But his legs were moving, faster than they'd ever moved before.

"Emma!" His scream was a rock that skipped across the waves and sank.

The *Liberty* was gone.

CHAPTER TWELVE

PHILADELPHIA, PENNSYLVANIA

Clayborn Tanner pulled his sporty black Lexus into the drive of his suburban Philadelphia home. With the recent addition to his family, maybe it was time to consider getting a bigger vehicle. The baby had come early, but everything had worked out. His mother had managed to get on a flight last night, after his phone call, and made it in from her post on the *Liberty* to help out. Their three-year-old loved his new sister. But most important of all, his brand-new beautiful daughter had been born healthy, and she and his wife had already been released from the hospital.

He opened the front door and the aroma of bacon and eggs awakened a flood of wonderful memories. No matter how poor they'd been when he was growing up, his single mother had always managed to keep good food on their table. She was a wonder, his mother. He'd chosen to become a doctor because he was determined to pay her back for every single sacrifice she'd made. He'd given his daughter his mother's name in tribute. Little Bria Loraine Tanner, didn't know it yet, but she had a lot to live up to.

"Daddy!" Benson left the piles of Legos scattered around the fireplace and launched himself into his father's outstretched arms. "Can I go see my sister?"

"She's sleeping for now, but when she wakes up you can," Clayborn said.

"When is she gonna wake up?"

"I don't know, but I'll let you know."

His mother stepped from the kitchen, wiping her hands on a towel. "This fine young man has not let his little sister so much as whimper."

"Hey, Mama. I got the milk."

"You didn't have to go out this early for milk."

"I didn't mind." Clayborn gave her a quick visual exam. Dark circles under the eyes. Knitted brow, like she was fighting a headache. "You look a little tired after your flight. You need to go sleep for a while."

"I didn't come here to sit around." She poked him in the ribs. "But I wouldn't have it any other way. I love slaving over a hot stove to fix my boy his favorite food."

"You know we really appreciate your coming to help."

Jasmine walked into the kitchen, a dreamy smile on her face and her hair askew. "Clayborn, do not think that this untenable spoiling will continue after your mother returns to Africa."

"I know better." Clayborn gave his wife an appreciative grin then leaned in and kissed her full lips. "How are you feeling?"

Jasmine wrapped her arm around his waist. "Tired, but good."

"I think you need to consider staying permanently, Mama," Clayborn said. "You could move into the pool house. See the kids all the time. Save yourself the wear and tear of these grueling international flights." He stopped short of adding *and live in a safer neighborhood*. "Let me take care of you for a change."

"I've taken four weeks of shore leave. By the time that's used up, I'm sure you'll be ready for me to—" Mama dropped the spatula she'd been using to flip a stack of pancakes. "I'm so clumsy today. Must be jet lag."

Her hands were shaking, but instead of making a move to pick up the utensil, she grabbed hold of the counter.

Clayborn rushed to her aid. "I'll get it, Mama." He tossed the spatula into the sink and retrieved another one from the drawer. Before he handed it over, he gave her a more extensive visual exam. This time he noticed his mother looked more tired than usual. The trip seemed to have aged her. Or was it as he feared, that she was too old for the rigors of life on a medical mission ship? Either way, once she rested, they would have to revisit his concerns about how much longer she could keep up her mission work.

"I think you're right about the jet lag, Mama." He eased her away from the stove. "Why don't you go lie down and let me finish up here."

"I'll admit I may have started my trip a little behind the curve." She wiped her hands again, then dabbed at the tiny trickle of sweat slipping from her temple. "At our current port, I've had to spend quite a bit of time in the village helping the local teachers. I love it, but that tropical heat can really wear a person down."

He touched her forehead. "No fever." He untied her apron. "A long nap is what the doctor is prescribing for you, Mama."

"If you think I'm going to let you put me to bed without breakfast and miss out on any chances to hold that new grandbaby, you can think again, young man."

"Fine," Clayborn agreed reluctantly. "You hold the baby while I finish up the pancakes."

"That's more like it." Mama pushed past Jasmine and Clayborn and went to the nursery.

Ten minutes later, Clayborn found his mother passed out in the rocking chair with his newborn daughter crying her lungs out in her arms.

CHAPTER THIRTEEN

SOMEWHERE IN THE GULF OF GUINEA

MAC PULLED HER ATTENTION AWAY FROM THE ARMED MEN AND STARED AT the man she'd once called Daddy, as the ship headed to sea. It had been ten...no, eleven years since she'd last seen Edmonton Scott. Not that she really cared. He'd always put his career first, country second, and his family last. In fact, she hadn't even known where he was until a second ago. But all the medals this third-generation military man had received as a Navy admiral meant nothing to her. She'd always remember him as the man who walked out on her family.

What he was doing aboard a medical ship, she had no idea.

He looked different, so much so that she probably wouldn't have recognized him if she'd simply passed him on the street. He'd lost weight and his red hair had grayed, making him look older than his fifty odd years. But their relationship—and their past for that matter—didn't matter. He was a coward. She wasn't. Her goal was to do everything in her power to save everyone on this ship and then find a way to revenge Mo's death.

"Why are we leaving port?" her father asked the pirates. From his shaken expression, her father had recognized her too. How, she didn't know. She was no longer that foolish girl who hoped he'd come home someday. But all of that would have to be dealt with later.

Dabir's jaw tensed. "No questions. Just keep heading out to sea."

"To what end?" her father asked. "We've activated the security alert system. There are already people who know about the takeover and are right now following a pre-determined plan to put an end to this."

"If they had received your signal, that would be true." Dabir said. "The jammer we've set up blocks radio communications, GPS signals, and Wi-Fi, which has disrupted all signals from this ship. You are invisible. No one can see that I have taken a ship full of hostages or that two dozen of my men are currently isolating sections of the ship."

"Unless you're lying." The handsome yet somewhat disheveled civilian standing next to her father took a step forward. "I think there are only four of you, which means the security team on this ship will be able to stop this."

"Your security team has already been neutralized. Besides, do you really want to risk the lives of everyone on this ship with your assumptions?" He turned to the captain. "So, unless you want a bunch of dead bodies, make an all-ship announcement that everyone who's not in the hospital or tending to patients, needs to go immediately to their quarters."

"We have critical patients dependent upon this ship operating at maximum performance, we can't simply abandon our posts," her father said.

"Do it," Dabir said. "Now."

Edmonton Scott made the announcement, the hesitation unmistakable in his voice. She couldn't understand why a humanitarian organization intent on doing good would have hired someone like her father, but she knew she couldn't rely on the man who'd abandoned her to stick with his responsibility to his patients and crew.

The woman lying on the floor pulled at Mac's attention as she tried pushing herself up with her arms and started retching. Harper shoved a trash can in front of her.

"Your wife needs medical care, and we can't give it to her on the bridge," Harper said.

Mac took a step forward, and the lead pirate raised his gun, aiming at her chest. "What's wrong with her?"

"Don't take another step," Dabir said.

"I just want to help," Mac raised her palms. "Rachel's a doctor. Can she look at her?"

The sick woman looked up at her husband. "Dabir, please."

Dabir hesitated, then nodded. A moment later, Rachel was crouching down next to the woman.

"What is your name?" Rachel asked.

"Abeje."

"Can you tell me how long you've been sick?"

The woman's hands shook, and sweat beaded across her forehead. "Three. . .maybe four days."

"Do you have a headache? Fever?"

The woman nodded.

"Diarrhea and vomiting?"

"Yes."

Rachel turned back to Dabir. "I can't do anything here. It's possible it's malaria, but she needs IV fluids at a minimum until we can confirm what's wrong."

"We can take her down to the hospital level." Mac caught Dabir's gaze and held it. If she couldn't fight her way out of this, maybe she could negotiate. "Put an end to this, Dabir, and Rachel will see that your wife gets the best treatment available."

"You're not in a position to make demands," Dabir said.

"Then what else do you want?" Mac took a step forward. "She will die if you don't do something. It's up to you."

Dabir paused, as if weighing how much to say. "She's not the only one sick from my village. My son is there, and people are dying."

Rachel stood and walked to Dabir. "How long have your people been sick?"

"Three, maybe four weeks."

"And the people who have died," Rachel said. "Do you know what was wrong with them?"

"The same as my wife. They have headaches and fever. They vomit until it turns to blood, and then they die."

A shudder swept the room.

"How many?" Rachel asked, her voice growing in insistency.

"I don't know. Many."

"How far is your village?" Rachel was not backing down.

"It's up the river. Two hours by boat."

"Rachel. . .what are you thinking?" Mac asked.

"It could be a number of things, malaria, cholera, a virus. I can't say for sure. It concerns me that there have been so many deaths in such a short period of time. I'm going to need to do some tests in my lab." She looked at Dabir. "That's what I do here. I can find out what's wrong with your wife, but I need to take her down to my lab now and do some testing."

"My wife would not be sick if the foreign ships didn't send their boats to dump their trash," Dabir said. "There is a film on the water that washes up on our shores and fills our water wells. The fish and even our crops are dying."

"Has the water been tested?" Rachel asked.

Dabir shook his head. "Those in charge are paid to look the other way."

"What about Ebola?" Mackenzie's father blurted out. "A spreading virus...people dying..."

Rachel held up her hand. "We can't rule it out, but I don't think we need to go there. Not yet."

Mac's jaw slacked at the theory. If there was Ebola in the capital city...or on this ship, they could be looking at an epidemic that could wipe out dozens, if not hundreds of people. It was a word that struck fear at its mention. She'd been through Senegal in 2014 when there was an outbreak across west Africa that had killed over ten thousand people and had included isolated outbreaks in the UK, Italy, and the United States. If she remembered correctly, the fatality rate had been as high as forty percent.

And there was a chance that the woman laying half a dozen feet from her was infected with the same deadly disease.

"But if it is some sort of virus—" her father started.

Rachel held up her hand. "We can't jump to any conclusions at this point, but you might have a point. There are a number of things I want to look at first, and maybe the toxic water is a place to start. Dr. DeMarcus told me about rumors that toxins were being dumped from the ships and then washing up on the shore in one of the villages he'd visited."

Mac caught the concern in Rachel's eyes. It mirrored her own. When she'd signed up to extract hostages from an oil tanker, she'd expected to get in and get out in a matter of hours. If this woman was sick with some kind of communicable disease capable of killing off a village, she had far more to worry about than trying to take these pirates into custody.

"Is it possible that toxic waste is behind this illness?" Mac asked.

Rachel nodded. "There have been plenty of situations where companies dump waste in the water that makes people sick."

Mac pulled Rachel aside. "What are the chances this is Ebola?"

"Like I said, it's a possibility, but until we test her, there's no way to know."

Mac turned to Dabir. She'd had enough of his games and threats. "You need to let this doctor take your wife down to the hospital so that she can figure out what we're dealing with."

Dabir glanced at his wife. "Cédric and I will come with you, but the captain and everyone else stay in this room."

Questions spun in Mac's mind while she glanced at the four armed men. This wasn't simply a bunch of men who'd showed up on the ship, angry because their leader's wife didn't have an appointment with a doctor. These men had AK-47s, and if they were jamming communications, they clearly had some experience in hostile take-overs. There was a ridge on Dabir's shoulder where it looked like a bullet had struck. Mo had clipped someone on the oil tanker. No. They wanted more than just medical help.

"What happened to your shoulder?" Mac asked. "It looks like a fresh gunshot wound. You should get someone to look at it. It could get infected."

"So you're a doctor too?"

Mac lowered her gaze. "Just trying to help. That's all."

"You don't act like a doctor. You handle yourself more like a soldier."

Mac's jaw clenched.

"I know who you are." He pulled her onto the small balcony outside the bridge and shoved her against the railing. "You were on the oil tanker, weren't you?"

Mac blinked at the bright sunlight, but didn't answer.

"Answer me," he repeated. "Were you on that oil tanker?"

Rachel ran out on the balcony behind them with Cédric right behind her before Mac could answer. "Please leave her alone. Let me help your wife."

"Rachel, you need to go back inside the bridge, now."

"Don't move." Dabir pointed his weapon at Rachel, then back to Mac. "Either of you."

"Why are you doing this?" Rachel asked. "You could have gone to the local clinic in town if you found out there were no appointments here."

Mac watched his gaze harden before he spoke to her again. "You were on that tanker. And you're responsible for my brother's death."

CHAPTER FOURTEEN

DOUALA, CAMEROON

JOSIAH SCOURED THE CROWDED DOCK A SECOND AND THEN A THIRD TIME, then finally found a policeman. Something had happened here, but what had triggered a ship filled with hundreds of people to put out to sea? He had no idea.

"I need to know what's going on," Josiah said, stepping in front of the armed officer. "Where is the *Liberty*?"

"*Monsieur, nous sommes*—"

"English, please."

"We are trying to find out, sir," the man answered brusquely then turned to walk away.

"Wait. You have to know something." Josiah took a breath and lowered his voice. "A ship like that doesn't just disappear. I left to do onshore patient care, and when I returned to board the ship where I am currently working as a surgeon, they were gone. My six-year-old daughter and my sister are on that ship!"

The man's face scrunched in concern or irritation, Josiah couldn't tell. "All we know right now is that there was some kind of disagreement at the gangplank and three security officers were shot."

"Shot?"

Josiah glanced in the direction the man was looking and made out the motionless body of one of the uniformed Gurkhas lying on the ground.

"Wait a minute. . .they're dead?" Josiah pushed his way forward, but the officer grabbed his arm.

"Sir, you cannot go near the bodies. That is all the information I have for now. I am sorry."

Josiah pushed back at the panic. Sorry wasn't going to help him find Emma.

Ignoring the officer's glare, Josiah continued down the crowded dock to where a thick tether rope had been severed. The rough edges had a frayed look, like someone had hacked through the fibers. The hooks where the heavy chains from the ship had been moored were nearly pulled from the dock.

The Liberty had left in a hurry.

But why?

Josiah tried to think of what could have happened. An SOS of another ship at sea. No, the *Liberty* wasn't equipped for maritime rescues. A serious virus outbreak of some kind farther down the coast. Maybe, but from what he knew, the *Liberty* wasn't equipped for dealing with a contagious disease, especially anything that could escalate.

Josiah let his gaze travel the ebb and flow of the waves.

Pirates.

The idea hit him so hard he gasped.

Everyone had tried to assure him that the *Liberty* was not at risk for pirates, but why not? There was a boatload of valuable equipment aboard the ship. Medical help to be had for anyone living in an obscure, hard-to-reach place. Or perhaps, someone believed they could extort a hefty ransom for highly trained and skilled health care professionals.

Why not steal a medical ship?

If it had been pirates who'd taken the ship, they wouldn't waste time before disappearing. They could slip into one of those secret coves he'd heard about on the news, and he might never see Emma again. Life without Emma was no life at all.

His ragged inhalations refused to fill his lungs with air. His head started to swim. He knew the symptoms of hyperventilation, and he was going down if he stood there and did nothing. He cupped his hands around his mouth and nose and made himself breathe in and out. The fog slowly began to clear, and he knew what he had to do.

He'd hire a boat and go after Emma and Rachel himself.

His head whipped right then left. He needed a boat. He would offer them whatever they wanted to help him.

The Chinese trawler.

Josiah ran to where the fishing boat still sat, next to where the *Liberty* had been anchored.

"Ahoy!" he shouted from the dock. No one answered.

He tugged on the mooring rope and the boat groaned close enough for him to make the leap onto the deck. He landed in an ugly roll and hit his head on a rusty interior wall. He took the six outside stairs two at a time. Surely someone would be at the bridge. He pounded on the windows and shouted for help. No one answered. He plastered his face to the glass. Whoever owned this boat was either sleeping or enjoying some hard-earned R&R.

He started to leave and search for another boat to hire when he noticed a motorized skiff tied to the back of the trawler. Without hesitation, Josiah raced to the back of the boat, grabbed the tow rope, and reeled the skiff in to within jumping distance. In one big leap, he landed with a thud. He untied the boat, climbed over the pile of plastic bottles and nets in the bottom, then went for the outboard. Memories of his father flooded his mind. His father had taught him to steer their skiff up and down the Amazon River, but then he'd watched his father die in one. And he hadn't summoned the courage to step into one again. Until now.

Josiah wrapped his hand around the throttle rope and gave it a hard yank. Nothing. He checked the fuel. Full. He yanked again. This time giving his pull everything he had. Black smoke sputtered out behind the motor until the engine finally caught. He eased the boat forward. Once clear of the harbor, he cranked the throttle and set sail for the open waters. He didn't know how long the ship had been gone. But he knew that a state-of-the-art ship like the *Liberty* could put some nautical miles behind it if someone was pushing.

And he feared someone desperate was pushing.

Josiah shifted the motor into a higher gear. The bow of his skiff rose and fell, beating its way through the waves. Behind him the harbor was shrinking. Josiah was in open water before he spotted the sun's gleam off the shiny white paint of the *Liberty*.

Salt spray stung his eyes and lips as he bounced across the water toward the open sea. He pulled out his phone, hoping to reach someone on the ship's security team. Squinting against the sun's glare he tried to read the screen. No signal. He crammed the phone back into his pocket.

Rachel was on that boat. That was the only thing keeping him from completely panicking. Emma would not be alone. Rachel would lose her own life before she let anything happen to her niece.

Why had he agreed to come to Africa?

Josiah kicked the motor up as high as it would go. The whine of the engine drowned out the sound of the wind, but if he let himself think about the water splashing over the sides of the skiff, he'd completely lose it. A boat. He was on a boat—and after Rachel had promised him that he wouldn't get his feet wet.

Suddenly, the ship appeared in the distance to his right. Relief flooded through him, but what was he supposed to do now? Climb up the side of the ship? And even if he could, then what? Board like he was some sort of superhero? He didn't have a weapon or even a good-sized stick. Was he crazy?

Yes. Crazy mad.

They had his daughter and sister. He was not going to sit around and wait for help that may never come.

Without a plan in place, he rode the skiff to within shouting distance of the moving ship. Hoping to see someone on deck, he slowed the motor to keep pace. Where was everyone?

His gaze traveled the seven stories to the bridge and a wall of glass. Out on a small, narrow deck he could see a man, waving what looked like an AK-47.

Pirates!

Josiah pressed the motor up a notch, anxious to get a better view. He eased the skiff through the wake until he was even with the bridge.

He gasped.

Two women. Both dressed in scrubs.

The brunette was in pink. The blonde in red with black splotches that looked like Mickey Mouse ears.

Rachel.

"Rachel!" he screamed. "Rachel!"

The wind, the *Liberty's* engines, and his skiff's motor drowned his plea. He pulled even with the place where Rachel stood and began to frantically wave his arms.

The man holding her hostage pushed her to the railing and Rachel turned.

She'd spotted him down below. She was mouthing his name and struggling to break free of the man who had her by the arm. She lunged for the railing and shouted something he couldn't make out.

The pirate guarding the brunette aimed his gun at Josiah and pulled off a rapid-fire round.

Josiah dove into the bottom of his boat. He could feel the skiff veering, and he could only pray that the boat was not going to plow into the ship.

Listening carefully for more gunfire, Josiah raised his head. The skiff had fallen back, and he was no longer parallel to the bridge. He had no idea what had happened to Rachel or the brunette. He eased back into position and pressed the skiff once again toward the bridge.

He could see now that Rachel and the brunette were still on the balcony, but he couldn't see Emma anywhere. Where was Emma?

Not knowing what else to do, he decided to create a distraction. Give Rachel an opportunity to jump overboard. Then he could swing by and pick her up. No. No. No. If Rachel bailed, that would leave Emma alone on a boat that had obviously been hijacked.

Josiah looked up and realized he'd let the skiff come within gun range again. It was too late to back off now. He had no choice but to try and help Rachel. His sister knew the ins and outs of this ship far better than he. Together, they'd figure out how to get to Emma.

He pulled close and yelled, "Rachel, jump!"

The man with a gun lifted to fire again, but the brunette raised her pink-clad leg and kicked him so hard in the stomach that he nearly fell over the rail.

"Jump, Rachel!" Josiah screamed. "Now."

The man with the gun righted himself and came up swinging his weapon at the brunette. She ducked and rammed her head into his belly. The gunman doubled.

"Now, Rachel!" Josiah ordered.

Rachel had one leg over the rail. Another man burst from the bridge door. He yanked Rachel back so hard she slammed into the glass wall of the bridge and crumpled to the balcony floor.

"Rachel!"

This new man on the scene stepped over Rachel and went to where the brunette was fighting with the other man. He raised his rifle over the head of the brunette.

"No!" Josiah screamed.

The brunette wheeled, and the man rammed the butt of his rifle into her forehead with such force that she crashed into the rail, lost her balance, and toppled over the rail. She hit the water with a bone-cracking splash. Then sank.

Josiah looked from where he'd seen the woman enter the wake to the bridge where the two men had Rachel on her feet and were dragging her back inside the *Liberty*.

He could hear the ship's engine rev into high gear.

Foam and waves churned around him.

Save his family? Or save the woman sinking into the sea.

Josiah stood. Before he could change his mind, he dove.

CHAPTER FIFTEEN

PHILADELPHIA, PENNSYLVANIA

"Mama!" Clayborn dropped the towel in his hand and rushed into the nursery. "Mama!" He took his crying daughter from his mother's limp arms. "Jasmine!" he yelled. "Come get the baby."

His wife rushed into the room, her open robe trailing behind her like wings. "Oh, Lord. What's happened?"

"I don't know." He thrust the baby at her. "Get Bria out of here. If my mother has the flu, I don't want our newborn anywhere near her."

"Your mom looks awful." Jasmine's face had drained of color. "Should I call 9-1-1?"

"Yes." He snatched his mother's wrist. Pulse weak. "Then bring me my bag."

"Clayborn?" His mother's eyes fluttered open. "What's going on?"

"You passed out, Mama." He turned to take his bag from Jasmine then sent her from the room with orders to let him know when the ambulance arrived.

"I don't need an ambulance." His mother tried to push herself up out of her chair, but she fell back, either too weak or too dizzy to stand. "A few hours of sound sleep, and I'll be good as new."

Clayborn ran a thermometer over her forehead. “100.2.”

“Give me a little Tylenol, and I’ll finish flipping your pancakes.”

“Mama, I’m the doctor, and I say you’re going to the ER.”

“No, Clayborn.”

“You’ve been out of the country for months. It could be malaria, maybe even typhoid fever.”

“I passed all the airport screening tests.”

“That’s good, Mama,” he told her. What he didn’t say was that even the new CDC protocols for international travel sometimes missed viruses in the early stages of contagion.

Fifteen minutes later, two burly paramedics had his mother strapped to a gurney and lifted into the ambulance.

“I’m going with her,” Clayborn told his wife.

“What about the baby?” His wife’s face was a map of all the worst-case scenarios.

He kissed her forehead. “Call your mother to come help with the kids, and try not to worry.”

Mama winced at every bump in the road. Clayborn held her hand and tried not to let the list of infectious diseases and their symptoms he’d memorized in med school scare him worse than he already was.

The ambulance sped to the hospital where Clayborn worked, and he followed his mother’s gurney into the ER waiting room. The place was a beehive of sick kids, construction injuries, and the usual homeless people seeking a place to spend the night.

“Dr. Tanner?” Tanya, the nurse who happened to be hanging around at reception, recognized him and got them straight back. After a few check-in questions, including the triage protocol questions that had been instituted by the CDC after outbreaks like Ebola in 2014 and COVID-19 in 2020, Tanya turned back to them. “Has your mother been out of the country?”

“She’s been working in Cameroon,” Clayborn admitted. “Just returned early this morning.”

“It could be one of a dozen different things,” Tanya said.

“That’s what has me worried.”

A flicker of fear flashed in Tanya’s big blue eyes, but she immediately tamped it with her legendary steely professionalism. “Who do you want me to call?”

"I think we need an epidemiologist. Is Dr. Maxwell on duty?" He and Liz were friends from med school days. Liz Maxwell was, without a doubt, one of the best in her field.

"I'll check."

"In the meantime, let's do a nasal swab to make sure it's not just the flu, and get a CT scan of her abdomen."

"On it."

In the next hour, it was confirmed that his mother did not have the flu. Her CT scan came back with no acute disease of the abdomen or pelvis and "unremarkable" for the head. It was also confirmed that her temp had risen to 102.2.

"Clayborn?" Mama waved him close. Her eyes were closed and her voice sounded weaker than it had before the ambulance came. "Can you turn off the lights? My head is killing me."

"Headache?" he asked.

She answered with a pained little nod.

He flipped the switch to the overheads and turned on the single lowlight above the bed. "Any nausea?"

"My stomach hurts." She winced. "And I need a bathroom. Now."

"You don't have to get up."

"I've got the flu, Clayborn, not paralyzed limbs."

"You don't have the flu, Mama."

Her gaze shifted to his. "What is it then?"

"We don't know yet."

"Try not to worry, Son."

"You've been in Africa."

"If you'd come to visit, you'd discover it's not as dangerous as you think."

"You can convince me once you're feeling better." He helped her from the bed and led her to the small bathroom off the busy hall. "I'll be right outside." He waited by the door, nodding to nurses and doctors as they passed. His mind ran through the list of possibilities, but his heart kept saying, *Boy, you're in trouble. Your mama's been kissing your baby.*

He was pinching the tension at the bridge of his nose when he heard jet-force retching followed by a deep and painful moan. Before he could yank the bathroom door open, he heard his mother fall.

"Mama!" Clayborn burst in to find his mother in a pool of vomit and diarrhea. He pulled the emergency call chain that summoned a nurse immediately.

Tanya helped him lift his mother and guide her trembling body back to her sick bay. Mama sat on the edge of the bed, covered in her own mess, and shaking her head. She was mumbling something about being sorry that she might have dragged something awful home from Africa.

"What if I infected the baby?" A tear spilled down her cheek.

Clayborn was fighting his growing sense of panic. "We're going to get you cleaned up, Mama." He took a tissue and reached for a splatter in her hair.

Tanya stopped him with a freshly gloved hand. "I've got this doctor."

He nodded, threw the clean tissue in the trash, then stepped on the other side of the curtain. It was time he called Dr. Maxwell himself.

She answered on the second ring. "I'm at a conference, Clayborn. I saw the text from the nurse, but decided you'd keep hounding me if it was important. What do you think we're dealing with?"

"She's been in Africa."

"Malaria?"

"Malaria. . .typhoid. I don't know. That's why I'm calling you."

There was a pause on the other end of the line. He could hear a deep intake of breath, and he felt his own chest constrict.

"I can't do anything until I see all of her labs." His friend hadn't told him anything he didn't know, but she'd told him everything he didn't want to hear in that carefully crafted answer. "I'll keep my phone on vibrate, Clayborn. Text me the lab numbers as soon as they're all back."

"What if it's cerebral malaria, Liz?"

"Then we'll hit her hard with every anti-malarial we've got."

Clayborn knew he hadn't told her everything. He forced his next words around the lump of fear stuck in his throat. "She's vomiting and has bloody diarrhea."

This time a pause was so long he could hear the wheels turning in Liz's head. "I'm required to notify the CDC and initiate that all care providers use masks, gowns, and gloves." His colleague heard his sharp intake of breath. "Try to breathe, Clayborn. It's protocol. Earliest I can get to Philly is probably this afternoon. In the meantime, remember your mama's a tough one."

She tried to cheer him up by brightening her voice, but it didn't work.

"Liz..." Clayborn could barely hold back the tears, but holding back information wouldn't help Mama. The best epidemiologist in Philadelphia had to know everything. "Mama's been kissing on my toddler and newborn."

"And you?"

"Yes."

"Let me look over the blood results before I order a mandatory quarantine," Liz said. "In the meantime, tell Jasmine not to let anyone in the house. And Clayborn, you stay in your mother's hospital room until I tell you it's safe to come out. Wash your hands in hot, soapy water, then gown and glove up yourself." She let out a long breath. "I'm ordering Tanya confined to your mother's room as well."

CHAPTER SIXTEEN

SOMEWHERE IN THE GULF OF GUINEA

Bullets pierced the water all around Josiah as he kicked toward the sinking flash of pink. Ignoring his burning lungs, he kicked harder. If whoever had been shoved overboard sank a few more feet, he would lose the surface light and not be able to find her.

"Consider the problem. Execute the moves. Summit," he told himself.

Another big kick put him within reach of swirling ebony hair.

Stretching, he snagged an arm. He tightened his hold and climbed for the surface.

All around him the water seemed to be closing in. He was suddenly a boy, getting ready to step from the small boat his father used to visit the sick up and down the Amazon. The gunmen had burst from the jungle, surprising them. Josiah remembered his father pushing him over the side of the boat. The sounds of rapid bullet fire hitting above him. Down into the murky river he'd sunk. He hadn't been sure which way was up. He'd felt a hand reach down and grab him. Haul him over the side of the boat. He thought the hand had been his father's, but when he scrambled to his knees, his father lay dead in a puddle of blood.

Rachel believed it was God who'd pulled him up and saved him that day. But it was hard to credit a god who'd save one person and not another.

Josiah clawed at the water with his free hand. Reaching for someone he no longer believed was there. Praying he was wrong.

His head popped above a wave and he gasped for air. He gave a big tug on the limp body he'd hauled. The woman's lolling head broke the water line. He couldn't tell if she was breathing, but he couldn't help her if someone was still shooting at them.

Treading water, Josiah quickly glanced around. The ship must have traveled out of shooting range because the rapid fire had stopped. Now to find the skiff. It was idling about fifty feet away and still afloat. If it was riddled with bullet holes, they were sunk. He hooked an arm under the chin of the unconscious brunette and swam toward the skiff.

It would be no easy task to flop her limp body into the boat, but thankfully his adrenaline was still pumping. He pushed and shoved. After an unproductive minute of heaving, he realized her pink scrub top was caught on a protruding loose nail. He ripped the scrub top until she was freed, then pushed her up and over into the boat. Relieved to hear her sputtering cough, he flopped into the boat and landed on top of her face-down body with a thud.

"Sorry," he huffed and rolled off. Trying to catch his own breath, he scrambled to his feet.

She was coughing up water but unable to raise herself more than to her knees.

"Hold on." He clambered to her side and lifted her to a sitting position. "You need to clear those lungs. Cough it out."

She doubled over and coughed. Red water pooled at his knees.

"You're bleeding." He waited until her breathing had leveled out and then lifted her chin. In his hands he held the beautiful face of the security operative who'd chewed him out for losing her partner on the operating table. "Mackenzie?" Blood trickled from the gash on her head, just above her left brow. "Why were you still on the ship?"

"Why weren't you on the ship?"

She stiffened as he wiped away the trail of blood with his finger, relieved it didn't look serious.

"I was sent to work the onshore post-op clinic. When I came back, the ship was gone and a couple Gurkhas were dead."

"Oh." The fire in her accusation flickered out. "I guess you weren't expecting pirates to come after a medical ship." She swayed and leaned into him. "Nobody was."

He took her by the shoulders. "Before you pass out again, tell me what happened, and who was just shooting at me."

"Armed men brought a sick woman onboard. Demanded medical attention. Things escalated." She took a breath. "They've done this before. Hijacked a ship."

"How do you know?"

"At least one of the pirates is from the raid that got Mo killed." She swallowed hard. "His name's Dabir. He says I'm responsible for his brother's death, and he's pretty angry."

Josiah's heart thundered in his ears. His daughter was on the boat with a killer. "What about Emma?" he demanded. "Did you see her? Is she all right?"

She nodded. "Rachel and I hid her in an air duct. If she stays put, she'll be safe."

"You left my little girl in an air duct?" He couldn't let himself think of the terror his little girl must be feeling, sitting in a dark tunnel, all alone and not knowing what was going on. "What if she doesn't stay put?"

"She's a smart girl."

He frowned, but it wasn't Mac's fault that he'd brought a six-year-old to pirate-infested waters. The blame belonged to him.

"Your forehead took the brunt of a rifle butt." He ripped off his shirt, forcing himself to stay focused on the injured woman because if he didn't, he'd crawl out of his skin. "Staunch the bleeding with this." He tossed her the shirt and turned to rev the skiff's motor. "We've got to catch that ship."

"More than you know."

"What do you mean?" he shouted over the roar of the outboard.

"The woman they brought on board is very sick."

"Everyone who comes aboard the *Liberty* is in need of medical attention."

"Do they have fevers and headaches? Are they too weak to stand?" She paused, letting her list sink in. These symptoms, on their own were not usually deadly, but they would disqualify the patient from becoming one of the *Liberty's* surgery candidates. "And she's vomiting."

"Vomiting?" Josiah tallied the symptoms. It'd been a long time since he'd had to use his general medicine diagnostic skills. "Could be malaria."

"People are dying in their village," she said. "Dabir said he thinks it's connected to toxic dumping near where he lives. He said there's a filmy substance on the waterways. Fish and crops are dying, but that isn't the only possibility."

Mac looked up and he caught the fear in her gaze.

"What are you saying?" he asked.

"The possibility of Ebola was mentioned."

"Ebola?" Terror ripped through him. Every MD in the world knew the magnitude of that diagnosis. His sister knew its deadly capabilities better than most. "My daughter and sister are on a ship with Ebola?"

"It's just a possibility."

"Where is your team? The authorities?"

"The hostiles are using a jammer. The ship's cut off from all communication."

Josiah dug in his pocket and pulled out his phone.

"What are you doing?" she asked.

"We've got to find a way to get help. It shouldn't affect us this far from the ship." He punched the power button. "This could quickly escalate into an international crisis if we don't get things under control right now."

And they were at the epicenter.

He punched the power button a second time. Water dripped from the stainless-steel case. His phone was toast. He cursed and threw it into the sea.

He turned to Mac who'd been watching his tirade with wide green eyes. "You better be good at your job."

"Why?" she asked.

"Because you're going to help me find a way to get my daughter and sister before either the pirates or whatever virus is on board takes them both."

CHAPTER SEVENTEEN

SOMEWHERE IN THE GULF OF GUINEA

THE DIMLY-LIT PASSAGEWAY WAS EMPTY AS DABIR AND ANOTHER ONE OF the armed men escorted Rachel, Harper, and Dabir's wife to the lab. While Abeje struggled to walk with her husband's help, Rachel was busy processing everything that had just happened. She'd watched the gunmen hit Mac over the head with the butt of his gun, then push her overboard.

And she'd seen her brother. In a small boat. Frantic and as frightened as she.

She knew he'd gone to the post-op clinic in town today and hadn't even been on the ship, but what had Josiah been doing on a skiff bobbing below them in the ocean? He must have returned to take her and Emma to lunch, discovered the ship had left the port, and found a way to come after them. Which gave her hope that he'd been able to inform the authorities of what was going on before he left. If nothing else, it was a large port with dozens of witnesses to the *Liberty's* unscheduled departure. Someone was going to ask questions as to why the ship had just pulled out of the dock unannounced.

But at the moment, they had another pressing issue to deal with. The captain had made an announcement that everyone was to remain in their quarters until further notice. Isolation was the best course of action if they were dealing with a hemorrhagic virus like Ebola, but even that precaution didn't begin to address all of her concerns. And while she wanted to dismiss the theory entirely, she was in West Africa in the middle of the 2014 Ebola outbreak and knew firsthand how quickly the illness could spread. And how terrifying the aftermath could be. Which meant that making any assumptions at this point could prove deadly. She glanced back at the armed man walking a step behind her, unable to shove aside the frightening question. How were they supposed to control both a virus and the pirates?

A minute later, Rachel paused in front of the lab, took a deep breath, and stepped inside the state-of-the-art space made up of donated diagnostic equipment and supplies used to run simple blood tests. The fear that had been spreading through her gut for the last hour was slowly shifting into anger. There was no way Dabir and his men were going to get away with this takeover. The *Liberty* had too many protocols in place. Somewhere on the ship, the security team was implementing a plan, and the captain had put out a security alert, which meant the authorities had been notified. Or at least that was what she told herself. Dabir had mentioned a jammer, and they were now well out to sea. If the authorities couldn't track the ship, it could potentially take hours, even days to find them.

Dabir stepped into the lab behind her, waiting while she and Harper quickly settled Abeje onto the padded examination table normally used to draw blood for transfusions.

Rachel turned back to him. "Have you or any of your men had symptoms like your wife?"

"I was sick for a few days," Dabir admitted. "Why?"

"If she has the same thing you did, testing your blood might help me figure out what it is."

Dabir hesitated, then nodded.

Surprised at his compliance, but also worried he might change his mind, she quickly masked and gloved, then began to set things up to draw his blood.

"I'd wait outside if I were you," she said, as soon as she'd finished drawing the tubes. "There's a good chance that whatever she has is highly contagious even if you've already had it."

Dabir hesitated, then he and the other armed man stepped into the passageway, shutting the door behind them. Rachel let out a sharp sigh. She had no idea if her last statement was true or not, but at least she wouldn't have to work with armed men breathing down her neck. She turned back to her patient, her mind making a mental checklist of what needed to be done. The room was smaller than the lab she'd worked in at her last job, but was adequate to meet the ship's needs. The diagnostic equipment and supplies crucial to running a hospital were laid out around the perimeter of the room beneath tall rows of cabinets as well as on the large, rectangular workstation in the middle of the room. All of it allowed them to provide doctors with the information needed to treat patients.

But her efficient little lab wasn't set up to control a spreading virus.

Abeje groaned as Rachel adjusted the table.

"What can I do?" Harper asked, reaching out to calm the woman.

Rachel pulled her back. "Until we know what we're dealing with, we need to treat this like it's an infectious disease, which means gloves, masks, gowns...the whole works." Rachel grabbed the supplies Harper needed out of a cabinet. "As soon as you're dressed, you can start taking her vital signs so we can establish a baseline. We'll get her as comfortable as possible, start an IV, then try to figure out what we're dealing with."

"I'm on it."

Rachel worked to keep her focus while she finished garbing up. She pulled out a couple test kits they had in stock, but all she could think about was Josiah and Emma. She'd been the one who'd convinced her brother to come, promising him that this experience would be good for both him and Emma. A new start as they did something he and Camilla had always planned to do. She'd thought that making a difference in the lives of the patients on this ship would motivate him to start living again. Instead that decision might cost him his life. Or Emma's. Or both.

Rachel's heart raced at the thought of her sweet niece, who'd had to grow up so fast. She couldn't be sure if Emma had stayed where they'd hidden her, but she was certain the girl was terrified, wherever she was right now. But as worried as Rachel was about her brother, Mac, and Emma, her attention at the moment had to be the sick woman in her lab. And figuring out what was causing her rapid deterioration and if this was what was spreading in the woman's village.

"Her blood pressure's low," Harper said.

"What about her temperature?"

"A hundred and one."

Rachel made a mental note of the results as Harper wrote them down, got Abeje set up on an IV for hydration, then drew a vial of blood from the woman who lay silent on the table. A blood smear would give results for both malaria and Ebola. If those came back negative, she'd broaden the search. Knowing exactly what to test for next was one of the challenges of identifying a disease. Initial symptoms for Ebola, for example, were non-specific. Fever, weakness, and headaches could mean any number of tropical diseases, including malaria. But the terrifying thing about not knowing exactly what she was dealing with was that often before a hemorrhagic disease could be identified the patient was already infectious.

Which was why she'd put precautions in place, though she knew neither the exact infection or the source of the infection. If they were looking at Ebola, they were going to have to do everything possible to contain the risks of it spreading. The one positive thing about Ebola was that it wasn't airborne. It spread by contact with bodily fluids, which in some ways, made it easier to contain, but even taking blood samples was a potential risk. Every time she drew blood, it created another chance for her to come in contact with the virus.

"What if this is Ebola?" Harper asked while checking Abeje's oxygen levels.

"Odds are it isn't, but we'll just continue taking every precaution possible."

Harper glanced at the strips Rachel had set out that looked like pregnancy tests. "How long for the results?"

"Not too long ago, it would have taken a minimum of twenty-four hours to test for Ebola, but thankfully, we have a limited supply of ReEBOV Antigen Rapid tests that will give us an answer in fifteen minutes by detecting the Ebola protein. We'll have an answer for the malaria test about the same time."

What she didn't mention was that there was a margin of error that often resulted in false positives. But the false negatives were worse. Those results could send infected patients back into their communities.

"You seem pretty competent for a second-year med-student," Rachel said.

Harper shot her a weak smile, but Rachel had been impressed with the young woman's calm composure and ability to jump in and do exactly what she'd been asked to do.

"My father taught me virus transmission protocol from the time I could walk. Wash and dry your hands thoroughly and often, cover your mouth when you cough, don't share glasses or eating utensils. . ." Any trace of a smile faded. "Ebola doesn't always play by the rules."

"We'll deal with that if we have to." Rachel caught her gaze. "What's wrong?"

"You mentioned on the bridge that my father had told you about toxins that were being dumped from ships and then washing up on the shore."

Rachel nodded. "Did he mention it to you?"

"No, but security called me this morning. My father never checked in last night, and he didn't show up at the post-op clinic. I don't know where he is and haven't been able to get ahold of him."

"Josiah mentioned that he wasn't at the post-op clinic. I was going to check, but then—"

"As far as I know, he didn't make it back before we were forced out to sea. It isn't like him not to tell me where he is."

Rachel felt a catch in her throat. "We'll find him."

"You can't promise that."

No. Just like she never should have promised Josiah that the risks were minimal, and he and Emma would be fine. But there had to be a way out of all of this. For all of them.

"I'm not blaming you. None of us could have ever imagined something like this happening or that my father would go missing. What if he's sick with what Abeje has. He could be in danger and waiting on me to help him." Harper dropped her hands to her sides. "Like your brother and your niece."

"We're all in this together, and we can't forget that we're not the only ones trying to put an end to this."

"I know."

But Harper was right about one thing. They had no idea how far this had spread. The key to any outbreak was stopping it as quickly as possible, and to try to keep it from spreading into major travel hubs.

Like Douala.

Not only did the city have an estimated population of almost three million people, it also had the largest port in Central Africa and a major international airport. In a matter of hours, an infected person could take the virus to Lagos, Accra, South Africa, or even the United States.

"I'm taking an infectious disease class in the fall, but I don't know the specifics of Ebola beyond what I've seen on the news," Harper said. "What do I need to know?"

"It starts out like most viral infections, which often makes it hard to diagnose. Fever, vomiting, diarrhea, body aches. It targets the immune system and infects white blood cells and actually has the ability to replicate itself. Which is why patients end up with high levels of the virus in their bodies. It also effects the blood's ability to clot, which is why you sometimes see profuse bleeding."

And the virus's mission wasn't just to keep replicating in one person. Its purpose—its only purpose—was to find the next person to host it and its deadly ways. This piece of terror Rachel kept to herself.

"Sounds like wearing protective equipment was definitely the right call."

Rachel changed the subject while she went through the lab's inventory list in order to determine what they could test for, and Harper rechecked Abeje's vitals. "Tell me about your family. You have some older siblings, don't you?"

"Darby's two years older than me. She just graduated from Harvard Law School. Liam's the oldest. He's a journalist. He spent five years in the military and is somewhere in West Africa right now, working on an assignment."

"So you're the baby?"

Harper let out a soft laugh. "Yes, and my family never fails to remind me."

"What about your mom?" Rachel asked. "I haven't seen her on the ship."

"And you never will," Harper said. "She thought Dad was throwing away his potential on the *Liberty*, so she divorced him and married a rich New York banker with three grown kids."

"Blended families can be tough," Rachel said. She and Josiah had never fit in with the kids of the Kansas man their mother had married.

The timer dinged, interrupting their conversation. Rachel read the results. "She just tested negative for both Ebola and malaria."

"That's good. Isn't it?"

"Yes and no." Rachel hesitated with her answer as she logged the time and results. "Yes, because the *Liberty* is not set up to handle a possible pandemic like Ebola. No, because now I have no idea what we're looking at.

But false negatives are always possible with both Ebola and malaria. I'll need to test her again several times over the next seventy-two hours to make sure what we have is an actual negative."

"And in the meantime?" Harper asked

Rachel moved back to where Abeje lay, still going through their limited options. "We need to broaden the search and keep testing. Yellow fever, cholera, typhoid. Or it could also be a different strain of a hemorrhagic fever. I'll also run some initial tests on Dabir's blood."

And then there was still the possibility that the illness spreading through the remote village was connected to toxic dumping. The problem was with either route, her options of testing remained limited. They routinely digitalized samples and transmitted them via satellite to specialists halfway around the world for results, but with the jammer, there was no way she could contact outside help.

Abeje groaned.

"Abeje try to lie still." Rachel moved back across the room to her patient.

The woman turned toward Rachel and retched. Blood sprayed the front of Rachel's paper gown.

"Harper get out of the way. Now!"

Hemorrhagic syndrome, as they called it, wasn't as common with Ebola as most people thought, but when a patient did bleed, it was usually dramatic. And it usually happened at the very late stages of the disease.

Rachel's heart hammered inside her chest. Whatever Abeje had, the woman was dying. Even if she had the resources to stop the disease from spreading, which she didn't, Rachel wasn't sure there was anything she could do to save her.

CHAPTER EIGHTEEN

SOMEWHERE IN THE GULF OF GUINEA

MAC OPENED HER EYES, THEN BLINKED AT THE BRIGHT SUNLIGHT AND water glistening beneath a cloudless sky. She held her hand up to block the light. Everything that had happened the past twenty-four hours rushed through her, pressing against her chest. Their attempted rescue of the hostages on the oil tanker. Mo being rushed into surgery. Having to call his wife and tell her he was dead. Realizing that one of the pirates they'd shot was onboard the *Liberty*.

She shifted her gaze to the man steering their small boat.

He'd risked his life to save her, a stranger. She saved people all the time she didn't know. She wasn't used to being the one in need of rescue, and she didn't like how vulnerable it made her feel.

Josiah stood at the helm, staring out across the water at the *Liberty* still looming in the distance. His chiseled features were set in a mixture of worry, anger, and determination. His daughter and his sister were captives on a ship with some trigger-happy pirates and an unknown virus that was killing its victims. Josiah didn't think twice. He was coming for his family. And he wasn't going to stop until they were safe. No matter what. Just once, Mac wished her father would have done the same for her. But it would be dereliction of her duty to allow Josiah to charge into a hostage situation without a plan. He'd get them all killed.

She stood, whacking her head on the awning above her.

"Hey." Josiah switched the boat to idle, then headed toward her. "Slow down."

Holding her hand against her throbbing forehead, she walked to the edge of the boat, trying to find her sea legs. "You shouldn't have let me sleep. We need to get on that boat."

"You needed to rest."

"Even with a concussion?"

"I checked your symptoms. You were awake, able to hold a conversation. No dilated pupils." He stopped in front of her. "Any numbness or weakness since I last checked you?"

She shook her head.

"What about blurred vision."

"None."

"Any dizziness or headache?"

"Slight headache from the whack I just gave myself." The boat dipped, and she turned to grab the rail, wincing at the pain shooting up her side. "And I feel like every time I move I discover a new bruise."

"I'm not surprised. You just fell seven stories into the water after being bashed on the head. You're lucky to be alive. I guess a few side-effects are to be expected. I just wish I had a way of making sure you don't have any internal injuries."

"I think I'm okay. Really."

"Said every concussed person I've ever treated." He moved in closer until those blue-gray eyes of his were right in front of her. "I need to check your pupils again."

She let out an exasperated huff of air. "I thought you were a plastic surgeon."

"Granted, it's been a long time since I took a basic first-aid class, but overall, I'm a pretty capable doctor."

"Fine." Her fingers squeezed the rail as he wrapped his hand around her wrist and gazed into her eyes. "So how serious are my injuries, Doc?"

"Doc?" He checked his watch, let her sarcasm go, but held her arm firm. "A bump on your head. More than one scratch. But pulse is still steady."

He released her wrist.

She was pretty sure it was racing.

"You're going to live," he said.

"That's good news, and thank you, by the way," she said, turning away from him. "For fishing me out of the water."

"I thought about throwing you back, but Emma would have killed me."

"Your daughter's against catch and release?"

"Emma's taken a liking to you, and once she takes up with someone, she doesn't let go."

"She is pretty adorable. I think it would be impossible not to like her. She's a smart kid who seems very grown up."

"The smarts came from her mother. Growing up too fast is on me."

She shifted her attention back to the *Liberty,* wondering why he was so hard on himself. He may have screwed up by bringing his child to a pirate-riddled, third-world country, but at least he'd wanted to be with his daughter enough to bring her with him. Her father, on the other hand...No. Mac stopped herself. Recounting all the ways her father had failed her would suck up all the room left in her fuzzy brain for making a plan. She couldn't change the past for her or Josiah, but she could do what she could do to help him secure Emma's future.

"I'll work to come up with some kind of rescue plan," she said. "While you keep an eye on the ship. We need to stay out of gun range, but don't let us fall so far behind that we lose sight of them."

Josiah headed back to the helm. "Do you think following them is the best idea?"

"As opposed to what?" she asked, following him to the front of the boat.

His hand grasped the throttle. "Going for help." The boat sped forward with such speed that Mackenzie had to place her hand on his shoulder to keep from being thrown to the back.

"There are dozens of coves along this coast big enough to hide a cruise ship," she shouted. "We lose them, and it's over." Spray hit her face as the boat bounced across the water, and she went through their options. She had no idea how far away they were from Douala, or where the *Liberty* was headed. "Our best bet is to board that ship. Which means we need a plan."

"What kind of plan?"

She glanced toward the stern of the boat that was cluttered with a couple of jerry cans, some rope, fishing nets, and buckets. Someone was going to be unhappy when they went to go fishing tonight. But what they needed was a couple of weapons.

"The first item of business is to get aboard the *Liberty*. Then I need to locate the pirates' jammer and disable it so I can call my team."

"But if there is Ebola on that ship, your team could accelerate the spread if they don't know what they're doing."

"Do you know how to contain Ebola?"

"Isolation for the symptomatic. Proper protective gear for the caregivers. No contact with bodily fluids for anyone," he said.

"Then I guess we're the best shot of stopping a pandemic. Once we board, we'll find a way to arm ourselves. Then we'll free the ship's security people and while they're helping me take out the bad guys, you can figure out how to take out a deadly virus."

He frowned. "You make it sound easy."

"I'm not expecting it to be easy. Just doable." She started toward the front of the boat. There had to be something in all of the stuff left in the skiff they could use to their advantage. "In the meantime, I'll rig up a way to get us aboard that ship."

"Mac?"

She hesitated, then turned around. "What's wrong?"

"Why hijack an entire medical ship?" he asked. "Why not just ask for help?"

"Desperation." She pulled on the end of a coiled rope. "His wife is dying." She saw Josiah's expression change and she wanted to kick herself. She knew he'd lost his wife. How could she have been so inconsiderate? She filled in the silence with, "I'm going to assume this was more than likely the straw that broke the camel's back."

Desperate people always complicated a mission, because they were willing to take risks that the average person would never take. It was what happened when you got to the place where you felt you had nothing more to lose. When you'd already lost—or were convinced you were going to lose—what was most important to you. Hopefully, Josiah wouldn't let his desperation put his sister and daughter at greater risk.

Anticipating the pirates' next move wasn't going to be easy. Desperation also brought with it unpredictability. She'd already seen that. While someone thinking rationally might have simply asked to speak to someone in charge and look to a solution, he'd hijacked a medical ship.

And that wasn't the only issue they were facing. There was a potentially deadly disease on board that couldn't be stopped with a negotiator.

"Mac, what are you thinking?"

She glanced up at him. "I was thinking about how out of control this has gotten. We went on that ship to save the hostages and now they've taken an entire medical ship hostage. My partner is dead. Your daughter and sister are on that boat."

"If I let myself think about how scared she must be that I left her..." His voice trailed off.

The familiar feeling of guilt resurfaced. "I'm sorry."

"Sorry?" Josiah asked. "How is this your fault?"

"If I had done my job and captured all of the pirates, we wouldn't be in this situation."

"Things rarely go as planned. Trust me. I've learned that firsthand."

Silence settled between them, as Josiah worked to stay out of the wake of the *Liberty*, but close enough that they could still see the ship.

"Do you pray?" he asked, finally.

His question caught her off guard. "My mother used to pray, but it didn't ever seem to change anything."

"My parents were missionaries. Named me Josiah. It's Hebrew for 'Jehovah heals.'"

"Do you believe God heals?"

"I used to." Sadness flickered in his eyes.

"And did it change anything?"

"Camilla still died."

It didn't take much to read between the lines of his pain. She might not know him well, but she knew that losing his wife had to have sent his world spiraling out of control.

She gazed out across the sparkling water, lit now by the sun that was quickly dropping in the west. She knew how Mo would have answered her question. He would have told her that God had a way of taking the odd pieces of your life and using them for His plan. That God had her right where He wanted her. In a place where she simply had to turn to Him.

But Mo's faith had never been shattered like hers.

"Tell me about her," Mac said.

"Camilla?" He blew out a sharp breath as he kept the boat steady. "She was smart, witty, and knew exactly why she'd been put on this earth. From the time she was a little girl, she wanted to make sick kids well. That's why she became one of the best pediatric heart surgeons in the country."

"I can't imagine what it's been like for you to lose her."

"It's been hard on Emma. On both of us."

"Why did you bring your daughter to Africa?"

"That was my sister's doing. She's convinced that I'm unhappy in my life and need a change of pace. A challenge to make me want to live again. I admit, I've just been going through the motions, and Emma deserves more from me. But honestly, I don't have the energy to dig deep enough to find it."

"I'm guessing this wasn't the solution Rachel had in mind."

"Hardly." His laugh rang hollow. "She assured me it was safe, and that Emma and I would thrive. Camilla and I had always planned to do something like this, but the day never came. At least not for the two of us."

"New chapters are always hard to start, especially when they weren't part of the plan." Like when life pulled you off course and threatened to drag you under.

"Why do you do what you do?" he asked, breaking into her thoughts again.

Her brow rose at the question. "You mean what is a woman doing dropping out of planes and into hostage situations?"

"I meant why do you regularly put your life on the line for others? It's pretty admirable."

She was used to fighting prejudice against her gender, her bi-racial features, injuries, and even her fears. His admiration was unexpected and unsettling.

"I guess I'm just a soldier at heart. I joined the military when I was twenty-one, then eventually became a paratrooper. I had to be medically retired after a bad jump shattered my ankle. But once I healed, I decided I missed the adrenaline rush and joined an international security group. We do a lot of consulting, evacuations, kidnappings, mainly for businesses working in places like Africa and the Middle East. When negotiations go south, we go in. Like we did on the oil tanker."

Sometimes they won.

Sometimes people died.

She turned back to him and caught his gaze. He was counting on her, and for some strange reason, she wanted him to know he could. “Help me rig up a way to get us on that ship once night falls. We’re going to go save your daughter.”

CHAPTER NINETEEN

SOMEWHERE IN THE GULF OF GUINEA

JOSIAH KILLED THE MOTOR AND LET THEIR BOAT IDLE IN THE ROCKING waves. The blistering equatorial sun had reddened his bare shoulders, but he was only slightly aware of the pain. What cut deeper was the pain of helplessness. He hadn't believed it was possible to feel more vulnerable than he had when the rope snapped and Camilla sailed off the rock face.

But he did.

He couldn't stand to think of Emma sitting in the dark, her arms wrapped around thin little legs drawn to her chest, and crying that she had been left behind. Again. She'd sat and cried like that for days after Camilla died. His inability to comfort his child had broken his heart. And shamefully, the helplessness of the situation had driven him to bury himself in the operating room.

And what about Rachel? He could barely allow himself to think of his sister. If it was true that this man had brought Ebola onto the ship, Rachel's terror meter would be pinging off the charts. She'd know the odds of the authorities stopping armed pirates were far better than the odds of the limited staff of the *Liberty* beating a killer virus.

No one on that ship was safe.

Josiah pursed his chapped lips to hold back a scream of frustration. He needed to be on that ship.

His gaze drifted to Mackenzie. The gash above her brow had stopped bleeding. Without a CT, he'd have to take it as good news that she wasn't exhibiting concussion symptoms. But she had turned into a drill sergeant tough as any charge nurse he'd ever faced. After she'd delivered her marching orders, she'd become extremely focused and very quiet. Josiah couldn't figure her out. On the one hand, he'd seen how extremely kind she'd been to Emma. On the other hand, she could rappel onto the deck of a dark ship in the dead of night and shoot people.

Was she an introvert? Maybe. Tough as nails? For sure. Out to prove herself in a man's world? Absolutely. Why? He'd like to get to know this impressive woman after he had his daughter safely back on dry, pirate-free land. That he'd felt interest in another woman brought a lightning bolt stab of guilt to his heart. He'd not felt drawn to another woman since the day he first set eyes on Camilla. Even considering the possibility felt like a betrayal of everything good he and Camilla had shared. He shook off his attraction as one of the irrational feelings that can occur when people face traumatic events together. His heart would forever belong to Camilla. End of story.

Josiah tented his hand and squinted into the distance. "I think they've anchored," he announced quietly, keeping in mind Mac's curt reminder that sound carried over the water. "Now what?"

Mac looked up from the knots she made in the rope they were going to climb. "Now we wait."

"For what?"

"Darkness."

His forced dive into the deep had gone a long way in eliminating his usual avoidance of water. But floating around in the ocean, in the middle of the night, in a boat not much bigger than his California bathtub, brought his preference for dry land rushing back. He let out a long, slow breath.

"Here." She handed him the anchor, then wrapped a few turns of the rope around her hand. "Pull on my command."

"Aye, aye, sir." His sarcasm reminded him of Rachel and the reason he was out here.

"It's got to hold if you don't want to get dropped into the drink from seven stories up. Trust me, it's no fun." Not giving him time to argue the merits of trying to scale a cruise ship, she stood and got herself balanced in the skiff. "Pull."

"Wait," he said. "You're bleeding." He nodded toward the huge bloodstain on her scrub.

"It's just a scratch."

"From the size of that stain, it's my medical opinion that it's more than a scratch." He set the anchor at his feet. "I'm not sure how I missed it, but I need to have a look."

"I'm fine."

"Don't argue. The sun is going down. Before long I won't be able to see my hand in front of my face." He nodded again. "You could bleed to death before sunup."

Mac let out a frustrated whoosh of breath and dropped the rope. "Turn around."

"I'm a professional."

"Turn around."

"Fine." He turned and crossed his arms.

He heard her release a whoosh of breath, then groan as she slowly peeled the pink llama fabric over her head.

"Okay," she said.

He turned around and tried not to stare. A black tank top clung to her sculpted torso. Smooth olive skin covered her long neck and toned, graceful arms that looked as if they belonged to a prima ballerina. He cleared his throat. He was a professional, resolved to stay true to the memory of his wife. The perfections of a certain patient's curves had no power to penetrate the shield around his heart.

"You might want to sit down," he stammered.

She dropped the bloody scrub top and lowered herself onto the pile of rope. "Have at it, Doctor."

Josiah realized he'd been so preoccupied by the faint outline of a lace bra beneath the skin-tight tank that he'd not moved in for the exam. "Right."

He made his way to where she sat and knelt in front of her. They were eye to eye. Each assessing the other. He couldn't read everything behind her hard stare, but he could see that she didn't trust him completely. Was it him, or men in general? He'd stood by the operating table of countless women who'd wanted to trust his ability, had even paid a lot of money to prove that they believed in his medical skills. In the end, they would always grab his hand right before the anesthesiologist put them under and say, "Don't hurt me."

There were lots of ways to hurt a woman. He'd hurt Camilla plenty. If he could do it all over again, he would have filled every second of their time together with joy instead of busting his tail to become the world's best plastics doc. But there were no do-overs for the hurts he'd caused the dead.

He raised his palms to allow his skeptical patient to prepare for his examination. "Take a few deep breaths and try not to look."

"I'm not afraid of a little blood."

"Suit yourself." Josiah gently lifted the hem of her tank until he came to the place where the black fabric had adhered to the dried blood. "This might hurt."

He freed her shirt with a tug.

She winced.

"Sorry." He let her catch her breath, then lifted her shirt along the blood trail that led to a deep gash just below her rib cage. "The nail you got hung up on when I was trying to put you into the skiff must have put a hole in you, and then in moving around you pulled it open. I don't think it went deep enough to hit anything vital." He snatched up her scrub top and ripped a long piece of fabric from the hem. "I'm going to wrap this around you to try and stop the bleeding until I can stitch you up."

She nodded, obviously in pain but unwilling to admit it. "It better not leave a scar."

"You can sue me if it does." He finished wrapping the wound. "Hope you're up to date on your tetanus," he quipped.

"Security operatives have to stay current on their shots."

"In case you need to bite someone?"

She smiled. "Exactly."

It was the first real smile he'd seen from her, and it was a beautiful and dangerous assault upon the internal argument he'd been having with himself.

They spent the remaining daylight, preparing their equipment. Mac checked and rechecked the knots. She started to go over the plan again.

Josiah held up his hand. "I got it the first five times."

"Scaling the side of a ship is not going to be easy."

Her lack of faith in his ability could not go unchallenged. "You ever heard of El Capitan?"

"The sheer rock face in Yosemite?"

"I've climbed it." That he hadn't climbed in the two years since his wife died and never wanted to climb again, he kept to himself. "More than once."

If she was impressed, she didn't let it show.

They bobbed in silence. Josiah kept an eye on the ship and Mac kept an eye on the disappearing light.

"I've been thinking," Josiah finally said.

"That sounds dangerous." Her sarcasm had softened.

He'd always been a sucker for sarcasm. Found the teasing banter especially attractive. Camilla had wielded it like a scalpel to his heart.

Josiah buried Camilla's sexy taunting of him from the ledge and forced his thoughts back to the nagging connection between the sickness in the pirates' village and what was possibly happening on the ship. "When I went to the out-patient clinic, the nurse had me look at a patient she suspected had contracted malaria. Febrile. Headache. Nauseated." He paused, weighing whether or not he really wanted to think this was possible, let alone say it out loud. "The test came back negative. What if that patient has Ebola?"

Mackenzie's face drained of color. "That would mean the virus has moved from a small remote village to a heavily populated city."

"The patient I examined was probably already infected when they took her aboard ship and operated. She probably wasn't showing symptoms, since they went ahead with her operation, but. . ." He thought of all the people on the *Liberty.* Gracious, selfless people, who had no idea they'd been exposed to something so horrible. "When we're in the OR, we're careful not to come in contact with body fluids or blood products, but it only takes a spec to the eye to give an aggressive virus a chance to leap from person to person."

"Then shutting down any possible means of contamination with the crew and passengers has to be priority number two."

"The ship's captain seems well-trained."

"I wouldn't count on this particular captain."

"Why would you say that?"

"Because I know him."

"How?"

Mac frowned. "He's my father."

"Why didn't you tell me you had a dog in this fight?"

"My father has nothing to do with my decision to go after these pirates."

The feelings he'd toyed with cracked and popped in his head like a downed power line. He didn't know this woman and he never would. "Your need to avenge your partner's death could get my daughter killed."

CHAPTER TWENTY

SOMEWHERE IN THE GULF OF GUINEA

PANIC PUSHED RACHEL INTO ACTION. SHE LOOKED DOWN AT HER LAB COAT that was now splattered with blood. Fear of what they were facing had morphed into full-blown anger. International health protocol dictated that local health authorities in Douala be notified immediately when a case of Ebola or another hemorrhagic fever was suspected. On top of that, she needed to be in contact with the CDC and inform them that there was a chance that they were looking at a possible repeat of the tragic 2014 Ebola epidemic. Stepped-up airport protocols needed to be initiated in order to stop the spread of the infection. But she didn't have a way to verify what they were dealing with.

And nothing was going to change as long as they were stuck on a ship with no way to communicate to the outside world. But for now, she couldn't think beyond the need to clean up every trace of blood and other fluids. Once she had sterilized her lab and herself as best she could, then she'd make a plan to correctly identify the disease.

"Harper, I need you to remove your gloves and gown, leave them in that bin, wash your hands with the disinfectant, then get out of here."

"I'm not leaving you—"

"Harper, do what I say. The keys are on the cabinet by the door. Go straight to my room, then shower from head to toe and use a thick layer of the hand sanitizer I keep under the sink. Lock the door, and don't leave my room for any reason. You'll be safe there until this is over."

Harper planted her feet in the middle of the room. "I'm staying."

"You're risking your life—"

"You need me, and I can't just sit in a room. I came on this ship to be useful. Not to hide."

Rachel frowned. The girl wasn't budging, and she didn't have time to argue. "Fine, but you're going to need to scrub down, then put on a fresh gown and mask."

"I might have only finished my second year of med school, but I know enough to take precautions. And enough to know the seriousness of this situation."

"Okay." Hopefully, she wouldn't regret this concession. "The first step is detection, and even though we don't know what this is, going forward we're going to assume it's contagious and deadly. We're going to need to follow CDC protocol for cleaning and disinfecting the waste. We have only a limited supply of personal protection equipment, but we'll use everything we have, PVC aprons, gloves, goggles, and masks. Everything. We'll go ahead and change, then start disinfecting the room as best we can."

Rachel glanced at Abeje, thankful the woman had drifted back to sleep. She needed to further her diagnosis in the lab by testing a wider range of tropical illnesses that needed to be considered, like arboviruses, dengue, and chikungunya, but first they needed to disinfect the room and set up a more secure isolation area. While maybe not the most efficient plan, she had access to plastic sheeting and duct tape in the lab. Their limited supply of PVC aprons and gloves were resistant to pathogens and could be sterilized after use.

She was thankful Harper was here, but she wished she could go find her regular lab techs. They knew the lab, the equipment, and how to safely deal with blood. But at the moment, she couldn't risk their lives too. Not only were they dealing with some kind of spreading disease, but they also had armed pirates on board who had already killed at least one Gurkha. Still, she wished she had someone to bounce ideas off of.

Someone like Aiden.

Once she had on the suit, gloves, and goggles she'd found for both of them in one of the cabinets, Rachel started cleaning with the disinfectant they kept in the lab. She knew from past experience how important it was to ensure that the virus was completely disinfected, but still let her mind slip back into the not-so-distant past. Because this wasn't the first time she'd found herself in a situation where she'd been terrified that a virus would win.

She and Aiden had met at a party in Washington DC at the home of a woman who'd donated to the private lab Rachel worked for. She'd almost not gone that night. Stuffy parties and fundraisers had never interested her. Instead, she was perfectly content to spend her free evenings getting caught up on her reading. But a co-worker had insisted she go. And when she got there, she found out that introducing her to Aiden had been her friend's plan all along. But Aiden hadn't been there for the party.

She shuddered at the memories of Aiden's discovery of the source of a lethal outbreak that had already decimated a remote Tibetan village. And how it had almost cost them their lives. She was comfortable in a lab setting, not fighting for her life, and those frightening days had proved it. But now, once again, she was terrified she was facing something completely out of her control.

Aiden had always said it was a game he believed deep down they could never win. That one day, some dormant or yet-undiscovered virus would wipe out half the population. As far as she was concerned, that wasn't going to happen. Not if she could do anything about it.

"Despite everything, I wish you were here to help me, Aiden," she whispered to herself as she swabbed the floor with disinfectant.

But no matter how easygoing Aiden appeared, he was obsessed with the accuracy and precision of his work, down to the smallest detail. Whether it was collecting samples in the darkness of a bat cave or blood draws at a small clinic in the bush, he'd always told her that the precautions they took were only as good as the person who took them.

"Don't worry, Rachel," he'd said on their last static-filled call. "I'm not going to be the one who gets caught by the disease I'm chasing."

But he'd been so obsessed with his work that in the end, he'd chosen it over her.

"Rachel?"

Harper's voice jerked Rachel out of the past and back to the dark road she was navigating with a possible out-of-control virus bearing down.

"I'm sorry. . ."

"I just took her vitals again. Her temperature's spiking."

Rachel headed for one of the cabinets, praying she had what they needed. "We'll give her 400 mg ibuprofen through her IV."

But the pain medicine was just a mask for the symptoms. Treating her patient effectively meant she had to quickly find out what was making Abeje sick if she were to have a chance of stopping this woman's rapid deterioration. Terrifying as the ramifications of losing the pirate's wife could be, a virus like Ebola—or whatever this was—made it almost impossible for a caregiver to avoid the blood, vomit, and sweat of the dying. She and everyone on this boat could get infected.

No matter how much she cleaned up from Abeje, the virus was still going to cling to the walls, the floors, and across Abeje's weakened body. But if they weren't dealing with Ebola, what were they dealing with? Diagnosis in a health crisis was crucial. How could she treat this woman, and anyone else who might get sick, if she had no idea what had been brought onto the *Liberty*?

CHAPTER TWENTY-ONE

SOMEWHERE IN THE GULF OF GUINEA

THE BIG WHITE SHIP WAS A GLOWING TARGET IN THE MOONLIGHT. Hopefully, the wave noise was loud enough that anyone standing guard wouldn't hear the skiff's outboard motor. Josiah eased their small boat alongside the anchored *Liberty*. The rope ladder, the one he'd seen in the orientation video, had been removed. Just as Mackenzie had insisted it would be. He was more familiar with the ship, but he had to admit that she knew pirates. These brigands were smart, and they wouldn't make it easy for anyone to thwart their plan.

"We'll have to go aft," Mackenzie whispered with a hint of I-told-you-so.

He motored the skiff around to the dark side of the ship. He cut the motor and let the skiff drift against the ship. His eyes traveled up the slick white walls. Higher and higher until the smoke tower disappeared into the velvety blanket of stars. Climbing the *Liberty* presented a challenge as treacherous as any rock face he'd ever scaled. And bobbing about in an unstable skiff was certainly starting the attack of this problem from a position of disadvantage. Whether or not they could execute enough moves to summit remained to be seen.

"Hand me the anchor rope," he whispered to Mac.

"You've got one shot," she said, holding the heavy three-pronged weight in her hand. "If this anchor hits the side of the ship it will ring like a dinner bell." Mac gave him the makeshift ladder. "Hope your aim is as good as your self-proclaimed rock-climbing skills."

"You might want to stand close to me," he said.

"I don't."

"I'm not hitting on you. I'm going to have to generate a pretty big swing to launch a twenty-pound anchor that high, and I don't want to have to fish you out of the drink again."

"Want me to throw it?"

"Have you ever thrown a grappling hook before?"

"Yes," she said confidently.

He considered her challenge. "Well, it's my daughter." His argument was weak, but it was all he had. "I'll do the throwing."

She stomped into a crouch position close to his side.

He waited until she was tucked up beside him. Trying not to think about her body pressed against his, he swung the anchor around and around their heads. When he thought he'd reached maximum momentum, he released his hold and sent the anchor sailing. As it flew high overhead, the thought crossed his mind that he might not have thought this through. In this poor light, they wouldn't be able to see the anchor fall should it not catch and come tumbling down. Holding his breath, he waited. One of the three-pronged hooks clanged against the railing, snagged, and caught.

"Oh, yeah," he whispered, pumping his fist.

"Now we have to climb it." Mac reached out and grabbed the swinging end of the rope and tugged hard with two hands. "I think it will hold both of us."

He stepped aside. "Ladies first."

If she noticed that he sounded more hesitant than gallant, she graciously didn't comment.

He watched as Mac tucked into the waistband of her pants a slender metal rod she'd found at the bottom of the skiff. "Last one to the top buys dinner," she whispered.

He snagged her arm. "That jerk who shoved my sister around is mine."

"Only if you beat me to him," she said. "I owe him for my new forehead scar." She hoisted herself from the skiff, then swung between ocean and ship until the momentum carried her close enough to plant her shoes against the shiny white paint.

She was like a spider scrambling up a web. Her sinewy arms worked in perfect tandem with her muscled long legs. Each move carried her higher up the side of the ship. Visions of Camilla, roped to the side of El Capitan and laughing at him for staring at her, flashed in his mind.

"Coming?" Mac's whisper-shout snapped his attention to the end of the rope dangling in front of him.

He wouldn't have come to Africa if he'd known he'd be forced to take to the water and a climbing rope. But he had come to Africa. His daughter and sister had been kidnapped by pirates. He hadn't died in the water and, with any luck, he'd survive this climb.

Emma and Rachel were counting on him. For their sakes, he'd risk everything. . .even letting a woman egg him on to scale new heights.

He grabbed hold of the rope above the first knot.

Consider the problem. Execute the moves. Summit.

Camilla's voice whispered in his mind and he leapt from the skiff. The combination of wind and momentum slammed him into the hull.

"Ouch!"

"Shhh," Mac hissed.

"Right." Heart pounding, he didn't let himself look down at the dark water swirling only ten feet below. "Eyes up," he muttered. "Think of Emma."

Hand over hand he pulled himself higher. The burn in his arms forced his feet to seek a crevice between two of the riveted steel panels. He dug his toes into the hold. To relieve the strain to his arm muscles, he released his right hand and shook out his pumped forearm. The move was second nature. He hadn't even had to think about it. He was thirty-six years old and getting back on a bicycle for the first time in years and doing wheelies like he was ten again. Relief surged through his fingers. He clasped the rope with his right hand, then shook out his left arm. This time, the move sent a chunk of the grief he carried plummeting to the foamy water below. Feeling lighter than he had in months, he took a deep breath and looked up.

He could do this. For Emma's sake, he would do this.

Mac's reverse rappel was a jackknife form above him. She was using her feet as much as her arms to walk her lean body up the ship's slippery metal side. He employed the same method and was quickly within a body-length below her.

"Only one more deck." Her smile at his progress was a shot of adrenaline.

"No problem." Though he'd always been lead climber whenever he and Camilla took to the rocks, Josiah followed Mac's every move. Hand over hand. Step by step. He was sweating and breathing hard, but he was doing this. He was climbing again, and it felt more than good. It felt right.

Mac's foot slipped. Her heel came down and hit him hard in the face. He managed to keep his feet against the ship and not let go of the rope, but once his vision cleared, he could see that she was struggling to hold on.

"Stay calm," he told her. "I'm going to catch your foot and put you back on the wall."

"I'm losing my grip."

"Hang on." Her foot sailed past his face again. He let go of the rope with one hand and snagged her ankle. "Here."

He palmed the sole of her foot and pushed up. It was just a smidgen of help, but it instantly put her back on track. Within seconds she reached the railing, heaved herself over, and disappeared.

"Clear." Her voice shook him from thoughts of almost losing her. "Josiah?" She was leaning over and reaching for him.

He grabbed hold of her hand and she hauled him over the rail. They toppled onto the small deck at the back of the ship, Mac landing first and him piling on top of her.

For a second, they didn't move, his labored breath mingling with hers.

"We have to go," she whispered.

"Right." He pushed himself off her and got to his feet. "You hurt?"

He reached for her, but she batted his hand away. "I'm fine." She scrambled to her feet. "I left Emma on deck four." Mac pulled the metal pipe from her waistband. Their only weapon. "But my plan is to find the Gurkhas first."

"You don't even know if any of them are still alive." He jerked free. "I'm getting Emma."

"You know nothing about tactical operations."

"You know nothing about how determined I am to find my daughter."

She faced him in the semi-darkness. "Trust me."

He hesitated a second longer, then followed her down a hall dimly lit by emergency lighting. Thirty seconds later, he spotted a ventilation grate that had been pushed from the wall and now blocked the passageway.

Mac turned to him. "This is where I left her."

Josiah crouched near the opening. "Em?" he whispered into the tunnel. It was so dark inside the opening he couldn't tell how far back the shaft went. "Emma? It's Daddy. Come out." No answer. He wished he had a flashlight. What if she'd fallen asleep? He tried to squeeze in, but it was only big enough for a child. "Emma!"

Nothing.

Had he really expected her to still be here?

He backed out, raked his hands through his hair, and wished he knew his six-year-old daughter well enough to know what she would do if she got scared.

"I'm sorry," Mac said. "We didn't exactly have a lot of time to debate the options."

"Maybe she went to Rachel's room. It's just down the hall, and she'd know how to find it." Frantic, he took off at a sprint. He checked each locked door until he came to the room labeled ALLEN. "Ray," he whispered. Nothing. He pounded on the door.

"Shhhh," Mac hissed.

"Ray?" Nothing. His mind was whirring with possibilities, none of them good. "Maybe they're in Rachel's lab."

"Why would they go there?"

"Because Rachel wouldn't let a man with a gun keep her from figuring out what had made Dabir's wife sick. And Emma would figure out a way to get to her aunt's lab." He took Mac's hand. "Deck 3."

They descended the blue stairs to the hospital floor.

"How many pirates?" Josiah asked as he checked every locked door.

"They said they had two dozen men on board, but I only saw four."

"You can take 'em, right?" Even as he said it, Josiah knew his question hadn't made either one of them feel any better. "Sorry. Let's go."

He moved through the semi-darkness. Why hadn't he paid closer attention on his tour of the hospital floor's layout? He felt his way past the lecture room, the operating bays, and a cargo hold. All of them unlocked but empty.

"Wait." Mac grabbed his arm. "There's an armed guard ahead, and I don't think it's one of ours."

They pressed their backs against the wall and held their breaths, praying the man didn't see them. They heard his retreating boots a moment later.

"Let's go," Mac urged.

"I think this is it." Josiah tried the next door, but it was locked. Was Rachel being held in her lab? Or were she and Emma hiding and too afraid to open the door?

He knocked lightly. "Ray, it's Joey."

The clatter of stainless steel hitting the floor sounded from inside the lab. Someone was in there.

Mac stayed his hand. "Wait."

He couldn't wait. His daughter and sister needed him now.

"Ray," he whispered again.

The door cracked open. The putrid smell of vomit hit Josiah's nose and turned his empty stomach.

"Josiah?"

Soft blue light from a workstation with vials and machines silhouetted a figure to his left. To his right, a second figure stood in front of plastic sheeting and what looked like a makeshift isolation chamber. Both were dressed in yellow gowns. Heavy green gloves covered their hands and arms, and their faces were shrouded behind masks and goggles.

But he recognized the woman's voice.

"Rachel!" Josiah started to her from the doorway. "Is Emma here?"

"Don't." She held up her palms and quickly backed away. "I need you to get out of here, Joey. Both of you. Now." Her voice was shaky, tired, and very frightened.

"Not without you and Emma."

"Emma's not here. I don't know where she is. I'm sorry."

"What's going on, Ray?"

"One of the pirate's wives is feverish and vomiting blood."

"Ebola?" Josiah asked.

"The test came back negative."

The woman laying behind the plastic sheeting groaned and blood trailed from her nose.

"What else could it be?"

"I don't know," Rachel said. "A virus that's mutating? Something I don't have a test for?"

"Leave her, Rachel, and come with me. Both of you."

"I can't." She held up her hand, warding him off. "Go find Emma and find a way off this ship. Now!"

The hall lights flickered on. "Nobody's going anywhere."

Josiah wheeled to see a wiry black man with well-muscled arms standing behind him and pointing an AK-47 at him and Mackenzie.

"Dabir," Rachel said as a second armed man joined the first. "Stay back," Rachel warned. "It's not safe here."

Dabir pushed toward Josiah. "I need to see my wife."

"You don't want to do that," Josiah said.

The barrel of the automatic aimed at Josiah's chest. "I'm the one who says what I do and don't do now." Dabir's gaze moved beyond Josiah. "Abeje!" He pushed past Josiah and strode to his wife's side.

"Dabir." The woman behind the sheeting weakly raised her hand to keep him back. "You must go."

Rachel turned to Dabir. "I'm doing everything I can to help her, but I'm almost certain whatever she has is contagious and most likely it's what's killing your village."

Josiah swallowed hard. Toe to toe, he knew the man would have to put a bullet in his sister to get her to back down.

"She's my wife."

"And you want what's best for her, right?" Josiah fought memories of trying to get to Camilla after the fall and paramedics holding him back. "It's best for Abeje if you wait outside."

Dabir's eyes darted from Josiah to his wife and then to Rachel. "Many in my village said I was a fool to bring her here. People come to the hospital to die, they said. But I thought you could help her."

"I want to help her, but I haven't had time to figure out what's wrong yet."

"Then you better get busy." Dabir took a step back from the bed. "Because if she dies, you die."

"Dabir!" His wife coughed, and blood splattered onto her gown. "Go home. Take our son far from the sickness in our village."

"But Abeje—"

"Please." She turned away from him, pulling her knees up toward her chest.

He spoke to her in a language Josiah did not understand, but he could tell from the man's quivering lips that he was afraid. Josiah remembered the void he'd fallen into the day he lost his wife. And that hole would never be filled.

"Abeje!" Dabir's voice rose as he kept talking to her, but it was as if his wife had already sailed over the cliff.

The proud man stepped away. When he turned, his fear and hurt had already hardened into an anger Josiah knew and understood far too well.

Dabir pointed his weapon at Rachel. "Could you fix this sickness, if you knew what it was?"

Rachel held up her palms. "Maybe, but I'd need to examine more sick patients and draw samples of their blood and urine."

Dabir reached to grab her arm. "You need to come to my village."

From the corner of his eye, Josiah saw Mac reach for the metal pipe behind her. He blocked her entry into the discussion. Not wanting to set off a confrontation that could get them all killed and leave Emma with no one, he held up his hands. "Rachel needs to stay here. I'll go to your village and get the samples."

CHAPTER TWENTY-TWO

SOMEWHERE IN THE GULF OF GUINEA

MAC FELT HER STOMACH HEAVE AT THE SMELL OF VOMIT LINGERING IN THE lab and at the blood stains on Rachel's gown. She wasn't a doctor, but even she could see that in just a few hours Dabir's wife had deteriorated. Whatever had made her sick, they were going to have to move fast to keep it from spreading further.

"How is letting Josiah leave the *Liberty* going to help?" Mac asked Rachel. "We need to transport this woman back to the hospital in Douala. They'll have the resources to treat her."

Rachel shook her head. "Better to keep her isolated on the ship for now and limit further exposure until we can figure out what we're dealing with."

"Except it may already be spreading." Josiah turned to his sister. "Remember that female patient at the post-op clinic I called you about?"

"Yes," Rachel said.

"She presented with these same symptoms." Josiah nodded toward Abeje.

"Were you careful?" Rachel asked.

"Yes, but if this is some hemorrhagic virus—"

"Dabir is right," Rachel said. "We need to find the source."

Dabir waved his gun at Josiah and Mac. "I'm taking these two to my village—"

"You don't need Mac," Josiah argued.

"You don't need to go alone," Mac argued back before she realized the pleading in Josiah's eyes was asking her to stay behind to protect his daughter.

Dabir pointed at Rachel. "You will stay and help my wife."

"You don't understand," Rachel said. "I don't have a treatment. I don't know how to fix this by myself."

"What *can* you do?" Dabir asked, his sharp eyes alert to any sleight of hand any of them might try to pull.

"We're already doing everything we can." Rachel looked at the woman who now lay quietly on the bed behind the plastic sheet curtain Harper had rigged to the ceiling with duct tape. "We're treating symptoms—blood pressure, fever, and headache, but that's like putting a Band-Aid on a bleeding artery. Supportive care might temporarily slow down the symptoms, but it won't heal her. On top of that, there are strict global health protocols that need to be followed in situations like this, so this doesn't spread further. I need to let the local authorities know what's happening so they can contact your national government. I need to contact the CDC—"

"You think the world cares what happens to my wife?" Dabir took a step forward. "My first wife died because no one would treat her at the hospital. Now, I finally have someone's attention, and you're the one who's going to save her—"

"You don't understand." Rachel shook her head. "She has all the symptoms of a viral hemorrhagic fever, including vomiting blood. No one wants to see another global epidemic. And even if I had blood samples of everyone who is sick in your village, my lab isn't set up to stop a pandemic. And if the virus on this boat has already spread to the capital city, that's exactly what we're going to have."

Mac studied Dabir's face and tried to read his expression. If Rachel's threat of catastrophic outcomes had frightened him as much as it frightened her, he didn't let it show. He'd come this far, and had to believe he was in too deep. That there was no way out of this. And clearly, he was going to do anything to stay in control, even if he caused the whole world to crash down on all of them. If she was going to keep others from dying, she needed to find a way to come alongside this desperate man.

"What do you need us to do in Dabir's village?" Mac asked Josiah's sister.

Rachel's frown deepened. "Normally, I would advise against sending non-trained personnel into a hot zone. This is a job for trained virus hunters."

"But this isn't normal," Mac reminded her. "And I don't think our friend with the gun is going to allow that, do you?"

Rachel released a resigned sigh. "You're going to need to follow proper testing protocols and that will require you act as a team."

Josiah cut his gaze to Mac and then back to his sister. "How do you think we got on this ship?"

"All right then." Rachel pulled off her gloves. "I'm going to need blood samples." She turned on the tap and started scrubbing her hands. "Mark and label every tube, but you're going to have to be careful. I can't emphasize just how quickly this can spread if precautions aren't made. You'll need to minimize the number of blood draws and needle pricks, because every time you're exposed to bodily fluids your risk goes up. That means you also need to stay covered with gowns, masks, and gloves at all times. Am I clear?"

"Crystal," Mac said.

"There are barrels that wash up along the river," Dabir said. "Like I said on the bridge, dying vegetation and a film on the river. Something is killing the land and the animals." His focus shifted from Mac to his dying wife. "What if whatever is killing the jungle is also killing my wife and the people in my village?"

"We can't overlook toxic poisoning," Rachel said. "But it will be impossible to tie environmental toxins to this sickness without samples of the water." She started putting supplies in a plastic tub. "We'll also need a way to communicate. I need to know what you find—"

"No." Dabir nodded at Josiah to take the first box. "We'll take the supplies and return with your samples." He waved his rifle at Josiah and Mac. "We need to go."

"There are so many things that could go wrong—"

"I studied tropical disease, Rachel. Remember?" Josiah said, interrupting his sister. "I need you to stay behind and take care of things here."

Mac could tell from Rachel's reaction that taking care of things was Josiah's code to his sister for her to take care of Emma. Mac's brain raced through the limited options to keep the child safe. She wasn't sure how many armed men were on the *Liberty*, but if her team could find the ship, they'd be able to put an end to this madness. The problem was the jammer. It was acting as a cloak that concealed the ship, making them virtually invisible. If she could find the device and disable it, they'd be able to contact her team. She hadn't seen land or any other navigational markers from the skiff. Pinpointing their location in a million square miles of water would be like searching for a needle in a haystack.

She made a mistake in volunteering to go with Josiah. The fastest way to shut all of this down was to locate the jammer and notify her team. To do her job, she would have to remain on the ship.

"Rachel's going to need help here," Mac said, ready to put her plan into place. "Someone who's already been exposed to whatever this is. I'll stay."

If she was right and there were only four armed men, then Dabir would still have to take at least one with him and leave two on the ship. She could find a way to take two down even if they were armed. Then once she found the jammer and disabled it, they'd get the help they needed.

"She has help." Dabir pointed at the young woman who'd kept silent through all of their negotiations.

"But she's just a student," Mac argued.

Dabir grabbed Mac's arm. "You'll come with me and help the doctor in the village."

Josiah started for her, but Mac gave a little shake of her head and he stayed put.

She understood Josiah's frustration. It was all she could do not to jerk free and go for Dabir's gun. But it wouldn't take much to push this desperate man over the edge. To put them all in even greater danger. For now, the odds were not in their favor. What she needed was a plan B. Something to even those odds. Something that would give her time to figure out how to send a silent S.O.S. Dabir knew she wasn't part of the medical crew. Knew she'd been on that tanker. He didn't want her out of his sight and yet somehow, he thought she was going to be useful to him.

"We'll also bring along the captain and the other man who was on the bridge. Having them as hostages will make sure this ship stays put." Dabir squeezed Mac's arm tighter. "We'll take the boat you used to track us and go to the village."

"At least take a proper team from the ship, Dabir," Rachel said. "We have trained lab techs—"

"No," Dabir said. "We'll keep it small. Just enough to get what is needed."

"Wait a minute," Josiah said. "There's another problem we haven't even talked about. There are almost five hundred people on this ship currently confined to quarters. How long do you think that's going to be feasible? First of all, the ship doesn't have an indefinite power source, or food, or water. And second, with a disease on board, we need to keep the crew isolated."

"Put Samuel, our chief medical officer, in charge," Rachel said. "Let him assemble a small medical team that delivers water and food to each quarter. His delivery team can also cordon off the gym and isolate and treat anyone who is displaying symptoms. That will allow us to initiate immediate supportive care and keep track of any spread."

"Fine." Dabir's reluctant agreement told Mac he did have a reasonable side, a compassion for others, that might be the key that would unlock a positive outcome to this nightmare.

Rachel turned to Josiah. "You need to hurry."

"Dabir." The soft plea came from behind the plastic barrier. "If Taiwo gets sick—"

"He's not going to," Dabir answered her. "I will make sure of that." He released his hold on Mac's arm and stepped up to the plastic sheeting. He raised his hand as if contemplating the cost of touching his wife one last time. "I need to do this to save you. To save Taiwo. I'll be back. I promise."

Twenty minutes later, Mac, Josiah, Sid, and Mac's father had used the winch to lower the tubs of supplies and themselves to the skiff. Dabir and one of his armed buddies ordered them to follow. Mac sat next to Josiah. Across from her sat Sid and her father. He offered her a hopeful smile, but she turned her gaze away.

"We'll leave you untied." Dabir pointed his gun at Mac's head. "But try anything and you'll end up as fish bait." He cranked the motor on the skiff then pulled away from the ship in a swirl of foam.

Mac studied Dabir's body language as they headed toward the shore. She wasn't sure how long he'd played the role of pirate, but she'd seen a surprising tenderness between him and his wife. And when he spoke of his son. If she found a way to tap into his compassion, she might just find the key to ending this without more bloodshed.

Moonlight filtered through the trees on the delta as the skiff slid through the dark waters. Eventually, they turned and headed into a wide tributary that dumped into the ocean. Tree roots of mangroves and palms elevated above the water. Tethered boats bobbed with the tide. Mo would have loved exploring this part of the world and taking photos for his kids. Had it been less than forty-eight hours since her extraction partner told her that this stint looked like paradise compared to Iraq? If only she'd thought to count the hostages a second sooner. That mistake had cost Mo his life and put her in the middle of an impossible situation. If she made another mistake, many more could die.

She glanced at Josiah's profile beside her, knowing he was thinking about his little girl and his sister. She wished she could end this for him. Frustration forced its way through her as easily as Dabir sat in the back of the motorized boat and navigated the watery maze. She needed another plan.

There could still be security officers on the *Liberty*. She wasn't sure where they were or how many of them, if any, were still alive. Her problem was, even if she did manage to escape from Dabir, she had no idea where they were now or how to navigate her way out of the delta. Even if she made it back to the ship, without a phone she couldn't call in her team. She could see the position of the first rays of sunlight and was pretty sure they were north of Douala, probably toward Nigeria, heading northeast, upriver. Dabir had said he lived a couple hours from the coastline, which fit her calculations as well.

What she didn't understand was how Dabir had managed to take hostage an entire medical ship with only four armed gunmen. And she hadn't stopped them. By now, she hoped her team knew that something was wrong. Hopefully, when they arrived back at port and saw that the *Liberty* was gone, they'd search for her.

But it wasn't the armed men on the boat that worried her the most. She'd seen Rachel's bloodstained gown. Whatever was in that blood...whatever virus was running through Dabir's wife...was going to kill her. Which meant it could kill anyone who came in contact with it.

She'd also seen the fear in Rachel's eyes when she had Josiah repeat her long list of instructions on what precautions must be taken at Dabir's village. His inexperience with deadly viruses had her worried. From what Emma had said, her father was a plastic surgeon. It might be true that he'd taken a class on hemorrhagic diseases, but what did he really know about containing a virus that was potentially running out of control?

Josiah leaned forward next to her. "What are you thinking?"

Wishing that Rachel had come with us, but she kept that to herself. "I'm planning our escape."

"I'm all ears."

"I'm just finding it a little tricky when I've got an AK-47 pointed at my head and no real escape route," she said, barely above the roar of the motor. "My original plan was to stay on the boat and deactivate the jammer. I was hoping my team would show up and put an end to this, but now—"

"There's a good chance your team will be there by the time we get back, right?"

"I hope so, but by then we could potentially come in contact with a couple hundred people who are contagious with the virus."

"Maybe it hasn't spread that quickly."

"Maybe. But while I'm trying to find an escape route, you need a plan to stop this disease because Dabir's wife's not going to make it, is she?"

"Probably not."

"Dabir and his friends won't like that."

"No man wants to lose his wife."

Mac frowned. Josiah had way too much skin in the game. He had empathy for the pirate, and that would not serve him well if this dangerous foray into the village went south. His daughter was on the *Liberty*. She needed to keep Josiah focused on what was to be gained rather than what he'd lost.

"What's your story with the captain?" Josiah's question jarred her. He nodded in the direction of Sid and her father sleeping against the side of the boat. "The two of you aren't exactly on speaking terms, are you?"

She shifted her gaze momentarily. It had been years since she'd seen Captain Edmonton Scott. He was thinner, grayer, and sober. But he still had the disgraceful scar above his right eye. She knew she needed to confront him at some point. Demand an explanation for his complete disappearance from her life. But this wasn't the time or place.

"It's a long story," she said, not ready to tell any of it. "Believe it or not, I didn't even know he was on the *Liberty*."

"Looks like the *Liberty* is just full of surprises."

"None of them good as far as I'm concerned."

First light revealed a slimy film on the top of the water as the boat slowed and skimmed the sandy shore.

"Time to wake up," Dabir said. "This is where we get off."

Mac rested her hand on Josiah's arm for a brief moment. "Notice the water."

"Maybe Dabir is on to something."

Several people ran toward the boat, including a woman whose frantic voice carried across the water as she shouted something at Dabir.

"Dabir, what's going on?" Mac stepped to the front of the boat.

"It's my sister." Dabir turned to her. "She lives up the river about three kilometers. My nephew is sick. And the death toll is rising."

CHAPTER TWENTY-THREE

PHILADELPHIA, PENNSYLVANIA

"EBOLA?" THE TERROR IN JASMINE'S VOICE MIRRORED THE FEELINGS THAT had ripped through Clayborn when his mother's last PCR came back positive for the world's deadliest virus. "Loraine held our baby, Clayborn."

He squeezed his cellphone tighter. "Listen to me, Jasmine. I don't have long to talk." Keeping a grip on his emotions was the only help he could offer his family. "They're transporting me and Mom to Bethesda."

"Maryland?" Jasmine's voice cracked. "You're leaving me with a toddler and a newborn?"

"I know you're scared, baby. I am too." Clayborn did his best to keep his voice calm. "But if Mom is going to have a fighting chance, the National Institutes of Health is the best choice." What he wasn't telling her was that he was under a mandatory quarantine and couldn't come home. "It's a facility staffed with contagious-disease specialists who are totally devoted to the latest in clinical research. They're equipped with negative-pressure patient rooms, high-efficiency germicidal lamps that can eliminate harmful pathogens from every surface, and here's the best news: they have access to every new or experimental antiviral."

"What if I get sick, Clayborn?" She wasn't buying his clinical approach to this emotionally charged problem. "Will I have to go to Bethesda?"

He couldn't let himself imagine his kids left alone. "You're not going to get sick. Ebola only spreads when a person comes in contact with the blood or body fluids of a person or animal who's sick or has died from the disease. Mom didn't start with the vomiting and diarrhea until she got to the hospital."

"Did you come in contact with Loraine's body fluids?"

He swallowed hard and looked at the hand he'd scrubbed a thousand times since he'd scooped his mother up from the bathroom floor. "Yes."

"That's why you're not coming home, isn't it?"

"I've been put under a twenty-one-day quarantine."

"Twenty-one days!"

He took a deep breath. "Remember the infectious disease doc I introduced you to at the last hospital Christmas party?"

"Not really."

He couldn't blame his wife for not making this easy. She was tired. Ticked. And terrified. "Her name is Liz Maxwell, and she's coming to stay with you for a few days."

"You told me to call my mother. She caught the next flight out of Florida, Clayborn. I don't need a babysitter."

"Right. I forgot about your mom." Clayborn raked his hand through his hair. "I'm glad you've got help with the kids, because Dr. Maxwell isn't coming to babysit."

"Then why is she coming?"

"She's coming to maintain a..." He hesitated to say the word again. "Twenty-one-day quarantine on you and the kids. And now your mother."

"Because we might get sick?"

He wanted to reach through the phone and hold her. To reassure her with promises that everything was going to be alright, but from what Liz had told him about Ebola, he couldn't hurt his wife more by giving her false hope. She deserved the truth.

"The CDC isn't willing to take any chances," he finally managed.

"So, the government's answer to managing a possible world-wide pandemic is to send me a jailer? If that's supposed to make me feel better, it doesn't." Jasmine paused. "Wait, Clayborn. There's some guy from the CDC on the TV."

"Let me turn up the sound on my screen." Clayborn found the remote, took a quick peek at his mother who was sleeping fitfully, then cranked the television's volume.

The Director of the Center for Disease Control and Prevention stood at the podium. His face was ashen, his demeanor sober. Cameras clicked as he began to speak.

"An individual traveling from Cameroon to the United States has been officially diagnosed with a new strain of Ebola." The epidemiologist's expression was neutral, but Clayborn recognized the flicker of terror in his eyes. "The passenger was not sick on the days of travel and passed all airport screenings. Shortly after the passenger's arrival, she began to experience symptoms consistent with several tropical diseases. Specimens were sent to our lab for testing. Unfortunately, the results came back positive for Ebola."

As reporters shouted questions, the director shuffled his notes then clenched the edges of the lectern. "Thinking this was the only case, we immediately initiated isolation protocols for the extended family." He paused to check his notes. "Since then, we have received another positive PCR test result from Dallas and one from California. Both patients arrived in the States from another airport in Central Africa."

Clayborn felt his heart skip a beat. The virus was spreading.

"Our next steps are three-fold," the director continued without stopping to answer any of the questions reporters fired at him. "First, we are committed to providing the most effective care for these patients. They will be transported to Bethesda, Maryland, via an aircraft designed to reduce the risk of infecting healthcare workers. Second, we are asking the public's help in identifying everyone who may have had contact with the infected patients. And third, once these contacts are identified, they will be monitored during a mandatory twenty-one-day isolation period. If they develop fever, they too will be transported to Bethesda and cared for." He lifted his eyes and stared straight into the camera. "We have assured the president that the U.S. has the best doctors and public health infrastructure in the world. We are prepared to respond to this outbreak of Ebola."

While the director went on to list the dates and times of his mother's flight, Clayborn knew that what the world's premiere epidemiologist had just promised the American public was only partly true. Some doctors believed ZMapp had been effective for Dr. Brantly, the American physician infected with Ebola in Africa and brought to the States in 2014. But there was no proof it had been the drug that had saved him.

For now, there was no known cure for Ebola.

No guarantee anyone could save his mother or spare his wife and children. Jasmine was right to freak out. This was bad. Worse than anything they'd ever faced.

"Clayborn?" Jasmine's voice whispered in his ear. "I love you."

"Don't worry, baby. It's going to be all right," he lied, and from Jasmine's sobs on the other end of the line, they both knew it.

CHAPTER TWENTY-FOUR

GULF OF GUINEA, COASTAL REGION

HEAT AND HUMIDITY HUNG HEAVY LIKE AN ANCHOR AROUND JOSIAH'S neck as the skiff beached on the river's sandy shore. His knuckles ached from hours of clutching the side of the small craft as they traversed miles of murky waterways through a dense rainforest populated with screaming monkeys. Several people spotted them, shouting as they swarmed the boat. Josiah did not have to speak their language to understand their panic. Fear was a universal emotion. He knew because he was fighting a pretty serious case of panic himself.

"What do they want?" Captain Scott asked Dabir.

"I called ahead. Told them I was bringing help." Dabir poked Josiah with the barrel of his AK-47. "Out!"

"Then we better not disappoint them." Josiah slung the large bag of Ebola protective gear and other supplies Rachel had managed to piece together over his shoulder. From the corner of his eye, he caught Mac sizing up the chaos. From the twitch in her clenched jaw, she was probably plotting another plan to break free. He didn't want to be here any more than she did, but he couldn't let her shoot-first-ask-questions-later training screw up his chances of getting Emma back.

"Remember," Josiah told his ragtag medical team comprised of a ship's captain, an oilman, and a pirate fighter, "Try not to touch anyone or anything until we get suited up."

"Right." Mac shouldered the backpack containing the portable Ebola testing station then jumped out of the boat.

People rushed her. Begging for medicine, they pulled at her backpack. Mac spun around and yelled for them to step back.

"Crap," Josiah leapt out of the boat and elbowed his way through the crowd. Once he reached Mac, he shouted to Dabir, "We need to find a place to set up a makeshift clinic. Somewhere away from this crowd."

Someone pushed a sick child into Dabir's arms. The flicker of helplessness in Dabir's eyes was quickly replaced with determination. "You can use the school."

Josiah and Mac followed Dabir and the other armed men who'd come to shore up Dabir's two-man crew, to a single-story cement-block building topped with a metal roof. Rusty iron bars covered glassless windows. Dabir, still holding the boy, led them through one of the four open classroom doors. Inside this small room, the air was sweltering and the smell of body odor overwhelming. Seventy children were crammed into a small room meant to accommodate less than half of that. The kids sat four to a desk. Their big dark eyes surveyed the foreigners with suspicion.

Josiah's experience of helping his father set up clinics in third-world conditions kicked in. "Captain Scott, we need the school emptied of all students."

"Will do." The captain cut a longing look at Mac, which she returned with a cold stare. He let out a weary sigh and began to gently motion children toward the door. "Children, let's play a game outside, shall we?"

Josiah turned to the oilman. "Once this room is vacated, I need you to push every student desk against the walls. Move the teacher desk to the center of the room. I'll use it to set up the portable blood-draw station."

"Seems easier than babysitting." The oilman stepped out of the way of children noisily filing past. "My ex-wife would be happy to tell you that I'm no good with kids."

"What do you need me to do?" Mac asked Josiah, but her narrowed eyes remained trained on her father, who had children happily following him outside like he was Mother Goose.

"The room next door will be our triage station," Josiah said. "You'll take temperatures. Record symptoms. Separate those who have fever from those who don't."

"On it." Mackenzie sprinted from the room as if relieved to be out of the presence of her father.

"Now, for the sick." Josiah turned his attention to the small limp child in Dabir's arms. "We'll need another room for those with advanced symptoms. Have someone empty one room of all the furniture and line the floor with reed mats that can be disposed of properly." He took a step toward Dabir, who was not moving. "Do you understand?"

"Yes." Dabir gazed down at the boy in his arms then looked Josiah in the eye. "Can you help my nephew?"

"Your nephew?"

Worry carved deep lines in Dabir's forehead. "He's my sister's boy. She says if he were my boy, I would take him to the ship where I took my wife." The words were heavy with the weight of a man conflicted between what he knew had to be done and what he wanted to do.

Josiah understood the pain of that conflict well. Since Camilla's death, he'd done whatever he could to escape the pain instead of doing what had to be done. He should have been taking care of Emma, putting her need to heal above his own. This desperate man standing before him was facing the possibility of losing his wife and he wasn't running off to hide. He was thinking about how to help his family.

The sudden urge to get Emma back was a scalpel that sliced Josiah open and let him feel something other than grief for the first time in months. "Where is your son?"

"I haven't seen him yet."

"Go find your son and make sure he's okay." Josiah held out his arms. "I'll take care of your nephew."

Dabir's eyes softened slightly. "I'll set up the sick room and leave him there."

Within twenty minutes the school had been rearranged, swept out, and converted into a poor excuse for a clinic. Josiah set up the portable blood-testing center on the teacher's desk. The clear plastic structure was the size of an old-fashioned oxygen tent. On one side of the tent, the patient would sit in a chair, unzip the enclosure, then insert an arm for the blood draw. He would stand on the other side of the tent, stick his gloved hands into the two gloves made of heavy Kevlar. This set up would allow him to administer the needle stick and fill the collection tubes inside a sealed environment.

Josiah surveyed the room. He hadn't drawn someone's blood in years, but wishing Rachel were here would only put her at risk. He could do this. For Emma's sake, he had to do this.

Josiah called his team together. As they suited up in paper gowns, masks, protective eyewear, and gloves, he went over Rachel's instructions again. "I cannot stress how important it is to avoid any and all body fluids." He had a mental list of new assignments. "Sid, I need you and Captain Scott to keep the soap dispenser filled and buckets of fresh hot water changed out regularly. We also need a separate handwashing station for those coming for testing."

"Where do you suggest we get hot water?" Sid asked, obviously not interested in getting his hands any dirtier than he already had. "There's only a pump outside."

"Have someone build a fire."

"Don't worry, Doc." The captain took Sid by the arm. "We can boil water."

Mac pointed the thermometer gun at him. "How do you work this thing?"

He wrapped his hand around hers. Her strong grip and even gaze helped to calm the frantic feelings he'd been fighting since leaving his daughter behind. "Try not to let it touch the skin surface of any patient." He pointed the tip at his own sweaty forehead until the beep sounded.

"Got it." She slipped her hand out from under his, but her eyes remained on him. "After I take their temperature, then what?"

Despite the tough-girl persona, Mac was as nervous about all of this as he was. At least, that's how he explained the flush on her cheeks and the increase in his own pulse.

"We'll funnel people through your room. After you record their symptoms, you can send them to me. I'll test a few blood samples on the spot and store the rest in the cooler we brought."

"That ice won't last long in this heat."

"Guess we better hurry, then," Josiah agreed. "But first, I need to examine Dabir's nephew." Josiah gathered an IV kit, a bag of saline solution he'd taken from one of the ship's operating rooms, and a clean set of infusion tubing. "Haven't started an IV in years. Hope I haven't lost my touch."

"Need help?"

"All I can get, but promise—"

"Not to touch him," Mac said.

Dabir had placed the boy on a mat in the room Josiah had designated as their isolation bay. To his surprise, Dabir had also left the child with a full cup of water and an empty wooden bowl for vomiting. Luckily, the bowl was still empty. The child shivered despite the heat.

"Hey there, little man." Mac knelt beside the boy, her voice soft, kind. "We're going to help you feel better, okay?"

Josiah nodded, praying that was true. "I'm Dr. Allen," he said as he prepared the IV tubing. "You look like you can kick a ball really far."

The boy nodded weakly. Josiah lifted his tiny hand. He could feel the boy's high temperature through his gloves. He searched for a prominent vein. "Mac, can you stand and suspend the fluid bag for us?"

"Sure."

Josiah handed Mac the IV bag he'd attached to the tubing. Saline solution filled the tube properly. Josiah tapped the line until all the air bubbles were removed. Luckily, Rachel had grabbed a thinner gauge catheter, perfect for children. The boy barely winced when Josiah stuck him with the needle and taped everything into place.

"You're a tough one. Now I need you to hang on while we rig a way to suspend this bag." Once they'd solved that problem with a stick and some duct tape attached to the back of a chair, he took his assistant aside. "I only have half a dozen Ebola tests and four more bags of fluids."

Mac's brow furrowed under her goggles. "Is that going to be enough?"

"Not by a long shot."

"If we're not going to be able to treat everyone—"

"We're going to have to stick to getting the samples we need and getting out of here. This boy is already pretty far into the virus progression. I can almost guarantee that whatever this is, it's spread far beyond what we're prepared to handle."

"Maybe we should go now. Steal the skiff, hightail it back to the *Liberty*, overtake the two pirates left behind, save your daughter, and fly you two back to America where it's safe."

Her concern kicked at the wall around Josiah's heart. He glanced out the window, weighing what she was offering. He'd been playing it safe since Camilla died. Keeping his memories of that horrible day shut up behind an OR door. Being safe had made him an incredible plastic surgeon, but it hadn't brought his wife back or eased his guilt. Safe wasn't always saved.

Outside, a child was crying. Compassion he thought long buried bubbled up inside him, bringing with it his father's voice. "We're all they've got." Josiah inclined his head toward the box of latex gloves on the windowsill. "Wash your hands. Change your gloves. And start sending them in. We're going to get the samples *and* do what we can to help."

"You're one hard-headed man, Dr. Allen."

A smile lifted his spirits and bolstered his courage. "You're not the first woman to accuse me of being stubborn."

All through the rest of the morning, Josiah and his team funneled people through their crude little clinic with remarkable efficiency. Sid had quit his whining. The captain was keeping the children entertained with games of kickball and tag. And Mac, when she wasn't gazing out the window watching her father play and laugh, was actually very good at triage.

Every patient was anxious. Some reported varying degrees of headache or nausea. So far, every patient they'd tested had come back negative for Ebola.

He had no idea what he was dealing with, and no way to contact his sister to find out what he should do next.

Between patients, Josiah ran to check on Dabir's nephew. Two older women from the village had offered to help, but as grateful as he was for their assistance, it was impossible to keep up with the boy's vomiting and intractable diarrhea. Soon his liver and kidneys would fail. Then he would die.

"He's getting worse, isn't he?" Mac's question didn't need an answer. He could tell from her face she knew the boy was dying.

And that wasn't their only problem. With each visit to the sick room, another patient mat had been filled. If this kept up, they would have to start putting people outside on the porch. Tensions were rising. People were shouting and demanding his attention. If the help he and his team provided didn't make a difference, then Dabir had no reason to keep them alive except for the samples Rachel needed. The pirate still had an entire medical ship filled with people he could hold for ransom.

"His uncle told me his name is Duna." Mac stood beside the mat where the young boy lay. "It means 'capable of anything.'" Mac lifted her glimmering eyes to Josiah. "Isn't there something you can do to save him?"

"We need help." Josiah pulled off his gloves. "Maybe I can convince Dabir to let me call in Doctors Without Borders."

"And if he doesn't agree?" she asked.

Josiah snapped on a fresh pair of gloves. "Just do your best to keep the sick quarantined from those who are currently without symptoms. We'll find a way to figure this out."

Chomba, one of Dabir's brothers they'd come to learn, entered the room, still carrying his weapon, a reminder that this was no ordinary hospital setup. He stopped in front of Mac. "Come with me. My brother wants me to show you where they dump the barrels of waste."

Josiah took a step forward. "I don't think we should separate."

"We need those waste samples," Mac said.

"It could be dangerous out there, depending on what you find," he argued.

"And it's not dangerous in here?" Mac shook her head. "I'll be fine."

"I'll take the captain as well," Chomba said.

"I can handle getting the samples on my own."

"My brother wants you both to go," Chomba said.

"He's right," Josiah said. "There's safety in numbers."

"There's nothing safe about the captain. Better he's with me than left with you." Mackenzie thrust her clipboard at Josiah and caught his gaze. "Don't do anything stupid while I'm gone, like poke yourself with that needle."

"Too late," Josiah said.

"You poked yourself?" Mac's eyes were wide behind the lens of her goggles.

Josiah shook his head. "I brought a six-year-old here. That's about as stupid as it gets."

Mosquitos buzzed in the thickening afternoon air as he watched her walk away, worried that his assistant was the one who'd just done something stupid.

CHAPTER TWENTY-FIVE

GULF OF GUINEA, COASTAL REGION

In any other situation, Mac would have been captivated by the lush jungle landscape. Growing up with a father in the military, she'd had the opportunity to travel the world. But while she enjoyed bustling cities like Paris and London, it was always the non-touristy places she'd loved the most. And today, the peacefulness of the river as they headed farther upstream in the dugout pirogue made her feel as if she'd stepped into a scene out of National Geographic. A place she'd be tempted to explore if given the opportunity.

The trees and sky reflected in the water that was clear for the most part, while a sprinkling of lily pads floated near the shoreline. If she closed her eyes, she could feel the breeze coming off the water and, with the remoteness, almost believe she'd been transported to a different century. There was no real sense of time here. No rush hour traffic, or rich oil executives screaming for her attention. Just the quiet lapping of the water against the side of the boat, and the haunting sound of a lone bird crying out in the distance.

But having Dabir's brother sitting behind her with an AK-47 pointed at her back shattered any peaceful illusions. She was on this little excursion for one reason. Rachel was counting on her to bring back samples that would hopefully lead to answers. The possibility of failing was enough to sober her and let her see this jungle and its desperate people for what they were. Dangerous.

"Are we just going to keep on pretending we don't know each other?"

Her father's voice pulled Mac out of her thoughts. The man she'd managed to avoid having a conversation with from the moment she'd seen him on the ship would be avoided no longer.

"I don't really have anything to say," she said.

"I was just trying to remember the last time I saw you."

Eleven years.

Her father tried again. "You're as beautiful as your mother."

She shifted in the seat that was nothing more than a wooden bar at the bottom of the boat. "Don't talk about my mother."

"Fair enough." He took a deep breath. "Mind if I ask when you started rescuing hostages from oil tankers?"

She glowered at him. He had no right to ask her anything, but something in her wanted him to know the pain she'd suffered trying to be shed of his shadow. "A botched jump ended my military stint, but my training led me here."

A pleased smile lit his face. "I knew, one way or another, you'd reach your dreams."

She remembered being five years old and begging her father to let her try on his Navy dress white hat. It had fallen across her eyes, but she'd raised her chin and offered him her version of a crisp salute. She'd wanted to be just like the heavily decorated Navy admiral and spent her military career proving to him she was as tough as the son he never had. Trouble was, he'd already abandoned her and had no idea of what she'd accomplished.

"You know nothing about me or my dreams."

"I know you care deeply about the teammate you lost. I'm sorry. It's not easy to lose those we count on to have our backs." His voice sounded as if he'd personally suffered a similar loss, and she realized how little she knew about his years of active military service. His experiences in the field. The battles he'd seen. Or the men he'd commanded and lost. "Was he a friend as well?"

She swallowed hard. "He was."

"No matter how good you are or how much you train, there are some hard jobs in this life, and they come with extremely high risks. I have a feeling you're very good at what you do, and what happened wasn't your fault."

She shifted again, wishing Josiah had not insisted her father come along. "Unlike some people, I'm not afraid of hard situations."

She closed her mouth, not sure why she'd felt the need to draw blood. She'd stopped thinking about him years ago, when he gave up his role as her father, and nothing was going to give her back the time she'd lost with him, no matter what he said. Not even the fact that he was now the captain of the *Liberty*. She really didn't care what this stranger thought about her.

"This isn't exactly how I pictured our reunion," he said.

"Being held hostage by a bunch of armed pirates is hardly a family reunion."

He leaned forward and lowered his voice. "You've had your life planned out since you were five. Knowing you, you're working on a plan to get us out of here. How can I help?"

"Like I've already said. You don't know me."

"It's just that I've prayed God would give me the chance to change that, and look, here you are."

His admission wasn't exactly an apology, but it did free her tongue just a bit. "Keep praying, because we don't exactly have a lot of options right now."

"I've missed you," he said after a few moments of silence as they sped up river.

"In case you forgot, you're the one who left."

The moment she said it, she wanted to take back the sharp words, but they were true. And guilt was a game she was tired of playing. As a thirteen-year-old, she'd believed his leaving was her fault, but not anymore. He left of his own volition.

"I haven't forgotten." He swallowed hard. "It's a load of regret I knew I'd carry the rest of my life when you didn't answer my letters."

"Letters?"

"I've been sending you letters for years."

"What letters? Where did you send them?"

"Home."

Their eyes locked. If this was true, it meant her mother hadn't given her the letters. But instead of blaming his ex-wife for keeping them secret, Mac's father simply shook his head.

"When I looked up and there you were, standing on my bridge, I knew God had heard my prayers. That, once again, the Lord had given me more grace than I deserved."

Mo's sermons on forgiveness and grace ricocheted through Mac's head.

"Once again?" she asked.

"It's a long story. There are so many things I'd like to say."

Whatever his excuses, they'd have to wait. "Let's just call a truce for now."

Disappointment flickered in his eyes, but he nodded.

There was too much at stake to get distracted by the past. And, in the end, their relationship didn't matter. As soon as they delivered the samples to Rachel, she planned to find a way to put a stop to this nightmare, return to her life, and never look back.

She stared at the growing film of oil floating on the water. A childhood memory popped through the fog of emotions swirling in her mind. She was ten. Her father had risked taking his black wife and their bi-racial child to Scotland to visit his homeland where his ancestors had been red-headed and red-blooded farmers from the Highlands. He'd taken her to Loch Ness for a glimpse of Nessie, the Loch Ness Monster. During the boat ride she'd seen a side of her father she'd never seen before–his love of water, along with his fascination of the history surrounding them—and it took root inside her. Because while she'd always been uncomfortable in the sky, she too was drawn to the water. Sometimes when she hadn't heard from him in months, she'd remember that visit, think of him on the sea, and pretend that the reason he couldn't come to her was because he'd been swallowed by Nessie.

He didn't come home because he didn't want to be around her or because he didn't love her, but because a sea monster held him captive.

Mac shoved back the memories and glanced again at her father's profile. There was something different about him, but what did she expect? She'd certainly changed over the past decade. Surely, he had as well. There was one thing she could give him credit for. She'd always longed for his approval, and in her mind had always fallen short. It had been that hurt and longing for approval that had propelled her forward and made her the person she was today.

"How's your mother?" he asked.

Mac bristled. So much for the truce. Maybe he hadn't changed that much after all. "She seems happy enough. Though maybe it's because she can't remember everything there is to be unhappy about."

Her mother's loss of memory was the one thing that had helped to alleviate the guilt of not settling down and working a regular job so she could be closer to her. She hadn't forgotten how taking this career path meant she'd done the very same thing her father had—left someone helpless behind for the sake of career.

"She's in memory care," Mac continued. "Has been there for eighteen months now."

"Your Aunt Grace told me. She updates me now and then."

"I didn't know you were still in contact with her."

Her father shrugged. "Does your mother still know who you are?"

"On a good day. Most of the time she stares at me like I'm a stranger. She seems happy though. At least with Aunt Grace nearby, I don't have to worry quite as much."

"I am sorry. I never wanted things to end like this between us. Between her and me. Between you and me."

Mac blinked back the tears, determined not to let him see what she was really feeling. "It doesn't matter anymore."

A bird shrieked in the distance, shifting her attention to the thinning tree line, but the distraction wasn't enough to erase the hurt he'd left behind. She couldn't even remember the last time they'd been together as a family. Before he'd walked out on them.

"The dumping grounds are ahead," Chomba said. "We are almost there."

She cleared her throat, focused once again on why they were there. "The trees are dying."

"They say the river is poisoned here." Chomba shut off the boat's motor and let the current carry them toward shore. "Soon you will see why."

They rounded a bend and Mac felt her jaw slack. Chomba was right. The lush green forest had given way to naked trees jutting from mounds of trash heaped around the deep inlet. Smoke snaked from smoldering trash fires and smudged the sky with a hazy film. The rancid smell intensified as they headed toward the shoreline.

"This is one of the places where they dump at night," Chomba said. "The worst place."

Mac brought her sleeve to her nose. "This is horrible."

She could see black plastic bags, clothes, and shoes among the piles of trash that stretched upriver as far as a football field and climbed up the embankment. Abandoned pirogues bobbed up and down in the murky water beside clumps of garbage.

"Does anyone still fish here?" her father asked.

"There is nothing left here. No fish, no fertile soil. Nothing."

And yet the piles of trash hadn't stopped children from playing along the shoreline while women washed their clothes. Young boys rummaged through the piles of trash like they were on a treasure hunt.

"What are they looking for?" Mac asked.

"Anything they can sell at the local market."

Dead fish floated around them as Dabir's brother maneuvered the boat to the shore.

Her stomach churned. "What exactly is being dumped here, Chomba?"

"Whatever the rest of the world doesn't want."

She turned to her father. "The fallout from this could be environmentally catastrophic to the region."

Could a virus lurk in these piles of burning trash, or were they simply looking at a different kind of health crisis?

"I read about a cargo ship that was caught dumping toxic waste in Abidjan." Her father shook his head at the devastation around them. "It ended up killing over a dozen people and poisoning thousands," his voice had a tinge of sadness. "International treaties have been set up to stop this, but there's always someone who wants to save money. Illegal dumping has affected everything from air quality to the fishing grounds and soil quality."

And, from the ruins of the surrounding jungle, that's what was happening here.

"Do you know who's behind this?" she asked Chomba.

"Ships from other countries carry their garbage to the mouth of the river. They pay smaller boats to haul it upstream. The authorities are paid to look the other way." He nodded at them, his weapon still in hand. "Come. I will show you."

Mac scurried out of the boat behind her father, her boots sinking into the muddy bank as she took her first step. The smell was enough to make her sick, but the thoughts of standing in the source of the illness spreading through Dabir's village was terrifying.

Sweat beaded across the back of her neck as she followed Chomba through a narrow trail toward the top of the embankment.

He stopped for a moment and pointed toward the river. "This used to be prime land for growing food."

Mac surveyed the blackened acres. "And now it's a burning trash heap."

"Farther upriver, people plant," Chomba said, waving at her to keep going. "But the soil isn't good."

She took a step past him, hesitated, then turned. "I'm sorry, Chomba."

"For what?"

"That someone did this. That someone thought they could dump their problems here and get away with it."

"Who can stop them?" From the set of Chomba's face it was more of a resigned statement than a hopeful question. "First the trawlers drained the ocean of our fish. Now they poison the river so the fish can't come back. It gets harder and harder to feed our families."

As they walked up the ridge, Mac dissected the judgment she'd placed on Chomba and his brother. It would be easy to say she'd never stoop to something like pirating to feed her family, but what would she do? The only real difference between this skinny boy with an AK-47 and her was that she'd never been hungry, sick, and frightened.

Surveying the destruction before her, Mac dug into the small bag she carried and pulled out the clear glass vials Rachel had sent with them. Wishing Josiah was there to direct the collection wasn't going to do anyone any good. "I'll take samples of both the water and soil."

Her temples throbbed from the smoky air as she capped the murky vials. The sooner they got the samples to Rachel, the sooner they would have answers as to what was going on. At least that was what she hoped.

"Taiwo, what are you doing here?"

Mac turned to where Chomba was addressing a barefoot young boy wearing shorts and a dirty T-shirt. "Who's this?"

"Taiwo. Dabir's son."

"Taiwo." Mac crouched down in front of the boy. She didn't like using children as leverage, but she needed something to convince Dabir to let them get the help they needed. She glanced around the mounds of trash for a moment, wondering what Dabir's son was doing so far from his village. "How old are you?"

"Ten."

"You're a long way from your home, son," her father said from behind her.

Taiwo shrugged.

Chomba said, "Your father wants you home. You'll come back with us now."

Mac started to stand, then paused at the small circular metal disc hanging around the boy's neck with a piece of twine. "Your necklace. Where did you get it?"

"I found it." He pointed toward a large smoldering mound. "Over there."

"In the trash?"

Taiwo nodded.

Her father lifted the disc from the boy's chest and examined it carefully. "Looks like some kind of medical tag."

"That's what I was thinking," Mac agreed.

Rachel hadn't seemed sold on the idea that the virus had come from a trash heap. But what if there was more than old clothes and garbage dumped here?

"You're not in trouble, Taiwo," Mac said calmly. "But I need you to show me where you found it. Can you do that?"

Taiwo shrugged, then scurried off down another narrow trail that ran parallel to the water.

"Are you thinking someone's dumping medical waste?" she asked her father as they trotted after the boy.

"I think anything's possible."

A minute later they came across five green steel drums smelling like eggs left to rot in the sweltering sun.

Mac turned to Chomba. "Do you know what's in these?"

"No."

She kicked off the lid of one of the drums that lay on its side and felt a sick feeling washed through her. Inside she identified gloves and medical gowns, plastic packaging, swabs, and what looked like petri dishes.

"Medical waste," she said to her father.

"Which might mean nothing—"

"Unless it's infectious waste. . ." She couldn't even finish her sentence. What if a lab or a hospital had decided to cut corners and dump their biohazardous trash here? What if they'd been working with an infectious disease? She shook her head. The scenario seemed impossible.

"It wouldn't hurt to take a sample," her father said, holding out his hand for one of the vials. "I'll do it. We have no idea what that is."

Even if she could ignore her father's sudden willingness to put her well-being before his, she couldn't ignore the possibility that they might have just found the source of the virus.

CHAPTER TWENTY-SIX

KENEMA, SIERRA LEONE

Liam DeMarcus checked the internet connection on his phone from a padded chair in the guest house lobby, frustrated it was still down. Not that he should be surprised. Local power had finally come back on thirty minutes ago, after being out for almost forty-eight hours. Now he just needed the internet to come up.

He took a sip of his lukewarm Coke, wishing he had time to go take a shower before his next interview. Benjamin Moiba was a local who ran an agriculture project promoting sustainable practices for farmers and was newly sponsored by an NGO in the US that hoped to extend the reach of the project. Liam's job was to communicate the story through interviews and video footage for the NGO's website, board members, and supporters.

A glance at his watch told him the man was fifteen minutes late for their five o'clock appointment, but time ran slow on the African continent, and the town nestled in the eastern province of Sierra Leone was no exception. Not that he was complaining about a chance to catch his breath. Four towns in seven days across the country had left him wishing for a day off.

A news station played on the television in the corner of the lobby, its volume turned up too high. He glanced at the open door that led to a small courtyard with a couple of chairs and a table. Maybe he should go outside and wait so he and Moiba could talk without the interference of the television. Plus, they might catch a breeze and get a break from this heat.

He started toward the door, then a photo of a large, familiar white ship flashed on the flat TV screen.

The Liberty?

He stopped to check it out, but the channel flipped to a football match.

"Wait a minute." Liam held up his hand and walked toward the TV, signaling to the other guest he'd met the night before. "Would you mind turning it back to the news for a moment. Please."

"It was just a story about some missing boat."

"My father might be on that boat."

The man shrugged, flipped the channel, then dropped the remote on the padded chair next to him. A reporter stood next to a string of boats, addressing the camera.

. . . While there is still little information on the disappearance of the floating hospital, the one-hundred-and-sixty-meter-long ship with five hundred plus crew and patients seems to have vanished without a trace. The US-based medical ship, the Liberty, has been docked at the port here in Douala, Cameroon for the past four months where it has been providing both free health care and community health education. Local authorities have informed us that the ship left port unexpectedly due to an emergency, but the strange twist in the story is that now they have no idea where the Liberty is. Several witnesses also claim that shots were fired near the ship's gangplank shortly before the ship left port. We will update the situation as the story unfolds. This is Michel Nzouankeu—

"You said your father is on that ship?"

"Yeah. . ." Liam turned to the British tourist who'd come for the country's well-known yearly charity marathon. "My father and my sister."

"I wouldn't worry too much at this point," the man said in his clipped accent. "A ship that size can't just disappear."

"One would think, but why did they leave without following proper protocol?"

"I'm sure they'll show up, and it will all be nothing more than a miscommunication."

Maybe, but Liam wasn't convinced.

"I did hear there were some pirates who hijacked an oil tanker in the gulf a few days ago," the other man said, "but a security team was sent in and put an end to it."

Liam stopped in the middle of the room while a rusty fan clicked overhead. Was there somehow a connection between the oil tanker and the *Liberty*?

"Internet's back on, by the way."

Liam nodded. "Thanks."

He pulled out his phone and tried calling his dad and then Harper on WhatsApp.

Neither answered.

He blew out a sharp breath, then quickly dialed another contact on his list. His mom picked up on the third ring.

"Liam, how are you? Or I guess I should ask, where are you?"

"I'll be in Kenema for the next day or so, then I'm heading to Bo, my last stop in Sierra Leone. The electricity's been on and off the past couple days along with the internet, which is why I'm calling. I just saw a news report that the *Liberty* has gone missing. Have you heard anything about that? News can be difficult to access here."

"I was just getting ready to call you, actually. I saw a news clip this morning on the internet, but it didn't say much, so I called the *Liberty's* headquarters here in the US."

"Did you find out anything?"

"Just that there was some kind of emergency on the ship that required them to leave for another port—"

The connection went out for a moment.

"Liam?"

"Sorry. Phone and internet are sketchy here," he said. "What else did they say?"

"That was it." His mother's voice broke. "I told your father I didn't want your sister on that ship, and now...if anything happens to her..."

"I spent almost a year on the *Liberty*, and I was fine."

His mother had never liked the fact that his father had "wasted" his career in medicine on a non-profit surgical ship.

"It's different with Harper."

"Why, because she's a girl?"

"That's not what I mean, and you know it. She's a lot more sensitive than you were at that age. She's around sick patients and—"

"She's studying to be a doctor, Mom. Sick patients come with the job."

"All I know is that if your father has placed her in any danger, I swear I'll—"

"There's no need to jump to any conclusions that something's wrong," Liam said. "Listen, I need to go for now, but keep me updated on anything you find out."

"If you'll promise to do the same for me."

He ignored the little jab at how his defense of his father always upset her. But since his parents' divorce, his mother's choices had been harder to defend. "Love you, Mom."

He clicked off his phone before they got into it again and stared at the TV screen that was now playing highlights from a local football match. He couldn't ignore the questions pinging in his head. He needed to take his own advice and not worry, but huge ships that port for months at a time didn't just disappear.

He grabbed his laptop and headed toward the small courtyard lined with coconut trees and colorful bougainvillea that clung to the brick wall surrounding the property. He sat in one of the wooden chairs and set his laptop on the table in front of him. His parents had divorced when he was six, so he didn't have many memories of the two of them together. But to their credit, they had both done everything they could to be a part of his and Harper's life.

He'd spent eight months on the *Liberty* after his army stint, thinking at the time he might follow his father into the practice of third-world medicine, but getting involved in the ship's communication team ended up changing the direction he wanted to go. After serving his time on board, he'd spent the last five years working for a news organization in hopes of making a difference in the world through storytelling.

He moved his chair half a foot to the left so the shade cloth above him blocked the sun, then opened up his laptop. He needed to check his emails.

Scrolling through the new ones that had just come in, he stopped when he found what he was looking for.

To: Liam DeMarcus
From: Matthew DeMarcus
Hey son, thought I'd take advantage of your keen investigative skills and ask a favor. Internet's pretty slow here, as you know. What can you find out about Dema Diagnostics Research Group? Keep this between us.
Dad

Liam reread the message, glad now his contact was late. But why did his father want information on a research group? His father was an orthopedic surgeon. What kind of research would he need to fix another case of windswept legs? He'd reset the bones of hundreds of kids over the years. He was an artist.

Liam clicked onto his internet browser, thankful when the search bar popped up, and typed in the company's name. The first page was full of the standard information on the company with links to their website, contact page, and an overview of their projects.

He clicked onto Dema Diagnostics's website. From a cursory glance, it looked as if they were a lab that specialized in infectious diseases and investigated the causes of outbreaks in an effort to increase response times as well as develop vaccines and even possible cures of some of the most dangerous viruses on earth. He sat back in the chair and frowned, still uncertain why his father wanted to know about an international pharmaceutical company and why he'd asked him to keep it confidential.

Liam typed out a response.

To: Matthew DeMarcus
From: Liam DeMarcus
Dad, is everything okay? Not sure why you're looking for this information, but here's what I found. Looks like the bio-tech group is involved in research connected to infectious diseases. I can dig deeper if you want. Just let me know.
Liam

He went back to his home screen and rested his hands on the keyboard. Had the *Liberty* left port because of a possible outbreak? It was probably his nose for news working him into a frenzy over nothing, but something wasn't adding up. He smelled more than a story. He smelled danger.

Liam typed *Liberty and infectious disease* into the search engine. A second later, a list of articles popped up. One out of Baltimore caught his attention.

The CDC has just confirmed that a school principal recently serving on a medical ship in central Africa, the Liberty, *is currently in isolation and has been diagnosed with a previously unknown strain of the Ebola virus. No names have been released at this time, and there is no further information as to whether there are others also infected with the deadly disease.*

The article continued with terrifying facts about the hemorrhagic virus as well as a history of the 2014 outbreak in West Africa that killed over eleven thousand people.

There had to be a connection between the principal from the *Liberty* and the ship's disappearance.

Liam clicked back to the information on the *Dema Diagnostics* website, searched for a moment, then found what he was looking for.

Trials for an experimental vaccine are currently being conducted on chimpanzees in the UK and several African countries. Researchers are replacing specific viruses with an Ebola virus gene...

Liam's jaw tensed. What had his father stumbled into?

He searched through old emails for something from his travel agent and quickly found the phone number.

"This is Liam DeMarcus," he said when she answered his call. "I need a big favor. I need to be on the next flight out of the country."

"Where are you wanting to go?" asked the chirpy voice.

"Douala, Cameroon."

CHAPTER TWENTY-SEVEN

SOMEWHERE IN THE GULF OF GUINEA

RACHEL STARED AT THE TEST THAT HAD COME UP NEGATIVE A SECOND TIME and blew out a huff of frustration. She hoped the problem was that her current lab wasn't set up to run tests like this. She had emergency test kits that could screen for Ebola along with a number of other deadly viruses, but the focus of the *Liberty*'s mission had never been dealing with an outbreak. Clearly, they'd underestimated the odds of being in the crosshairs of a possible epidemic. She needed the help of the World Health Organization and the CDC.

Harper stepped up next to her, still wearing a gown and mask. "Are you okay?"

"Honestly, no." Rachel rested her gloved hands on the counter. "I tested Abeje again for Ebola, but the results are still negative."

"What does that mean?"

"Either we're not looking at Ebola, or I'm getting a false negative because this test isn't able to catch certain strains of the virus. There are also higher instances of false-negatives during the early and late stages of the disease."

"She's in the late stage, isn't she?"

Rachel glanced at her patient who now lay still on the bed. "I can try and keep her comfortable, but beyond that, there's nothing more I can do."

"What do we do in the meantime?" Harper asked.

"I don't know." Rachel disposed of the test in the biohazardous waste container, then peeled out of her soiled gown and gloves. "Three-quarters of the new viruses that affect humans come from animals. Apes, for example, have been known to be hosts to viruses like Ebola, anthrax, and yellow fever, to name a few. And there's always the potential of it being something yet undiscovered."

"My knowledge of infectious diseases is limited. How does it get passed on to humans?"

"Lots of ways. Virus transmission has been connected to the bite of a fruit bat or the consumption of bushmeat, like eating chimpanzees or gorillas."

Rachel caught the repulsed look on Harper's face as she thrust her hands in hot water and soaped all the way to her elbows in hopes extra scrubbing was enough to kill every trace of the clinging virus.

Hoping the damage wasn't already done.

"So, a human would have to come in contact with an infected animal?" Harper asked. "Or like you said, eat one?"

"In remote areas in particular, bushmeat is a large source of income for families. But unfortunately, eating bushmeat is also how an outbreak can start. Then once a human is infected, the virus can spread to other humans by contact with blood or bodily fluids of someone who has contracted the virus or who has died of the virus."

"How does the source get it? Say a chimpanzee?"

"We don't know. There are still more questions than answers."

Aiden would have found a way to get here and find the source of the outbreak. Rachel shoved away the painful thought and said, "I had a friend who was a disease tracker."

"He tried to stop outbreaks?"

"That was always his goal. When you can foresee where there might be an outbreak or a region at high risk, then steps can be taken that will hopefully stop an outbreak before it starts. For example, the CDC tracks diseases like TB, HIV and influenza in an effort to stop outbreaks. There are even outbreak trackers that compile data in order to be on top of the next hot spot. Ebola, though, has always been a difficult virus because it's been known to completely disappear for years."

"How does it do that?"

"That's the mystery of viruses my friend was trying to answer, because a virus has to have a living host."

"Like a monkey?"

"Probably not, because the animal wouldn't survive. We don't know where it hides." Rachel grabbed a couple paper towels, dried her hands thoroughly, then sat down on the metal stool next to the young woman. "Harper, when we were on the bridge, I mentioned your father had come to me about some questions concerning a possible outbreak. Did your father mention anything to you?"

"No, but I don't think he would have." She tugged on the front of the clean gown she was wearing. "He never wanted me to slip and give mom something else to worry about."

"Do you know what he was doing out in the villages?"

"He said he wished he'd brought more malaria test kits, but that he wasn't sure that's what was making his patients sick. I think he was cautious about coming to any conclusions. But if this is Ebola—or a hemorrhagic virus—he wouldn't have thought malaria. Would he?"

"It's actually very possible." Rachel pressed her fingers against her temples that had started to pound. The air-conditioning on the ship had gone off, leaving the room feeling humid and sticky. Without the ship's crew keeping the ship in top running condition, would the ship's plumbing and electrical systems shut down? If they did, people wouldn't be able to stand it in their rooms. They'd have to come out. Once they were in contact with each other the virus could quickly leapfrog from person to person. "The problem with many of these diseases is that Ebola, for example begins with influenza-like symptoms. Fatigue, fever, weakness, pain, and headache."

"Which could also mimic malaria," Harper said.

Rachel nodded. "Or a number of other things. So, without the right testing kits—and even sometimes with the right testing kits—it's hard to tell at the beginning until the symptoms start deviating."

She glanced at Harper and realized what a terrifying situation she'd been thrust into. She was in a room with a woman dying of something deadly, her father was missing, and the ship she loved was being held by pirates. Rachel forced out a sharp puff of air.

There's got to be a way out of this, God.

Except she was trained to research disease, not take down pirates. She'd never even touched a gun.

"I'm sure your father's fine, Harper," Rachel said. "He's probably aiding the authorities in locating us. He's probably far more worried about you than anything else."

"It's possible. I don't know. And maybe I've been reading too many suspense novels, but I can't not worry. I guess my mom was right after all."

"Meaning?" Rachel asked.

"When my father decided to serve on the *Liberty*, my mother wasn't happy. But she was really unhappy when I decided to spend the summer with him. She wants me to go to some Ivy League school and study law. Not finish med school and work for a non-profit where you have to raise your own support."

"And you?" Rachel asked. "What do you want to do?"

"Find a way to make a difference in the world. Being here has made me look at so many things in a different light. I don't think I'll ever be the same again." Her gaze shifted back to the bed where Abeje slept. "But I also can't help but be a little scared that I might catch whatever it is that is killing her. What if we all do?"

Rachel stared at the bright yellow biohazard container, wishing she could promise Harper everything would be fine, but she couldn't. "At this point, God is the only one who knows what's going to happen. I have to believe He hasn't forgotten us."

"I wish I could say I'm not afraid of dying, but I want to see my dad, my brother and sister, and my mom again. I want the chance to come back and work on this ship as a doctor if that's what I decide. To do something noble with my life. Like you. Like my dad."

Rachel frowned. "I'm not sure coming to Africa was noble."

"Why did you come?" Harper asked.

"Same as you. I thought I could come and make a difference."

"That's happened for you, hasn't it?"

"I think I make a difference being here, but I think I'm the one who's been changed the most. I wake up every day and see our patients as the real heroes. They go through life with so little and yet they never completely give up hope."

Her own words struck her to the core. Which meant she had to dig up just as much courage as the patients on this ship. She had to find a way to get help.

"What are you thinking?" Harper asked.

Rachel hesitated. "I need to find a way to get out of the lab and get help."

"How? They said they put up a jammer. That's why we can't call out. No one's coming to help us."

Rachel's gaze shifted to the door. "I know. But if I could find the jammer and turn it off—"

"You need a distraction." Harper stood.

Rachel shook her head. "It's a long shot, and far too risky. I don't know where they hid the jammer, and your father would not be happy with me if I allowed you to get involved."

"I'm already involved." Harper gripped Rachel's arm. "What if we told the guard we needed something for Abeje?"

"He'll say no."

"All you need is a little distraction to slip out. And I can always go back into the lab. He won't follow me in here."

"True."

Rachel's mind raced through possible scenarios. The pirates had insisted they had a dozen armed men on board, but she didn't believe them. And if she was right...

"You won't take any chances," Rachel said. "And you'll get back in here as soon as I'm gone?"

Harper nodded, then stepped outside the lab, leaving the door open a crack.

The action was met by a booming voice. "You're not supposed to come out here."

Rachel fought the urge to pull the young woman back into the lab, but stopped herself.

"It's Dabir's wife." Harper sounded all business. "There's a drug we need to treat her with called Regereron."

"What's that?"

"An antiviral drug for patients with Ebola."

"I was told to make sure you didn't leave. You need to get back inside. Now."

"I wouldn't want to be you if Dabir returns and his wife is dead because she didn't get her medicine."

Rachel watched through the crack of the door as Harper strode past the man down the hallway.

"It won't take me long, I promise," Harper said over her shoulder.

The guard's back was to Rachel and his attention solely on Harper hurrying down the hall. Rachel took a breath then slipped out of the room and hurried in the opposite direction.

Her heart pounded as she scaled the stairs two at a time at the end of the deck, praying Harper would be okay. But there was no turning back now. She was looking for two things. The Gurkhas, and the jammer. In order to shut down the entire ship's communication ability, she was going to assume that the device was larger than a cell phone, yet small enough that the men could have easily carried it onto the ship. And it would need a power source. It also made sense that it was located near the reception and communication's office. But she wasn't sure that knowledge was going to be enough to narrow down the location of the device that had knocked out their emergency communications system, internet and probably the ship's GPS system.

Emergency lighting lit the empty stairwell as she made her way to deck five and the reception area. Rachel poked her head around the door. No one was manning the reception desk. She raced to the counter. Having never seen a jammer, she picked up the receiver of the phone, but it was dead. The jammer had to be nearby, but where? A black box with antennas shoved under the desk caught her eye.

Something rustled behind her. "Step back."

Rachel turned slowly. "I just need—"

"I said, step away."

She turned slowly. "I've been in the lab with Dabir's wife."

"Then what are you doing here? No one is supposed to be outside their rooms."

Rachel prayed for the right words, wishing she had Mac's combat skills so she could possibly take him down. She decided to go with Harper's plan. "I was heading to the pharmacy. Abeje needs some antiviral drugs. Without them, she'll die."

His weapon shifted until it was aimed directly at her chest. "If you try to play the hero, you will die."

CHAPTER TWENTY-EIGHT

GULF OF GUINEA, COASTAL REGION

MAC LET THE COOL WATER RUN DOWN HER BACK INSIDE THE CEMENT shower, wishing it could somehow wash away the images of children playing next to burning heaps of trash, dead trees, and oil and waste floating on the river. Even more frightening was the possibility that they'd found the source of the illness spreading through the region. Whatever the source, though, the virus had already made it to the capital and possibly beyond.

She pushed her wet hair off her neck, thankful for Dabir's offer of a shower in the nearly completed cinderblock house he was building. The enticing scent of onions and garlic sizzling over an outdoor fire drifted through the air. Mackenzie realized she hadn't had a hot meal since before she'd hopped on a plane to Africa.

That seems like a lifetime ago.

When she'd arrived back at the village, she'd been told that Josiah had left their makeshift clinic to go and eat. Her father had argued against her determination to go straight to Josiah and give him a full report. "Shower off any possible contaminates," her father had said, urging her to take Dabir up on his offer. "Protect yourself. I'll shower next."

Her father's sudden concern for her well-being was not what sent her to the shower. It was the realization that she wanted to do everything within her power to keep Josiah safe. She'd never forgive herself if she inadvertently carried the virus to the man she was coming to admire. Was her sense of urgency to talk to Josiah based on what she'd discovered at the dumping site or was it based on something even scarier? She couldn't allow the seeds of interest in a man to take root. Allowing herself to be distracted by attraction was a sure way to get them all killed.

Mac turned off the water, then dropped the new bar of soap she'd been given onto the windowsill. A shiny silver watch with a thick leather band had been pushed into the corner. She hadn't noticed jewelry on any of the pirates. They wore all black and nothing that would capture the light of a search beam and give away their location. She picked up the watch and held it up to the light. It was a Longines Heritage Pulsometer watch. She knew because she'd dated a doctor once who'd made a big deal out of being able to afford one. She turned it over and noted the inscription. *To our favorite M.D. With love.*

Mac frowned. She hadn't noticed Josiah wearing a watch. And he clearly hadn't taken the time from caring for patients to shower. Had another doctor been to the village recently? She needed to make sure the watch didn't belong to Josiah. If not, they could decide together whether getting to the bottom of an obviously stolen watch was worth the risk of confronting Dabir.

A minute later, she was clean and cooled off, but when she had to dress in the same clothes she'd worn since yesterday, she couldn't claim to be toxin free. She shoved the watch into her front pocket. As she grabbed one of her boots, she winced at the pain radiating beneath her ribcage where the nail had ripped a nasty gash. She pulled up her shirt and ran her finger across the tender spot.

For a moment, all she could think about was how badly she wished she was back in Atlanta before all this had happened, grilling steaks and playing with Mo's kids. She'd had no idea at the time what was about to transpire. No idea that Mo's life would end here, and hers would never be the same again.

She swiped at the unwelcome tears. She was used to handling things by herself. Just because Mo no longer had her back didn't mean she couldn't focus on the job at hand. Emotions always got in the way, especially when the consequences were too great. Her ability to take risks and save lives without getting personally involved was why she was able to do what most people couldn't. It was why she wouldn't explore a relationship with Josiah or the scared little girl she'd pushed into an air duct.

Mac made her way through Dabir's sparsely furnished three-room house with its tin roof. In one room, there was an unmade bed and a little pallet on the floor beside it. A flowered skirt hung on a peg. Abeje had made this place home. From the way she'd begged Dabir to look after their son, she'd probably fought her husband on leaving her home to go in search of medical care. Leaving Taiwo behind had not been Abeje's first choice.

Mac stepped through the open door and onto the porch, needing another few moments to get her thoughts focused. A mosquito buzzed in her ear and she slapped it away. She might not get out of this place without coming down with whatever disease they were facing, but she would make certain she didn't lose her heart.

She leaned against the porch railing and stared out into the darkness at the moon reflecting against the water. Night sounds mingled with people talking and babies crying. Dabir had given Josiah and her the freedom to come and go between this house and the makeshift clinic, but the group of armed men huddled around an open fire was a reminder that they weren't here by choice.

"Mac?" Josiah stepped onto the porch and stopped in front of her. "You okay?" His scrubs and hair were darkened with sweat, his shoulders were slumped with exhaustion, and he held a first aid kit in his hand.

"Are you finished at the clinic?" she asked.

"Just took a short break. Decided I needed to shower and grab something to eat if I wanted to keep going. Then I ended up taking a short walk to clear my head."

"We brought samples back with us," she said.

"That's going to help Rachel." His eyes searched hers. "I just saw your father. How did things go with him?" The compassion in his voice was a rope tugging her closer to the desire of a relationship she'd just told herself could never happen.

"For the sake of the job at hand, we were civil." A change of subject was the only way to keep her feet from sliding toward his tired smile. "Did he tell you what we saw?"

"Metal drums containing pharmaceutical waste."

Taking care of business was the best way to keep the gate to her heart slammed shut. "You realize the implications. It might be a stretch, but if this is related to the virus that's spreading. . ."

"It definitely seems possible, and we can't dismiss it, but we're going to need results from the lab."

"Agreed."

He reached out and brushed his thumb across her wrist. "I was worried about you. I know you're used to risking your life, but this is different."

"I'm fine. Really." She pulled away from him, hating how easily his touch could derail her determination. "I'm sorry it took us longer than I expected to get the samples. I know you're worried about Emma and your sister."

"And you." Including her in his concern left no room for argument. "I told myself this was the great adventure I needed. Instead it's turned into one big nightmare."

"They're going to be okay."

She tried to force a degree of confidence into her voice, but knew she couldn't predict how this was going to play out, any more than scientists could predict where the next Ebola outbreak would emerge.

"Have you eaten today?" he asked.

"No."

"There are fried plantains, some kind of fermented cassava, and a peanut and greens sauce." He gave her an impish grin. "It's not bad."

"Compared to what? Hospital cafeteria food?"

"Way better."

She let out a surprised laugh. "Do you think it's safe to eat?"

"Hope so, but I figure whatever this virus is we've no doubt been exposed to it, so we might as well keep up our strength. But before you eat, why don't you let me check your battle scars?" He held up the small box in his hand. "After wading around in toxic muck, it can't hurt to put some antibiotic cream on that laceration."

"My side's a bit sore, but it's not bleeding anymore."

"It still needs to be cleaned."

"Josiah—"

"No arguments." He scrunched his face into mock seriousness. "Doctor's orders."

"How are you still standing?"

"Used to pulling long hours," he confessed. "But I wouldn't blame you if you'd rather wait for the doc coming on at the shift change..."

She laughed at the irony of two exhausted and ill-equipped humans being all that stood between a desperate pirate and a global pandemic. There was no one else coming to help them. They both knew that until she could get back to the *Liberty* and disable the jammer, they had no choice but to trust each other.

Mac slowly lifted the bottom of her tank top and exposed the spot where the screw had torn a gash across her abdomen.

"Scaling the side of a ship didn't help," he said.

"I'll live."

Josiah moved closer, his arm skimming hers as he crouched for a better look at her wound. She blew out a breath. Fear had always been a motivator for her. A motivator to do better, and to take risks. She'd learned to keep her feelings stuffed inside and control everything she could, but the emotions stirring within her refused to be tamed. Something about this man made her feel vulnerable and safe. Except for her combat partner, no man had ever made her feel that someone had her back. Josiah's blue-gray eyes and dimples invited her to take a risk on him. But what did she really know about him? A widower, a father, a plastic surgeon guilted by his sister into making a difference. A son of a missionary who seemed uncertain of what God wanted from him.

"It's slightly red around the edges, but you're right, it doesn't look like it's infected." He stood and ripped open an alcohol pad. "You're going to have to be extra diligent to keep this clean. Infections tend to thrive in hot, humid conditions."

She could feel his breath warm the skin he cleaned with a cold alcohol pad. Why was it every time he got close to her, her heart raced and her insides melted?

"Tell me about where you grew up," she said, looking for a distraction.

"Columbia. The Amazon rainforest was my backyard, and every boy's dream. We ate fish straight from the river, learned about the wildlife from locals, and spent half our time on the water."

"So, you're comfortable in remote places like this?"

Josiah laughed. "I admit I've become fond of running water and air conditioning."

"How old were you when you left?"

"Thirteen. Seems like forever ago."

"And your parents? How did they meet?"

He reached for the antibiotic cream. "My father was a general surgeon. He met my mother at Kansas University when he was in med school and she was an undergrad. They both spoke fluent Spanish and worked in the Amazon for years."

"Where are they now?"

"My father. . ." Josiah stopped what he was doing and looked at her. "Died in Columbia."

"I'm sorry."

"I still miss him. My mother married a Kansas farmer because his wheat fields were about as far from the jungle as she could get."

"Do you miss it? Columbia?"

Josiah gently dabbed the wound with the cream, then stepped back. "That country took a part of me. I went back to see it when I was twenty-one. Took a boat upriver and visited the village where we'd lived. The house was rundown and empty, but one of the young Colombians my father had trained finished his medical degree and came back to run the clinic."

"Your father left quite a legacy," she said. "Raising up doctors in third world countries and doctors in his own family."

"I went into medicine to put change in my bank account, not to change lives."

"I'm not sure I believe that. You did agree to work on a humanitarian ship?"

"My sister believes she can save me from myself." He quickly applied clean gauze, taped it down, then gently tugged her tank top back into place. "I need to clean your forehead as well."

"Do you need to be saved?"

He capped the antibiotic tube. "Don't we all?"

She considered the multiple layers of hurt this healer carried. If there was a cream that would ease his pain, she'd buy a tub full of it. "Think I'll need to look for a good plastic surgeon once this is over?" she teased in an effort to shift his attention to the cut above her brow.

He chuckled. "I might know one."

Longing stirred inside her. He'd come to Africa in search of a place where he and his daughter could find purpose. A bold move she admired. But she'd leave here when this was over, risking her life with another assignment. Risking her life for strangers came easy, but when was the last time she thought about risking her heart for love?

She leaned toward him. Josiah stopped repacking the first aid kit and closed the distance. Desire pulsed in the sliver of air between them. Her gaze shifted to his lips and the day-old beard, rugged and untamed as the jungle. As much as she wanted to reach up and smooth away the prickly edges, Josiah Allen wasn't a risk she could take.

There was just enough light on the porch to reveal the conflict in his eyes. "Mac. . ." his whisper brushed her lips. With the hands that had just tended her wound, he gently cupped her face.

She swallowed hard. "This—us—it can't—"

He pressed his lips against hers, effectively cutting off her argument. Every resistance tactic she'd spent a lifetime cultivating were dried kindling that ignited in flame. Longing pushed past the walls she'd built around her heart, as she wrapped her arms around his neck and kissed him back. The taste of longing surged through their connection like a restored powerline.

Josiah pulled away abruptly, the shock of her touch seeming to bring him to his senses. But still, he lingered in front of her, as if he were searching her face for an answer to what he'd just done.

"I need to head back to the schoolroom." He reached for the first aid kit. "It's going to be a long night."

"I can help."

"Mac, about what just happened." Self-condemnation weighted his voice.

Did he regret kissing her because it somehow betrayed the memory of his dead wife? She knew better than to get involved with a grieving man. There was no place for her in that complicated equation. If he was ever ready to commit to someone new, Emma deserved a mother who'd risk her own life before she'd leave her little girl alone in an air duct.

"Forget it." Mac couldn't stand the guilty look on his face. "We're both exhausted, and all of this has been incredibly emotional."

"Exactly," he nodded. "When people are under duress, especially when their survival depends on helping each other, their bodies start producing oxytocin. It's a chemical that can make them feel...connected."

His relief was the very reason she'd never allowed sexual attraction to come into play while on the job. "But they're really not?"

"Right."

She shoved her shaking hands into her front pockets. "Good to know."

"Yeah." His eyes bore into hers. "Good to know."

Her right hand fisted the object she'd crammed into her pocket. "I almost forgot." She pulled out the watch and handed it to him. "This was on the window ledge in the shower. It's got a pulsometer on it. Something a doctor would use, I think."

His fingers brushed her with heat as he took the watch from her. "Surgeons love these. They're waterproof and made for intensive medical use." He turned it over and held it up to the bare lightbulb hanging from the porch ceiling. "Probably costs a couple thousand dollars."

"Read the inscription," she said.

"To our favorite M.D. With love."

"What's the missing doctor's name?"

He looked at her. "Matthew DeMarcus."

His answer punched another hole in her belief that this entire situation was a fluke, including her growing attraction to him. "This isn't just another coincidence, is it?"

"I don't think so, but how did it get here?"

"You think Dabir and his men are responsible for Dr. DeMarcus's disappearance?"

"Maybe, but why?" she asked. "I still don't understand how all this fits together. DeMarcus's disappearance...the drums of pharmaceutical waste...the virus..." *Us?* "There has to be a connection to all of this."

Josiah's hands dropped to his sides. "Rachel said Dr. DeMarcus had come to her with some questions. He had patients who were sick, and he couldn't figure out what was wrong with them. He'd mentioned toxic dumping as a possible source."

"But Rachel didn't feel that toxic-waste symptoms matched Abeje's."

Josiah shrugged. "She doesn't know these people are living in a pharmaceutical waste dump."

A shiver swept through Mac despite the night's oppressive heat. "What if

Dr. DeMarcus was looking into what was making his patients sick and discovered something? Something that might have even cost him his life?"

"I guess, but—"

A shout interrupted his answer. The porch light caught Sid running up the stairs behind them.

"Sid?" Mac spun around. "What's wrong?"

"It's Dabir's nephew. His fever spiked, and he won't wake up."

CHAPTER TWENTY-NINE

GULF OF GUINEA, COASTAL REGION

JOSIAH FLEW TO THE OPEN THRESHOLD OF THE DIMLY LIT ISOLATION ROOM. It reeked of excrement. A single bulb powered by a gas generator gave off just enough light for him to see one of the village volunteers sitting beside Dabir's nephew. She was humming and patting the boy's hand.

"Josiah!" Mac's voice stopped him from charging across the room. He turned to see her ripping into a packaged paper gown and mask. "What can I do?" she asked as Josiah quickly wiggled his body into the flimsy protection, impatient for her to secure the ties as his eyes assessed the boy's labored respirations.

"I won't know until I examine him." Josiah snapped on the gloves. "Don't come into this room until you gown up."

"Doctor," the woman called.

Duna was convulsing.

Josiah quickly wove around mats filled with curled-up patients. The volunteer moved to give him room. He crouched beside the mat and laid a hand on Duna's bucking shoulder. "Hey," he whispered. But the boy did not respond or settle.

Without a CT scan, he couldn't know if the convulsions were encephalopathy or the direct effect of the virus on the brain.

Big bruises bloomed from the naval of the boy's distended abdomen. Dark purple blotches also covered his thin arms and legs. Blood seeped from the corner of his chapped mouth. Josiah gently pried his lips apart and discovered that the boy's gums were bleeding.

The life was literally seeping out of this child.

Josiah clasped the boy's thin wrist. He was hot as a furnace and his pulse was racing. Duna needed to be in an intensive care unit staffed with the best infectious disease docs in the world. He deserved more than a filthy mat in the middle of a jungle and being treated by a Hollywood plastic surgeon who could only guess at what should be done next.

Josiah couldn't hold back his frustration. "Mac, get Dabir, now!"

She wheeled, and he could hear her boots hitting the porch planks at a rapid pace.

The boy's eyes popped open. "Naa," he croaked.

Josiah assumed he was asking for his mother. "I'll get her for you, soon as I get you feeling better, okay?" He glanced around the room. How was he going to fix this? He didn't even have a glass of filtered water to offer this child, let alone what he really needed: a sedative to relieve his anxiety, a syringe of morphine to lessen the pain, and something to stop the internal hemorrhaging. "Hold my hand." He scooped the boy's hand into his. It was swollen so big the child's knuckles had disappeared. His small, calloused feet were also shiny black balloons.

Renal failure.

If the virus was destroying Duna's kidneys, they'd soon stop filtering waste products from the blood. It wouldn't take long for him to suffer a multi-organ shutdown.

Fighting the helplessness welling up inside of him, Josiah stroked Duna's puffy hand. "I have a little girl," he said, not sure how much English the boy understood. "Her name's Emma. About your age, I suspect." The same way a bedtime story settled Emma, Duna stopped his thrashing. His labored respirations eased, and his stiffened body relaxed.

Grateful he could give some comfort, Josiah continued. "Emma loves crowns. Bright shiny tiaras. Wears them everywhere." He tried to swallow around the lump that had been in his throat since Camilla died. Losing his wife had been hard. Losing Emma Grace would kill him. "My little girl makes toast. It's burned sometimes. I tell her, she shouldn't use electrical appliances without supervision, but she likes to bring breakfast to me in bed after I've been in the OR all night. It's not right for the child to have to parent the parent, right?" He could command whole operating teams, but he couldn't make himself move forward. Get on with life. Death was a wall he couldn't seem to climb. "But she's stubborn...like her mother," he said softly.

The hand he held became limp.

Dabir's nephew lay still upon his mat. Josiah reached up and checked for a carotid pulse.

Nothing.

Josiah launched himself into a one-man Code Blue. He laid Duna flat on his back and began frantic chest compressions. He was sweating and begging him to wake up when he felt a firm hand on his shoulder.

"He's gone." Dabir's face was blank of emotion. "I'll see to his burial."

Josiah tried to stand but the strength had drained from his limbs. "You must wear a mask and gloves and bury him soon. He must be wrapped in plastic, buried far from the village, and buried deep."

Dabir turned and left without a word.

Josiah slumped beside the small boy. He looked at the peace that had replaced the anguish on the still face. What great things had been lost to the world because of this child's early death? He needed to go find Duna's mother, but he couldn't bear the thought of telling her that he'd not been able to save her son. Unable to leave him, but unable to continue staring at the lifeless form, Josiah let his gaze drift to the open door. Mackenzie stood in the moonlight, her arms hanging limp at her sides. Tears streaming down her cheeks.

"I'm so sorry," she said.

Josiah shook his head. "He was just a kid."

Loud voices sounded outside the window. Josiah could hear a man and a woman shouting.

"Dabir!" Mac disappeared from the doorway.

Josiah pushed to his feet and ran to the porch. Dabir was holding an angry woman at arm's length. Duna's mother. She was wailing and tearing at her clothes.

Dabir pulled her close and let her cry into his shoulder.

Josiah remembered how Rachel had begged him to cry after Camilla's death and he never had. He envied this woman who could let her grief go. Josiah turned from the scene and headed back to the isolation room.

Mac caught up with him. "What can I do to help?"

"Don't touch me!" Josiah snapped.

Palms raised, she backed away.

"Sorry," Josiah managed to say. "I'm covered in his blood. It's not safe."

But she could see he meant he wasn't safe. His heart was still so raw. "Tell me what I can do," she repeated.

"Convince Dabir to get us out of here." He turned and went back inside the schoolroom.

The two women who'd been helping in the clinic wrapped Duna's body in a tarp then carried the body outside.

Josiah conducted rounds in the isolation room. The sick were in various stages of decline. He did what he could to make them comfortable, then hung his last four IV bags for the ones who seemed to be in the best shape. Maybe the extra hydration would give them a tiny chance of beating this monster. By the time he finished, he was so exhausted he could barely move.

He removed his soiled gown, mask, goggles, and gloves and tossed them into the bin he'd designated for daily burning. He stepped onto the porch and scrubbed his hands and face with soap and fresh water Mac had thought to fetch from the pump. The night was heavy with residual heat and loss. Mosquitos buzzed his throbbing head like a cloud of bad choices. Monkeys screamed accusations from the dark jungle beyond the compound. He rubbed the back of his neck and started toward the house for a shower and the futile hope that he'd ever feel washed clean again.

The flicker of fire at the far edge of the compound caught his attention. He squinted to make out what was going on. Flames leaping from a barrel threw off enough light that he could see a man digging a grave under a mangrove tree.

He needed to make sure that Dabir's nephew and the others who had died were buried properly in order to keep the contamination from spreading. Josiah walked past the pump and to the spot where the grave was being dug. The gravedigger had his back to Josiah, lifting a shovelful of dirt and tossing it onto a mound beside the grave.

"Dig it deep," Josiah said.

The man standing waist-deep in the hole turned. Sweat and sorrow trickled down Dabir's black face. He nodded toward his nephew's small body lying on the other side of the opening. "He was a good boy."

Something inside of Josiah snapped. Grief, old and sour, punched an angry hole in the wall around his heart. He picked up a shovel propped against a tree. Without a word, he pulled a pair of nitrile gloves from his pocket. Snapped them on, then lowered himself into the hole alongside his captor and began to dig.

CHAPTER THIRTY

GULF OF GUINEA, COASTAL REGION

THE SUN WOULD BE UP IN ANOTHER HOUR. JOSIAH IGNORED MAC'S PLEAS to sleep after he'd showered the grave dirt from his body. Even if he'd taken the time to close his eyes, the image of burying an innocent child would haunt his dreams. His own child was on a ship carrying the same deadly virus that had drained the life from Dabir's nephew. He had to find a way to get back to his daughter. To protect Emma better than he'd protected her mother. If he lost his daughter too, the gravediggers would have to put him in the same hole.

Since his return to his makeshift clinic, a dozen new sick people had lined up outside the schoolroom door. He'd already used almost everything Rachel had hurriedly packed in his medical kit, leaving him to divvy up the last small bottle of acetaminophen among the critical patients writhing on the mats. But he'd had so few tablets, the relief was insignificant. Fevers continued to rise. Most suffered vomiting and diarrhea. All moaned in pain.

Josiah crouched beside a thin woman with dried vomit on her cheek. He gently lifted her head and pressed a cup to her chapped lips. "Drink."

She was so delirious, she swatted the cup across the room.

Josiah eased her down upon the mat then rose wearily. Too tired to change into fresh gloves, he slumped against the teacher's wooden desk that had been shoved against the wall and closed his eyes. The torturous sounds of people slowly dying would not let him escape for even a second. The only thing left to do was pray. Pray that the suffering would cease. Pray that somehow, some way, he could convince the pirates to let him call in professional help. Pray that Emma had tucked herself far away from all of this. He cleared his dry throat to start a prayer, but it had been so long since he actually tried talking to God that he'd forgotten how. Maybe, at this point, the words didn't matter.

He squeezed his eyes shut for a moment and drew in a deep breath. No words seemed adequate and he didn't have any answers.

Hopefully God did.

"I need your help."

Josiah's eyes flew open. "Dabir?"

"My son, Taiwo." The pirate, who'd obviously not slept either, stood at the threshold of the schoolroom holding a small boy whose forehead glistened in the light of the single bulb. "He's sick."

Josiah sprang into action. He strode past a row of mats, pulling off his soiled gloves and snapping on a fresh pair. He placed his stethoscope on the child's belly. He couldn't hear any sign of angry bowel rumblings, but it was obvious the child was burning up. "If you don't want to bury your son next to your nephew, we're out of options. We have to take Taiwo to the *Liberty*. Now." Josiah stuck his stethoscope in his scrub pocket. "We also need to get the samples back to the *Liberty*, and get the authorities involved. Otherwise, this suffering you see here isn't going to end until everyone you care about is dead."

Dabir's frantic gaze darted between his moaning boy and Josiah. "Then we leave now."

Josiah nodded. "Thank you." He knew that the compromise didn't solve everything. In fact, dragging more sickness back to the *Liberty* would simply endanger more innocent people and put Emma in even greater danger.

But he was out of IV fluids, pain meds, and ideas. And Dabir's son was the only leverage he had to convince the man to get the help needed to stop this nightmare.

Josiah ripped off his gloves and threw them in the bin. "I'll leave instructions on how to care for the sick until we can return with a proper medical team."

The sky was pinking over the trees when they shoved off from the shore with ten extra men sporting assault rifles and desperate expressions. Josiah couldn't quit thinking about what he was going to find when they got to the *Liberty*. There wasn't a scenario spinning in his head that didn't turn his empty stomach.

Captain Scott and Sid were squeezed between two of the armed men. Mac sat cross-legged by the pallet she'd made for Taiwo in the bottom of the boat. Josiah took measure of the woman he'd kissed beneath a jungle porch light. She was exhausted, but insistent on sticking close to the sick boy. She was irritatingly stubborn, but almost always right. She had more courage in her little finger than most women possessed in their whole body.

Josiah studied his scrubbed-raw hands to keep from staring at the leafy shadows the sun cast upon Mac's beautiful olive skin. If he didn't regret kissing her, why did he feel so guilty?

"What should we do?" Mac's question brought his eyes up to meet her intense gaze.

Was she asking him not to let one kiss make things strained between them when their current situation was strained enough? "About what?"

She nodded toward Taiwo. "He's burning up."

"Without an IV we'll have to try and initiate oral hydration." He lifted the plastic container one of Dabir's men had filled from the well, splashed some into a tin cup, and held it out to Mac. "See if you can get him to drink."

As they traveled the sludgy ebb of the river, Josiah noted how the smells and sounds of this section of the African rainforest matched his memories of the lush Amazon. Until Mac had expressed genuine interest in his youth, he'd preferred to not revisit those years. It had been almost two decades since his family had lived and worked in Columbia, but if he allowed himself to breathe in deeply, which he seldom did, he could still smell the distinctive scents of the South American jungle. From the tangle of green vines and trees competing for the sunlight, the Amazon rainforest had emitted enticing odors of flowering vegetation and mesmerizing sounds of bickering monkeys, chirping insects, and wild game. He'd come to believe his father loved the jungle wildlife nearly as much as he loved the tribes who made their home there.

The landscape of this African jungle felt similar to its Amazonian counterpart in that both could be equally deceiving. Both could swallow a person whole and leave no trace behind. And the virus currently spreading like wildfire across this untamed land had been hiding here like a deadly viper, coiled and ready to strike. Josiah didn't want Emma to lose her father in this place of death and spend the rest of her life thinking he'd left her on purpose. If he had contracted the virus, at least she'd know her father died fighting to live. Fighting to give them a shot at being a family again.

Mac set Taiwo's empty cup down then squeezed in next to Josiah. "Once we're on the boat, I'll need your help." She stared straight ahead as she spoke, her voice low. Her gaze razor-focused on the horizon.

Trying not to think about the heat of her bare arm against his, a response tripped out. "With what?"

"I have to find the jammer and turn it off so I can call my team. I'm going to need a distraction."

"I can do that. When?"

"We'll have to play it by ear, but when I give you the nod, don't hesitate."

"Nod. Got it." He'd managed to shove a measure of confidence into his voice, but he had no idea how he was going to distract a dozen armed men. But if it meant saving his daughter's life and possibly those aboard the *Liberty*, he'd do anything at this point. If they were lucky, the fact that he'd tried to save Dabir's nephew had meant something to the man. Maybe they could put an end to this without any more violence.

Raindrops hit the awning that covered where Taiwo slept. The crowding of everyone but Dabir under the roof put an end to his and Mac's covert conversation. The heavens opened and blinding sheets of rain soaked all of them to the skin. Dabir remained at his post, driving the skiff as if a downpour was the least of his worries.

The sun had burned off the clouds by the time they reached the place where the river dumped into the ocean. A few minutes later, the *Liberty* came into view. Thanks to Dabir's communication device that somehow operated on a frequency outside the jamming tool the pirates had installed on the ship, one of his pirate buddies had already opened the gangway, allowing them to easily board from the skiff.

Inside the reception area, Dabir started barking orders to his men.

Josiah wished he could understand their language, but he could tell from the shouldering of rifles that Dabir had not softened as much as Josiah had hoped. This was still a hostage situation and everyone on this ship was still at risk.

Dabir grabbed his arm. "You have the samples?"

Josiah nodded.

"You and I will go see my wife first."

"What about your men?" Josiah asked.

"They'll wait here."

Josiah's eyes cut to Mac and he caught the subtle shake of her head. Not the nod, but a shake. Not the time to create a diversion.

Dabir scooped up his son from one of the other pirates while Josiah carried the cooler with the samples they'd gathered. Chomba followed behind with his AK-47, a reminder that the camaraderie Josiah had felt last night at the gravesite between Dabir and him was not mutual. They were fathers who loved their families, but they were not friends.

A minute later, Josiah pushed open the door to the lab, stopping in the doorway at the sight of his sister. The sharp smell of disinfectant lingered in the air.

"Ray?"

"Stay there, Joey." She held up a gloved hand where she stood next to Harper. Both women looked exhausted. "We've just finished disinfecting the room, but I don't want to take any chances."

"I have the samples." Josiah held out the cooler. "Dabir's son is sick."

He looked at the bed where Abeje had lain when they were here last and saw the black body bag.

Dabir let out a groan beside him. "Abeje is dead?"

"I'm sorry." Rachel clasped her hands together. "I did everything I could to save her."

"Your wife didn't get here in time," Josiah said, trying to read the man's expression. "Don't let that happen to your son."

Dabir pulled Taiwo tight, as if releasing him was releasing his last bargaining chip. "I want to see her."

"No." Rachel stepped between Dabir and the body. "You can't. If this is Ebola, it can be transmitted postmortem. We need to focus on your son now. The sooner we get him IV hydration, the better his chances, but not in here. I need a proper isolation room."

Dabir looked at Taiwo moaning in his arms. “He dies, your brother dies.”

“Threats will not solve this problem.” Rachel pushed between them. “If you don’t let us contact the World Health Organization or Doctors Without Borders, you’re going to lose your son, too.”

“Let her help, Dabir,” Josiah said.

“Like she helped my wife? What good are you? What good are either of you?”

“We might have answers,” Josiah said, stalling for time. “We have the samples my sister needs.” He turned to Rachel. “Mac found a landfill site where someone is dumping pharmaceuticals, Rachel. There has to be a connection.”

“It’s very possible.” Rachel turned to Dabir again. “But my lab is limited on what it can do. This is why I need outside help. This illness behaves consistent with the progression of a hemorrhagic fever, but every Ebola test I ran on Abeje came back negative.”

“How is that possible?” Dabir asked.

Rachel shook her head. “I don’t know. It’s possible that the rapid diagnostic tests I have produced a false negative, but it could also be a new strain.”

“Which means we have nothing to fight it,” Josiah said.

“I will not lose my son,” Dabir said. “My wife is dead. Someone has to pay. Once my demands are met, I’ll let your team on this ship, but until then we will do things my way.”

“What are you demanding?” Rachel asked.

“My wife back. My village back. My ability to make an honest living. But since I can’t have those things, I have a ship full of hostages. Keeping them alive has to be worth something.” Dabir turned to Josiah. “Right, doctor?”

Josiah fought to keep his expression blank as Taiwo stirred in the man’s arms.

“All the passengers are going into the three lounges. You can keep two of the wards open for patients and a few doctors and nurses.”

“But you’ll be breaking the quarantine,” Rachel argued. “Isolation is the only weapon we have against this virus. If it can’t find another host, it will eventually die out.”

“While it rages in my village?”

“At least let me set up an isolation room outside my lab and outside the wards for Taiwo and anyone else who is sick," Rachel said. "It's the only way for your son to receive the best care."

Dabir hesitated then handed Taiwo to Rachel. "Go with her, Chomba, and watch her. As for the two of you..." He nodded at Josiah and Harper. "You'll come with me upstairs."

Josiah took Harper's arm and started down the passageway in front of Dabir. "It's going to be okay," he whispered to her.

"Is it?"

A sick feeling washed through him. He couldn't truthfully answer her question. Between Dabir, his men, and the virus, he had no idea how this was going to end.

Mac stood at the reception desk next to Sid and her father, a worried expression on her face.

"Captain, you will address the ship again." Dabir shifted his weapon at Mac, then quickly gave the man further instructions. "Say something I don't like, and I will shoot her."

The captain nodded as he turned on the ship's internal communications. "This is your captain. I'm asking everyone to leave their quarters immediately and come to the lounges on deck six. Medical personnel already stationed in the two wards will stay with their patients at their posts. If you have any symptoms of fever, headache, or nausea, go straight to deck three. Do not engage with the armed men you come in contact with. I repeat, I need everyone to immediately leave their rooms and come to the lounges on deck six. . ."

A minute later, Josiah scanned the people being herded into the conference room where the pirates had taken him, Mac, Sid, and Captain Scott after the captain's announcement. Several of the terrified crew and patients were crying. Most were sober faced. He was sure all were praying. None of them were Emma.

Dabir pushed his way to the middle of the room and stepped upon a chair as the room began to fill. "I run this ship now. I want everyone to follow the orders of my men. You do as we say, or you die."

Dabir's men shoved a few of the people with the butt of their rifles, and they stumbled into the center of the room. People gasped and a couple of women cried out.

"Dabir." Sid held up his hands in front of him and approached the man.

"Tell me what you want. I know a negotiator," he offered. "Let me contact him. You can tell him what you want. We can end this without anyone getting hurt."

"I'm supposed to trust you?" Dabir asked.

Across the room, Josiah caught the flash of something sparkly poke up from behind the coffee bar as Dabir and Sid continued their conversation. It was Emma's tiara. Josiah wanted to yell, "Stay down!" but he knew that could be fatal. Instead, he held his tongue and his breath.

Slowly, Emma's head raised just high enough that Josiah could see the fear in her big blue eyes. She scanned the crowd. He knew that if she spotted him, she would shout out. He couldn't let Dabir get his hands on his daughter.

Josiah cut his gaze to Mac, who stood less than three yards from him. She, too, had spotted Emma behind the coffee bar. She turned and gave Josiah a slow, barely imperceptible nod.

There was no time to think. Josiah launched himself at Dabir, knocking the pirate to the floor. The man's AK-47 went flying out of his hands. People scattered, pushing themselves against the wall. Dabir reared back and slammed his fist into Josiah's face, but not before Josiah saw Mac fly across the cafeteria and snatch Emma from behind the counter.

Gunshots pummeled the ceiling. Josiah froze. Gaining the advantage, Dabir pushed him off and scrambled for his gun. He lifted the butt, but before he brought it down hard on Josiah's forehead, Josiah caught a glimpse of Mac and Emma disappearing out of the lounge.

CHAPTER THIRTY-ONE

SOMEWHERE IN THE GULF OF GUINEA

MAC HELD TIGHTLY TO EMMA'S HAND AS THEY RAN OUT OF THE CAFETERIA and into the passageway lit only by emergency lighting. She wished she had a better grasp of the layout of the ship. All she had was a rough blueprint in her mind from her brief time on board. What she did know was that it wasn't going to take long for Dabir to notice she was missing.

Mac grabbed the first door they came to, trying to find a place where they could hide while she made a plan.

Locked.

She ran to the stairs and hesitated for a split second at the bottom step, tried to recall everything she knew about the ship, then headed up, hoping she'd made the right decision. Most of the crew had been quarantined to their quarters on decks three and four, and they were currently being herded into the lounges on the sixth deck. She didn't know where the jammer was, but logic told her going down would pretty much guarantee she ran into the pirates. A wrong move could easily get her killed and now that she had Emma, she wouldn't let the girl be left alone again.

Hurried footsteps echoed in the stairwell. Mac quickly pulled Emma into the shadows of an alcove on deck seven, praying whoever it was would pass. But the odds of avoiding Dabir's men were slim. The bridge was on this deck as well as the officers' accommodations. If Dabir's men weren't up here yet, they would be soon.

Emma tugged on her hand. "I'm scared."

Mac bent down and pulled her close. "I know, sweetie."

"They grabbed my daddy. Everyone was yelling."

"I know."

"What if the bad guys find us?"

"I'm going to do everything I can to make sure that doesn't happen. That's why we need to be very quiet, okay?"

Tears filled Emma's eyes as she nodded.

"Mac?"

Mackenzie took a step forward at the familiar voice. "Harper?"

The young woman appeared at the top of the stairs. "I saw you leave and managed to slip out in the confusion. Thought you might need someone who knows their way around."

"I do. We need to find the jammer and disable it. It's the only way we're going to get help."

"Rachel told me where it was."

"What?"

Harper waved for them to follow. "Come with me. We need to get off this deck before we get caught."

"Where are we going?" Emma asked.

"This ship used to be a ferry," Harper said. "There's a network of service corridors and stairs that aren't used very often. My brother found them the summer he served on the ship."

Harper pushed open a door that said *Do Not Enter* and motioned them down a steep staircase.

"Where's the jammer?" Mac asked.

"Under the reception desk. Deck five. This will lead us there."

"They'll see us," Emma said.

"They don't know about this secret stairwell," Harper said. "And besides, they're busy trying to get everyone to deck six."

"Do you have any idea where the Gurkhas are?" Mac asked.

"I overheard someone say they were being held in the engine room, but I don't know."

They went down two narrow flights of stairs then Harper stopped at a door marked *Deck Five*. "On the other side of these doors is the reception counter. That's where Rachel said it was."

"Okay. I can turn off the jammer, but I'm going to need you to do something as well."

"Of course."

Mac hesitated, not wanting to worry the young woman, but at this point she didn't have a choice. "I believe your father discovered people were getting sick and was trying to find the source. I need to know if he has a laptop."

Harper's eyes grew wide. "He does. It's in our cabin."

"Can you get it for me? I need to look at his emails. See if he'd been in contact with anyone about a sickness. I know it's asking a lot—"

"If it helps get us off this boat—if it helps find my father—I'll do anything."

"Go get the laptop and meet me back here in this stairwell as soon as you can."

"Wait. You're going to need this." Harper pulled something out of her pocket. "My phone. You should be able to call out once the jammer stops working."

"Good thinking," Mac said. "Be careful."

"You too."

Mac watched Harper continue down the stairs then shifted her gaze to Emma, wondering if it would be safer to leave her here in the secret staircase or take her with her to disable the jammer.

Emma grabbed Mac's hand and tugged on it as if reading her mind. "I want to stay with you. I don't want to be alone."

"I'm not going to leave you alone," Mac said, decision made. "You and I are going to stick together."

"And find Daddy?" Emma asked.

"We are." Mac knelt down and faced the little girl. "I promise."

Forty-eight hours ago, she was jumping out of a plane, prepared to stop a hijacking situation. Today, she was protecting a little girl who'd somehow managed to completely win over her heart.

Mac eased the door open an inch. An eerie silence greeted her. A moment later, she pushed the door open, then slipped into the reception area with Emma still clinging to her. Harper said the long counter would be to her right. In the darkness, Mac did her best to hurry Emma across the tile floor. Once they were safe behind the counter, Mac wished she had a flashlight.

"Do you see it?" Emma asked.

"It should be right here under the counter." Mac felt around. "Here it is."

Voices echoed from behind the glass double doors separating reception from the counter. Mac left the jammer and pulled Emma under the corner of the counter then positioned a tall trash can in front of them. She held up a finger, signaling Emma to be quiet as they huddled under the overhang of the counter.

She'd expected them to search for her once Dabir noticed she was missing. He knew she had military experience and that she would go for the jammer. She pulled Emma closer, not wanting to think about what had happened to Josiah after Dabir's man struck him. He was going to be okay, she told herself. He had to be. He had a little girl who needed her father no matter how grown up she seemed.

And herself?

She didn't want to admit the flood of feelings Josiah awakened when he'd kissed her.

Boots pounded the floor on the other side of the counter, forcing her to keep her focus on the present. A second later, she could see the black boots of one of the men as he stepped behind the counter. A green light flashed between the man and Mac, shifting her attention momentarily. The jammer was six feet away, but if they moved or made any noise, the guard would catch them, and she'd lose her chance to turn it off.

"Do you see them?" one of the pirates said.

"They're not here," the man behind the counter answered. "They could be anywhere on this ship."

"Dabir will shoot us if we don't find them."

The man behind the counter hesitated then followed his friend. The door clicked behind them, but Mac didn't move until their voices disappeared.

Emma leaned forward and whispered in her ear. "I think they're gone."

Mac nodded. "I think you're right. And you, Emma Allen, are very brave."

"I'm trying to be."

"Let's get this done so we can go find your daddy."

The jammer was no light-weight model, but was made to block large areas with its eight antennas...like an entire ship. She yanked out the battery and stuffed it in her pocket so the machine couldn't be turned on again, then hurried Emma into the stairwell. It was only a matter of time before Dabir realized the jammer had been disabled, and he sent someone to see what had happened.

They sat on one of the narrow steps, then Mac grabbed Harper's phone out of her pocket and punched in her boss's number back in the US.

"Ethan?"

"Mac?"

"I can't believe how good it is to hear your voice, sir."

"Where are you?"

"On the *Liberty*, somewhere in the Gulf of Guinea. I don't know how long I'm going to have to talk, but I guess you have heard at least part of what's going on. I've just disabled the jammer."

"I know your team has been frantic trying to find you. A jammer explains why they haven't been able to locate you."

"Hopefully, you'll be able to track the ship's GPS now, but you're going to have to bring in an army."

"What's the situation?"

She turned her head away from Emma, but knew there was no way for the child not to hear the conversation. And besides, the girl had already seen too much. "A dozen or so armed pirates have taken over the ship, and they're not playing games. They killed several security guards, and Ethan...these are the same guys who were on the oil tanker when Mo was shot."

"It sounds like bringing in an army would only exacerbate the situation. We don't need more people dying. You need a negotiator."

"I think they're already working on that."

"Do they know you've turned off the jammer?"

"I don't think so, but it's only a matter of time before they discover it. And there's something else, Ethan." She drew in a deep breath as she pulled her jumbled thoughts together. "I'm not sure at this point if there's more than one jammer covering the ship, but the one I found is pretty advanced. Looks like it's able to block multiple frequencies, including cell phone, internet, and satellite, and probably has about a hundred-and-fifty-meter radius. This isn't common equipment you can buy at your local hardware store, and certainly not anywhere around here. And something like this isn't cheap, either. This is on par with the equipment we use. We're talking military grade."

"You don't think they're working on their own?"

"I think it's a possibility we can't ignore. And that's not the only problem we're facing." She paused, wondering how the situation could get any worse. "We've got at least one dead patient on board from what looks like Ebola or some type of hemorrhagic virus."

"Then there has to be a connection."

"A connection to what?" Mac asked, remembering the conversation she'd had with Josiah about the strange watch she'd found and the possibility it belonged to the missing doctor.

"A new strain of Ebola turned up in the US. The woman who brought it in was on the *Liberty*. Protocol has been put in motion in the local hospitals in Douala, and WHO is already responding and working with the Ministry of Health. Details are still sketchy, but my team is working with the authorities to put all the pieces together."

Was this what Dr. DeMarcus had stumbled onto?

"Keep your eyes and ears open," Ethan said. "We're tracking you now and will get a team in the air immediately. But you're going to need to be careful. This could turn ugly quickly."

She glanced at Emma huddled beside her. "I'll keep this phone with me and stay under the radar as long as possible."

"Stay safe."

"Thank you, sir." Mac clicked off the phone and sat in the darkened silence.

A little hand found hers. "What do we do now?"

She squeezed Emma's hand and sent up a prayer for wisdom. "We need to find Harper."

"What about my daddy?"

"You heard me talking to the man on the phone?"

"Yes," Emma whispered.

"He's my boss, and he's going to bring help."

They heard a door swing open from above them, then Harper whispered, "It's me." She sat beside them and opened a laptop. "I think I found what you're looking for."

CHAPTER THIRTY-TWO

BETHESDA, MARYLAND

CLAYBORN TANNER PACED THE LENGTH OF THE THICK GLASS WALL keeping him from his mother. The Bethesda team had separated them the moment they'd deplaned from their biohazard transport charter. His mind embraced the well-documented ability of isolation to stop the spread of a virus, but his heart couldn't bear the thought of his mother dying alone. He'd thrown such an unprofessional fit that he'd probably ruined his career, but at least having the room next door meant he could see his mom through the glass and talk to her via intercom.

Around midnight, the intercom in his room had buzzed. Clayborn had stirred from a fitful sleep and staggered to the glass.

"I'm sorry to wake you, Dr. Tanner." A man dressed in full hazmat gear stood at the intercom box. "We're upgrading your mother's condition to critical. She's in and out of consciousness, but I'm sure she'd love to hear your voice."

Clayborn had fought a headache ever since. He told himself it was because he hadn't had a decent night's sleep since his mother arrived. But his worried breaths left a steamy circle on the glass. What would happen to his wife and kids if he got sick?

His mother's potassium levels continued to drop. The docs had done everything they could, but nothing seemed to replenish the falling numbers.

At two a.m., he was informed his mother needed renal dialysis. If they couldn't save her kidneys, acute respiratory distress wouldn't be far behind. His mother had continued to weaken since they left Philadelphia. She no longer had the strength to use the bedside toilet or grimace in shame when the nurses had to roll her over and clean her up. It was torture watching this virus strip his strong, brilliant, vibrant mother of her dignity.

Clayborn pulled out his phone. It was too early in the morning to text Jasmine an update or to ask the question both of them dreaded: How are you feeling? If, by any chance, his wife had managed to put the terrible realities of their situation out of her mind long enough to catch a few winks, he wanted her to sleep. To keep up her strength. From everything he'd read—and he'd read everything he could find about Ebola on the internet—the stronger you were going into this, the better your chances of coming out of it alive. And they were all going to come out of this alive. Right?

Clayborn dragged a chair to the glass and propped up his socked feet. The team of hazmat-suited medical staff were working on his mother. He hit the internet icon on his phone and resumed his search for a solution. He read every article he could find on the recovery of the 2014 Ebola patients that had been brought to America and survived. The supportive care in the States was better than what Africa had to offer, but the surviving patients also received plasma transfusions from previous survivors and an experimental drug called ZMapp. Since then, the World Health Organization had approved survivor's blood transfusions for Ebola patients. Bethesda's crackerjack medical team had followed protocol and supported his mother's antiviral treatments with this same passive immunotherapy in the hopes that the antibodies the survivors' plasma contained would fight the virus.

And still his mother continued to decline.

When Clayborn asked the lead doc about their next step, the lead doc said that he suspected a rapidly mutating form of the Ebola virus coupled with his mother's advanced age—she was only fifty-seven for Pete's sake—was the reason they weren't making better headway.

Clayborn wasn't having any of this. He owed his mother too much. She'd worked two jobs and put herself through a master's program to give him and his brother a shot at a better life. For years, she'd navigated school politics and taken grief from parents and school board members who doubted the ability of a black woman to effectively lead a predominantly white school. She deserved every ounce of effort she'd poured into his future to be poured back into doing all he could to save her. She'd never given up on him, and he would never give up on her.

An hour later, sweat trickled down the crick in Clayborn's neck. A hot, sticky sweat drop slid down his nose and landed on his phone screen. He wiped the moisture away and continued reading a fascinating website he'd stumbled upon.

Dema Diagnostics, a bio-research firm based in Maryland, touted its active development of an antiviral that was currently undergoing clinical primate trials in the Congo basin. Early results had been very promising. However, after the containment of the 2014 Ebola outbreak, the FDA's approval had slowed to an imperceptible crawl. The article claimed that since people were no longer dying of Ebola, nobody was in a hurry for the drug. Dema Diagnostics challenged the bottleneck: *What will it take to nudge the FDA to bring this remarkable drug to the market? A new outbreak in the underdeveloped regions of the world?*

Clayborn leapt to his feet. He pounded on the thick glass, but the heavily geared attendants working around his mother's bed could not hear him.

He jabbed the intercom button. "I need to talk to the doctor."

The goggled faces turned toward him. The man he recognized as the leader of the team by his tall, thin body structure nodded. He spoke to the two nurses in the room, then made his exit.

It took several minutes for the doctor to complete the hospital's change-of-room protocols. By the time he entered Clayborn's room, Clayborn felt as if his head would explode.

"What is it?" The doctor stepped in and closed the door. "Are you feeling ill, Dr. Tanner?"

Clayborn held out his phone. "Look at this."

The doctor took the phone with his gloved hand, but he held it away from him as if it were a virus bomb. He began to read aloud. "In late August 2014, both Kent Brantly and Nancy Writebol became the first people to be given the experimental drug ZMapp. They both recovered, but there was no confirmation or proof that the drug was a factor. Up until that time, ZMapp had only been tested on primates and looked promising, causing no serious side effects and protecting the animals from infection." He handed the phone back to Clayborn. "We've tried ZMapp. We've even tried the latest drug brincidofovir. We're getting nowhere."

"Wait." Clayborn scrolled to the Dema Diagnostics site. "Look at this."

As the doctor read the information silently, a scowl formed above his goggles. He looked up and held out the phone. "You want me to give *your* mother a drug that's only been tested on primates?"

"That's what you did for Brantly and Writebol."

"There were many factors that played into that decision."

Clayborn snatched his phone. "Somebody has to go first." He didn't care that he sounded desperate. "My mother has always been a ground breaker."

"Even if I could get my hands on this new—"

"Look." Clayborn scrolled back to the first article. "The Bill & Melinda Gates Foundation donated $150,000 to help Amgen increase its antiviral production. Don't tell me you don't know how to get this done."

The doctor shook his head. "I don't think—"

"Doctor, please don't make me stand on this side of the glass and watch my mother die."

The doctor let out a weary sigh. "I've been told that the World Health Organization has boots on the ground in Douala."

"It's about time!"

"They've investigated reports of a strange sickness at the *Liberty's* abandoned post-op clinic. Tests have confirmed it is the same mutant strain of Ebola that we've isolated in your mother's blood."

"Are you saying they think the *Liberty* sailed off and left sick patients behind?"

"That's what the authorities are trying to figure out."

Clayborn felt nauseated by the possibility his medical colleagues had abandoned those in need. "Doing medical harm to a third-world nation is completely contrary to the *Liberty's* mission. People on that boat are so committed to helping medically underserved nations that they raise their own support and volunteer their time to work on the *Liberty*. Something is terribly wrong."

"I believe you're right, Dr. Tanner." The doctor stepped forward and gently laid a gloved hand on Clayborn's clammy face. "When did *your* fever start?"

"Fever?"

The doctor took a temperature scan of Clayborn's forehead. "101.2"

Clayborn sank into the chair near the glass wall. "But my tests have all been negative."

"It took three days after the first sign of symptoms to get a positive on your mother." The doctor took a step back. "Much as I don't want to give you something untested, I can't keep fighting this forest fire with a garden hose. I'll see what I can do to move the FDA toward approving human trials of Dema Diagnostics's new treatment."

Clayborn let out a relieved sigh. "Thank you."

The doctor shook his head. "It's not a magic bullet."

Clayborn was no infectious disease specialist, but he knew enough about the human body to know that a person's response to a certain virus was one of countless mysteries the drug companies may never solve. "Don't tell Mom about me until we get a positive read."

"At this point, Dr. Tanner, your mother has enough worries."

CHAPTER THIRTY-THREE

SOMEWHERE IN THE GULF OF GUINEA

MAC TOOK THE LAPTOP FROM HARPER, THEN SAT ON THE STAIR STEP below Harper and Emma. "Did you run into anyone?"

"I had one close call, but no."

"What about my daddy?" Emma asked.

Harper squeezed the little girl's shoulder. "I'm sorry, sweetie. I didn't see him."

Mac opened the computer. In the blue glow of the screen she saw the worry on Emma's face. "I haven't known your daddy for very long, but I do know something important about him."

"What's that?"

"He is a very strong man."

"He works out at the gym sometimes."

Mac smiled, then pointed to her heart. "I mean inside. Even though he's been sad lately, he's strong and brave. I've seen that in him as he's risked his life to help other people."

"Like coming here?"

"Like coming here."

Emma's brow furrowed. "God let Mommy die. What if he lets my daddy die too?"

The question struck Mac like a bullet to the heart. "I had a friend who told me to have faith. No matter what happens."

"Your friend, Mo?"

Mac swallowed hard. "Yes."

"But he died."

"You know what Mo would say if he were here?"

"No."

"Sometimes bad things happen, but that doesn't change who God is."

"She's right, Emma." Harper squeezed Emma's hand. "No matter what's happening around us, God is still good. He doesn't change. Sometimes life is scary, like right now. And sometimes life makes us happy. But no matter what is happening around us, God is right here with us."

"Even now?"

Harper nodded. "And he can help all of us be brave right now too. Just like your father is trying to be."

"I'll try to be brave."

Mac mouthed *thank you* to Harper, wanting desperately to believe everything she'd just said. Wanting to believe that God was right here in the middle of this and would somehow redeem the situation no matter how bad things got.

Harper's phone vibrated in Mac's pocket, jerking her back to the urgency of their situation.

"Who is it?" Harper asked.

"A message from my boss," she said, reading through the message. "They're coordinating a team on their end and are heading here now."

"How long is that going to take?" Harper asked.

"I don't know."

She knew what Harper was thinking. With almost five hundred people on the ship, things couldn't keep running indefinitely. It wasn't going to be long before the ship's systems shut down completely. Toilets wouldn't flush, food and water were going to run out. . .

"What did you see out there?" Mac asked Harper.

"As much as I could. It looked like they've been able to round everyone up and herd them into the three lounges on deck six. Two wards are filled with patients that are staffed by some of the nurses."

"You're quite the spy. That would mean two or three armed guards in each section." Mac spoke her thoughts out loud. "Perhaps a couple doing rounds on the boat to make sure they didn't miss anyone. Do you know where they took Taiwo?"

"Rachel's setting up an isolation area for him and anyone else who displays symptoms."

Mac quickly sent a text to her boss, with the logistical update on the situation. The more information the team had, the easier it would be for them to infiltrate the ship and put an end to the standoff. Ethan was right about one thing. With so many civilians involved, putting an end to this without someone else getting hurt—or killed—wasn't going to be easy.

She dropped the phone into her pocket. "You said you found what I was looking for on your father's computer?"

"I just had time to briefly glance. It took a few tries to get into my father's account. There are emails between Dad and my brother."

Mac shoved aside the guilt of looking through the man's personal emails and scrolled through the messages. The conversation began with Harper's father asking Liam to look into Dema Diagnostics Research Group.

TO: Matthew DeMarcus
FROM: Liam DeMarcus
SUBJECT: Re: DEMA DIAGNOSTICS
Dad, is everything okay? Not sure why you're looking for this information, but here's what I found. Looks like the bio-tech group is involved in research connected to infectious diseases. Not sure what you're looking for, but I can dig deeper if you want. Just let me know.
Liam

The next message was dated yesterday.

TO: Matthew DeMarcus
FROM: Liam DeMarcus

SUBJECT: Re: DEMA DIAGNOSTICS
Dad, I've tried calling several times, but it always goes straight to voice mail. I don't know what's going on, but please call me as soon as you can. I found out some more info about this tech group you asked me to look up. It looks like Dema Diagnostics is involved in trials for an experimental antiviral that is currently being tested on chimpanzees in the UK and several African countries. I don't know how all this works, but the website says they're working to develop an antiviral that would treat all strains of Ebola.
Liam

"So my father was looking into a research company that was working with Ebola?" Harper sounded stunned.

"Sometimes our fathers don't tell us everything." Mac thought about all she didn't know of her own father's story as she scrolled through more messages to see if anything stood out to her, then stopped. "Look at this." She swiveled the computer. "Your father also was in touch with Sid Ramsey, the oil executive."

TO: Sid Ramsey
FROM: Matthew DeMarcus
SUBJECT: Toxic Waste Dumping

Sid,
I don't know if you remember meeting me, but I'm one of the doctors working on board the Liberty. I've recently discovered a number of patients who are experiencing illnesses I believe could be tied to caustic waste dumping from oil tankers. I've been reading about similar cases, but know that you would be far more knowledgeable than I am on the subject and might be able to help me discern what is going on. Is it possible we could meet?

Sincerely,
Dr. Matthew DeMarcus

TO: Matthew DeMarcus
FROM: Sid Ramsey
SUBJECT: RE: Toxic Waste Dumping

I'm actually scheduled to be on the Liberty on Tuesday. Would be happy to meet you then if you are free.

Mac worked through the timeline in her head. "Your dad and Sid met the day before the oil tanker was hijacked. Sid was one of the hostages on that tanker."

"There's one more where my father thanks Sid." Harper pointed out.

"That proves they met, but we still don't know what they talked about."

And then the doctor had gone missing.

"I need to try to call my brother." Harper held out her hand for the phone. "It's possible he found out something that isn't in the emails."

"It's possible."

Harper called her brother, then switched the phone to speaker, keeping the volume so low Mac had to crowd close.

Liam answered on the fourth ring. "Liam?"

"Harper. . .where are you?"

"I'm on the *Liberty*."

"How are you calling?"

"I'm here with Mac."

"Mac who?"

"Long story short, she was one of the security team members that just ended a hostage situation on a nearby oil tanker."

"I saw that in the news, but what about the *Liberty*? It's missing?"

"Pirates are on the ship. Mac managed to take down the jammer they'd installed." Harper blew out a sharp breath. "We read your emails to Dad. I need to know if you have any more information."

"There's an Ebola outbreak on US soil. Apparently one of the crew members who was on the ship brought the virus home."

"Are you sure it was Ebola?" Harper whispered.

"That's what the news is reporting. It's apparently a new strain of the virus. What about Dad? Is he on the boat?"

Harper just stared at the phone.

"Harper? Where's dad?"

"I don't know. I was hoping you'd heard from him. As far as I know, no one has seen him since Tuesday."

"Where are you, Liam?" Mac asked.

"I just arrived in Douala, actually. I flew all night to Cameroon. I've managed to talk my way onto the helicopter that's leaving soon with the negotiator."

"No, Liam. People have been shot. People are sick—"

"Don't worry about me, Harper. Just promise you'll stay safe."

Mac's mind raced as Harper finished the call and hung up. She needed to get Harper and Emma somewhere safe and then try to find the ship's security team. With her working on the inside, they just might be able to put an end to this without anyone getting hurt.

"Let's get you two somewhere safe."

Emma looked up at her with wide eyes. "You said you wouldn't leave me."

Was this the kind of conflict real mothers dealt with? Juggling heartfelt promises with immediate realities? "You won't be alone, Emma. I need to find the security team and see what I can do to free your daddy. Do you think you and Harper can take care of each other?"

"I think so."

"Good girl. I want you to go to Harper's cabin, lock the door, and don't leave for any reason. They should be done going through the decks, which means you'll be safe there until your daddy and I come for you."

"I have Fruit Loops and Pop Tarts, and a bunch of DVDs," Harper said.

Voices sounded from outside the stairwell, from the reception area.

Mac leapt to her feet. "We need to go." She grabbed Emma's hand. "Now!"

The metal door just below them swung open and slammed against the wall. Dabir stood in front of his brother, pointing his AK-47 at them.

"Don't move." Dabir's shout echoed in the stairwell. "What have you done?"

Mac started to pull Emma and Harper behind her, but Dabir shouted his order again to not move.

Her heart pounded as she caught the man's piercing gaze. "It's over, Dabir. You need to take your men and get off this ship. I've contacted my team. Without the jammer you can't hide. They're on their way here now."

"You're wrong. I'm still in control. I have hundreds of hostages, and I will start shooting them, one at a time, until my demands are met, starting with the three of you."

Mac shook her head, fighting to keep her voice steady. "I don't believe you. I don't believe you're the kind of person who could kill a child."

"You don't know me at all."

"I know you loved your wife," Mac continued. "That you love your son. I know you're angry that she's gone, but you know it isn't the fault of anyone on this ship. In fact, Rachel and Harper both risked their lives to save her, and Rachel is still trying to figure out the source of the disease so she can save your son and the others who are sick."

"She had no choice."

"Maybe not, but do you know what else I've noticed? You're not trigger happy. A couple of your men are, but not you. You're smart and calculated, but your motivations are different. You care about your family and the people in your villages."

Dabir grabbed Harper and pulled her toward him. "If you don't think I'll follow through with my threats, you're wrong."

"Hurting one of us isn't going to help your family. You've lost your wife, and your brother. Do you want to lose your son too?"

"Keep my son out of this." Dabir aimed his weapon at Mac's chest.

"This isn't an oil tanker. It's a ship filled with doctors and nurses who've donated their time and lives to bring medical help to your people."

"Help!" Dabir scoffed. "My people are hungry and dying and no one notices. I will not sit back any longer and watch everything I've ever known and loved be stripped away from me."

"I saw your village. I saw what was being dumped in the water and on the land, and it's not something I will forget. And I'm not the only one." Mac paused, trying desperately to find a way to connect with the man. "Josiah, Sid Ramsey, the captain...they've all seen what's happening, and they have the connections to help you do something about it. But this isn't the way. Hostile demands are not the answer."

"Then what do you suggest I do, because your promises don't mean anything to me."

Mac drew in a deep breath. "Help me find the truth. Help me find out who's behind the dumping, who's been poisoning your land, and hold them responsible."

"Even if the truth comes to light, the government will only look the other way."

"I promise I'll help you, but please, not this way. No one else needs to die, Dabir."

She studied his face, knowing that the realization that his options were quickly shrinking had to be sinking in. Her team was coming. He'd seen them in action. Lost men. He had to know there was no way he was going to win in the end.

Chomba started to say something, but Dabir motioned for him to be quiet.

He took a step backward, dragging a wide-eyed Harper with him. "If you're lying to me, you're going to learn firsthand what it's like to stand by helplessly and watch someone you care about die."

CHAPTER THIRTY-FOUR

SOMEWHERE IN THE GULF OF GUINEA

DABIR STEPPED BACK INTO THE LOUNGE WITH THE WOMEN, THEN ORDERED them to sit down against the wall. He told Chomba to watch them, then moved to the middle of the lounge that was filled with over a hundred people. Some sat at the rows of tables talking in small groups, while others sat on the floor and leaned against the walls. He knew they all felt the thick tension lingering in the air as his men patrolled the deck. They weren't the only ones. When he'd stepped onto this ship, his only thought had been to ensure his wife received the medical help she deserved. Now that Abeje was dead, he'd somehow been sucked into a situation that had completely escalated out of control.

But there was no time to grieve her loss. No time to think through what was going to happen if his son died, because time was running out. He'd planned to fight this battle on the *Liberty*, but he was beginning to question how he was going to be able to stay in control once the authorities arrived. The last thing he wanted was more bloodshed, but neither was he ready to simply walk away from the help his people needed.

He needed a plan. Mac had told him to find out the truth, but he still wasn't sure how to accomplish that. Sid Ramsey had offered to bring in a negotiator, but he knew he couldn't trust Sid any more than he could trust anyone else around him—no matter how noble their reasons for being here.

He reached for his arm where the bullet had skimmed his shoulder, forcing himself to ignore the steady throb. An idea had begun to form in his mind. Balik's attempts to hijack the oil tanker had failed, but his couldn't. Not with his son's life on the line and the lives of those in his village.

Ramsey was sitting at one of the tables. Calm. Proud. Twisting the thick gold band on his finger. The man had influence. Dabir had seen that on the oil tanker. Balik had mentioned that the tall white man was the president of the African division of a large American oil company and had the connections they needed to get their money. The kind of connections Dabir needed now.

Dabir tightened his hold on his AK-47 and strode across the room to where Ramsey sat. He signaled for him to follow him out into the empty reception area adjacent to the full lounge.

"You mentioned you could help me with a negotiator," Dabir said, jumping right to the point once they'd left the lounge.

A slow, pleased grin lifted the corner of the oil executive's mouth. "I have contact with someone who has helped my company in the past. He can get you what you want. And my company will pay top dollar for my release."

"You sound like you're offering to go as one of my hostages."

Ramsey didn't hesitate. "If you'll allow me to make the situation worthwhile for both of us."

"How?"

"I ensure you a negotiator willing to fight for you. And you give me twenty-five percent of the ransom money. Seventy-five percent of—say—ten million, will leave you with a heavy windfall."

Dabir's finger pressed against the side of the weapon, a reminder he was still in control. Was that the deal Balik had made with the man when they'd attacked the oil tanker? Or was Ramsey simply trying to take advantage of the situation? Either way, he would never believe the oil executive was totally on his side. He'd lost too many men, including his brother, on that tanker, and had no desire to see that happen again. And besides, what guarantee did he have that Sid would keep any deal they made?

"You've taken Balik's place," Ramsey said, interrupting Dabir's thoughts.

"You knew him?"

"I made him a wealthy man, and I can do the same for you."

"Your promises mean nothing. Balik's dead."

"None of that was my fault. I can, though, help you fix this. A few million in your pocket could change your world."

"This isn't just about money," Dabir said.

"In the end, everything's about money. Think of what you could do for your son. For your community...whatever you want. But you're running out of time. If the extraction team boards this ship you won't win. It will be over."

"Ransom money won't bring my wife back."

"No, but think what you can do for your son with that kind of money."

Dabir frowned. No matter how friendly the man standing in front of him seemed, whatever he was offering was no favor. Ramsey wouldn't think twice about betraying him.

"What kind of deals did you make with Balik?" Dabir asked.

"Let's just say that I helped him line his pockets, and he helped do the same for me."

"You were the one financing Balik."

"How do you think he knew where to find my ship?"

"I can only imagine what your bosses would think if they found out you were making money by ripping off insurance companies." Dabir hesitated before continuing. "What about the illegal waste dumping? It's a lucrative business, and I know Balik's boat was involved."

"Perhaps." A pleased smile lifted Ramsey's lips. "But just like you'll never be able to prove we had this conversation; you'll never be able to prove I knew anything about toxic waste. It will simply be your word against mine."

"Is that a threat?"

"I'm giving you a chance to get out of this rich and alive. You take a handful of hostages and leave on one of the skiffs. I'm going to assume you have a satellite phone you can use to negotiate."

Dabir glanced at the clock hanging on the wall, knowing he needed to make a decision. And Ramsey's suggestion had merit. He might not have control of the ship much longer, but he'd still have some control if he left the *Liberty* with hostages. "Fine. I'll do it your way and use the negotiator. But you won't be coming with me."

"Why not?"

"You'll work with the negotiator. I have a SAT phone, one I'm going to assume you paid for. Arrange for your negotiator to call me in an hour."

"And in the meantime?"

He motioned for Ramsey to head back to the lounge. "I'm leaving the ship with my men and hostages."

"And the twenty-five percent?"

"You keep your word." Dabir shouldered his gun. "I'll keep mine."

CHAPTER THIRTY-FIVE

SOMEWHERE IN THE GULF OF GUINEA

TWO OF THE PIRATES ESCORTED JOSIAH TO THE ROW OF OPERATING rooms where he'd been told Rachel had set up an isolation room for anyone showing signs of the disease. Dabir had ordered Josiah to help her save his son. All he could do was pray Mac got Emma hidden away. So far, Dabir didn't know he had a child on this ship. Hopefully, he never would.

Inside the scrub room adjacent to the five operating rooms, Josiah tapped on the glass of the room where Rachel stood over Taiwo's bed. Two other patients filled two more beds.

A moment later, Rachel stepped out of the room, still wearing her protection garb. "What happened?"

Josiah cast a sidelong glance at the man holding an AK-47 and a pretty big grudge for the blow Josiah had managed to land in the guy's belly. "I was escorted here so I wouldn't cause any more trouble."

Rachel's frowned deepened. "What did you do?"

"I got in a bit of a brawl with Dabir, but I'm fine. I was sent here to help."

"We've got to close that gash first." His sister quickly changed her gloves and ushered him toward the scrub sink. "What were you thinking?" She mopped blood from his forehead. "You could have been killed."

"I was thinking that if any of these jokers hurt my little girl, I'll kill them," he admitted.

"Do you know where Emma is?"

"Shhhh." Josiah glanced at their guards who had stopped in the doorway, apparently not eager to get any closer to a potentially deadly disease. "I saw her in the lounge. Mac went after her, but I don't know if Dabir saw Emma."

"Mac will take care of her." She pulled the edges of his wound together. "This is going to leave a scar."

"That's the least of my worries."

His sister applied a couple of sticky strips, then whispered, "I have three patients with varying symptoms. Dabir's son tested positive for malaria, but negative for Ebola. Although I can't be certain we're not looking at another false negative, his symptoms line up with malaria, and the prophylactic seems to be working."

"Let's pray to God the tests are right this time."

Rachel's brows raised in surprise. "When did you start talking to the man upstairs?"

"You don't have to be in tight with God to dislike seeing kids die." Josiah hated the hurt he saw flash in his sister's eyes. "Sorry, Ray."

"I'm not giving up on you, and God won't either." She leaned in close and Josiah was reminded once again that his little sister was always on his side. And that if he was honest with himself, so was God.

"I've started Taiwo on a quinine drip and his fever is dropping," she said. "If all we're looking at is malaria, it will continue to drop. I need to move him to his own isolation spot so that he doesn't get Ebola, but he will also need repeated Ebola testing until he's completely in the clear."

"Let's keep that to ourselves for now." Josiah nodded toward their guards. "Does that guard look sick to you?"

"Sweating. Clutching his belly. Swaying like he can barely lift that rifle," Rachel observed.

Josiah turned back to the sink. Hot water and soap sluiced his own blood from his hands. He dried them, then snapped on fresh gloves. Then he put on a gown, mask, and clean goggles. With palms raised he walked over to the guy who'd brought him to the clinic.

"You look as bad as my head feels." The guy scowled at him but said nothing. "Do you have a headache, sore throat, feel feverish?"

"It is hot in here," the sweating man said.

"You're sick." Josiah lifted the thermometer gun from its charging station. "Let me take your temperature."

The pirate shook his head. "Stand back." He tried to raise his rifle but it clattered to the floor. The other pirate bent to snatch it up. By the time he raised to his feet, his sick friend was slumped against him.

Josiah called for Rachel and she immediately came to his aid. They'd just finished starting an IV on the sick pirate when Dabir stormed into the room holding Mac by the arm. Mac had Emma by the hand.

"Get them out of here!" Josiah shouted.

"Daddy!" His daughter started for him, but Mac held her back.

"Don't, Emma!" Josiah shouted. He saw her face crumple and then Mac pulled a sobbing Emma closer to her. Josiah felt Rachel's grip on his arm.

A sly smile formed on Dabir's lips. "You have a daughter?" he asked Josiah.

All sorts of lies zipped through Josiah's mind. None of them were convincing. "Yes," he said. "You hurt her and I'll kill you."

Dabir's glower dared Josiah to try anything. "I'm leaving the ship and my son is going with me."

"Your son is sick," Rachel said. "Taking him off this ship is a death sentence."

"I'm out of options, which means it's a chance I have to take. I can't leave him here, and it won't be long until the authorities show up. And I'll be taking your daughter, Doctor."

"No, please. No." Josiah begged. "Take me."

Dabir smiled. "Our weaknesses never serve us well, Doctor." He tried to tug Emma away from Mac, but she started crying and Mac wouldn't let go. "Very well, I shall take you both," he told Mac. "I've seen how the doctor looks at you. He will not try anything that will get the woman he loves killed."

"No." Josiah strained against Rachel's tightening grip on his arm. "Take me."

"Josiah," she warned.

"Please. Don't take them." Panic mushroomed as Josiah's gaze locked with Mac's. He tried to communicate with his eyes what she'd come to mean to him, but if she'd understood she kept her face neutral. He could only hope that, for Emma's sake, she was purposefully not letting his feelings tie his decisions to her. He didn't believe it possible to admire her even more, but he'd been wrong. About so many things.

Josiah turned to Dabir. "You have options. You don't have to do this. Stay on board. We'll treat your son. Make sure you get help in your village."

Dabir motioned for one of his men to get Taiwo. "It's too late for that."

"What about your man?" Rachel asked, pointing to the pirate receiving IV fluids. "He's sick as well. Much sicker than Taiwo."

Dabir hesitated. "I have to leave him. And if the Doctor wants to see his little girl again, he'll make sure Wilson lives."

Mac tried to pull away from Dabir's grip. "You're making a mistake. Take me. Take the captain, but don't take Emma."

Dabir lifted Josiah's chin with the barrel of his gun. "Don't test me or try to follow me. I'll leave a guard outside your door." Dabir let his gaze slide to Emma and Mac. "I'm prepared to follow through...whatever the cost."

CHAPTER THIRTY-SIX

SOMEWHERE ABOVE THE GULF OF GUINEA

THE RHYTHMIC SOUND OF MI-17 PROPELLER BLADES THUDDED ABOVE LIAM as the helicopter sped toward the *Liberty*. From the short briefing they'd received before leaving Douala, he'd learned that the pirates had left the ship with hostages once the jammer had been disabled. But that wasn't all he knew. The limited correspondence he'd had with his father concerning *Dema Diagnostics's* meddling with Ebola made him anxious about what they were going to find aboard the *Liberty*.

Liam stared out the window, but his white-capped waves of worry refused to calm. Both his father and sister had been pulled into the epicenter of a deadly situation. And while he might have managed to convince the team heading out to sea with him that this was a story that needed to be told through the eyes of a journalist, to him this was far more personal than today's headline.

A moment later, the helo shifted directions and a ship with a large blue cross on the side came into view.

The guy sitting next to him dressed in a US Army uniform nudged Liam's shoulder. "These waters are swarming with militia, armed gangs, and pirates.

It's hard to believe someone would be crazy enough to risk the lives of civilians, even for a good cause."

Liam swallowed hard. "My father and sister work on that ship."

The guy's eyes widened. "You have family on the *Liberty*?"

Liam nodded. He turned back to the window and stared out across the water. Before leaving Douala, he'd scoured the news for reports on the internet, looking for anything that might give him an update on the Ebola outbreak. From what he'd read, the CDC had already deployed a field team to Douala, enhanced screening at airports across West and Central Africa, and had issued a level three travel warning. In the US, there had already been several confirmed cases. The reports had also been quick to claim they'd caught the outbreak early, but there were indications that the virus was a far more aggressive hemorrhagic fever than the 2014 Ebola strain that had killed thousands. Here on the African continent, there were already confirmed cases in Nigeria, Equatorial Guinea, and Central African Republic. The virus was clearly spreading.

The helicopter circled in above the top deck of the ship, then hovered a few seconds above the platform before landing. Liam grabbed his backpack and followed the security team and hostage negotiator. Two uniformed Gurkhas greeted them, shouting instructions above the noise of the spinning helicopter blades. Liam followed them down a narrow staircase and into a darkened deck that felt familiar and eerily quiet. Too quiet. Tension fueled his adrenaline as their boots echoed in the corridor. They passed a large lounge where dozens of people sat at tables and chatted in small groups, ready and waiting, he was sure, to get off this ship. He had reported in conflict zones across Africa and the Middle East and he'd seen the faces of people who'd had enough. He scanned the room. Once he knew Harper was safe, he would go in search of their father.

Their group stopped at the ship's reception area where several of the *Liberty's* crew waited to greet them.

Someone from the ship's security team started the initial introductions. "This is Samuel Methu—"

"Samuel!" Liam dropped his pack and threw his arms around the chief medical officer he'd known from his time with his father on the *Liberty*. "It's good to see you, man."

"Look at you." Samuel held Liam out at arm's length. "All grown up."

"What's going on here, Samuel?"

Samuel's face sobered. "Let them bring you up to speed."

Liam had an uneasy feeling, but he listened as the man on the security team went on to introduce Ricardo Nunes, the second officer who was new to Liam, and Sid Ramsey, who'd arranged for the negotiator, Jackson Meade.

The lieutenant Liam had met before boarding the helo finished shaking everyone's hands. "We're a part of the Army medical readiness training exercise team already in country. Brandon Knight's leading up the security extraction team that was already on board, and obviously, some of you know Liam DeMarcus. He's officially here as a journalist, but he also has family on board."

Samuel caught Liam's gaze. "I'm sorry to tell you, Liam, but your sister is one of the hostages."

This news was an unexpected gut punch. "Harper's not on the ship?" Liam took a step back, trying to take in the information he'd just been given. He'd worked in a dozen war zones as a correspondent, but had always been able to keep his feelings about a situation at an arm's length. He should have known the impossibility of separating family and emotions. He'd accepted the reality his father and Harper had been exposed to the virus, but he'd never considered the possibility Harper would be taken as a hostage.

"Why would they take a med student?" He blew out a huff of anger. "Dad is not going to be happy about this when we find him."

The chief medical officer placed a hand on Liam's shoulder. "You know Dr. DeMarcus is not here?"

"Harper was able to call me after she and some woman figured out how to disable the jammer. She said Dad left the *Liberty* four days ago. But he never reported to his post-op shift."

Four days ago. That was the last time Liam had heard from his father. The room spun. Voices echoed around him as the nightmare he'd been thrust into seemed to escalate. He pushed back the panic. His sister and father were going to be okay. They had to be.

"That's true," Samuel said.

"Why didn't you check on him?" Liam heard his own voice cutting through the noise in his head.

"Everything spiraled out of control so quickly," Ricardo explained. "The pirates boarded the ship and immediately forced us out to sea."

"I'm sorry we don't know more, son," Samuel said.

Liam raised his palms. "I'm not your son." He rubbed the back of his neck. He shouldn't have talked to his old friend that way. "I'm sorry, Samuel. If my father was okay, he would have responded to my calls and emails, wouldn't he?"

"If he could, yes," Samuel agreed.

Liam tried to work through the limited information he had. "There has to be a connection between my father going missing and this situation. The last time I heard from him, he was looking into some research group dealing with infectious diseases. And then the next thing I know, some kind of hemorrhagic virus is spreading from the *Liberty*." Liam raked his hand through his hair. "Where could he be?"

"I'm sorry," Samuel said. "But we have no answer for you."

"Maybe my sister knows something and that's why they took her." Liam did not work to hold back the frustration in his voice. "What's the plan to get the hostages back?" he asked Ricardo.

"We're getting the ship ready to head back to port," the second officer said.

"Has the virus been contained?" Knight asked.

"It'll take twenty-one days of no new cases before we can assume the virus has been contained," Samuel said. "Protocols have been put into place, and thankfully we were able to spend the last couple hours evaluating the passengers. We have six in isolation, but no one else has exhibited any symptoms."

"And the hostages?" Liam asked, his anxiety growing. "We're going after the hostages, right?"

"Once we establish a connection between our negotiator and the pirates," Knight said, "we should be able to trace the phone they're using, and put an end to this."

Should be able to.

Liam tried to grab onto the man's optimism, but he'd read about the pirate attack that had taken place last week. Several hostages had been killed, including one of the members of the private security extraction team involved. And while he was certain they were qualified for the task at hand, with his sister's life on the line—and possibly his father's—he wasn't sure what the alternative was, but neither was he convinced their plan was going to be enough.

CHAPTER THIRTY-SEVEN

SOMEWHERE IN THE GULF OF GUINEA

WHEN SHE'D TRIED TALKING DABIR OFF THE LEDGE, BEING FORCED OFF the *Liberty* wasn't the result she'd expected. Mac sat on a small boat skimming farther and farther away from the possibility she would ever see Josiah again.

Saltwater sprayed across the deck, then quickly dried beneath the heat of the sun that seemed to burn away every plan she'd considered since this whole mess began. There was no way she could win this now. Not with eleven armed men pressed in around her and Emma and Taiwo on board. Keeping these children alive had to be her focus now. Desperation was a wild card. She had to be ready when her captors forced her to play her hand.

Dabir stood at the helm with one of his men, a satellite phone to his ear. He was animated and shouting at someone on the other end. By now, her team should have arrived on the *Liberty*, including the negotiator. From Dabir's angry expression, she assumed he wasn't pleased with the negotiator's offer. The negotiator didn't know any of the man's motivation like she did. But even if she could capitalize on her limited understanding, she and Dabir came from two different worlds. He didn't trust her any more than she trusted him.

Emma pressed into Mac's side, as if she were attempting to get as far away from the armed men as possible.

This isn't the place for a little girl, God. How could You allow this to happen?

A spark of anger lit inside her, fueled by the pent-up grief over Mo's death, then quickly followed by stark feelings of emptiness. Why was it always easier to blame God when things went wrong?

Have a little faith, Mac. No matter what happens.

She shoved Mo's last words further into the recesses of her mind. The tiny bit of faith she'd tried to dig up hadn't been enough to save him.

"I miss my daddy."

Emma's words pulled Mac back to the present. "I know he's missing you."

"Do you think my daddy's okay?"

Before Dabir dragged her away, she'd tried to communicate to Josiah through her eyes that she'd do her best to protect his daughter. But if she'd learned anything about this man, she knew without a doubt that he would move heaven and earth to come for Emma, and she couldn't help but hope that same man was coming for her. "He's safe now," Mac whispered. "And he and my friends are going to make sure we're safe too."

"Are they going to have to fight these men?" Emma whispered back.

Mac struggled to find a response. Six-year-olds shouldn't have to know how dark the world could be.

"I hope not."

Harper, whom Dabir had grabbed at the last minute to take care of Taiwo, maneuvered her way past them with a bucket of water.

"How's your patient doing?" Mac asked the tired med student.

Harper grabbed the metal rail in order to keep her balance. "Much better, actually."

"He doesn't have the same symptoms as the others."

"Can you two keep a secret?"

Mac and Emma nodded.

Harper glanced toward the helm. "Rachel said Taiwo tested positive for malaria. She said if he had the virus, he'd already be showing symptoms."

"So you're treating him for malaria?"

Harper nodded. "Yes, and it's working."

"Taiwo looks sad." Emma pulled away from Mac a few inches. "Can I talk to him?"

Mac took the little girl's hand. "Not now, sweetie."

"Maybe I can make him feel better."

"Even if it is Ebola, without symptoms, he isn't contagious," Harper said.

Mac let her eyes settle on Emma for a few seconds. She felt responsible to ensure her safety. "I'm not going to use children as a bridge in this negotiation."

"Please?" Emma begged. "He doesn't have a mama."

Mac felt her resolve soften. Emma knew exactly what that felt like. "Remember, you can't tell Taiwo he has malaria."

Emma nodded. "Promise."

Mac let Emma go, but her muscles remained taut, ready to spring into action if one of the pirates even looked at Emma wrong as the little girl moved to the back of the boat with Harper.

Emma crouched beside Taiwo and started talking to him. He smiled and started talking to her. There were no walls between them. No animosity. No mistrust or suspicion. Only acceptance.

"Mind if I sit here?"

Mac looked up as her father sat down next to her, taking the empty spot where Emma had been sitting. "Do I have a choice?"

"How are you doing?" he asked.

"Fine."

"I'm not sure I believe that. Not after everything that's happened."

She wanted to argue with him, but he was right. She was far from fine. She was the one who was supposed to fix situations like this. Instead she was stuck in the middle of a no-win scenario.

"I know what you're thinking," he said.

"How could you possibly know anything about me?"

"Because we're a lot alike."

Mac cut a glare his way. "We're nothing alike."

"You want to take responsibility for what's happened, but this isn't your fault."

"Don't lecture me about taking responsibility."

Her response had nicked him, but she could see he wasn't going to give up. "My mother always told me not to ask *what if*. Especially when you can't change anything."

She frowned at the irony of the statement. There were too many things she couldn't change about the past, let alone the last couple of days. Mo was dead. A deadly virus was running rampant. She was on a small boat with someone else's child and a dozen armed pirates who no longer had anything left to lose.

"You're wrong." She leaned forward and clasped her hands into one fist. "I should be able to fix this. It's my job to fix situations like this."

"Sometimes all you can do is pray."

"You really think God is listening?" Mac pressed her lips together to keep from telling him all the ways God hadn't come through.

"The girl I knew would have believed He was listening."

She looked him in the eye. "I'm not that naïve girl anymore."

Silence hung between them for the next few seconds, blotted out only by the sound of the waves slapping against the boat and the murmuring of the men around them.

"Can I ask you a question?" she said finally.

"Anything you want to know."

After all these years, did she really want to know why he'd disappeared from her life? With everything that was going on around them, devising a way for Dabir to save face and Emma to safely return to Josiah should be her focus.

But she might not get another chance to ask the burning question that had simmered in the back of her mind for as long as she could remember.

She blew out a short breath. "Why did you leave us?"

His eyes filled with tears, but he began to share as if he'd been waiting for this day and now that it had come it was a relief. "I wish I had an easy answer. It wasn't something that happened overnight. It was a steady veering off course, until one day I woke up and was too lost to find my way back. I didn't even recognize who I was anymore."

"You could have turned around. Come back home."

But he never had.

"There are things you don't know, Mac. Things that took me a lifetime to see. It would be easy for me to tell you I've changed, but there's no reason for you to believe that. I've spent the past decade regretting so many things. Like you, I can't fix everything, no matter how desperately I've tried."

"What have you tried to fix?"

"Us."

A memory surfaced as she stared past him. She'd been Emma's age. Her father had come home with a puppy for her birthday, and he and her mom had laughed together, glad to see Mac so happy. In that moment, everything had been perfect.

Perfect until everything had come crashing down. He'd walked out, leaving her and her mom alone. That act had broken her mother, and Mac would never be able to forgive him for that.

"I was caught up in a career and the prestige I wanted. I was traveling too much. Drinking too much. I couldn't see what I had in front of me."

"What changed?"

"One morning, I woke up in a ditch outside of town with my car wrapped around a tree. I realized at that moment I should have been dead. Or even worse, I could have killed someone else. Everything changed after that. I started going to AA. Went back to church. I quickly realized how lucky I was to not only be alive, but to also still have my career. But by then I'd lost everything that really mattered. Your mother. You."

"Is that the reason you work on the *Liberty* now? Is it some kind of...I don't know...atonement?"

She knew her words were laced with the judgment he thought he deserved.

"At first. But I've come to love doing some good in the world."

Mac studied her father's face. Lines were etched into his forehead and his fiery red hair had turned white. But the toll of the years was softened by a peace that had never been there before. Whatever he'd done to find his redemption, it was too little too late to redeem their relationship. So why did she feel a thawing of her heart?

"How do I get Dabir to call this off?" she asked this changed man sitting next to her. "Every approach I've made to appeal to him has failed."

"Find the common denominator between you."

"We don't exactly have much in common."

"Then maybe you need a common enemy to unite you."

She leaned forward. "Like what?"

"I don't know, but if anyone can figure it out, I have a feeling you can."

A commotion drew her gaze toward the front of the boat. A second later, one of the men was marching across the deck toward her. He grabbed her arm and started dragging her to the front of the boat.

"Hey!" Her father started after them.

"It's okay." She motioned for her father to stay back. Something told her Dabir wasn't going to hurt anyone in front of his son. "Dabir, what's going on?"

Dabir held up the phone, and put the call on speaker. "You're my proof of life. Tell him your name."

"This is Mackenzie Scott. Who is this?"

"My name is Jackson Meade. I'm a negotiator. I need to know if everyone is okay."

Mac glanced behind her. "We're all fine for the moment, but—"

"That's enough." Dabir pulled the phone away from her. "You got what you wanted. You have twelve hours to give me what I want."

Dabir hung up the phone, then shouted out another order. The boat shifted course and headed toward the shoreline.

"My son," Dabir said, avoiding her gaze. "He doesn't have the sickness, does he?"

She weighed what to tell him. A lie would keep him scared, but the truth could help him trust her. "We know he has malaria, but he'll need monitoring to make sure he doesn't have the virus that killed your wife." She took a step forward. "Give your son a shot at a good ending to this story, Dabir. Let us go."

His dark eyes bore through her. "This ends with me finding the truth."

"How? By going in circles? Because that's all we're doing out here. Literally. Your brother's dead. Your wife is dead. How many more people are going to die before this is over? I don't think that's what you really want. You can stop this before anyone else gets hurt."

Dabir fisted his hands at his sides. "This has never been about what I want. It's always been about my wife. My son. My village."

"How is putting your son at risk going to help your village? My team will find this boat. You can't win."

Dabir's fingers grasped the metal rail next to him as the boat skimmed across the water. "Balik knew something."

"Who's Balik?"

"He was killed on the oil tanker, but he was making money on the side. If I find his boat, maybe I can figure out who he was working with and who paid him."

"Paying him to dump the waste near your village?"

"That and other things. But enough with all the questions." He aimed the weapon at her. "Don't think I won't pull the trigger. You think I can't win, but if my demands aren't met in the twelve hours, you'll be the first."

"Do you want Taiwo to see you kill a woman?"

At the mention of Taiwo's name, Mac saw a flicker of struggle in Dabir's eyes. "I don't have a choice."

"There's always a choice."

"For you, maybe," Dabir said. "But my son does not have enough to eat. Or clean water to drink. Violence is the only way to make a life for my boy."

The wind whipped against her face. She had no answers, but one thing was clear. Her father had been right. She and Dabir agreed on the rights of everyone to have access to decent food and water. Now all she had to do was help him fight whoever had denied his people these basic rights.

Five minutes later, Dabir maneuvered them into a small cove along the shoreline then pulled next to another boat and anchored the two together with a rope.

"We're here. This is Balik's boat." He signaled to her to follow him. "You and your father are coming with me."

Mac stepped into the deserted boat ahead of Dabir and her father. She had no idea what Dabir thought he was going to find aboard this rusty fishing boat. Traces of toxic material? Pharmaceutical waste? She'd already captured the proof of this atrocity in the test tubes that were safely back in Rachel's lab. This was an exercise in futility. She walked toward the bow, past piles of nets and crates, a couple of faded life jackets, and several barrels similar to the ones they'd seen near Dabir's village.

"Mac!"

She turned around and headed back to where her father stood, the color draining from his face as Dabir pulled back a sheet of plastic. The face of a dead man stared up at them.

Mac lifted the man's ID badge and felt a wave of nausea wash through her. "We just found our missing doctor."

CHAPTER THIRTY-EIGHT

SOMEWHERE IN THE GULF OF GUINEA

Josiah paced the makeshift isolation room. He didn't care about Dabir's threats. He would get his daughter back. But he needed a weapon. He spotted a metal IV pole and yanked it from the stand.

He turned to Rachel who was handling her stress by bleaching the room for the second time. "I'm going after Emma."

Rachel lifted her eyes from the counter. "What about the guy with the AK-47 guarding our door?"

Josiah ripped the fluid bag and tubing from the metal pole. "He's going to have a headache after I get through with him."

"Getting yourself killed is not going to help Emma."

Josiah felt the rumble of the floor beneath his feet. "What's going on?"

Rachel took a step back. "The ship's engines have started. We're moving."

Josiah fisted the IV pole. "This ends now." He started for the door.

"I'm coming with you."

"No."

"Not your call, big brother." She ripped off her gloves. Grabbed a fresh pair and stuck them in her scrub pocket. "I can create a diversion and maybe you can get out without having to kill anyone."

Josiah raised the pole and poised himself to swing. Rachel slowly opened the door, then stuck her head out.

"He lied." She stepped into the hall. "There's no one out here."

"That sorry—"

The intercom crackled to life. Josiah and Rachel froze.

"This is Chief Medical Officer, Samuel Methu. The pirates have left the ship, and a security team and negotiator have just arrived. The *Liberty* is now secure. Medical staff is free to return to your posts. Non-medical staff needs to return to their quarters immediately and will be given further instructions as we put a quarantine into place. Our infectious disease protocol is still in place. Gowns and masks are required for all medical staff. Vigilant hand-washing is a must. If you begin to experience flu-like symptoms, you must report immediately to the hospital ward." He paused. "Our captain asked me to convey his continued pride in the admirable behavior of every crew member." The medical officer cleared his throat. "Our captain also asked for our prayers for the three who have been taken hostage with him."

Emma.

Josiah pushed past his sister, his heart about to explode. "I'm going after my daughter if I have to take this ship hostage myself!"

Rachel scrambled after him as he shot out of the OR. "The bridge is this way."

He wheeled and followed her up several flights of stairs. By the time he and Rachel reached the bridge, she'd called in someone to check their patients and he was winded and angrier than he'd ever been in his life. Through the glass door, he could see several people gathered around the control panel. He yanked the metal handle. The door was locked. At his jiggling of the door, all heads swiveled in his direction.

He pounded the glass. "I need to speak to someone!"

The second officer, Ricardo, spoke to a brawny man with a buzz cut and decked out in the same heavy, black tactical gear Mac had been wearing when they first met. The night he'd failed to save her teammate. He would not fail her this time.

Josiah pounded again. "Let me in!"

The brawny guy gave an assenting jerk of his head and one of his subordinates came to the door. "What's the emergency?" he mouthed through the glass.

"The pirates have my daughter!" Josiah shouted.

The subordinate relayed something to his commander. The man looked at Josiah and Rachel standing on the other side of the glass, then gave a reluctant nod of the head.

Josiah burst onto the bridge the minute the door opened. "Where are we heading?"

"Back to port in Douala."

"My daughter is out there."

"We know." Second Officer Ricardo stepped in front of him. "We've already got a security extraction team on board as well as a medical readiness training team with the US Army led by Sergeant Hill. Their helicopter delivered them twenty minutes ago. We've also brought in Jackson Meade, a negotiator."

Josiah let his eyes dart around the room, wondering how it had come to this. A dozen men armed and dressed like they were ready for war. He recognized Mac's team in their tactical gear. The US soldiers all dressed in fatigues. A man he didn't recognize sat in front of an open laptop with a phone the size of a brick to his ear. The negotiator. Between the *Liberty's* second officer and chief medical officer stood a young guy, about Rachel's age, wearing jeans and a T-shirt. He looked like he'd seen chaos before, and it didn't faze him. And finally, sitting in the captain's chair, was Sid Ramsey. The oil executive who'd helped Josiah clean up vomit and diarrhea in the village.

"I'm the father of the little girl who's on the boat with the pirates," Josiah managed. "And so help me if—"

Rachel cut off his tirade. "We're doctors, and we believe we have significant evidence that some of the men who escaped this ship could be carrying a deadly virus. They must be stopped immediately and put into mandatory quarantine."

The brawny man stepped forward. "Brandon Knight. There are four hundred plus people aboard this ship. Our priority is to get this ship to port and let the World Health Organization decide how to keep everyone from getting sick." He nodded toward the man on the phone. "Our negotiator is first rate at his job. He's working to track the pirates via their SAT phone, and will do his best to meet their demands and put an end to this as quickly as possible."

"You don't understand! They're too desperate to negotiate." Josiah fished in his pocket, pulled out the watch that Mac had found in Dabir's shower and held it up. "They kill whoever gets in their way."

"Wait a minute." The guy in the T-shirt lunged for the watch. "Where did you get this?"

Josiah released the watch at the panicked look on the guy's face. "Why?"

"I'm Liam DeMarcus." He ran his finger over the inscription on the watch. "M.D. stands for Matthew DeMarcus." He stared Josiah right in the eye. "I know, because I told the jeweler what to inscribe. He's my father."

"Look, Liam," Josiah said. "I'm sorry, I don't know that your dad's dead, I just said that because I'm desperate to get my child, and—"

Liam held up the watch. "Tell me where you got this!"

"In one of the pirate's—Dabir's—village."

"I need to find my father," Liam demanded.

"I'm afraid that's not possible, son," Knight said. "Trust us. Once Jackson gets a lock on their location, my team and I will take to the air and hunt them down. We won't do anything that would put the hostages at risk."

"If they're heading to Dabir's village, the jungle is so dense they could easily hide out of sight," Josiah argued. "I've been there. Let me go with you."

"Not up for negotiation. We're following procedure on this one." Knight took a bold step forward. "Doctor, you need to let the professionals handle your daughter's extraction. You and your medical team are all going back to port, where I'm sure your expertise will be needed. My team will take care of the hostages. I give you my word."

Josiah's fists balled at his sides, but the memory of Mac's friend bleeding out on his table refused to be so easily set aside. "Your word isn't a bulletproof vest for my daughter."

"He's right, Joey." Rachel put her hand on his arm. "The best thing we can do for Emma and the others right now is to find a way to stop this virus."

"That's not going to get Emma back."

"Wait a minute." The negotiator, Jackson Meade, turned from the laptop and swiveled his chair toward Josiah. "If you went to the pirate's village, then you've spent some time with Dabir, right?"

"Yes." Josiah's mind replayed the night he and Dabir dug his nephew's grave. "Why?"

"Does Dabir have a weakness, something we can use as leverage?"

"Family," Josiah said without hesitation. "His brother and his son. His village. People are dying there, and he wants answers."

Knight took a step forward. "And you know where his village is located?"

"It's a couple hours up the coast from the capital."

Jackson Meade stood up and crossed the bridge, stopping in front of Josiah. "Do you think he'll go there?"

"It's possible, because it's remote and fairly isolated, but I don't think so."

"Why not?"

"The last time I saw him, he said he needed to find out the truth."

"The truth about what?" Meade asked.

"The truth about what was killing his village. What killed his wife." Josiah studied the negotiator's face for a moment, then turned to Knight. "If you can track him, I want to go with your team."

"Joey—"

"I need to go." Josiah ignored his sister's warning. "And I can help."

Knight shook his head. "You're a civilian."

"A civilian who's been to Dabir's village. I've spent time with the man."

Knight's hands dropped to his sides. "So from what I'm hearing, even though you don't have the experience of a negotiator, you want me to stake everything on your rapport with Dabir."

"Exactly," Josiah said. "If we don't move quickly it could take days, maybe even weeks, to get them back. And with a virus on the loose out there, you could be looking at hundreds more dead."

"Then I'll need to go as well," Rachel said.

Josiah glanced at his sister. "Rachel, no—"

"Why not? You said it yourself. There's a virus on the loose, and we know that at least one of Dabir's men is showing symptoms. We can't let this go unchecked."

"They have a point," Liam said. "There are already confirmed cases in the US. And I'm sure everyone here knows about the Ebola epidemic in West Africa in 2014. It's not going to take much for this to spread like wildfire."

"It's in the States?" Josiah asked.

"According to the latest reports, yes," Liam said.

"You think you can do better than our negotiator?" Ramsey asked from his perch in the captain's seat.

"I know Dabir's scared, and out of options," Josiah said. "I was there when he buried his nephew, his wife is dead, and now he's worried about having to bury his son as well. Believe it or not, I don't think he wants anyone else to die."

"That's quite an assumption about a man who's left a trail of bodies behind him. We've both seen that," Knight said.

"Yes, but Dabir isn't in this just for the money. I think I can use the leverage of the virus and his people to work out a deal."

"That would be a huge gamble," Knight countered.

"One that might be worth taking, the more I think about it," Ramsey said.

Sergeant Hill rubbed the back of his neck. "We're not talking about heading out to an afternoon tea. These are armed pirates with hostages—"

"I think these doctors are right. You've got a roomful of military expertise in this room, but you're going to need medical support if you encounter the virus."

"Then I'm coming as well," Liam said. "Former Staff Sergeant DeMarcus. US Army. I spent five years as a civil affairs specialist. My sister's out there. And if there's any chance my dad is still alive, I'm going to find him."

"Don't discount the fact that the four of us have scores to settle with these brigands," Ramsey said. "I just spent almost two weeks on a hijacked oil tanker."

"I'm guessing you want added to be added the list," Knight said. "But I'm not sending someone out there bent on revenge."

Ramsey stood. "This isn't just about revenge. We're talking about putting an end to this. I was the one who spoke with Dabir about bringing in a negotiator, but maybe that was the wrong approach. I know Jackson Meade personally, and he's the best at what he does, but he's not dealt with the man on a personal level. Some of us have, which gives us an advantage. On top of that, I've spent my life negotiating in the boardroom. Like Josiah, I'd like to think I've built some trust with the man. We might be able to tip the balance in this situation."

Josiah caught Knight's frown, but the man didn't argue.

"While I normally wouldn't agree, we aren't exactly dealing with an everyday situation," Sergeant Hill said. "Working out of the box might be our only way to stop this."

"There's a fifteen-seat dinghy tethered with the lifeboats you can use," Ricardo said.

Knight turned to one of his men. "Get the team ready. We leave in ten minutes."

Nine minutes later, the winch had lowered the dinghy and the team into the water. Josiah glanced up at the *Liberty* as they sped away, hoping that their plan to end this with Dabir was rational and not pure foolishness.

CHAPTER THIRTY-NINE

BETHESDA, MARYLAND

The blare of a pressurization alarm sounded in Clayborn's isolation room. Since he'd tested positive for Ebola yesterday, the medical team had been coming in and out so fast that the room's negative-pressure balance had struggled to remain uncompromised. Everyone but him would have to evacuate until the pressure had stabilized. On the staff's hurried way out, they mumbled apologies to Clayborn for having to leave him, but they'd promised to get him more comfortable the minute the pressure was restored.

Lying flat on his back, Clayborn tugged at the thin paper sheet. He was shivering despite the continued rise of his body temperature — 104.6 last he'd heard. He stared at the air exhaust grill located in the ceiling and tried to calm himself by counting the little squares in the grid. But his pounding head and roiling stomach refused to be ignored. He turned on his side where he could see his mother lying unresponsive in her bed. Watching her suffer had given him the disadvantage of knowing how this illness progressed, and he was terrified. He knew he should ask to call his wife, but Jasmine would hear the fear in his voice the moment he said hello.

An inward whoosh of air fluttered Clayborn's sheet as the door between the anteroom and his isolation room opened and closed.

"Dr. Tanner." The face of the nurse with the kind voice was completely obscured by her protective suit. But he could see her big brown eyes behind the clear plastic shield, and they were terrified. "You have a call from a Dr. Maxwell. Do you feel like talking to her?"

When the doctor had given him the bad news that he had Ebola, Clayborn hadn't shed a tear. But the prospect of being told his family might be ill caused hot tears to seep from his eyes.

"Of course." He nodded and the nurse handed him a cellphone wrapped in protective plastic. "Liz?" He sniffed. "Is it Jasmine?"

"Calm down, Clayborn. Jasmine and the kids are fine," Liz said. "It's you I'm worried about."

"The test finally came back positive."

"So I gathered."

"They called you?"

"No. Jasmine got a call and a detailed email," Liz said. "Tell me you're not letting them give you an experimental drug."

"How did you find out about that?"

"Someone had to sign the consent. After Jasmine read the consent form they were asking her to sign, she asked me what I thought it meant."

"What did you say?"

"That they'd sent it to her because they weren't sure you were of sound mind." Liz didn't give him time to respond. "And I have to tell you, Clayborn, you know I'm all for the advancement of medicine, but this is crazy."

"ZMapp was experimental when Brantly and Writebol took it. And they both recovered."

"A Spanish priest took it, and he died."

"*Dema Diagnostics* believes this new antiviral is a promising treatment for those already infected."

"And I've got oceanfront property in Arizona for you too."

"Liz." He swallowed the urge to vomit. "Mom may not make it."

A few seconds of silence passed. "Maybe the FDA will save you from yourself and shut this fool request down before it's too late."

"Eight vials are being express shipped from the California lab as we speak."

"Who pulled those strings?"

"I won't say."

"Don't do it, Clayborn."

"Mom and I don't have a choice."

CHAPTER FORTY

SOMEWHERE IN THE GULF OF GUINEA

MAC SWATTED AWAY A FLY HOVERING OVER THE DOCTOR'S BODY AND tried to stuff down the wave of nausea. The pieces were finally coming together, and the emerging picture was terrifying. She knew Dr. DeMarcus had been out in the villages, trying to figure out the reason behind his patients' decline. He'd contacted his son, Liam, and Sid Ramsey, looking for answers. He'd even gone to Rachel and mentioned the need to investigate some toxic dumping. Had he actually seen the dump site? Asked one too many questions? It all had to be connected, because her gut told her this was no natural death. The man in the bottom of Balik's boat had been murdered, but by whom?

Mac's foot crunched down on a plastic water bottle, as she took a step back. She kicked it out of the way because she couldn't kick whoever had done this. "We can't let Harper see this."

"Agreed," her father said. "But we can't just leave him here either."

Mac turned to Dabir, working to keep her anger in check. "What did you think you were going to find here?"

"Answers, but not this."

Mac swallowed the bile that always rose whenever she was forced to think about the losses that came with her line of work. "Why would Balik—or one of his men—risk the trouble that is sure to come with killing an American doctor?" she asked.

Dabir just stared at the body. From his refusal to meet her gaze, she knew he knew more.

"What do you know about the illegal dumping, Dabir?" Mac asked, desperate to find the common enemy that would unite them. "Is that what Balik was doing?"

Dabir walked toward the bow of the boat, then turned back to them, his AK-47 now at his side. "He told me he was making money on the side. I thought if I could find his boat, I could find out who was paying him."

"To dump the waste near your village?"

"That and other things."

Her mind raced as she waited for him to explain. "I can only help you if you tell me everything you know."

"Help me?"

"You and I both know there are only two ways for this to end. Either my team takes you out, or you give me a reason to testify on your behalf. Think of Taiwo."

Dabir studied her. He was a smart and proud man pushed into a corner. Mac had no idea what he would do. She tensed, ready to do whatever it took to protect the rest of the hostages. Especially Emma.

"Dabir, don't let your son grow up without his father. Tell me what you know, and I'll speak to the authorities about reducing your prison sentence."

He raised his eyes to hers. "I got in an argument with Balik right before we took over the tanker. I found out he'd been making money on the side dumping waste."

"Upriver from your village?" she asked.

Dabir nodded.

"Someone was cutting corners and found a cheaper way to dispose of illegal goods," her father said.

"Poison," Dabir said.

Mac glanced at the other boat where Harper still sat with Emma and Taiwo. "And possibly the source of the virus."

The young woman had no idea greed was going to crumble her world.

Greed was the reason Mo was dead, the reason Harper's father was dead, and the reason more were going to die if they didn't stop this.

"I found a watch at your house," Mac told Dabir. "It was in the shower and had the initials MD. Mathew DeMarcus. He was asking questions about toxic dumping."

"Balik might have been the one who killed the doctor, but if he did, he was paid."

Why did it always come down to money?

"Who was paying Balik?" Mac asked.

Dabir's jaw tensed. "Balik didn't get all the ransom money when he took a ship. His men had to be paid. There were supplies, boats, jammers and sat phones. It all costs money."

"And the financier gets a cut of the money?" Mac asked.

Dabir nodded.

"Someone is funding the attacks on the ships and oil tankers," her father said. "Putting innocent people at risk for a little money?"

"It's millions of dollars." Sweat beaded across Dabir's forehead. "I know who is behind this."

"Who?" Mac asked.

"Ramsey."

"Sid Ramsey?" The name took Mac off guard. "He works for an oil company. He's the president of his division. Why would he be involved in this? He doesn't need your money."

"You would have to ask him to explain his motives."

Mac studied Dabir's expression, trying to make sense of what she was hearing. She didn't believe him. How could she? She'd seen firsthand what Dabir had been involved in. And Sid Ramsey had been a hostage on an oil tanker and thrust into this nightmare. There was no way he'd financed his own hostage situation. He was a victim of these heinous crimes, not the perpetrator.

"Ramsey said you wouldn't believe me." Dabir's jaw tensed. "He said it would be my word against his, and he was right. You said you'd listen to me, help me be a father to my son, but when I tell you the truth, you don't believe me."

"I've seen what's happening in your village firsthand," she said. "And I can understand what's motivating you. I want to believe you, but you're not making it easy. You took an oil tanker hostage, people were killed, and now you're blaming the victim."

Her father stepped forward. "I believe you, Dabir."

"What do you mean?" Mac wheeled on her father, incredulous but not surprised that he'd not taken her side.

"I've known Sid Ramsey for thirty years, and trust me, no matter what you've seen, he's no boy scout. He comes across as a man in control of things, but he's deep in debt. He's a gambler, and everything he does is a façade. He's broke and desperate."

"That doesn't prove he's behind the dumping and the doctor's death," Mac said.

"All I know is that he isn't the man you think he is."

"Dabir!" One of Dabir's men shouted at him as he jumped onto the boat. "There's another call for you. You need to take it."

"Stay where you are," Dabir ordered. "Both of you."

Mac watched as Dabir took the phone. Her team would be tracking them, which meant it was just a matter of time until they found them. All they needed was a little patience and this would all be over. But if Sid Ramsey was behind this...

She wheeled on her father. "What am I missing? You and Sid Ramsey are friends. Thick as thieves."

Her father sat down on a bench and leaned forward, his elbows on his thighs. "It's been years, but some things are hard to forget."

"What happened between you?"

Her father hesitated, before answering her question. "I told you about the car accident, but I didn't tell you everything. I'd drunk too much that night. Sid was in the car with me. I was driving. It was a stupid decision, but your mother had told me she was leaving me, and I lost it. Sid was trying to talk some reason into me. I hit a tree. Sid somehow talked me into switching places before the cops showed up."

"He hadn't been drinking?"

Her father shook his head. "Not that night. It had been a foggy night and hard to see. Because Sid hadn't been drinking, they deemed it an accident. But I knew the truth, and so did Sid."

Mac felt sick inside. "And now you owe him?"

"He came back to me a few months later. He'd been gambling and had run up a large debt. He needed money. So I gave him our savings. But it wasn't enough. Next, I gave him the stocks and bonds my father had left me." Her father caught her gaze, his eyes filled with shame. "I meant what I said about things changing after that. I went to AA, quit drinking, and turned my life around. But I've always been a coward, and I was convinced that if the truth came out, and my record was tarnished, I'd lose the only thing I had left."

"Your career."

Mac turned away from him, unable to process what he was saying. Or what she was feeling. She'd always felt like a victim growing up, something she later fought against, but she'd never totally shaken the feeling of abandonment. Nor had she ever stopped to think about what he'd lost. She wasn't sure if hearing this story made her feel sorry for him, or despise him even more. But at the moment, their past didn't matter.

"If you're right about Sid and his debts, maybe there is a connection to him and the toxic dumping," she said. "When Dr. DeMarcus was trying to determine why people were getting sick, he must have stumbled upon the pharmaceutical drums. He would have known what he found."

"What did you see in those emails Dr. DeMarcus sent?" her father asked.

"There were a couple from his son, Harper's brother, that mentioned a drug company called *Dema Diagnostics.* Something about an experimental vaccine that's being tested on primates."

"It makes sense."

"What do you mean?" Mac asked.

"I don't spend all my time on the bridge. I also do a lot of onshore volunteering. One of the basic things they teach at the off-site clinic is not to handle bushmeat. The virus can spread through bodily fluids and jump from primates to humans. The problem is that it's common to earn a living buying and selling monkeys and other kinds of bushmeat along the river."

"Do you think it's possible someone found dumped primates infected with an experimental virus and ate them?"

"It's very possible. All it would take is one person. For many, bushmeat is their main source of food. On top of that, many see Ebola as nothing more than witchcraft. They don't believe the disease exists, so they don't take precautions. Their fear of catching a virus certainly wouldn't stop them from eating the meat."

"Especially if they're hungry." Mac felt a shiver go through her. "So Sid takes a shortcut when dumping the waste, someone gets infected, and the virus starts spreading."

"It's all very plausible."

"There's just one problem. Dabir was right about one thing. We still don't have any proof, and without proof, no one will listen to him." She stood and headed toward the helm. "Balik and Sid would have had to have communicated. If we could find the phone—"

"We'd have proof," her father said.

"Exactly."

She started rummaging through the storage compartments at the helm.

"What are you doing?" Dabir asked, his voice edged with anger.

She turned to him and held up a disposable phone. "I think I just found the proof we need."

CHAPTER FORTY-ONE

SOMEWHERE IN THE GULF OF GUINEA

TWO HOURS HAD PASSED AND THERE WAS STILL NO SIGN OF THE PIRATES' boat. Rachel stared at the murky waterway, pondering how she and her brother had once again ended up deep in a jungle. Sitting on the side of a boat, with a heavily armed extraction team, ready to try and stop a hostage situation. The plan was risky, but what choice was there?

Her mind skittered to a day from long ago. A day when she saw the world come undone. Voices whispered from the living room of their two-room jungle house. Her mother held a crying Josiah on the couch. Her brother's clothes were stained and wet, and she couldn't understand why her father hadn't come home with Joey. Two days later, she and her brother followed their mother onto a plane and they left the Amazon. She remembered the hard pews of the church and her father's casket at the front of the pulpit. Her mother telling her and Josiah that Daddy was in heaven and that they should be happy. But if that was true, then why was her mother crying?

Rachel wouldn't know until a year later that someone had saved Joey the day their father died. Her brother didn't know who had pulled him out of the river. She believed the same God who'd saved her brother for her, could save Emma for her brother.

"It's Rachel, right?"

She sifted in her seat as Dr. DeMarcus's son sat down next to her. "Yeah."

"I'm Liam," he said. "You don't mind if I sit here, do you?"

"Of course not." She wiped away a tear and forced a smile. "Though I doubt I'll be very good company right now."

The rise of one dark brow told her he hadn't missed her tears, but he'd wisely chosen not to investigate further. "I'm not looking to be entertained." His worries about his father and sister sounded in his voice, and Rachel felt bad for her moment of self-centered reflection. "I'm still trying to take in everything that's happened over the last couple days."

"Me too."

"How old is your niece?" he asked.

"Six." Rachel rubbed a tight muscle in her neck, while images of Emma surfaced. "I know this probably won't really help, but your sister's been amazing through all of this. She's part of the reason we were able to turn off the jammer and call for help. I'm thankful Emma is with her right now, though I hate that they're going through this."

"I guess just knowing you worked with Harper...I don't know. I'm grasping at straws, but I just need to know she's going to be okay."

"She's strong. I've seen it firsthand. She's been through a lot, but she's showed courage and faith. Honestly, I'm not sure I would have made it through without her. You should be proud."

"Thanks." Relief eased the lines around his intense eyes. "Sorry about your niece."

Rachel swallowed the lump in her throat, the fear she felt mixing with full-blown anger. It was one thing for an adult to deal with trauma, but a little girl...That should never happen.

"Is there a chance she has the virus?" Liam asked. "Harper?"

Rachel hesitated, not wanting to tell him that she'd let his little sister get exposed to the deadly virus.

"I need the truth," Liam said.

"It's very possible."

"I need to know how to help my sister."

Rachel blew out a short breath, wishing they'd been equipped to take even more precautions. "She was in close contact with someone who died of the disease while working with me in the lab, but so far, she hasn't exhibited any symptoms. Neither of us have."

"And now she's out there somewhere with a bunch of men who wouldn't think twice about killing her if it worked to their advantage."

"Hey." Rachel laid her hand on his arm. "We're going to find Harper, Emma, Mac, and the captain. We have to keep believing that."

"I've seen enough of this continent to know what can happen in a hostage situation. There's no telling how long this is going to last, or what they might do to her."

Rachel fought back the panic, refusing to allow what she'd learned about the desperation to take over. "You said former military. What do you do now?"

"I work primarily for NGO's on the continent. I collect video footage and do interviews so they can tell their stories."

"Why Africa?"

"I've actually spent time on the *Liberty*. After I left the army. I guess I'd seen enough bad things, that I wanted to be a part of something good. Like what I saw on the *Liberty*. I might not be able to change the world, but maybe my stories can offer the world a different perspective."

"And the hope that goes with it?"

He caught her gaze and held it for a few seconds. "With all you've seen, I'm sure that hope isn't always easy to find, but my father says helping one person at a time is enough."

"I agree." She felt her pulse quicken slightly, not sure if it was because they were about to try and take down a boat of pirates, or because she felt as if he could see straight into her soul.

"What are you working on right now?" she asked.

"I actually flew here from Sierra Leone. I was planning on doing an interview with a local man who runs an amazing sustainable agriculture project and teaches his methods to other farmers in the area."

"Is what you do ever risky?" she asked.

"I have a few stories that might raise the hairs on the back of your neck."

Rachel hesitated, then forced a smile. "You remind me of someone I used to know."

"Yeah. How so?"

"He was a risk taker. Was convinced what he did would save the world one day."

"A boyfriend?"

She nodded. "From a long time ago."

It was funny how she could go for weeks without thinking of Aiden, and then suddenly his loss would careen into her consciousness and stir the ache to life. Today's ride through the jungle had already dragged her farther into the past than she wanted to go. Liam was an unexpected and much needed distraction.

She let herself notice his dark hair that needed a trim and day-old beard. How his deep voice felt calming on her spirit. And how he made her feel like nothing was going to go wrong. Like they were invincible. Aiden had been that way. No. He was impetuous, brilliant, and a foolish risk taker. It wasn't fair to expect anyone to live up to the things she'd loved about Aiden. But then he'd walked out of her life without saying good-bye.

"A shadow just crossed your face," Liam said. "I didn't mean to bring up bad memories."

"It's okay. He was someone I once cared about. Someone I haven't seen for a very long time. What about you? Anyone special in your life?"

"Not now. There was someone, but when I left the military, she decided to stay in, and eventually we drifted apart."

"That's never easy," Rachel said.

"Just like sitting on the sidelines isn't easy."

Josiah shouted from the helm. "I think we found them."

Rachel and Liam jumped up and headed to the helm where Knight stood next to her brother, who was studying the shoreline with a pair of binoculars.

"Are you sure it's them?" Liam asked.

"You can see the skiff from the *Liberty*," Josiah said, "but they've pulled up against another boat. I can see people on both of them."

"What are they doing?" Rachel asked.

"Not sure." Josiah handed the binoculars back to Knight.

Rachel let a whoosh of air escape. "What do we do now?"

Brandon Knight never got a chance to respond. An explosive boom ripped from somewhere on the water, and one of the boats they'd been surveying erupted into a ball of flames.

CHAPTER FORTY-TWO

SOMEWHERE IN THE GULF OF GUINEA

The boat shook beneath Mac like a violent earthquake. She grabbed for the metal railing next to her, hoping to catch her balance. Instead, the force of the impact slammed her against the rail, crushing her rib cage. Pain shot up her side as the deck tipped and water rushed across the starboard side of the boat, knocking her off her feet. They'd been hit by something, but what? A bomb? An RPG?

Screams filled the air, followed by a second loud boom. She braced for the impact. Nothing. Had the other boat been hit too? She strained to see what was happening, but the air was filled with thick smoke and smelled like petrol. Gushing water swirled around her knees. She needed to scramble up the deck toward the other side before the boat completely submerged, but something had pinned her foot.

"Mac!" her father's voice cut through the darkness. "Mac, take my hand."

Mac's head jerked up from where she clung to the railing. Her father perched above her on the slanted deck, hanging onto a metal pole for support as he reached for her. The force of the impact had ripped the boat from its anchor, and it was now moving with the tide, drifting away from the shoreline.

"Mac, I need you to reach out and take my hand."

"I'm trying." The rising water lapped against her waist as she tried to pull her leg away again, but her foot still wouldn't budge. "My foot is wedged under something."

Panic threatened to envelop her, but she couldn't let it take root. It would only slow her thinking. She needed to think logically. Not emotionally. And the first thing she needed to do was to free her foot. If the other boat had been hit, Harper and Emma were going to need her help. And Taiwo. She pulled as hard as she could, using the railing as leverage to break free, but her foot still wouldn't move.

"Come on, Mac!"

She caught the urgency in her father's voice. "I can't get loose."

"Don't worry. I'm going to get you out of here."

Her father dove into the water, disappearing before she could respond. A few seconds later, he popped to the surface.

"One of the barrels has your leg pinned against the side of the boat," he said. "I've got to go down and move it."

"There's not enough time. You have to get off this boat. In another minute, this boat will be completely submerged."

"I'm not leaving you again."

She glanced around. The shore couldn't be that far away, but all she could see was water. Water, and the lingering smoke from whatever had done this, leaving its hazy imprint behind.

"I'll be back," he promised.

He took a deep breath then dove once again beneath the surface. The water in the gulf was almost tropical, but she still felt so cold. It wasn't the first time she'd faced death, but this time...this time she wasn't sure she was going to beat it.

And those in the other boat?

Something slammed into her shoulder. She turned and let out a scream. Dr. DeMarcus's body, still partially wrapped in plastic, floated next to her, his bloated face staring up at her. She shoved his body away from her with her free hand and shuddered.

God, don't let Emma die too. Please.

Or Harper or Taiwo. They were all innocent.

But she wasn't.

She'd had the chance to stop all of this on that oil tanker and she'd failed.

I'm sorry, God...

A wave of nausea hit, as the doctor's body floated away. Why did calling on God seem so natural and yet foreign at the same time? She wasn't the first person to wait until she was in trouble to cry out for rescue. It had always been easy for her to blame everything bad that happened on a God she couldn't see and a father who hadn't been there for her.

She tilted her head back, trying to keep her face out of the water that was now almost to her chin. She'd fought against the idea of a faith like Mo's, while at the same time, somehow wanting a faith of her own so badly. But she didn't care what happened to her right now. She needed to get out of here and make sure the others were okay. Emma needed her father, just like Josiah needed his daughter.

Like she needed them both.

Memories flooded through her. Emma wearing her shiny tiara and telling her how whipped cream would make her happy. The way she'd felt found in Josiah's gaze and loved by his kiss. She wanted to tell him right now, before it was too late, how she felt about him.

The boat groaned beneath her, shifting her attention back to her surroundings. A few seconds at most was all she had left before the water engulfed her. She searched the water for her father, but couldn't see anything. Where was he? Had he come up? She needed to tell him things too. That no matter what he'd done, a part of her had never stopped loving him. Never stopped wanting to be his little girl.

Faith, Mac. No matter what happens.

She embraced the words repeating in her head and whispered, "Daddy," as the water submerged her into darkness.

CHAPTER FORTY-THREE

SOMEWHERE IN THE GULF OF GUINEA

JOSIAH HAD JUST RETURNED COMMANDER KNIGHT'S BINOCULARS WHEN A loud boom, immediately followed by flaming pieces of flying shrapnel, knocked him against the dinghy's wheel Sloan had been steering.

"Someone blew the boats!" Commander Knight shouted.

From the corner of his eye, Josiah saw a small motorboat with two men dressed in black speed away from the continuing explosions.

Dark smoke billowed from where the two pirate boats had been anchored. Men with guns strapped across their chests jumped into the water to escape the burst of angry orange flames.

"Emma!" Where was his daughter? "Mac!" He'd spotted them only seconds ago and was hopeful he'd have them both in his arms soon. Mac had been on one boat, along with her father and Dabir. Emma had been sitting by Harper on the skiff Dabir had taken from the *Liberty*. Heart racing, Josiah scanned the chaos. He could see none of them now.

"Daddy!" Emma's scream cut through the smoke.

He could barely make out a small body in a pink T-shirt standing at the rail of a sinking boat.

"Emma!" Before he could tell Sloan to floor it, the bow of his daughter's boat suddenly shifted. The abrupt change in the deck angle unsettled Emma's footing and she toppled backwards over the railing and fell into the water. She wasn't a swimmer. He'd always meant to get her swimming lessons, but his own fear of the water had made him put it off.

"Emma!" Josiah couldn't wait for Sloan to shift the motor into a higher gear. He dove from the bow of the *Liberty's* drifting dinghy.

He heard the sound of someone diving in after him.

It was Liam who came up for air three feet away. "Harper!" He was stroking toward his sister, who was clinging to the quickly submerging boat she and Emma had been on seconds before.

Floating patches of fuel burned on top of the water. Twisted pieces of metal bobbed all around them. Liam plowed through the mess, calling to his sister while Josiah swam toward where he'd seen Emma fall into the river.

On what was left of the small boat that had exploded, Dabir burst through a plume of black smoke. Blood streamed down his face. He jumped from the burning boat to the sinking boat where Emma had been.

Taiwo pointed to a place it would take Josiah several more strokes to reach.

Dabir wheeled and scanned the churning water. "I see her." Without hesitating, he left his son and dove into the river for another man's daughter.

Josiah thrashed through the debris, petroleum and smoke fumes choking him with each stroke.

"Joey, there!" Rachel yelled from the back of the dinghy that had managed to maneuver through the burning remains of pirate boats. "I saw Emma go down there."

Josiah dove beneath water black as night. He felt his way through the darkness. Above him, he could hear orders being shouted and men hitting the water. Mac's team wouldn't be enough. He needed help.

God!

A small foot kicked his outstretched hand. He reached for Emma, but when he closed his grip, she was gone.

No! He couldn't lose Emma too. Please God, don't take Emma!

Lungs burning, Josiah pawed at the darkness he'd been fighting for almost two years. Loss. Grief. Guilt. Grief. They swirled around him, sucking away his ability to think.

Take my hand.

The voice coming to him lit the depths of his memories. He knew, without a doubt, that it was the same voice that he'd heard clearly years ago. The calming voice that had told him to kick toward the hand that had eventually pulled him from the Amazon River. It was the voice that had saved him then...He could trust that voice to save him now.

No longer lost and disoriented, Josiah kicked toward the orange glow above him. When his head popped above the waterline, he sucked in large gulps of petrol-tainted air.

"Joey!" Rachel was waving for his attention. "She's okay." Rachel pointed to where Dabir was treading water and hoisting a kicking, sputtering, screaming Emma up to Harper, Liam, and Taiwo, who had somehow made it to the dinghy.

Taiwo put his arm around Emma and she immediately calmed. Josiah's long strokes carried him quickly through the smoking debris field and to the boat where his daughter was safe. At the ladder, he stopped to acknowledge Dabir's heroic deed with a nod. The man was no angel, but neither was he a demon. He was a father who risked his own child to save another.

"Grab him!" Commander Knight yelled to one of his men who was in the water.

Dabir, still clinging to the dinghy ladder with one hand, raised his other hand in surrender. Mac's teammate in the water grabbed Dabir by the shirt and held him until Commander Knight could reach down and haul Dabir into the dinghy. Dabir's decision to save Emma had cost him the chance to try and escape.

On shore, winded pirates splashed from the water, pursued by the rest of Mac's team.

Adrenaline seeping away, Josiah worked to haul himself into the dinghy.

"Tell them it's over," Commander Knight ordered Dabir.

The weary pirate nodded and got to his feet. He shouted to his men in a language Josiah didn't have to be African to understand. Dabir's men dropped their dripping weapons and raised their hands.

As Josiah worked to get his legs under him, Emma launched herself into his arms. "Daddy!"

Josiah scooped up his daughter. "Are you okay?"

Emma nodded. "You have to find Mac."

He scrambled to his feet. His gaze sorted the crowd on the dinghy. "Where is she?"

"I don't know," Emma sobbed. "She was on the other boat."

Heart thundering in his ears, Josiah scanned the wreckage of the boat that had blown up, the boat where he'd earlier spotted Mac. All but the bow was completely submerged. "Mac!"

"There she is." Liam dove from the dinghy and stroked toward a body floating a few feet away. Within moments, Josiah helped Liam drag aboard the unconscious woman he'd come to love.

CHAPTER FORTY-FOUR

SOMEWHERE IN THE GULF OF GUINEA

"Mac!"

Eyelids flying open, Mac turned toward the voice. Josiah's face hovered next to hers as he pulled her against his chest and wrapped her in his arms. She took in a confused breath. Where had he come from? When Dabir had forced Josiah to stay behind on the *Liberty*, she wasn't sure she'd ever see him again. Was she dreaming...or dead?

"Mac, you're safe now."

"My father...I need to find him." She pushed against him, panicking now. "He was trying to get me off the boat. My foot was stuck. I couldn't get free—"

"You need to be still, Mac." Josiah laid his fingers against her neck, checking her pulse. "Liam pulled you out of the water, then you passed out. I need to make sure you're okay."

"I am." She fought again against Josiah's grip. "I need to find my father. He was there with me. And Emma...Where's Emma? Taiwo?"

"The kids are with Harper. Dabir pulled Emma out of the water when their boat started to sink. And one of your men was able to get to Taiwo."

Dabir saved Emma?

Emma was okay. Taiwo was okay. But her father...

"You didn't answer my question." She searched Josiah's eyes. "Where is my father?"

Josiah's hands moved to her shoulders. "I'm so sorry, Mac."

"Why?"

"They found Captain Scott in the water, not far from where Liam found you. He's gone."

Gone? No. She must have heard him wrong. Her father wasn't dead. He'd saved her.

She shook her head. "He can't be dead. My foot was wedged under one of the barrels. He dove down to move it."

"The boat was submerged, but you were floating on the surface when we got to you. He must have gotten you loose."

"You don't understand." She tried to push him away, needing to get up. Needing to go and find her father and tell him... "He can't be dead."

"We tried to save him, but he was already gone."

She was shivering. The sun was shining on her, but she felt so cold. So cold she didn't think she'd ever be able to warm up again.

"He wasn't supposed to die." Mac stared out across the deck. "I said things to him....things I shouldn't have. I should have been the one who died. He could have saved himself."

"I'm not exactly the one to talk about God, but it's a miracle you're alive." Josiah wrapped his arms around her and pulled her against his chest. "Slow, deep breaths. You're going to get through this."

She felt so vulnerable, but with his arms around her, she knew she could believe him.

"Where is everyone?" she asked, noticing that the only other people on the *Liberty's* dinghy was Sloan who stood at the helm, and Ramsey who was talking on his SAT phone on the other side of the boat.

"Dabir and his men surrendered," Josiah told her. "Your team has the men restrained on the shore until the helo arrives with a group of US military personnel coming from the *Liberty*."

"But who hit us?" She pressed her hands against his chest, her mind scrambling to keep up with what he was saying. "What happened out there?"

"I wish I knew," Josiah said. "There was a speed boat that we feel pretty sure was responsible—I saw them—but they're long gone. Your team said it was a rocket-propelled grenade."

The nightmare that had started with Mo's death still wasn't over. The boats had been hit, the evidence of the missing doctor was destroyed, her father was dead, and there was a virus on the loose. A sense of hopelessness pressed in against her. Her lungs fought for air. No matter how hard she'd tried, she couldn't fix everything. There was simply too much evil in the world. She dropped her hands into her lap. What if she'd been wrong about Mo's Sunday school God? What if a faith like he had was the only thing that could make sense out of the pain of this world, and bring hope?

Faith, Mac. No matter what happens.

The words she'd been thinking when she slipped beneath the water gave her the same peace now. She looked to make sure Harper wasn't listening. "There was someone else on that boat," she whispered.

"Who?" Josiah asked.

"Dr. DeMarcus. He's dead, Josiah." Mac lowered her voice as her head started to clear and the pieces started coming together. "I think Sid Ramsey had him killed."

"What?" Josiah pushed back a strand of her wet hair, pausing for a moment when his thumb touched the side of her face. "DeMarcus's son, Liam, flew in with the negotiator and your team. He's on shore with the others."

"We have to find the doctor's body."

"Agreed, but what were you doing on that other boat?"

"Dabir was looking for proof."

"Proof of what?"

"Proof of who was behind the illegal dumping near his village."

"And did he find anything?"

She nodded. "We found a phone on the boat. A boat that belongs to the person who'd been dumping the waste. A pirate named Balik. But Balik was following orders from someone higher up."

"And you think that person was Sid?" Josiah asked.

"Yes, and I think DeMarcus found out too much." She pulled the phone out of her wet pocket. She could only hope the waterproof case had protected the device. She pushed the power button and the black screen flickered to blue. "Dabir told me Ramsey was Balik's financier and that he'd made a deal to get a cut of any ransom money they brought in."

"Which would explain why Sid was trying so hard to organize a negotiator, but still, he doesn't exactly fit the profile."

"I said the same thing," she said, "But my father. . .he's known the man for years. He told me Sid Ramsey wasn't the magnanimous man people thought he was."

She motioned for Josiah to help her up.

"You need to rest, Mac—"

"I need to fix this for Harper." Once she was on her feet, she scrolled through the contacts on the phone, and pressed on one. "He was also making a profit on dumping the waste, by arranging for Balik to dispose of it."

A moment later, a phone started ringing on the other side of the dinghy.

Ramsey pulled his ringing phone from his pocket.

Mac held out the phone in her hand and smiled. The color drained from Ramsey's face. "Sloan!" she shouted at her teammate who was still at the helm. "I need you to restrain Sid Ramsey. Now."

Her teammate turned around. "What?"

"Just do it."

Sloan pulled out his weapon and ordered the man to hold out his hands.

"You're behind all of this," Mac said, stepping up in front of Ramsey. "The dumped waste outside Dabir's village. The death of Dr. DeMarcus. The death of my father."

"You've got to be kidding." Ramsey held up his bound hands in front of him. "You can't do this."

"That's not all," Mac said, scrolling through his phone until she found what she was looking for. "You're tracking someone. Someone right here."

"That would explain how they found the boat in order to blow it up," Josiah said.

"I have no idea what you're talking about," Ramsey said standing up.

"Sit down," Mac said. "This isn't over. You realized you needed to silence us, just like you silenced Dr. DeMarcus. He's dead."

"I never killed anyone—"

"No, but you hired someone to do it for you. Just like you hired those men to attack these two boats. Did you really think you'd be able to silence all of us?" Mac held onto Josiah's arm, but the truth coming out gave her the strength to continue. "You've been blackmailing my father for years. He told me about your large debt. When Dr. DeMarcus contacted you about the toxic dumping, you realized you couldn't risk this coming back on you."

"And the dumped waste is connected to the virus?" Josiah asked. "You sure?"

Mac nodded as she scrolled through the texts. "There are messages on this phone. Meeting places and instructions. Once the authorities follow the money trail, they'll have all the evidence they need to put you away for a long time."

"This wasn't supposed to happen." Ramsey shook his head. "People weren't supposed to die."

Mac caught the man's guilty gaze. "But now someone's going to have to tell Liam and Harper that their father is dead, and that you killed him."

CHAPTER FORTY-FIVE

GULF OF GUINEA SHORELINE

Josiah held Emma tight as the military chopper set down on a sandy strip of river shore in front of them. Two armed men jumped to the ground. Weapons raised, they strode to where Mac and her team held Dabir and his pirate crew at gunpoint.

"Come on, Cricket. There's something Daddy's got to do." Josiah felt Emma's arms tighten around his neck.

"Don't leave me, Daddy."

"We're a family, you and me. Families stick together."

She smiled and buried her tear-streaked face in his neck. "I love you so much, Daddy."

"Ditto, princess." Josiah and Emma made their way to the prisoners waiting to be transferred to Douala. "I need to talk to Dabir," he shouted to Mac over the whir of the blades.

She shook her head. "Best you don't."

His gaze went from the little girl clinging to him to Mac. "You know how important it is to have closure."

He could see the hurt that lingered in her eyes. She'd be sorting out unresolved feelings for her father for weeks to come, and he intended to wrap her in his arms whenever the grief threatened to overwhelm. He'd tell her how he felt about her when the time was right. For now, he'd help her get through this awful day.

Mac spoke to her team leader. He scowled, but then he personally escorted Dabir clear of the chopper blades.

"Can I talk to him alone?" Josiah asked the team leader.

"Afraid not."

Josiah gave a reluctant nod then took a step toward the man he'd wanted to kill. The defiance and desperation Josiah had seen in his eyes throughout this whole ordeal had been snuffed. They weren't so different, Dabir and him. Josiah fully understood a father's desire to do whatever it took to give his child a better life.

"Dabir, thank you for saving my little girl's life." He switched Emma to his left arm and held out his right hand. "I'll be forever grateful."

Dabir shook his head. "She would not have needed saving if I'd never gone to your ship."

"Look," Josiah said as they shook hands. "You needed help. I'm sorry we couldn't save your wife."

Dabir swallowed and inclined his head toward Taiwo. "My boy. Can you see that he gets delivered to my sister?"

"Absolutely."

"My brother Chomba only did as I ordered him."

"I'm not sure what I can do about that, but I'll try."

"Thank you." Dabir shook Josiah's hand again.

"Do you still want to help your village?"

Dabir held up his zip-tied wrists. "How?"

"My sister Rachel tested your blood. Turns out she was able to identify rare antibodies that can block not just one, but all known strains of Ebola."

"What does that mean?

"That your blood could be the key to stopping this virus. We can send some to your village and send some to the States."

"The States?"

"One of Mac's team told me it's spreading. If you help us stop this, perhaps the international courts will go easier on you. Get you home in time to help raise your boy."

Dabir hesitated, then nodded. "I'll do it."

CHAPTER FORTY-SIX

PORT OF DOUALA, THREE WEEKS LATER

Mac sat on a padded chair in Rachel's tight quarters on the *Liberty*, still groggy from a restless night's sleep on the empty bunks she'd been using the past three weeks. As of today, they'd finally made it through the quarantine.

"I'm making some tea before I finish packing," Rachel said. "Would you like some?"

"Yes, thank you." Mac shivered, and grabbed a sweatshirt from the pile of clothes Rachel had loaned her. "You know I don't know what I would have done without you, these past couple weeks. From company to clothes. . ."

"I agree. Keeping up with the outside world via the internet—including Emma and Josiah and others on the ship—has been a huge blessing." Rachel pulled the electric kettle off the stand and poured two cups. "But it's still hard, isn't it?"

Mac nodded. "I just received an email from Mo's wife. She's really struggling with the loss of her husband. I'm planning to go see her as soon as I can."

She might have finally been able to wash away the lingering scent of petrol and smoke, but she still was working to heal her shattered heart.

"You both suffered huge losses."

Unable to put her tumbling emotions into words, Mac slipped on the sweatshirt. Mo's loss was understandable, but how could she still mourn a man who'd chosen to walk out of her life? A man she didn't even know. It didn't make sense. She didn't have more than a handful of memories of her father before she'd arrived on the *Liberty*.

"I feel like I shouldn't cry for a man I didn't know."

"Captain Scott was a human being and now he's dead," Rachel said. "That's reason enough to cry."

"But tears can never take away the loss of what could have been."

Rachel added a couple spoonfuls of sugar to her tea. "Everyone has to grieve, Mac. We might not do it in the same way or in the same time frame, but we all have to work through the pain. It's okay. You've lost a close friend *and* your father. You have every right to grieve. You *need* to grieve."

"What if I don't know how?" She took her tea, surprised at her own question. How was it that she could jump out of a plane and storm a hijacked tanker, but she didn't know how to deal with any of this?

"Grief is never linear, and it's never simple, but maybe you need to start by not being so hard on yourself," Rachel said.

Mac swirled the teabag in her cup, waiting for it to brew. Maybe she shouldn't blame her father for trying to atone for his bad choices. Hadn't she done the same thing when she swore to hunt down Mo's killer? Hadn't atonement been at the root of Josiah's decision to bring his daughter to Africa? Maybe it was human nature to want to atone for our terrible mistakes. After all, what else could have compelled Dabir to save Emma when he had a chance to save his own son and himself? But had trying to do a whole bunch of good to make up for the bad really gotten any of them anywhere? Mo wasn't alive. Josiah had nearly lost his daughter. And Dabir would likely spend the rest of his life behind bars.

"Easier said than done," Mac finally said.

"God has a way of redeeming situations, and more often than not, by using people we'd never choose. I know your father's life was changed by the time he spent on this ship. I knew your father well, and I can promise you that he wouldn't want you to feel guilty in any way over his death."

"I pushed him away. Even to the very end."

"Captain Scott was a smart man. He knew why you felt the need to keep him at arm's length."

Rachel set her cup on the nightstand and pulled off a few magnetic photos off the wall behind her bed and set them in her suitcase.

"This is an adorable photo," Mac said, picking up one of them."

Two little girls, one white and one an Albino girl who couldn't be more than two or three, smiled up at the camera.

"It's from the wedding of some friends of mine, Race and Mia who met in Africa. He was a pilot who transported donated organs across East Africa. Mia—I went to college with her—is a heart transplant surgeon." Rachel laughed. "You can guess how they met. They were married a year ago, and now live in Dar es Salaam. They're expecting a little boy in a couple months. They met these little cuties in Tanzania where Kelsey received a heart. Kelsey and Jeme were the flower girls."

"They're adorable."

"I keep their photo to remind me of the importance of forgiveness. It's a long story, but they're legally sisters now."

Mac pulled her feet up beneath her, finally starting to feel warm again. "Mo used to always tell me to have faith. That Jesus was the answer when people failed us. Maybe it's time I started understanding exactly what it means to forgive."

"Trying to figure out how forgiveness changes the one who chooses to forgive is like trying to figure out how this virus really got started." Rachel shook her head. "Sometimes all we can know for sure is that choosing to love is better than the alternative."

Mac turned the possibilities over in her mind. She could continue to lug a load of disappointment and bitterness around, or let go of the hatred of her father for what he had done to their family. Hatred hadn't changed him, but the love of something greater had.

"Mac?" Rachel's touch brought Mac back into the conversation. "You okay?"

"Just thinking about how much has changed." Mac shot Rachel a grin. "Like for instance, I've noticed how much time you've spent over the past couple weeks talking to Liam."

"No fair, changing the subject like that." A blush spread across Rachel's cheeks. "I enjoy talking to him. He's nice. . .handsome. . ."

"Nice *and* handsome."

"Very handsome." Rachel laughed. "There is a connection I can't deny. Time will tell, I suppose. We're planning to Facetime and have even talked about meeting up back in the States once all of this is over. His family doesn't live too far from my mom."

"I think you should."

"He's going to take Harper back to the States to spend some time with their mother. And there will be a funeral for their father soon." Rachel opened a drawer and pulled out some more clothes to pack. "I've noticed I'm not the only one who's been spending a lot of time video chatting."

Mac felt her face flush. "What do you mean?"

"I've seen the way my brother looks at you, and I've seen the way you look at him. Plus Emma adores you."

Mac shook her head, not sure she was ready to go there. "After watching my parents' marriage unravel and then experiencing a couple of sour relationships, I've kind of given up on the whole two kids and a white picket fence dream."

Rachel dismissed her concerns with a wave of her hand. "Who says you need a white picket fence? Though I won't try to convince you that Josiah wouldn't come with a set of struggles. Losing his wife has been hard on him. And on Emma. And now all of this. . ."

"I can't even imagine."

A knock on the door pulled her attention away from their conversation.

"Come in," Rachel said.

The door opened, and Josiah stood in the doorway with Emma nestled next to him, her tiara tilted slightly on the top of her head. "We've just been given the all clear and thought we'd come see you both in person."

"Does that mean I can hug people now?" Emma asked.

"You certainly can."

Emma bounded across the room and pulled her aunt into a big hug before coming to Mac. "I missed you."

"I missed you so much too," Mac said. "It's been a long time."

Rachel glanced at Emma. "I need to go check on someone. Would you like to go with me?"

Emma nodded, then frowned. "Are you leaving the ship, Mac?"

"Soon, but I wasn't going to go until I could see you in person and tell you what a remarkable young lady you are."

"I told my daddy that you should come and visit us in California," Emma said. "We could go to the beach, go horseback riding, and get a pedicure."

"Wow. That sounds lovely, I just—"

"I'm pretty sure Mac has plans to get back to her life, Cricket." Josiah's eyes locked with hers, and Mac felt heat all the way to her toes. Leaving him was going to be harder than she was ready for. "Though...I agree with Emma. I wouldn't mind if you visited us."

Rachel scooted Emma out the door. "Why don't the two of you discuss your plans outside. The sunrise is beautiful from the deck and I think you might just catch it."

"What do you say?" Josiah had not taken his eyes off her. "Now that we're actually allowed to leave our rooms."

She stood up, forcing aside the feelings of vulnerability. "I'd like that."

They walked up the stairs in silence, then slipped out onto the deck. Rachel was right. The sun was just starting to paint splashes of orange and pink across the sky.

"I wanted to see how you're doing. In person." Josiah leaned against the railing. "I know you're going to have to leave soon."

"I'm headed out for a briefing of our next assignment in an hour. We've been called to work with the US and local military on continued security until the medical threat in the region is over."

"Sounds like you'll be busy, though the reports from the CDC are encouraging. It looks as if they have the disease under control."

"They believe they've passed the peak of the infection, but I think I'm going to need to stay busy."

"Everything that's happened is still a bit unsettling. Given our travel history, we'll be monitored by public health officials in the States as well. The *Liberty* will have to have a thorough inspection by the World Health Organization to ensure that there's no trace of the virus left. And after being cleaned and decontaminated, the staff is being given the option to go home, especially families with children, but from what I've heard many are staying. There's still a lot of work ahead, but with the proper containment, they believe the virus can be completely controlled."

"I also just heard that Doctors Without Borders and WHO have made huge progress with the massive clean-up effort conducted on the river and dumping site to ensure the origin of the virus is completely neutralized."

"That's all great news," Josiah said.

"It is." But she had no desire to talk about the virus anymore. She wanted to reach for his hand. Tell him she wanted to come with him. But this had to be goodbye and she knew it.

"What about your father's remains?"

Mac shifted against the railing, looking out across the water and listening to the sounds of gulls and tugboats. Life aboard this ship had restored her father's joy. "I considered a burial at sea, but after contacting my aunt, we've decided his body will be shipped back to the States. I'll work with some of the *Liberty* staff to plan his funeral. He was their captain and they're anxious to give him the honor due him."

"And after that?"

"My contract with the extraction team doesn't end for another ten months. So after I bury my father, I'll catch up with the team at our next assignment." The future was something they'd avoided talking about while in quarantine. "What about you?"

"I'm figuring things out as we go, but we'll be heading home soon. Emma and I are both going to do some trauma counseling, for starters. I'm going to make sure she gets the closure she needs. I don't want her to be saddled with the fear of living. I know those feelings all too well, and it's not what Camilla would have wanted for either of us."

"Emma's a lucky girl."

"I'm the lucky one. Despite everything that's happened, she's connected us to people in ways I've never thought possible. They feel like family. I wouldn't be surprised if she begs me to come back. But no matter what we end up doing, I'm pretty sure I'm going to sell my practice."

"Wow...That's a huge step."

"Yes, but one that's been a long time in coming, actually. I think it's time I spent my talents on something more...meaningful."

"Any ideas?" she asked.

"Not yet, but there is one other thing before I forget." He reached into his pocket and pulled something out. "One of the nurses asked me to give it to you on my way to see you."

Mac let out a sharp breath. "Mo's dog tags."

"I know it doesn't make up for what happened, but I hope it helps."

"It does." Tears spilled over Mac's cheeks. She wanted to throw her arms around his neck and kiss him, but she was afraid one more kiss would never be enough. "Thank you. So much. And please tell Emma I haven't forgotten about the bracelets she made for Tarrence and Jalen. I'll make sure they get them."

"She'll be happy to hear that, but you could always tell her yourself. And the whole California invite...that might not be a bad idea. Your coming to visit us. We have a guest room, and we live near the beach—"

"I might take you up on that offer."

"So I'm not overstepping with the invite?"

"Technically, Emma's already invited me."

Josiah grinned and shook his head. "Look...I'm not exactly up on the whole dating scene. I haven't dated, or whatever they call it these days, for well over a decade. And, honestly, I never imagined wanting to." He stuffed his hands into his pockets. "But I'm going to miss our video chats and getting to know you better."

"There's no reason they can't continue as long as I have internet."

"It's just that. . ." Josiah hesitated. "Since that day I kissed you, I haven't been able to stop thinking about wanting to kiss you again. I know you said that a relationship shouldn't happen between us while we were under such duress...and you were right. But, and maybe I'm way out of line here, but I can't ignore what I'm feeling. What I hope you're feeling too."

Mac sifted through her feelings. Josiah wasn't the only one leery of opening his heart. "I admit I didn't handle that night well. I was just...I guess, afraid that what was happening between us might interfere with our mission."

"What if you and me finding each other was a part of God's plan?" he asked.

Her mind scrambled for an excuse. "Or what if what we're feeling is, like you said, an infusion of oxytocin?"

He smiled. "Our oxy numbers have had time to level." His eyes took on an intensity that radiated heat. "I think we need to consider the possibility that we could be suffering from something even more life changing than a deadly virus." He took her hand and laced their fingers together. "Emma adores you and I...I know you've stirred a part of my soul that I thought had died. I can't stop thinking that you might be that missing piece I didn't even know I needed."

His words ignited the feelings she'd tried to shove aside. Hungry emotions kicked at the wall of her heart and demanded that she consider the possibility that she needed this man as much as he needed her. Funny how she never hesitated risking her life when it came to her career, but her heart...that was a different story. What would happen if she decided to open up her heart to him and give him a chance?

"I'm going to need time to sort out my father's estate," she said, forcing herself to catch his gaze. She could no longer ignore what his nearness did to her. "And then there's my security contract..."

He held a finger to her lips. "We'll take things one step at a time. Meanwhile, we can FaceTime and email, and see where it goes."

Her smile faded as fear tried to force its way back in. "And if it doesn't work out?"

"Maybe it won't, but what if it does?"

She rested her hands against his chest. "I'm always up for an adventure."

In the colorful glow of the sunrise above the horizon, he drew her into his arms and kissed her. His lips tasted of hope and the promise of a future. Peace, gentle as the waves lapping the *Liberty,* washed over her. Forgiveness and freedom might be hard to find, but maybe together, they could find what they'd both been searching for.

CHAPTER FORTY-SEVEN

BETHESDA, MARYLAND

CLAYBORN'S OLD FRIEND AND MEDICAL COLLEAGUE LIZ MAXWELL HAD not left his side in days. "Take it slow." Her gloved hands were clamped to the handles of his wheelchair while she waited on him to haul himself out of his hospital bed for the first time.

He sank into the seat with an exhausted huff. "I feel like I'm coming back from a war." His wasted leg muscles were so weak he could barely stand.

"It was a fight for your life that we almost lost." Liz was masked and gowned head to toe. He couldn't see her face, but from her tone, he knew she was smiling. "Every day you're growing a little stronger." Once he settled into the seat, she released the lock on his chair. "Now that the results of your polymerase chain reaction test came back negative for the second time, we can get your physical therapy started and rebuild the muscle strength you've lost." She pushed him toward the glass wall where his mother waved from her wheelchair. "Now, I believe you've kept that lovely lady waiting long enough."

He couldn't begin to express his gratitude to his colleague. The moment she'd heard he was allowing himself to become Dema Diagnostics's experimental antiviral first human guinea pig, she'd left the oversight of his family's quarantine in the hands of another epidemiologist and flown to Bethesda. Had Liz not intervened, he and his mother would not be alive.

Clayborn had spent the last few days piecing together what Liz and his medical team had done on his behalf after his fever shot so high his brain swelled and he lost consciousness. According to Liz, during the worst phase of the illness, he'd developed a rash over his entire body. A rash that was fading, but that had left irritating bumps he could still see and feel. While he'd drifted in and out of coherency, Liz had lived in the recliner by his bed, researching every possibility between short naps. Just when she and the Bethesda medical team thought they would lose him, plasma infusions donated by an atypical African Ebola survivor had arrived.

An epidemiologist working on the *Liberty* had discovered that this recently recovered man's blood contained the antibodies that blocked more than just one strain of Ebola. His antibodies had the ability to block all five of the known strains. She suggested to Dr. Maxwell that this survivor's plasma might possibly contain the antibodies needed to stop this unknown strain as well.

Clayborn's medical team credited this form of passive immunotherapy as the key to his turnaround. Only yesterday, had Clayborn learned that, ironically, the donor that had saved his life was the lead pirate who'd hijacked his mother's medical ship, the *Liberty*.

He and his mother owed their lives to a desperate man they knew very little about. But Clayborn understood the desperation that would drive a man to do whatever it took to save his family. Hadn't he done the same? He'd put more than himself at risk when he'd considered trying Dema Diagnostics's meds. He'd risked the life of his mother. Desperation was a dangerous thing. But the desire to protect those you love is universal. Humanity's common denominator.

Clayborn and his mother would probably suffer long-term side effects of the virus for years to come. His mother had developed inflammation of the tissue around her heart and a pulsating eye pain that had caused some vision loss. The doctors had assured them that, with proper treatment, blindness could be avoided. Both of them still suffered tremendous headaches, and it would take months to get them steady on their feet due to their massive weight losses and a residual lack of appetite.

"My boy." His mother's shaky voice crackled through the intercom. "My precious, precious boy." She raised her withered palms and pressed them to the glass. "Promise me you'll help me find a way to get back to Africa."

In his heart, he'd already committed himself to contact the doctors aboard the *Liberty* who'd fought with the international authorities for the right to ship the pirate's plasma to the States. Next, he intended to locate the man who'd saved their lives with the donation of his plasma and do whatever he could to thank him.

Clayborn had had plenty of time to lie in bed and think about the hostage scenario Liz had relayed to him. He'd tried to imagine the conversation Dr. Josiah Allen must have had with the pirate who'd endangered his daughter. Why would either of them have anything to do with the other?

Clayborn lifted his hands and pressed his palms against the glass to match the hands of a woman who'd given her life to making a difference in the lives of others. He thought of all the hours she'd spent in sweltering, understaffed schools and ill-equipped medical clinics. Countless lives had been impacted because of this sacrificial woman.

Truth be known, he didn't want his mother to go back to Africa. He wanted to keep her safe and assure a future where his kids got to grow up around their grandmother. But he also wanted his children to know that their grandmother was a woman who fulfilled her God-given purpose.

Clayborn smiled. "Mama, you make me that chicken dinner I didn't get to eat, and I promise I'll take you back to your beloved medical ship myself."

A tap sounded on the hallway observation window across the room.

"Surprise!" Liz shouted and wheeled Clayborn around.

Out in the hall, his mother-in-law held his three-year-old son Benson. The boy pounded the glass and shouted, "Daddy!"

Beside them stood Jasmine. His beautiful wife had dark circles under her eyes, but her smile was glowing. She blew him a kiss then turned her body so that he could see the face of his curly-haired daughter cradled against her chest.

"Bria," he whispered. "She's holding her head up by herself." He'd missed so much, but thanks to a man he'd never met in Africa, he wouldn't miss any more. "Wheel me over there, Liz."

He set the brake then pushed himself up from his chair. On shaky legs, he stood tall for his family.

Jasmine mouthed, "I love you." Then she pressed her lips to the glass.

Clayborn leaned in and pressed his lips against the cool surface. Love. It was the first real thing he'd tasted in days. And it was sweet.

CHAPTER FORTY-EIGHT

DABIR'S VILLAGE, NINE MONTHS LATER

"EMMA!" JOSIAH CALLED FROM THE PORCH OF THE NEW CLINIC SET TO open as soon as the contingency he'd invited from the *Liberty* arrived. "You and Taiwo stay away from the river's edge."

"But Taiwo is teaching me how to throw a fishing net." Emma's eyes sparkled, and Josiah's heart leapt at the sight of his daughter enjoying her childhood again.

Dabir would be proud of his son. Josiah pulled out his phone and snapped a picture. When he went next week to visit Dabir in prison, he'd take him a new stack of books to read and he'd give him printed photos of his boy and his continued progress.

A lot had happened over the past nine months.

Rachel had convinced him to stay and give the *Liberty's* psychologist a shot at his and Emma's trauma. The weekly therapy sessions had done so much for both of them. They still had moments of sadness, especially on days like this. Camilla would have loved being in the middle of helping underserved people acquire decent medical care.

Staying in Africa had allowed him to help Rachel pinpoint the source of

Ebola and trace it back to the unethical, antiviral testing and disposal of primates that had been infected with the virus. From the samples Mac had gathered at the dump site, the CDC was able to identify the previously unknown and mutant strain of Ebola the experiments had created. Within forty-eight hours, the World Health Organization and Doctors Without Borders had medical boots and equipment on the ground. Dabir's rare antibodies, it turned out, had been key in stopping not just one strain of the virus, but all known strains, in a therapy being used that actually attacked the virus.

After Dabir and his men went to jail in Douala, Josiah had hired the best international maritime legal counsel he could find. He wouldn't dispute the fact that hijacking a medical ship and kidnapping passengers should be considered a violent crime, but Josiah was convinced Dabir had already paid dearly. He'd lost his livelihood, his wife, and his way of life. And he'd saved Josiah's daughter when he could have swam away in the chaos and saved himself, something Josiah would never forget.

Worried oil companies had spurred an international debate that was still being fought. If nobody did anything, the oil companies claimed, what had happened to the *Liberty* would just be another case of pirate catch and release. How could the companies protect their valuable cargos that sailed the west African trade routes? Increased security would certainly raise the price of fuel throughout the world. So while the legal battles raged, Dabir and his brothers twiddled their thumbs in a Cameroonian jail, while Sid Ramsey sat in a US prison with a long list of charges, including murder.

It was Samuel Methu, the ship's chief medical officer, who'd shifted Josiah's way of thinking about how to remedy the lack of medical care in the outlying villages' situation. When he told Samuel about his idea of raising money from his wealthy clients to try and fix the problem, Samuel had convinced him that simply pouring money into an underdeveloped country was not the answer. The desperation driving the pirates was proof that foreign money never filtered down enough to address the root of the problem.

"These people need skills and jobs as much as they need medicine," the young Cameroonian doctor had said when he'd so eloquently made his case to leave his post on the *Liberty* and build a clinic in Dabir's village—a village not far from the one where he'd grown up. And that project was only the first of several business plans this bright young man would propose to Josiah over the next few months.

In conjunction with Samuel's best friend from college, Philip Gambo, an established coffee farmer, Samuel showed Josiah ambitious plans to restore the damaged soil and put Cameroon back on the map as a coffee and cocoa producer. They'd hammered out a detailed business plan where they proposed to connect African business leaders, investors, and entrepreneurs with local farmers in order to create hundreds of jobs throughout the region and expand not only domestically, but internationally. A successful result would impact hundreds of families along the river. Even Liam had offered his services and had produced an informative video on their plans to revitalize the impoverished region.

Through it all, Josiah continued to be impressed with how Samuel had managed to invest the seed money raised from Josiah's Hollywood A-lister friends and the significant settlement money *Dema Diagnostics* had kicked in. The plans being implemented would result in a desperately needed boost for the area.

Today was the plan's first step forward. The opening of the area's first easily accessible medical clinic.

Josiah turned and looked at the small cinderblock building with its sparkling clean windows and shiny tin roof. Memories, as big as Josiah's father's hands, pushed through the last crumbling layers of his grief. As they gently dusted the ashes from his heart, the scales fell from his eyes. For the first time since that horrible day when he and his father had been delivering groceries to the Amazon's native villages, he could see his father clearly. He watched his father smile as he brought medicine to a man who'd shot holes in his boat the week before, but later returned and learned how to patch them. He saw his father stop long enough to teach a very skinny boy to fish and then gave him his own fishing pole and tackle box. He saw his father lying in the bottom of the boat, looking up at him as his breath drained through the holes left by a drug lord's AK-47.

He saw his father's lips mouth the word, "Forgive." All these years, and he'd not remembered that life-changing part of the story until now.

A hand to Josiah's shoulder brought him back to the moment.

"Dr. Allen." Samuel had a big grin on his face. He held out a freshly washed and pressed white coat that matched his own. "The captain just phoned. Their dinghy is only ten minutes out. Is your speech ready?"

Josiah slid his arms into the crisp sleeves. "You're the one who should give the speech."

"Don't worry, I have plenty to say as well, but everyone is expecting to hear from you, too." He grasped Josiah's hand and pulled him into a hug.

"Dr. Allen?" Josiah released Samuel at the sound of his name and turned to see Loraine's son, Clayborn. "I'm sorry to interrupt."

"Clayborn," Josiah extended his hand. "I'm glad you made it."

"Me too."

Loraine's son had used his two-week vacation from his medical practice to bring his mother back to Africa. They both still wore out pretty easily from their bouts of the deadly virus, but they wouldn't hear of taking a break from unpacking the boxes of hospital and school supplies Clayborn's friend Dr. Liz Maxwell and his medical team at Bethesda had sent.

Clayborn wiped the sweat from his brow. "Mom says the village children have a song to share, but she's not sure where you'd like them to sit."

"They're going to steal the show." Josiah chuckled. "Harper DeMarcus is right over there. She'll have an answer for you."

"They're here!" Emma squealed from the river's shore.

As the *Liberty*'s dinghy motored slowly up to the newly built dock, Josiah noticed that Faoudu stood beside the Liberty's new captain, Ricardo. The boy with the windy legs as Emma called them, stood tall and proud.

After he'd sold his practice and signed a contract for six months aboard the *Liberty,* Josiah had been able to conduct a thorough examination of Faoudu's legs. He decided the boy's problem needed a consult from the best pediatric ortho he knew in the States. The doctor had readily agreed to fly in and do the work for free. The surgery had taken hours, and Faoudu's recovery had been long and painful, but every day Emma rushed from her schoolroom to the ward. She read to the boy, played card games with him, and goaded him until he finally took a step. Emma was her mother times ten.

Josiah smiled at his daughter, who'd run up the dock to greet her friends from the *Liberty*.

Rachel leapt onto the dock and scooped up Emma. His sister deserved a child of her own as much as his daughter deserved a new mother. That thought was quickly pushed away by thoughts of Mac. Her commander had granted a four-week leave for Mac to bury her father. She'd turned down Josiah's offer to attend the funeral, but two weeks later she'd invited him and Emma to come to the ceremony where Edmonton Scott received a posthumous advancement to the grade of four-star general due to outstanding service to his country. The week the three of them had spent together had been wonderful. He'd fallen deeper in love with her over late-night chats on the balcony and picnics in the park with Emma. They'd both wanted more with their relationship, but their timing couldn't have been worse. Mac was headed back to Africa, to fulfill her contract with her security team, and as far as he was concerned, FaceTime on Fridays with Emma for a *Faoudu* update and regular calls with him simply wasn't enough. And then there was the question he couldn't dismiss. How could he ask a woman created for danger to throw her lot in with a doctor who'd decided to do humanitarian work with his precocious daughter?

But today, he couldn't let himself dwell on whether or not they'd ever get their timing right.

"There's another boat coming!" Emma shouted. "She's here!"

"Who's here?" Josiah asked.

"Mac!"

Josiah felt his heart still. "Mac?"

"I invited her," Emma shouted back.

"How?"

"FaceTime." She grabbed Josiah's hand. "Come on."

Rushing onto the dock, Josiah didn't need to be pulled toward the beautiful woman stepping out of the boat. His legs were pounding the ground as if her smile was a magnet drawing him to her. The sundress she wore showed off her toned tanned arms and long bronze legs. She was coming toward them with her arms open like she was a woman coming to stay.

"Mac!" Emma threw her arms around Mac's neck. "I knew you would come."

"How could I not come?" Mac said over Emma's head, her eyes locked with Josiah's. "I know Mo's in heaven smiling at the thought of someone naming a clinic after him."

"Emma and I thought you'd like that," Rachel said.

Josiah gave his sister a why-am-I-always-the-last-to-know look, and she just smiled and shrugged.

"Aren't you going to hug her, Daddy?" Emma pushed Josiah toward Mac. "Hug her, Daddy."

They hugged. Mac's body fit perfectly against his. For a moment, they were the only two people in the world. Josiah felt the hope of a future surge through him. Then Emma tugged on his shirt.

"Let's show her the clinic, Daddy."

"Right." He let Mackenzie go and took a step back. "It's a beauty."

"I'm sure it is." Mac smiled.

With Emma in the middle, the three of them walked hand in hand to the clinic porch where people were milling around, waiting for the beginning of the ceremony.

"I don't understand. I thought you couldn't come," he said.

"I didn't think I could either. But then I received a call from the *Liberty's* headquarters. They're looking for someone to step in as head of security."

"But your other job."

"I know we haven't had time to talk, but since my contract was about over, Commander Knight pulled a few strings and I became a free woman. The *Liberty* needed a decision right away, and coming here seemed right. Emma and Rachel suggested we keep it a surprise."

"Are you surprised, Daddy?" Emma beamed.

"Trust me, I'm surprised." He held on tightly to Mac's hand, afraid if he let go she might disappear.

"Emma, we need you now." Harper motioned from the other side of the clinic.

Emma gave Mac a huge hug, then scurried off. "Thank you for coming."

"Someone's glad you're here," Josiah whispered.

Mac pulled Josiah aside onto the back porch of the clinic where they could see the water in the distance. "And you...are you glad I'm here?"

"Very."

Her smile lit her eyes. "This clinic is the beginning of freedom for these people. Freedom from the threat of terrible diseases." She took both of his hands. "I think it's time we both grabbed onto that gift of freedom and peace as well. Together."

Forgiveness meant freedom.

Forgive those who'd killed his missionary father whose sole purpose for taking his wife and two kids to the Amazon had been to help.

Forgive his sister for insisting he bring his daughter to Africa.

Forgive himself for the things he could not control...like Camilla's accidental death.

Forgiveness.

His search over the past few months had brought him an unexpected freedom and peace as he'd learned once again to trust his heavenly father. That peace had filled in the empty spaces where guilt and anger had once dwelt.

"You sure this isn't some oxytocin induced decision?"

Her eyes sparkled. "Oxytocin is not the molecular equivalent of love."

"You may have a future in medicine."

She tilted her lips toward his. "I'm the girl who's going to have your back for the rest of your life."

"Then I better buckle up because it's going to be an adventure." Josiah drew this beautiful woman into his arms. As he kissed her deeply, he silently thanked God for considering the problem, executing the moves, and helping them summit together.

EPILOGUE

BALTIMORE, MARYLAND

HARRY SPENCE DROPPED THE EMPTY BAG OF CHEETOS INTO THE TRASH next to his office desk and pulled the keyboard toward him. He stared at the computer. No matter how many times he went over the data, no matter how many tests he ran, something in the formula was still off. He just wasn't sure what.

He was good at what he did, but there were still limits. Certain scientific rules in his field that couldn't be broken. Which meant there were no short-cuts, and cutting corners was not something he was willing to do.

He tugged on the front of his turtleneck. This wasn't the first time he'd been pressured to speed up the process. Two years ago, he'd been ordered to finish the new formula ZAR 242, an anti-rejection drug for organ recipients. But pushing through a replacement drug too fast had come with a cost. Why couldn't those above him understand that the process of getting a drug to the approval stages took time and that cutting corners always came with a price?

That stint had cost him nearly everything. In fact, if it wasn't for Valerie he was pretty sure he would be in prison or dead right now. Her meticulous record keeping had convinced the DA that he hadn't been involved in the scandal. In the end, the lab he'd worked in had shut down after being accused of illegally pushing FDA approval with the flawed replacement. His boss had been arrested, at least two people had died, and multiple indictments filed against the company.

He'd thought that his career as a researcher was over until he'd been approached by a different lab, looking for someone with his expertise. Because of his previous work, he'd been tasked to work on a replacement to the anti-rejection drug, ZAR 242. One that would increase the longevity of a transplanted organs and lower the risk of side effects, particularly the risk of post-transplant cancer.

His new boss had even sweetened the pot, by offering him more money and shares in the company. He'd been given a specific case file. Someone with unique heart issues after a failed transplant. They needed something that would increase the longevity of a transplanted organ, but once again the anti-rejection drug had too many flaws. He was starting to wonder if the money he'd been offered was really worth it.

He squirmed in his chair. Maybe Valerie was right after all. Maybe he should walk away from the endless politics and start a new career as a novelist. At least there, the risks of life and death stayed on the page.

But that's not what Axton Blade would have done. Axton would have faced the enemy.

Harry grabbed a pen off the desk and started tapping it against the table. Axton might be nothing more than a figment of his imagination, but it was the novel he'd written that had been the catalyst that changed his life. When Valerie had discovered his secret, the five-hundred-page, hand-written novel, he'd tried to convince her it was nothing. That he was just a science geek who'd written a novel about a hero who saved the world. He might not be able to save the world himself, but he could dream. She'd told him he might not be that different from Axton after all, and that he had just as much power with his brain as Axton had wielding his sword. He just needed to believe in himself.

Max's crying interrupted his rambling thoughts.

Harry rubbed the back of his neck as he slid out of his chair and headed for the living room. "Valerie?"

"Is he bothering you?" she asked.

"No. Never."

He took in the perfect image of his wife holding their five-month-old son in the middle of their living room. Marrying the woman of his dreams had completely changed his world. He had no idea how she put up with him and his long list of phobias, but she did.

She walked up to him, still bouncing Max on her shoulder. "I've told you this before, and I'll tell you again, Harry Spence, you're a good man. While everyone else focuses on the profits, you are in it to save lives. It's why the politics of your job is hard for you. But it's also why you will always do the right thing."

"Even when I'm not sure what the right thing is?"

She smiled up at him. "You'll figure it out."

Harry kissed Max on the top of his bald head, then let his gaze shift to a photo of his mother that sat on the fireplace mantel. He wished she was here to see his little family. Before Valerie, his mother had been his motivation. But Dorothy Spence had died due to severe left-ventricular dysfunction after a heart transplant at the age of thirty-two, three days after his fifth birthday. His pursuit of finding a cure for her sickness had never diminished, which was why he couldn't just walk away.

Axton Blade might not put up with what he did, yet Harry knew he wasn't the same person he'd been two years ago. He turned back to his wife and kissed her slowly on the lips, still amazed that he'd won the girl.

"What was that for?" she asked as he pulled away a moment later.

He brushed back a strand of her red hair and smiled down at her. "I just love you."

Her smile broadened. "You better."

Harry's phone rang and he quickly pulled it out of his pocket, not wanting to wake the baby that had now fallen asleep.

"I'm sorry, but I need to take this," he whispered. "It's Frank."

"Of course. I need to put Max in his crib anyway."

Harry headed back into his office and took the call. "What have you got, Frank?"

"I think there might be something behind your paranoia."

Harry sat down in his chair and blew out a sharp breath. His concerns were worth nothing without proof, but this time he'd hired the PI to do the legwork for him.

"What have you found?" Harry asked.

"DEMA Diagnostics is still trying to cover their tracks, and you're not alone in believing that something is very off. There's a journalist whose father, a doctor, was killed in Africa in connection to that toxic waste that was dumped in pharmaceutical drums. He's been asking a lot of questions as well, and people are starting to notice."

"I read about that incident, but I thought that was limited to issues with an Ebola vaccine."

"That's what I'm looking into."

"What happened to the doctor?"

"He asked too many questions."

Just like he was doing.

"Who is this journalist asking the questions?" Harry asked.

"I'm trying to get ahold of him, but I'm finding it hard to track him down. Apparently, he's working out of the country."

"Where?"

"Somewhere in Central Africa."

Harry's brow began to sweat. He'd been to Africa once and had almost died. He reached for his inhaler. Cannibals, poachers, and voodoo dolls had ended up being the least of his worries.

"What's the journalist's name?" Harry asked.

There was a pause on the line before Frank answered. "His name is Liam DeMarcus."

THE AGENTS OF MERCY SERIES

"Gripping, riveting, unnerving."

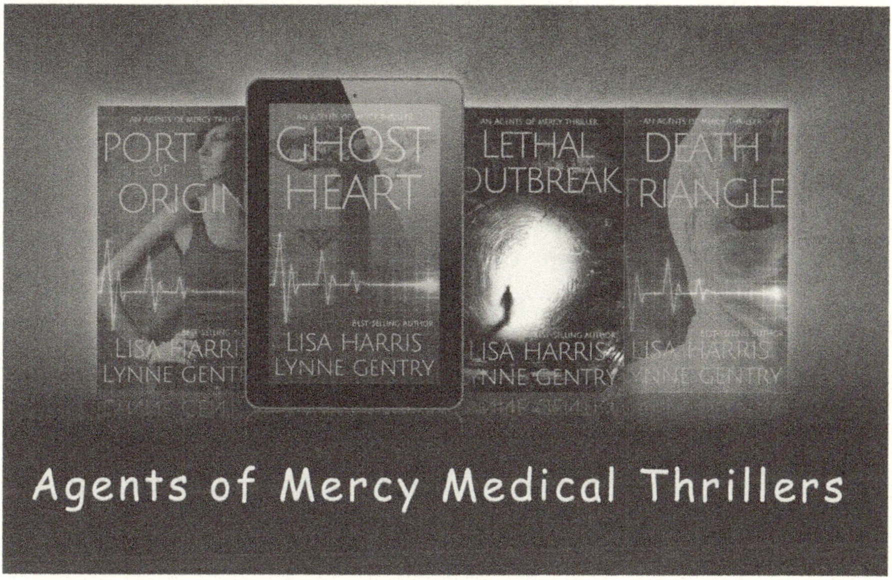

Ghost Heart
Port of Origin
Lethal Outbreak
Death Triangle

LETHAL OUTBREAK: BOOK THREE

You've read Port of Origin. Are you ready for the prequel? Find out the story behind Rachel and Aiden's romance and then watch for Death Triangle. The story that will tie the entire series together in one shocking conclusion!

CHAPTER ONE

Lethal Outbreak

Aiden Ballinger stepped outside the makeshift laboratory and felt the frigid winter air slip its icy fingers through the fabric of his heavy coat. He'd found every movement at the high altitude exhausting, but he'd also found a sense of tranquility he hadn't expected in the frozen tundra's barren landscape. The *roof of the world* was a fitting description for the Tibetan Plateau, standing over three miles above sea level and surrounded by the spectacular peaks of the Himalayan mountain range. But the very thing that mesmerized him, also terrified him.

Because this find was different.

He sucked in a breath and felt his lungs burn. He'd checked the results from the field testing a dozen times, then checked them again. It wasn't the first time an unknown bacteria or virus had been discovered in frozen tundra. Outbreaks like the one his Rapid Response Team had come to investigate were becoming more and more common. Industrial expansion across the globe was excavating viruses that had been buried for centuries as well as destroying the natural habitats of animals. With the ease and increase in international travel opportunities, it wouldn't take much to turn a small, localized outbreak into a worldwide pandemic. His job was to isolate and eliminate deadly pathogens before that happened. But this time, he hadn't been quick enough. His team had evidence, in the form of some very sick villagers, that the genetic signature of the recently uncovered virus was dangerous to humans right out of the gate. And that had him more than worried.

Aiden's SAT phone buzzed, and he took the call from his boss, hoping for better reception than last time. "Shepherd?"

"Aiden. . .sorry it took me so long to get through. Tell me what you've got."

"I sent you an encrypted email with the test results from the virus, but we need to move fast on this. We've recorded at least thirty-five newly infected people in the nearby village in the past forty-eight hours, and it's not slowing down."

"So the results are conclusive?"

"Conclusive enough that we need to do further testing in the States. We've been able to do an initial match between the virus we retrieved and those infected. Once verified, we'll be able to better respond."

"Agreed. I'm working on getting you out of there as soon as possible."

Aiden hesitated for a moment. "I'll be honest, I've never seen anything quite like this. We're looking at a viable giant virus with the potential—as already seen—to spread rapidly—"

"We need. . .exposed. . .spell disaster. . ."

"Shepherd. . ." Aiden tried moving up a slight incline, searching for better reception. "Shepherd, you're breaking up."

"Check. . .get packed. . .I'll arrange. . ."

Aiden hung up the call, frustrated. But cell reception was the least of his problems right now. They had yet to attempt to revive any of the pathogens they'd found, even though that didn't matter at this point. Not when they had evidence pointing to the fact that the virus had already found viable host cells in humans.

Calum "Iceman" Lewis stepped out of the Quonset hut designed for arctic conditions, then pulled his hood tighter around his face. "What are you doing out here, man? It's freezing."

"Trying to get a better signal. Trying to clear my head." Aiden walked back to his long-time friend and caught his gaze. "You looked at the last round of test results?"

"I did, but it's still inconclusive. We need to study the DNA's degradation—"

"If the virus's DNA wasn't viable, there wouldn't be an outbreak."

"Agreed, but I still think you're jumping to conclusions."

Aiden shook his head. "I might not be able to conclusively prove what we've found, but we both know that if there's going to be a viral outbreak on a grand scale, it's going to come from this exact scenario. These giant viruses have proven they can survive for long periods of time in harsh conditions. And we have evidence that it can infect humans."

Scientists had been warning about the situation for years. Ancient bacteria, viruses, and infectious microorganisms thawing and being released. Some believed there was little threat to humans because most of these pathogens couldn't survive indefinitely in harsh conditions or without a host. But in nature, there were always exceptions. Ebola was the perfect example of a virus that went into hiding only to emerge somewhere else unexpectedly. Up until now, there had never been any clear indication of where it had been or where it would show up again. But Ebola, like every virus, needed a place to hide between deadly outbreaks. Both bats and primates had been thought to be the place it chose, but there were still as many questions as answers.

"What do you want us to do?" Iceman's question broke through his thoughts.

"I'm going to head back to the States with samples of the virus while you finish up here. I want to have our initial findings retested in a high-security biolab in the US. We need to know exactly what we're dealing with."

"Okay."

"And Iceman. . ." Aiden turned and caught his friend's gaze. "We can't talk about this. To anyone. At least not until we can unequivocally verify the connection. News of the discovery of a prehistoric giant virus that has already infected humans *and* is spreading rapidly will only cause panic. Shepherd is working with the local government to ensure measures are put into place to slow the outbreak, but we need to tread carefully. And quickly."

"Agreed, but maybe *you* need to slow down." His friend reached out and squeezed Aiden's shoulder. "I can tell that your mind has already gone well past a viable threat—which admittedly we have—to a worldwide pandemic."

Aiden shook his head. "If my gut is right, we just opened Pandora's box."

Want to keep reading? Grab your paperback or ebook copy now!

DISCUSSION QUESTIONS

1. While *Port of Origin* explores the prejudices that separate us, what are some things you believe unify us?

2. Josiah and Dabir are both experiencing tremendous grief. Discuss the different ways they handle it. What are the similar ways they handle their pain?

3. Recent international viral outbreaks have proven how quickly a fatal virus can spread. Do you feel the world was prepared for a pandemic? If not, why not? How could we work together in a health crisis?

4. Humanitarian medical ships like the *Liberty* do exist. Have you ever considered volunteering on a Mercy Ship?

5. Where should the world dump its waste?

6. If pouring money into an impoverished country does not improve the quality of life for its citizens, what are some suggestions for improving their circumstances and future?

ACKNOWLEDGEMENTS

We are always so grateful for our readers. Your enthusiastic support for our work keeps us at the computer working far into the night.

We are so grateful for the help of experts. Retired Air Force Colonel Steve Johnson and Gabriel Harris gave us military advice. Dr. Megan Maxwell answered multiple medical questions. Thanks to Ellen Tarver for her great edits. Beta readers Jana Leasure, Janet Johnson, Judy Gentry, and Ian Acheson gave us excellent feedback. Appreciate also our wonderful readers who continue to help us spread the word about this series.

A special thanks to our husbands who are our biggest cheerleaders.

ABOUT LISA & LYNNE

LISA HARRIS is a USA Today best-selling author, a Christy Award winner, and the winner of the Best Inspirational Suspense Novel for 2011 (*Blood Covenant*) and 2015 (*Vendetta*) from Romantic Times. She has over forty novels and novellas in print. Lisa and her family work as missionaries in southern Africa. Lisa loves hanging out with her family, cooking different ethnic dishes, photography, and heading into the African bush on safari. Visit www.lisaharriswrites.com to learn more.

LYNNE GENTRY is USA Today best-selling author who loves to entertain audiences with her books. In addition to the medical thrillers she co-pens with Lisa Harris, Lynne's varied works range from the highly-praised historical *Carthage Chronicles* series to several laugh-out-loud small-town comedy series. RT Reviews calls this Top Pick author one to watch. Readers say her writing is exceptional and her stories extraordinary. When Lynne is not creating enchanting new worlds, she's laughing with her family or working with her medical therapy dog. Find out more at www.lynnegentry.com.

INSIDER CHAT WITH THE AUTHORS

Where did you get the idea for this story?

Lynne has always been a fan of Mercy Ships and has followed their work via Facebook for years. One day she was scrolling through her FB feed and saw a picture of a boy whose body was bent into the shape of a Z. She read his before and after story. Through volunteer medical care the Mercy Ship had brought to his third-world country, he was given the gift of straight legs. At about the same time pirates were really upping their attack game on ships passing the Somalian coast, an Ebola outbreak that made its way to the States set off global panic. The three elements collided and *Port of Origin* was the result.

Is pirating in Africa real, or something you made up for this story?

Unfortunately, pirating is still a problem the world over, but it is especially dangerous for ships to travel the waters of the African coasts. According to a recent BBC News report, West Africa is home to the world's most dangerous seas. The oil-rich coastline makes easy targets of the oil and gas tankers.

What is happening to deal with the issue of pirating?

Effective policing of the seas from brigands has been a problem since ships first set sail. International waters make for international problems. Increased security by major shipping companies has slowed some of the pirating. While there will always be those who choose to make their living through illegal gain, we believe a lot of the pirating problem is driven by need rather than greed. Increased opportunities for Africans to support their families and the restoration of destroyed habitats will hopefully decrease the allure of pirating the seas.

Have you ever been on a medical ship?

Lisa has memories of close to thirty years ago when she visited the Doulos while it was docked in West Africa. What she remembers the most was going to their book store and buying a couple CDs. Her family had been living overseas for a long time, so walking into a bookstore that looked just like a bookstore in the US was very exciting. But what is even more exciting is that this ship held over 22 million people during its thirty years in service in 108 countries!

Tell me more about these humanitarian ships.

According to the Mercy Ship's website https://www.mercyships.org/ five billion people lack access to safe surgery. Many of these people will die from treatable diseases. Hospital ships rely on contributions and volunteers to bring state-of-the-art medical care to 50% of the world's population. Our hope is that you will consider helping Mercy Ships bring healing to those without hope.

Besides giving readers a fast-paced thriller, what do you want people to get out of this story?

One of the most thrilling parts of writing such a large cast of characters is the challenge of walking in so many different shoes, which is what you have to do to write authentically. What always amazes us is that no matter a character's skin color, educational background, or their finances, at the core of each of us is a longing to be seen, heard, and loved.

What is it like co-writing a book? What is the process?

LYNNE: There is a creative give and take that makes the storytelling process more difficult, but in the end, we believe also makes the story more powerful.

Since we live on different continents and in different time zones, we did a lot of the work via email. The skeleton of the story went back and forth between us many times. However, when we really needed to solve a plot point we would set up a Skype call, which also gave us a chance to visit and reconnect. And since we really do enjoy each other, those calls were a treat for both of us.

First, we decided we wanted our hero and heroine to each have a distinctive voice. The easiest way to achieve their separate voices was for each of us to choose which one we wanted to write. Next, it made sense for Lisa to write the scenes involving African characters since she lives there. Because of my connections to the medical world through my daughter and husband, I did the research and writing for those scenes.

LISA: A project like this definitely was something I loved doing since I don't have a lot of contact with other writers on a day-to-day basis. And having two people brainstorm ideas for a book is always a win-win situation.

So while writing a book is always challenging, this experience was also a huge blessing to me. It allowed us to each take our strengths and put them together, while also learning from each other.

Once we decided on who was going to write which characters, it allowed us to focus on that part of the story line, and on each specific character's backstory and personalities. Watching the story then come together was really exciting.

How long have you been writing?

LYNNE: I've always been a storyteller, focusing on dramatic works, but I didn't start novel writing until 2002.

LISA: I began writing after my husband and I adopted our oldest son back in 1997. Six years later, I had my first novella published and I've been writing ever since.

Tell me about your other books?

LYNNE: I've written in several genres. I have a historical series (*The Carthage Chronicles*) and two Southern small-town family sagas filled with humor and hope (*The Women of Fossil Ridge and The Mt. Hope Southern Adventures* series).

LISA: I'm currently writing a US Marshal series for Revell (Baker Publishing). This is my third series with them, (*Southern Crimes, Nikki Boyd Files*) plus I have written three stand alone novels for them, all romantic suspense. I also write for *Love Inspired Suspense*, and am currently finishing up a series set in Colorado about four brothers. Yes, I love suspense!

GHOST HEART: BOOK ONE

Agents of Mercy Book One

WEDNESDAY, DECEMBER 11TH, 5:52 PM
MAKURU, TANZANIA

According to legend, their kind could never die. When they grew old, they simply vanished from this world, like smoke from the cooking fire that snakes above the spindly baobab trees and slithers away.

But not all legends are true.

Or so Jeme prayed.

Squinting through the shimmering rays of the grueling African sun, Jeme balanced the bowl of dried beans on her head and pressed through the crowded marketplace. A maze of narrow paths twisted around her, each lined with dozens of sellers who sat in cramped wooden shops displaying wares on rickety tables.

The smell of curried meat roasting on the grills mingled with the pungent odor of dried fish baking in the late afternoon heat. Jeme's empty stomach roiled as she hurried past piles of tomatoes, peppers, oranges, and colorful bags of spices. If only she could escape the whispers competing with the buzz of the buyers and sellers. Whispers that spoke of the magical powers of albino blood spilled across the brown earth, and of potions that could bring untold wealth.

She stepped into a puddle left over from the late afternoon rains, barely noticing the mud oozing between her toes. In Makuru, fish and vegetables weren't the only things for sale.

There was a price for human flesh, promising the strongest magic.

A flash of red caught her eye then vanished behind one of the tin-roofed stalls. Jeme jerked around, her breath tangled in the fear that had long ago taken root. Her fingers pressed against the rough wood of the kiosk as her eyes searched for the hunters. If they trailed her to the home she shared with Mbui, Numa, and Zaina, they would uncover her secret.

Jeme willed her heart to stop its frantic pounding and slipped through the back entrance of the market. Without the cover of the pulsing throng, she would be easier to track. Nerves on high alert, she hurried down the dirt path that led to her compound.

Something snapped behind her.

A fleeting look revealed nothing more than a boy watching his herd of goats in the grassy field beyond the market. She fingered the charm around her neck. She couldn't be too careful.

She longed for Mbui's presence and his cunning way of making their path difficult to follow. Not so many months ago, her husband had walked her home from the market each evening to ensure her safety from those who believed in the legend. Then fever attacked him, and Mbui's strength left.

Doctors from the hospital in Dar es Salaam promised her husband a new heart and a new life, but two days ago the fever returned, hotter than ever. He was dying because of the curse. Today she'd called his doctor, begging her to come before she had to bury Mbui beneath the baobab tree.

A quick glance at the setting sun only added to her concern. There was still no sign of Dr. Kendall's plane.

Fifteen minutes passed before Jeme reached the end of the winding path. Uncertain whether or not she'd been followed, she crouched in the shadows edging the compound. She studied the home she'd grown to love. Mbui's once strong hands had built the three huts, with their thick thatched roofs and solid mud walls.

Everything looked the same as when she'd left before the sun had risen from its bed in the sky. Tattered pieces of laundry fluttered in the breeze. Chickens pecked the twig-swept yard. And their goat remained tethered to a sturdy papaya tree. There was no sign of her sister, but Numa rarely ventured into the sunlight.

Glancing over her shoulder, Jeme slipped from the dense foliage. Shooing chickens from her path, she quickly crossed the yard. She passed the hut she and Mbui shared and went straight to her sister's door. She stopped and stared at the crude wooden slab hanging slightly ajar.

She knocked. "Numa?"

Nothing.

Jeme knocked again, panic rising at her failure to rouse her sister's cheery response. She pressed on the door. It creaked open. A beam of light spilled onto the floor. She stepped across the threshold, letting her eyes adjust to the silent darkness.

"Numa?"

Jeme froze.

A skinned body lay in a pool of blood.

"Numa!" Jeme fell to the packed-dirt floor. "No!" Her legs refused to stand, so she crawled the short distance to her sister. Body trembling, she sought Numa's hands, but they were gone. Every limb was gone.

"No!" Her screams rose through the thatched roof.

Jeme pounded the earth, cursing the ancestors who had forsaken her sister. Tears streamed down her cheeks as the sobs shook her chest.

Zaina!

Terror sliced through Jeme with the force of Mbui's sugarcane machete. Where was her daughter?

Jeme jumped up, screaming for the child she'd left in the care of her sister. She tripped over a pile of cooking pots, barely managing to keep her balance as she frantically searched the dark shadows of the room for signs of her baby.

"Zaina!"

Chest heaving, Jeme stopped in the center of the hut. She couldn't breathe. She couldn't think. She couldn't live without her child.

A soft cry broke through the stillness.

She turned to her sister's tiny bed, threw off the thin blanket, and shoved the mattress onto the floor. On top of the wooden bed slats, Zaina lay wrapped tightly in Numa's *kanga*.

Jeme pulled the crying infant toward her pounding chest and quickly quieted her with the offer of her swollen breast. Rocking back and forth, she glanced from the lifeless body of Numa to the door. What should she do? Because it wasn't her own dark skin the albino hunters were after.

Jeme caressed the soft, pale skin of her daughter's pinkish feet. Eventually, the blazing African sun would bake her child's delicate skin until it was thick and leathery. Blemishes would rise and mark Zaina's beautiful face like inky splotches on white paper—like Numa.

Jeme tucked her towheaded daughter deep into the faded cloth and tied her securely onto her back. She would not allow her own flesh and blood to become the hunted.

But if she stayed here, it was only a matter of time before human poachers found this cursed child.

DECEMBER 11TH, 9:34 AM EST

cincinnati, ohio

Catherine Taylor maneuvered her daughter's stroller around the redheaded toddler squatting amongst the Legos scattered on the gleaming waiting room floor. Although five years of weekly visits to the cardiologist had failed to make the jungle-themed office feel like home, joining other parents in their fight against similar heart defects had spawned a sense of family.

"Look, Kelsey." Catherine peered around the stroller cover. Blonde curls framed the angelic face of the underweight child holding a stuffed monkey in one hand and her soothing blanket in the other. Normal five-year-olds had given up their blankets by now, but the gap between Kelsey and normal children was growing wider by the day. "It's your friend, Timmy."

Kelsey's frail little arm extended the toy she'd requested in her Santa letter. "Want to see my new monkey?" When Kelsey asked why Santa had brought her gifts early and not her brother's, Catherine had told her it was because Santa's sleigh would be too full. The truth was, Christmas was two weeks away, and she couldn't bear it if Kelsey died before she opened her gifts.

"Let's see if Timmy is feeling better before we share." Catherine quickly wheeled the stroller wide as she eyed the small boy for any signs of last week's runny nose.

Susan, Timmy's mother, left her seat and wrapped a protective arm around her son. "He's not contagious." Desperate eyes, sunken in the haggard shell of former soccer-mom beauty, searched Catherine's for a bit of understanding. Understanding Catherine could no longer afford.

Everything in Dr. Finke's lobby had been specifically chosen so that it could be sterilized on a daily basis. But neither mother could deny what worried them most. The unseen microorganisms. Those microscopic missiles of death that traveled the airwaves seeking to destroy weakened targets like Kelsey and Timmy. Contracting a single germ that normal children shrugged off could kill their babies.

Catherine parked Kelsey in the far corner...just in case. "How did Timmy manage to shake that cold?"

Susan nervously tucked a strand of mahogany hair behind her ear. "Two rounds of antibiotics."

"Whatever it takes, right?" Catherine offered Susan the same hopeful, but useless smile other mothers had once offered her. The clock was ticking and antibiotics wouldn't slow it down.

She removed her fur-lined gloves and dropped them into the giant tote bag she lugged whenever forced to leave the house.

"I want out, Momma."

If only Kelsey could run and play. "Hang on, punkin." Catherine unzipped Kelsey's pink parka and freed her twig-like arms. Ugly purple tracks from endless blood tests scored the tender flesh between her daughter's wrists and elbows. Longing to kiss away the painful bruises, she folded Kelsey's arms across the labored rise and fall of her little chest. How much longer could her child endure this medical poking and prodding?

Kelsey whimpered, but didn't complain. "Can you turn me to the wall?"

All sorts of animals were hidden in the foliage of the wallpaper jungle scene. Kelsey tried to spot a new creature every time they came for a checkup. Last time, she'd found the monkey. His ability to leap from tree to tree had so entranced her, nothing would do until she had one of her own.

"Sure." Catherine checked her watch and felt her own heart lurch. She'd nearly missed the morning meds.

"Punkin, it's time for your special milk." Catherine scooped her daughter into her arms and sank into the nearest chair.

"But I want to show my monkey to the monkey on the wall," Kelsey protested.

"Take a drink for Momma, and I'll help you introduce your monkey to the monkey on the wall." She kissed the nest of curls nuzzled against her chest, drinking in the baby-shampoo scent of her sweet girl.

Digging into her tote bag, Catherine sorted through an assortment of Ziploc bags until she found the one with the Sippy cup. If she could cajole Kelsey into taking half an ounce of the milky supplement, then maybe they'd have a shot at keeping today's meds in her child's distended tummy.

She held the cup to her daughter's clamped lips. "Please. Just one sip."

"I'm tired." A fussy shake of Kelsey's head signaled the start of the cycle of absolute refusal.

Pain, combined with the disgusting taste of the medicine regime, always transformed her child's normally sunny disposition into a full-blown tantrum. Within moments of the exertion, the panting spells would begin. Afraid Kelsey could no longer tolerate the trauma, Catherine withdrew the cup. "Maybe later then." She snatched the night-night from the stroller and offered the silky-edged blanket to her snuffling child.

Kelsey accepted one of the few things that could soothe her and drew herself into a ball around its soft comfort. Seconds later, she drifted off to sleep.

Holding her dormant child tight, Catherine resisted the urge to check for the faint irregular beat of Kelsey's struggling heart.

How long did they have before the deformed organ gave up its battle?

Carefully, she returned her youngest to the stroller, relieved when she saw Kelsey take a breath. She stroked the damp curls away from her daughter's pale, oval face.

Nothing so perfect on the outside could possibly have something so wrong on the inside. A lie, she knew. But easier to swallow than the truth.

Scrubbing the untouched drinking cup with an antibacterial wipe, Catherine refused to give in to the panic knotting her gut. According to Brad, their daughter was a fighter, inheriting her stubborn streak from Catherine. Thank God. If Kelsey had been born with Brad's everything-will-work-out personality, her shriveled blue body would have never made it out of the preemie unit of Cincinnati's NICU.

Catherine sealed the cup in the Ziploc then stuffed it inside Kelsey's bag.

Keeping Kelsey hydrated and medicated had become a vicious cycle of trying to stay on the clock. If she delayed forcing Kelsey's morning meds down her, the med schedule would be off for the entire day. She made a mental note to ask Dr. Finke to explain the feeding tube he'd mentioned last week. Maybe if Kelsey's meds could be pumped directly into her frail body, things would turn around. A desperate measure, but one she was more inclined to consider due to Kelsey's continued deterioration.

In an attempt to quiet the butterflies aloft in her stomach, Catherine picked up the same dog-eared parenting magazine she'd read every office visit for the last five years. Flipping the pages without actually reading a word, she watched Timmy quietly press together plastic blocks with older-child precision. Every week, he built imaginary cars he would probably never drive and lopsided castles he would never fill with his own children.

Catherine's eyes slid from the boy to his mother. Susan, perched on the edge of a green-leather seat, stared at Catherine's sleeping daughter. Susan teetered on the brink of a catastrophe similar to Catherine's, and from the pinched look on her face, she knew it. Any moment Susan's son could be lying listless in a stroller while other mothers looked on and thanked their lucky stars he was not their child.

In Susan's fearful gaze, Catherine saw what she'd been telling herself could not be true. Until a few weeks ago, Kelsey's limited play mimicked Timmy's. She'd play quietly with her baby doll, stopping every few minutes to fold herself into the squatting position. The pressure against her chest granted the swollen aorta of her boot-shaped heart a brief reprieve while forcing oxygen-deprived blood into hungry lungs.

Catherine adjusted Kelsey's blanket, her own heart sinking at her inability to rouse her daughter even a little.

Susan reached down and helped Timmy snap two Legos together. Envy, bitter as bile stung Catherine's tongue. Timmy still had a bit of rose in his cheeks. Catherine glanced at Kelsey's sleeping face and grimaced at the total void of color.

Terror clawed at her insides. Kelsey's worsening condition was not Susan's fault. The poor woman would soon have more troubles than any mother should ever have to bear.

"Is it someone's naptime?" Susan's attempt to sound upbeat fell flat.

Catherine stifled the urge to scream, her clenched sigh ruffling her stringy bangs in desperate need of a trim. "Twenty hours out of twenty-four."

Susan nodded, letting the snippy answer go unquestioned.

"Sorry, Susan...I..." Catherine closed the magazine and laid it on the table. Her friend didn't deserve the anger that boiled just below the steely exterior she worked to maintain. But try as she might, she couldn't shake the urge to hit someone. Even on those rare occasions when Brad put forth the extra effort to spell her, she couldn't escape the feeling that any moment she could blow.

Susan dismissed the apology with a wave. "Is she—" Her voice fragile as a brittle leaf. "—going to need a transplant?"

"We find out today."

Susan crossed the room and slipped into the chair beside Catherine. "I've been doing some research. On the Internet." She looked around the room as if it were bugged then quickly removed several printed pages from her purse and handed them to Catherine. "Just in case."

"What is this?"

"You can get a heart. If you have the money."

Trepidation rattled the papers in Catherine's hands. She quickly thumbed through them, trying to make sense of the printed words. She stopped on the page with a red, lopsided heart-shaped map in the upper right hand corner. "What are you talking about?"

"Did your insurance grant preapproval?"

"Brad's checking on the hold up." Catherine glanced at the page again. This wasn't a heart logo. This was a map of Africa. Her stomach cartwheeled. "But we've bought a supplemental policy just in case."

"Good thing, because in the States, a new heart is going to cost over a million dollars."

"I know. I've checked the numbers."

"Well, in some countries"—Susan scanned the room again—"hearts are more...affordable."

Catherine stiffened, folded the papers, and handed them back to Susan. "I'm not looking for a clearance rack special to replace my daughter's heart."

"How long can you afford to wait?" Susan tilted her head in Kelsey's direction. When Catherine said nothing, Susan dropped the papers in Catherine's lap. "I'm just saying, I'd think about it if it were me." She squeezed Catherine's arm and then quietly retreated to her side of the waiting room.

Hands trembling, Catherine crammed the papers into her tote. How dare Susan claim to know how much time Kelsey had left. She couldn't know that any more than she could know about Africa. Just because the woman had googled something on the Internet didn't make it true.

So why would she believe Susan?

Catherine straightened her blouse. Kelsey had time. Lots of it. She dug around in the tote bag and fished out a Ziploc of bottles and pill canisters. Kelsey had to have those meds.

Catherine blocked the hum of Timmy's pretend cars, but Susan's tendered advice continued its assault upon everything she hoped was true. Dr. Finke was the best pediatric heart surgeon in Ohio. He'd fixed Kelsey before...twice. Catherine was counting on him to do it again.

Taking her baby to some dirty, foreign country so some witch doctor could wave a magic potion over her was out of the question. Who in their right mind would let some quack who probably flunked out of an American med school operate on their child in a primitive, third-world facility?

Catherine fumed while Susan let Timmy drive his Lego car over her face. Susan was crazy. Why hadn't she noticed the woman's desperation before? The truth hit Catherine like cold water in the face. Taking care of a sick child had dried up her own well of common sense.

Think. She had to calm down and think.

From the moment Kelsey was born, Catherine had known something wasn't right. Clear thinking, along with her determination to find the best medical care, had brought them this far. And clear thinking would help her find the cure for her daughter. No frazzled, armchair quarterback could tell her what was best for her baby. She'd think of something. She always did.

Catherine took a deep breath and removed the biggest prescription bottle from the baggie. She shook it well then filled the oral syringe. Lifting Kelsey from the stroller, she worked to rouse her. "Here you go, punkin." She gently pinched Kelsey's cheeks into the formation her stepson Jonathan called "the guppy" and shot the contents into her daughter's mouth.

Holding Kelsey tight, Catherine waited for the retching. She felt the ragged expansion of her daughter's ribcage, bones so fragile they could be easily crushed under her grip. Tears, hot and angry, stung Catherine's eyes. She buried her face in Kelsey's hair, hiding her fear from Susan.

How much time? Did this question haunt every mother? If it didn't, it should. No one was promised more than the present moment, and if Dr. Finke didn't have good news, there would be no future.

She refused to dwell on the possibility. The ventricular septal patch was holding. If she didn't cling to the hope that this advanced prosthetic mesh would keep the hole in Kelsey's heart sealed, her own heart would fail.

ALSO BY LISA HARRIS

AGENTS OF MERCY THRILLERS

Ghost Heart

Port of Origin

Lethal Outbreak

Death Triangle

SOUTHERN CRIMES

Dangerous Passage

Fatal Exchange

Hidden Agenda

THE NIKKI BOYD FILES

Vendetta

Missing

Pursued

A NIKKI BOYD NOVEL

Vanishing Point

STAND ALONE NOVELS

A Secret to Die For

Deadly Intentions

The Traitor's Pawn

MISSION HOPE

Blood Ransom

Blood Covenant

LOVE INSPIRED SUSPENSE

Deadly Safari

Desperate Escape

Taken

Stolen Identity

Desert Secrets

Fatal Cover-Up

Deadly Exchange

No Place to Hide

The O'Callaghan Brothers

Sheltered by the Solider

Christmas Witness Pursuit

Hostage Rescue

Christmas Up in Flames

US MARSHAL SERIES

The Escape

The Chase

HISTORICAL

An Ocean Away

Sweet Revenge

Sign up for Lisa's newsletter and keep up with her latest news and book releases!

www.lisaharriswrites.com

ALSO BY LYNNE GENTRY

THE CARTHAGE CHRONICLES

A Perfect Fit (eShort Prequel)

Healer of Carthage

Shades of Surrender (eShort Prequel)

Return to Exile

Valley of Decision

MT. HOPE SOUTHERN ADVENTURES

Walking Shoes

Shoes to Fill

Dancing Shoes

Baby Shoes

WOMEN OF FOSSIL RIDGE

Flying Fossils

Finally Free

First Frost

AGENTS OF MERCY THRILLERS

Ghost Heart

Port of Origin

Lethal Outbreak

Death Triangle

Sign up for Lynne's newsletters and

keep up with her latest news and book releases!

www.lynnegentry.com